Julie

From the lush green farmlands of colonial Virginia to the glitter of Georgian London, *A Rose Without Thorns* is the dazzling, passionate, unforgettable saga of an extraordinary woman on an extraordinary journey to claim a life—and a love—of her own.

Daughter of a bankrupt Virginia tobacco farmer, Susannah Bry found herself on her own at sixteen, traveling abroad to the lavish country estate of her mother's family in England . . . only to find herself spurned by her aristocratic aunt and facing a life of humiliation and servitude as the companion to her aunt's cruel and domineering neighbor. Susannah manuevers her escape by entering into a loveless marriage to her kind, shy, scholarly cousin Harry. They soon separate, and Susannah enters the fashionable London underworld—a bohemian society of pleasure gardens and masked balls, brothels and love nests, opium and sweet, sensuous death. Here Susannah will lose her heart to the most fascinating man in town, the actor, dramatist, and sensualist Nicholas Carrick.

Now as the shadow of the French Revolution falls across Europe and a burgeoning new America beckons from across the sea, Susannah must fight with all the strength of her pioneer roots for her own life, liberty, and destined love, little knowing that her future rests on a question that may never be answered. . . .

A Rose Without Thorns

A Rose
Without Thorns

Lucy Kidd

BANTAM BOOKS

NEW YORK · TORONTO · LONDON · SYDNEY · AUCKLAND

A ROSE WITHOUT THORNS
A Bantam Fanfare Book / January 1992

FANFARE *and the portrayal of a boxed "ff" are trademarks of Bantam Books,
a division of Bantam Doubleday Dell Publishing Group, Inc.*

*All rights reserved.
Copyright © 1991 by Lucy Armstrong Kidd.
Cover art copyright © 1991 by Ken Otsuka.
No part of this book may be reproduced or transmitted
in any form or by any means, electronic or mechanical,
including photocopying, recording, or by any information
storage and retrieval system, without permission in
writing from the publisher.
For information address: Bantam Books.*

*If you purchased this book without a cover you should be aware that
this book is stolen property. It was reported as "unsold and destroyed"
to the publisher and neither the author nor the publisher has received
any payment for this "stripped book."*

ISBN 0-553-28917-9

Published simultaneously in the United States and Canada

*Bantam Books are published by Bantam Books, a division of Bantam Dou-
bleday Dell Publishing Group, Inc. Its trademark, consisting of the words
"Bantam Books" and the portrayal of a rooster, is Registered in U.S. Patent
and Trademark Office and in other countries. Marca Registrada. Bantam
Books, 666 Fifth Avenue, New York, New York 10103.*

PRINTED IN THE UNITED STATES OF AMERICA
RAD 0 9 8 7 6 5 4 3 2 1

To my parents, with love

A Rose
Without Thorns

Prologue

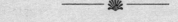

Albemarle County, Virginia—1787

Fire took hold of the house: crawling, leaping, dancing. It lay in wait on the wide stones of Bry's hearth, then seized its escape: a thin trail of gold liquid. The flames snatched at the cracks in the floor, gnawing at the thick, warped Virginia planks. They licked their way farther: faster, now more daring, tasting the dust on the windowsills, reaching for the trailing edge of a tablecloth. They curled through the dense wools of the room's one moldering, treasured Turkey carpet.

The yellow tongues leapt higher, gathering strength. They hurled themselves again now, with greater force, at the knobbed legs of the dining table, at the sides of the walnut spinet. Such English carvings, English fripperies—not to be recovered soon in such a place as Albemarle. But the flames were indifferent. The spinet, broken and neglected since the lady's death, fell to them first. Its walnut sides crumpled like paper. And the tongues reached farther. They sought curtains, plate, lacquered cabinets quick to the flame. But of these there were none, for all had been sold long before. So, lingering but a moment upon the odd, perishable morsel—the Bible, the slave papers, the daughter's half-finished sums—the fire moved higher, unsatisfied. Rising and beginning to roar, it hurled itself upon the stairs.

In an attic chamber, Susannah Bry turned in her sleep. She coughed and writhed against the long tendrils of hair that had caught about her face and neck. It was the heat, the hard humid heat of summer, beginning. This she thought, or sensed, or dreamed: forgetting, in the depth of sleep, that it was only March. She threw off the sheets and stretched out on the bed in her damp nightshift. Again she slept.

Downstairs, outside, the commotion began. George Bry had been the first to scent the flames; and woken, startled from another sort of oblivion, he charged up: out of the long slaves' outbuilding, to the front of the house.

"Oh, my Lord. My God, my sweet Lord . . ."

Bry's voice sputtered to nothing in the darkness. Its tones of London, where he had been born, its accent of Albemarle—both stilled. And then, strangely calm, he began again to cry out. He called for Adela, the house servant, and for Jacob, his oldest hand. And then, until his throat was hoarse with it, he called, "Fire! Dear God help us. Fire. . . ."

The slaves woke and crept silently, wide-eyed, toward the burning place. Most of them had never seen such flames. Adela, too, came from her bed in the outbuilding, her face calm and her hair bound up in a turban. She clung to the hand of her tall daughter, Claudine, watching as Bry called out, his voice breaking, his arms flailing in the strange golden light.

Still Susannah slept. The smoke pressed into her room in thick clouds. Timbers cracked and fell below, but she heard no sound until a stone smashed her window. She woke, and the smoke stung her eyes and throat.

She thought she could not breathe or move. This freezing of her limbs, perhaps it was fright. For she must move, she knew it. She *must*. Yet it would be so easy to sleep again. Through a crack in her door she could see the walls of the stairwell, glowing orange. A deathly shade. *Fire.* And she thought, with little sense: *Is all lost, down there?* The Turkey carpet, Mother's spinet? *No, I will fetch it, save it. Sleep . . . .*

At the side of the house, there was a hammering. Glass splintered and trickled away. With great effort, Susannah raised her head; her father was leaning in, through the broken sides of her window. She felt herself smothered in heat, in blankets. He was shaking her: slapping her face, shouting her name. *Susan, Susannah!* He held her up by the broken window, where the air was clearer.

"Father—" She struggled to breathe. "What—what's happened?"

"Christ, Susanny. Go! The ladder's there—"

"No," she breathed, incoherent. "I must have—Mother's things." She fought against her father's arms, turning, trying to reach it in the cupboard: a simple box, with a silver cover. It was all her mother had left her, eleven years ago.

"Damn yer affairs, Susan. Save yourself." Bry's voice was rough. But at last, leaving her at the window's edge, he gave in. Casting a quick, despairing look around the attic, he gathered what he could. He wrapped a blanket, and an armful of dresses, around the box, and hurled the bundle out through the window. "Now, go—"

He held her tightly round the waist as she moved out the window. The smoke had grown still thicker, and she was weak. She could barely feel her legs beneath her. She reached for a footing on the ladder; she felt the first few steps under her feet before the smoke overcame her.

She fell backward and seemed to roll and drift. There was the dim pain of hard ground: but still she fell. And when she woke again, she was far from the house, lying on the grass with her father and Adela bent over her, stroking her face and hands, fear in their eyes.

Just now she could not ask why. How the fire had started, where her father could have been—that he had not seen. No one had called, no one had shouted to her, *Fire*. . . . She did not understand. But it was too much, too hard to bear thinking. . . .

When Bry saw, now, that his daughter was awake, he smiled—an eerie, gap-toothed smile—and ran back to the house. He left Susannah with Adela and her daughter, Claudine, on the long grass behind the carriage path. And soon, again, they saw him: frantic, mad. He swore, and his limbs beat and thrashed at the air. For now the whole of the house burned. It would not be saved.

Every now and then something inside would burst into a fresh jet of flame, and Susannah, lifting her head, would wonder what it was. They had little left. . . . Was it the writing desk? Or that trunk that contained her trousseau? Or the bed-curtains her mother had worked? She remembered only dimly how her mother had sewn away at them—determined and clumsy, pricking herself—trying to make this place as grand as her old house had been, in England. . . .

It was too late. The fire had caught: It would have them all. Watching, Susannah knew it, inside herself, even though her father refused to see. Bry had sent his six men with buckets to the well: four times back and forth, to no avail. For the well was a quarter mile off through the woods: too far. When the men came back, spilling water on all sides, they found the fire grown, despite them.

But Bry would not let them rest. In his fury he had torn off one of the thin branches of an oak, and now he paced back and forth before the house, slashing the air.

"Please, Master Bry. It's for gone. We'se all—" A slave boy, thirteen or fourteen, quaked in his path.

"Damn me, boy. Are ye giving it up? Lazy, scurvy rats y'all are—" And Bry lunged into the boy with his branch, his blue eyes narrow and angry. Susannah watched, far from them both, and thought, *He is mad. My father is verily mad*. "Adela, what will—" she said. She was too weak to move from the ground.

"Shh, love. 'Twill come all right." Adela ran her

cool hands across her forehead, but could not stop her trembling.

That was not the worst of it: for as day was starting to dawn, two of the boys, exhausted with running back and forth to the well, sought liquid nearer. They ravaged the back of the outbuilding for the flasks of honey-gold liquid stacked inside: firewater, they called it. Bry's special store. No one noticed them scurrying in the darkness, or unstoppering their find, exultant. No one saw them, until the whiskey splashed onto the flames, and the downstairs bedroom burst in a blaze of white-orange. The firewater was not water at all.

Bry ran at the two. Though muscular and wiry, he was not much bigger than they. But when he slashed his oak branch at their shoulders, they cowered.

"Damn me, ye'll go to the devil! The godless bleeding lot of ye—devil take ye for a lousy, thieving roguing couple of bastards! I'll ha'e ye hanged, I will. I swear't. . . ."

And it went on and on. Bry's violence: his taut body hurling itself into theirs. He held the first boy by the neck of his shirt, whipping him, then dropping him to the ground. He turned to the second. Susannah could hear him—John, it was, Jacob's son—whimpering and pleading.

"But, Adela—" she whispered. "He's but nine. Make my father stop."

"Shh. 'Twill do no good," Adela said, pressing her gently down. The black woman, who had for eleven years been mother to all the house, and to Susannah, stood above her, grave and beautiful, unmarked by the night's smoke and soot. She was the calm at the center of Susannah's world. Only sometimes, as now, Susannah thought: *Why, I do not understand her at all.*

Bry had finished. He stood, bent with exhaustion, behind the two huddled slaves. Then he raised his head one last time and let out a sound. Wild and high as an animal's howl, his cry rose above the slaves' wails and the rumble and crackling of the fire.

His hands to his face, Bry fell to ground, sobbing.

* * *

Virginia's late-winter damp finally saved the sheds,
and the slave huts and fields. The mist in the air grew
heavier as the night wore on, turning gradually to
rain as morning came. And the rain beat down the
fire on Bry's farm more effectively than any number
of slaves with buckets could do. The flames backed
down, leaving the shell of the house still standing: its
two main rooms and the frame of its roof above a
gutted attic. *It still stands*, thought Susannah, with
joy. Then, all was not lost. They would begin again.

Afterward, as the sky was growing bright, one of
the slaves brought water for washing. Adela mopped
Susannah's face and tried to rinse out the red-brown
tangles of her hair. Claudine, who was smooth-
skinned and lithe, like her mother, stood a few paces
away. She tapped her foot, letting out an indignant
whistle between her teeth, until at last her mother,
glancing up, ordered, "You, too. *De l'eau. Vite!*" She
spoke in the half-French dialect she and her daughter
shared: a language both of Virginia and of the West
Indies, where she came from.

"What for?" Claudine scowled. "What's the use?"

Adela stopped combing Susannah's hair and stared
at her daughter, hard. "Because I say. *Vas-y. Va-
t'en!*"

Slumping, Claudine moved off in the direction of
the well.

The slaves had all wandered away now, seeing the
fire beginning to die; only the Brys remained to watch
the last of it. George Bry hunched on the grass, his
face hidden, while Adela mopped away the soot above
the stained homespun of his shirt.

Susannah shivered. She was wearing only her nightdress and a blanket. She couldn't bear to think, now,
of losing the house and all their things. Yet the black
shell stared back at her. As if to say, *You fools. I dare
you to dream of it again—setting yourselves up so*

grandly. It had been a blue-painted, wood-frame house: two attic rooms, a bedchamber, a kitchen. Plainer than Monticello or Castle Hill—and yet, a gentleman's house, with all the fine things that marked it out as one. The smooth-paned glass windows, the finely carved cornices. The brass door knocker and hinges—all imported from England. It was true, many of their English belongings had gone. The china and the silver—but her father had promised to buy them back. As long as they had the house, it had been all right. . . .

"We can build it again," said Susannah softly. It was half a question.

Bry lifted his face, and shook his head. The smoke had streaked his skin, and suddenly, to Susannah, he looked old. He was only forty-four. Once, she knew, he had been handsome. For hadn't it been his fine blue eyes—his gentlemanly air—that lured her mother away from England? Away from her family, to an unknown land that would take more hewing and building than she knew. . . .

Now Bry's fine, aristocratic features were beginning to disintegrate; an "aristocrat" he had never been, in truth. His dark blue eyes, so like Susannah's, had grown paler and redder; he had lost teeth; his face had grown long, craggy and lean.

"Surely, it's not the worst—" Susannah began again.

"You don't know, child. You don't know half," he said.

For Bry knew far more than he dared tell her. He knew by now that his land was mud, unsalable. He knew, also, that farming was no simple thing: it depended on lucky harmonies—a regular rain, strong seedlings, rich soil—which he no longer hoped to coax from the elements around him. He knew that his romantic venture to America with a baronet's daughter had failed. Yes, irrevocably failed; and something about the way in which it had failed could not help but please his still-lively, liquorous fancy. Sparing him, at least, a slow and dreadful decline, the farm had burst out in sudden flame: a shot of sweet and

God-merciful death. Flames—Bry gave a surly chuckle at the thought—flames of protest at his very ineptitude. Flames along a trail of whiskey, spilled on the hearth. A trail spilled, he supposed now—many nights. But tonight it caught. . . .

And now what remained to him? Nothing of use: acres of forest, a crew of lazy slaves. A dirty, kind, ill-educated daughter—ill fitted for the world she would have to face. And yet—he had thought it out—the world must have her. A lucky thing she was pretty. . . .

Gathering his thoughts, rubbing the bristles of his chin, Bry spoke. Adela knelt close by him, listening.

And Susannah, whose sixteen-year-old face had not yet hardened into firm lines, showed at first no expression at all. Her body—which was small, like her father's, but rounded—curled in on itself, her full mouth forming no words but only a small, vaguely outlined O. Only her eyes, the color of a night sky, spoke astonishment. Their pupils widened and they seemed to grow darker yet as he spoke. Her father's notion—she would never have conceived it. It could not be. For now she found that by a fire, which was none of her doing, and a sequence of financial troubles of which she had scarcely been told, her entire future life was to be changed: cracked and scattered in the wind, like seed. She was not to live in Virginia, to have this farm, to take a husband. Nothing that she had counted upon was to be hers. For her father had settled upon another scheme, and she was to go to England.

Chapter 1

———— ❧ ————

Susannah bent over her father's shoulder as he dug his quill, for yet a fourth time, into paper.

"The Marches." She read the words, with a strange tingling in her skin. "What is it? Is it where I am to go?"

"Aye, Susanny. I' Surrey. To your aunt, ye know." Bry lifted his pen from the words "Dear Maria" and frowned.

Surrey? Susannah wondered, and twitched nervously from one foot to the other. The names—*Surrey, England, Aunt Maria*—were no more than that to her, for all that her father had repeated them all through her childhood. For all that they had been a part of her parents' life, twenty years past, and though, when hard times came, Bry talked of them still. For Susannah, it was too distant, that land of lazy wealth. She could not imagine it. She twitched again and stamped—for always she had trouble staying still—and Adela, pinning up her new skirts, below, admonished her, "Stand *straight.*"

"But I don't want to," Susannah whispered.

Adela glared up. *"Bien sûr,* you will," she said. But whether she meant *stand straight* or *go to England,* Susannah did not know. And her father, who heard nothing, gulped from his mug, wiped his brow, and wrote on.

Already, in the long, dirt-floored room, the piles of needlework were growing, the small sea-chest filling with clothes for Susannah and Claudine. For Adela's daughter was to accompany Susannah to England, as her maid. It was true, she was scarcely older than Susannah herself: but just now the house could spare no older, abler hands. Susannah looked down the room, which had once been slave quarters; now it was here that she, her father, Adela, and Claudine all slept, each in a separate corner, on makeshift beds of blankets and straw. *The Marches,* she thought, and gave a faint smile. She wondered what her grand Surrey aunt would make of *this* place.

"Damn," muttered George Bry, crumpling this letter, like the others before, and tossing it at the fire.

He could tell Susannah little of her aunt Maria, except that she was—he drawled the word grudgingly— a "vy-*count*-ess." When the Brys had married and emigrated, she been only sixteen. But in the years since, she had married an elderly viscount, Warrington, who, Bry thought, was now dead. She had a son— how many other children, he did not know.

Bry scribbled steadily at his letter this time, until, near the middle of the page, he swore again. "Damn!"

Susannah stared; then she looked about the room: the table, the mantel. "Have we any more paper?" she said quietly. She saw none. With her father, it was ever so.

"Wha—?" Bry looked around himself, startled.

"Pay no mind," said Adela calmly, standing. She smoothed the wrinkled sheet with her broad hands. " 'Twill do! I will put the iron to it."

And Susannah could make no protest: even though this attempt, like so many of her father's others, was halfway done and failed. She watched him slump over the barrel-top, defeated, and she knew: she loved him too much. "I don't *need* to go," she said, kneeling by him. "Truly, Father . . ." *Let me stay,* she pleaded with her eyes: as she had pleaded before, only to be told, *Have faith, girl, 'Tis best.*

"Aye," was all Bry said, tiredly, this time. "Ye need to. There's nought for ye here, child." He drank again; for a moment he smiled, his bare gums gleaming. "Why, where's your spirit, Susanny? All gone and left ye?"

Susannah only shook her head.

"Then, think on it! 'Tis an entire different world." Bry sat up and, with sudden conviction, seized Susannah by the shoulders. "Now ye listen—"

He talked, and she knew he would not understand. He talked of wealth, of finding a husband, a fine house—when she could look out, now, through the doorway, at the dark-scorched shell of the only house she wished for.

"I know ye can do it, Susanny!" her father said, shaking her shoulders. "To be sure, they don't know ye. But ye're your mother's daughter. They'll have to treat ye kindly! Might be they'll buy ye frocks—take ye dancing. . . ." His eyes searched his daughter's, but found no light there. He took her chin in his fingers and looked hard at her. "Come. I know ye can do it. Ye're a good one. Ye'll survive."

Susannah looked down, and nodded, and tried to smile.

Six days later they left for Richmond. Susannah and Claudine huddled on the floor of Bry's cart, sheltering under a blanket in the rain.

"Blast! The infernal—" Bry started to swear, as he whipped the animals on. One of the horses was twenty years old, and the other limped; but it was not this, or the rain, that angered him. His head ached from lack of drink, and inside his belly the slow, gnawing pain had set in. "T'devil . . ."

"What's the matter, Father?" said Susannah, and

"How far to Scotts Ferry?" said Claudine, less solici-
tous.

Bry did not answer, but cursed again, below his
breath.

For miles they had passed nothing but trees and
muddy, stumped tobacco fields. The rutted road was
slowly broadening, and as Bry drove on, still cursing
silently, the pain in his middle eased to a sufferable,
dull ache.

Susannah had lost track of their route. She had little
sense of lands and distances, beyond the familiar acres
that were her own. She knew there was an ocean to
the east, but this seemed no more or less real to her
than the Jackson lands, beyond a forked tree at their
border, where she was forbidden to ride. For Jackson
was one of the local men who started the troubles of
war ten and more years past; and, for her father's
disinterest in fighting, called him a Tory.

That he was not: Susannah knew it in her heart.
He cared for his new country; but he had not fought
for it. His crops had been in too perilous a state to
leave behind. He had fought once, for England, in
the wars of the 1760s: and in the eyes of the patriots,
like Jackson and Cocke, that was enough to convict
him. In return, he had insulted and sworn at them,
drunk in the inns; so that, now the time was come to
make amends, and marry off Susannah, it was too
late. None of the landed men would have her.

I do not care, she told herself. She might never
marry. It did not matter. For one day, she and her
father would have the finest house and the richest
plantation in Albemarle. . . .

She shook her head now, in the rain, and tried not
to think of it. They were losing sight, with every step,
of the lands she knew: the bending Rivanna, the Blue
Ridge Mountains. They passed taverns, roadside
churches, and the half-built mansion of Monticello.
After the small town of Scotts Ferry, which was the
farthest she had ever been from home before, they
followed the line of the James River, past fields and
vast, comfortable plantation houses. She saw farmers,

aproned servants: factors counting tobacco and cash and loading up their low transit boats. Nightfall came, and they pulled up at an inn near the water. While Bry drank downstairs with the men, Susannah and Claudine were left alone in their room.

Claudine tossed her head, and a smile spread across her high-boned, thin face as she leaned out the window.

Susannah could only stare at the other girl. "Do you not miss home?"

"No!" Claudine skipped a pebble across the slates below the window. "*Your* home," she said. "What's for me, there? Myself, I mean to have a better one."

Later, when it was dark, Susannah looked out and was no longer so scared. She heard voices in the street, and ripples on the water as canoes passed. And she knew then that, in some mysterious way, she was moving toward . . . *the center of the world.* England: where music and books and fashion all came from. Where—said Adela—the ladies wore wigs six feet high. Where there was a city: her father called it the greatest in Christendom. *London.* Why, it must have thirty streets—or fifty. *People must get lost there,* she thought, *and never come out.* And, almost despite her, her head began to hum with excitement.

Late the next afternoon they reached Richmond, and their ship, the *Rosaline.* They were lucky: the merchant brig had arrived just when the newssheets said it would. Bry found its Scottish captain in a tavern near the harbor, and there negotiated the two girls' passage. Standing outside the door, Susannah heard him laughing, talking in the sailors' own rolling tones. She laughed, bewildered, at his mimicry, and found, when they climbed on board, that he had wheedled for them the best cabin on the ship: when, as she well knew, he had barely the coins to pay their passage.

But for the two days they spent waiting in port, Bry was drunk and sullen. Susannah felt queasy with fear at the voyage ahead, but she could not talk of it to him. He answered her in grunts; their last days together rolled past, and only as the ship was on the verge of leaving harbor did he hug her, and murmur in her ear, "Ye're American! Despite this, Susanny. . . . Don't let them make ye English, do ye understand? Ye're a Virginian bred, Susanny. An American!"

Claudine stood a few paces away and stared: perhaps at this sudden, strange access of patriotism.

A day into the voyage the ship lost sight of land, though Susannah and Claudine, both sick in their cabin, did not notice, or even know how much time had passed. For a few hours Claudine even forgot how much she expected for herself in England. Leaning into their chamber pot, she moaned that she wished to God she had never come. But Susannah revived more quickly. On the morning of the third day she was able to leave their stinking chamber. The sea air in the corridor smelled startlingly clean, damp and salty.

She moved outside, clinging to the doorway, taken aback by the vastness of gray sky and sea: of the brig itself, whose polished decks spanned and fought the leaping water.

"Good morning ta ye! I didna' ken whether to credit ye were on this ship or not! Two fine ladies fra' Virginny . . ."

Startled, clutching at a rail behind her, Susannah looked over toward the voice.

"Well, an' ye've both left home for good, or so's I hear." The blond, grinning sailor had leapt, with startling speed, across what space of deck remained between them; now he bent close to her in a bow—or a mock of one. She was not sure. He raised his head, and as he smiled, a gold tooth glinted. "Roderick Farquhar, second mate. At your service, my lady."

"Oh, I'm—not 'my lady,' " said Susannah and shyly returned his smile.

"Then what'd you want to leave America for?"

Susannah's smile dropped. The sudden question had surprised her. Frankly she answered, "I didn't—want. We had to."

"Why?" Farquhar's gaze flickered over Susannah, and when she didn't answer, he stepped back, more respectful. "Did you lose your chance?"

"Our chance—" Susannah repeated, intrigued by his Scottish way of putting it. And because so many answers rushed to her at once, she did not know how to begin.

Her father, a London innkeeper's son, hadn't deserved such a chance: the daughter of a baronet, a plantation in America. When, secretly betrothed to pretty, coltish Anne Skowland, George Bry first visited Albemarle, it had seemed to roll out before him in vast waves of wealth. He had bought seven hundred acres on the promise of Anne's dowry and left them in the hands of an overseer, who would buy slaves and begin clearing trees. He went back to Anne and her parents, full of plans. And though they cast doubtful looks on him, at last the Skowlands agreed. Sir John, a benevolent father, guessed the appeal of flashing blue eyes, and a daring army tale, to a dreamy girl like Anne. Besides, he thought this scheme of planting in Virginia had promise.

But numbers were no more Skowland's strength than George Bry's. The overseer had only bought twelve slaves, and they could not farm even a tenth of the acres. Bry had not counted on the labor of building a house or clearing land; on the time it took to raze forest; or the year-round, ceaseless labor that tobacco growing entailed. He didn't reckon on the flies that plagued his fields, nor on slaves dying. Nor on his wife . . .

*   *   *

Inside Susannah's chestnut box, with its silver cover, was a miniature of Anne Bry: a sweet oval face, pale straw-colored hair, a rosebud mouth. And now, when Susannah tried to remember her mother, somehow this painted face was all that would come to mind. In Susannah's fifth summer she had finally faded away; but long before that, fits of fever had kept her in her bed: faint, pale, ailing. So that, when she died, nothing was very different for Susannah. Adela fed her, and soothed her scrapes and cuts, as always; her father gave her lessons. And inside that chestnut box, under the Sermon on the Mount, were a last few tokens of Anne Bry: a rose-shaped pin, a silver spoon engraved S, for Skowland. Sometimes, searching in the trunks of her clothes with Adela, Susannah would think she had caught the scent of her, amid the folds of cloth: rose water and dust. But she would not speak of this brief imagining, of her mother. None of the others did.

Those few times her father spoke Anne's name, it was with a sad dutiful courtesy: as of God. And with that same, sighing duty he took Susannah to church, and taught her the Bible, and letters. Sums he taught her from his own account books; and perhaps because of the intensity, the length, of these few lessons, when they came—Susannah learned. Much she learned on her own. She taught herself to ride, taking her father's old horses bareback through the woods. She swam, and ran across the tobacco fields with Claudine at her heels. The two girls, both curly-haired and willful, looked for all the world like scruffy twins when they came in, dirt-covered, for Adela to wash. Their hair was the same wavy, dark reddish brown, their faces the same indistinct oval. Claudine was paler than her mother, her skin the creamy brown of milky coffee; but she was spoiled, not treated like a slave child, and Susannah forgot that she was one. But then, when they were thirteen or so, Claudine grew tall, standoffish, and they ceased being friends. Claudine would hover protectively around her mother in the kitchen, glowering at Susannah from the doorway.

Susannah turned to the horses, finally to books, in her loneliness. There were only three books in the house: *Paradise Lost, The Lady's Book of Devotions*, and one Mr. Greengower's *Arabian Tales*. She did not always understand them; she wondered, especially, why Araby was accounted so exotic when it had green trees, just like Virginia, and snow. But in time she learned the three volumes nearly by heart. And outside, in the kitchen gardens, she learned the herbs with Adela. . . .

"Su*sannah*!"

Claudine was calling from the forecastle doorway. Drawn and pasty, she clung to the wall. "Come *in*!" she hissed.

Farquhar, who had been telling Susannah of the Indies, grinned and gave Claudine a nod. "G'd morning, miss!"

Claudine ignored him. "We're not to talk to *sailors*," she said grandly. "Come away!" Pushing herself from the door, she stepped unsteadily across the deck. She grabbed hold of Susannah's wrist and gave it a wrench. "Well, then, come!"

"I'll make up my own mind, thank you," said Susannah, twisting free. She stared at Claudine. Even for *her*, this was insolence. Why, she had not tried so hard to start a fight since they were both little girls.

And yet they had a whole long journey to suffer, somehow, together. "You should go back. You're still ill," Susannah said. She could not make herself sound very sympathetic.

"And *you're* every nature of fool," said Claudine. "Talking to strange men." She shot a dismissive glance at Farquhar, who was already well away from them down the deck, joining a cluster of sailors.

"You needn't be rude," said Susannah.

"Huh! Common sailor." Claudine tossed her head at the retreating figure of the second mate, and looked even more put out when he didn't notice. "I'm to

watch for you. Your father said so. For as you know
nothing 'bout men, and what they'll do."

"And what about you?" Susannah was infuriated:
all the more so because she couldn't shout as she
wished, surrounded, as they would be, in an instant,
by sailors. "What do *you* know about them? No more
than I—"

"Huh! I know what they're after, more than any
gooney bird what's got her eyes shut blind." Claudine
tossed her dark head as she moved into the forecastle
door. "Y'have to be *blind* not to see what men as him
is after. What all men are after. Y'have to be stupid. . . ."

A retort leaped to Susannah's throat, but she
thought, *Be a lady. Be dignified.* She turned her back
on Claudine and let it pass.

At night, to escape the confines of the cabin, she ate
at the ship's table with the captain and mates. It was
the first meal she had felt able to try: greasy salt pork
and hard biscuits spread with rancid butter. After
dinner she stood on the deck, breathing deeply: the
illness had nearly passed now. As she felt her way
back to the cabin in the dark, she surprised Claudine,
who was stumbling out. They did not speak; and in
the next few days they seemed only to pass each other,
one always leaving as the other entered, sharing their
stifling cupboard of a cabin only at night.

Soon there was nothing to distinguish one interminable day from the next. Though Susannah, thinking
of Adela's various prohibitions, now kept her distance
from the sailors, Claudine, she noticed, was becoming
fast friends with all of them: dancing on deck, singing
with them—even acting in the plays they made up
together to pass the time. Often as Susannah wandered on deck she would catch sight of Claudine hiding in some hatch or passageway, chased closed behind
by Farquhar. Claudine would escape him, and run
the length of the deck: laughing, disappearing behind
a dropped sail. Yet Susannah, keeping to what she

thought were rules, was not allowed such fun. She wandered to and fro, feeling the injustice of it, trying uselessly to replait her hair as it blew loose in the wind; almost as uselessly, to guess by that wind's strength how long it would take to reach England. And the only man who ventured to approach her now was the captain, with his blurred Scottish talk of winds and moon-phases. Never had she imagined anything as long as a sea voyage.

Tonight the first mate had perched on the table with his fiddle, and Susannah knew it would not be long—before Claudine swept in, with a high unnatural laugh, to join the men, making her feel suddenly ill at ease, out of place. Then she would have to think of being a "lady," much as she liked the music, and . . .

"Miss! Where's your friend?" a sailor called, as she stood, undecided, in the doorway. He doffed an imaginary cap. " 'Scuse me, miss—"

"We'd want you to stay and hear," offered another. The first mate, on the table, shouted agreement.

Nodding, pleased and taken aback by so much respectful attention, Susannah hurried down the corridor to find Claudine. Yes, she thought. She would stay. It was a special night—the captain's birthday, the men said.

She bent in the low doorway. The cabin was strewn with clothes—far more so than usual. "Claudine, what have you been—" she began, annoyed, and then looked up.

Claudine was resplendent. The silver lid of the chestnut box, which she held up to her face, reflected it. Her hair, though dirty as everyone's on board, was piled high, with a long curl dangling at her throat. Her face was clean, her white collar was fresh, and . . .

"That's my dress," said Susannah. Claudine did not seem to hear. "It's *mine*," said Susannah. "What are you doing wearing it?"

She did not like to think herself vain of her possessions. Covetousness was the root of evil—Adela said so. But this was her best dress: her only new one, made up hurriedly by Adela and Susannah before the departure. The skirt was of pure sea-blue wool, to suit her eyes; the bodice, though not of silk, was of a good blue-striped glazed cotton, with silver buttons that had been Anne Bry's. . . .

"It goes on me specially well, do you not think?" Claudine smiled at herself in the lid of the silver box. In sudden exasperation, Susannah reached and snatched it out of her hand.

Claudine spun. "Why, what is wrong?" Her eyes widened as if in innocence.

"You know my clothes aren't for you to wear. I *need* them."

"Aye, to be a fine *lady* in England." Claudine gave a mincing curtsy. Then she curled up her lip, as if to spit. "What a fine mock of a lady *you'll* be. As if your father had any more than a penny to rub in his hand. . . ."

"Naught to do with you," said Susannah, and she knew it was a weak retort. Trust Claudine, she thought, to turn the argument always from what mattered. But the girl *would* hear her, this time. She vowed it.

"You take my things—" She stepped toward Claudine. "You *never* ask me. You've been rude to me all this journey, you scarcely speak to me. And I've been kind—"

Claudine backed up against the wall. She gave the blue skirt a defiant shake. "*Kind*. Well, that is good of you. To be *kind*—"

"I don't know why you always have to be so rude!" Susannah felt the blood rising in her face, and the tears of anger, and she fought them down. The words flew from her. "Why should I suffer you? We thought to do you a favor, letting you come to England. We could have chosen another. A proper maid, who would help me, and—"

"I am not your maid."

"Of course you are," answered Susannah, unthinking.

Claudine shook her head slowly. Then she smiled.

It was a slow, lean smile, and her brown eyes were still and wide, like a cat's. " 'Tis a rare thing for one sister to wait on the other."

"What—" said Susannah. No other words would come.

"Aye," said Claudine. "Your very blood. Your father's." She paused. "So you see, what's yours is mine. Or ought to be."

" 'Tis a lie," said Susannah. It was impossible: Claudine didn't *have* a father. For as long as they had lived together she was only . . . Adela's. Born but two months before Susannah; nursed and raised by the same two mothers, in the same rooms. . . .

It must be a lie, thought Susannah, again, but did not speak. She thought of her father—of Adela. It could not be. "Where has this lie come from? What gave you this notion?"

"It is only the truth." Claudine raised clear eyes to her. "Aye, it is good to be able to speak!"

Susannah could not answer. She leaned against the bunk, her face hot, her heart thudding in her chest.

Claudine smoothed an imaginary wrinkle in her skirt. "My mother was not a slave, you know. She was a free woman of Martinique. Served at the governor's house until your father's men came—and took her."

"Then—why mightn't it be them? Why mightn't one of those men be your father? Not . . ."

But Susannah saw Claudine's curled lip, her face of disdainful refusal. She stared, and searched that face: its even oblong, like her own; its slanting eyes; its one, quizzical, raised brow. Like her father's.

"No, it was not any of those men." Claudine's face was calm again, her eyes wide and blank. "*They* only took her. They told her they would take her to New York, where she would have money. But when she came off the boat, it was Virginia. The only papers she had were slave papers. But she didn't know." Claudine's voice turned belligerent. "She couldn't read."

"You still don't know it was—my father." Her father and Adela. The more Susannah's instincts told

her it was true, the more she revolted against it.
Against the thought of her father . . . at nearly the
same time he had conceived her. . . . "Claudine," she
said slowly. "If this is true, I will make it up to you.
I promise." She could set Claudine free—as Adela had
been, once. She could find her work at the viscountess's house. . . .

"No, Susannah. You can never make it up to me."
Claudine played with one button of the blue-striped
bodice, as if deciding. She did not undo it. And Susannah did not speak of the dress, for it no longer
seemed to matter.

It rained hard for three days. Susannah stayed in
the cabin and hovered about the peeling passageways,
feeling wretched. She tried, at first, not to believe
Claudine. It should have been easy to forget her and
all she said, for Claudine was almost never in their
cabin now, but up on deck, or in the galley or the
hold. Bereft of the blue dress, she was still the fine
lady in the sailors' plays: acting what parts they liked,
or climbing up on Farquhar's shoulders, singing.

Susannah watched her, and saw her father's face in
hers: his own lean features, and his tale-telling ways.
She began to believe her: so much that the sight, the
thought, of those two faces pressed on her mind without cease, until she felt dizzy and her whole head
ached. But she did not speak of it to Claudine.

Fifty-one days into the journey, the sailors began to
strain to see coast. The captain studied the stars and
made his hurried calculations. "We'll be there, aye—
tomorrow," he whispered to Susannah with a wink.

By the next day, the coast was rushing in to meet
them. Rocks, tall cliffs, even houses, were in sight; an
excitement like fever infected the ship. The seamen
started to comb and preen as they hadn't in weeks.
Their clothes were dank and limp, like Susannah's
dresses; Claudine grumbled ceaselessly about arriv-

ing, looking so ill. The brig moved into the Thames now, and a smoky fog surrounded them. Susannah strained but could see nothing but the dim outlines of quays and warehouses. *Is it London yet?* she wondered, but felt too foolish to ask. The salt scent and the fog-filtered light of this place were strange, and only now did she realize how far she had come. *England.* It was a real land, after all. And yet, with its chill—its dim, hazy sun—it was nothing like Virginia. It seemed to Susannah it must occupy some opposite, cold, dark side of the world.

The *Rosaline* jostled and bumped against the docks, and the sailors leapt to fasten her to her moorings. Susannah clung to one of the masts, watching, as the scene around her grew clearer. The wooden docks were teeming with people—passengers, sailors, hawkers—and the river, with boats: humble rowboats, fat cargo carriers, gigantic warships bristling with cannon.

A smoky fog surrounded the ship, invaded it—stung her eyes, and seemed to blind her to the city she knew was near. She could see almost nothing. There was a long, arched bridge, ahead; high steeples, and a great dome that towered over all the gray buildings of the bank. The deep, rotting scent of the air came at her in waves, and she breathed through the folds of her cloak to keep from feeling sick at it. Sailors with crates were pushing past her in the rush to disembark.

Claudine came to find her, with Farquhar. "You'd best find a coach," said the second mate, cheerfully. Susannah nodded, nervously rattling the coins in the deep pocket of her dress. And somehow she found herself on Farquhar's arm, feeling for a footing on the gangplank. She left Claudine with their boxes while Farquhar took her to a place called the Red Lion Inn, where he said there were coaches for hire.

The docks seemed to rock beneath her, and she felt heavy, unused to land. His gold tooth glinting, Farquhar pulled her ahead through the crowds. She felt bodies bump against hers, hands feel for her pockets, and she held tight to her coins and drew in her breath against the stench. On the stairs that ran up to the street a fishwife jostled against her, her cry rising above the groan of ships and clatter of cartwheels: "Cod! Mackerel, haddock. Cod!"

She sounded brave and merry, Susannah thought, though most of these people did not look so. The women were pasty-skinned, the men unshaven; round, yelling mouths, some bare of teeth, gaped round her.

"Buy my pretty eels!" they cried, and, "Tuppence! Tuppence a bag!"

She stared at their heaped carts, their loudness, their audacity. But Farquhar did not notice them. He led her along a bare, gray wall he called the Tower, into an alley of mud-colored houses. The smell of rot—fish bones, urine, and excrement—grew so strong now that the air stopped in her throat. They passed huddled shapes lying in the dirt, which she stumbled over, too afraid to look. At the end of the alley there was a lit window: a door. Farquhar opened it and let her in.

At once she felt fifty eyes upon her. The whole tavern was full of London men: red-faced sailors, shipbuilders, apprentices. Stepping forward, she heard bellows of laughter. When she turned to look for Farquhar—*How strange*, she thought. He wasn't there.

"Mr. Farquhar!" she called, and a few more heads turned toward her.

"Have ye lost yer friend, my pretty?" An old man with a mug gave her a leer.

"Please," she began, "can you tell me if there are coaches here—"

"Coaches, ha!" the man guffawed. She felt more men approaching, and she shrank back toward the doorway.

"Here, chicky, p'raps *I* can help," said another, more sinister voice. She felt a hand reaching to grope her, and before she could see where the voice came from, she ran out through the door.

"Mr. Farquhar!" Her voice rang, hollow, in the alley. Nothing moved; no one answered.

The silence was eerie, and she held her breath again, against the stench, and ran. Back down the alley, past the Tower, stairs, and quay. A cold night wind lashed her cheeks. She did not mind the men who called and hissed at her now, but only prayed that she would find the ship again, and Claudine. Then, somehow, they would get to that strange-named place, The Marches.

The ship was there but deserted: No one was on deck.

"Claudine!" she called, climbing the gangplank.

It was frightening, being here all alone. *Where were they?* She searched the forecastle passage and the cabin; she stopped a lone sailor and asked him if he had seen Claudine or Farquhar.

"Aye, she went tae the docks least ten minutes ago. Sorry, dinna mair, miss!"

Then Claudine had gone, and all of Susannah's things with her. But she might still be on the docks, where Susannah could find her. Susannah ran down the plank again. She would not let all the hawkers and sailors scare her; she would search this place until she found Claudine. For she knew no other soul in this city.

A half hour later she was nervous and queasy, on the point of tears. But she would not cry. London, this beastly city, would pounce on her if she did. It would drag her up with its claws, sneering at her—this naive colonial, this silly Virginia girl—and then it would hurl her into the mucky river. *Stop!* she thought. *You're bewitching yourself.* If only one of these people would answer her. The women all gave her frightened looks and ignored her; the men all asked her questions about herself instead.

"Pardon me, miss. But may I be of assistance?"

Susannah turned. The voice had come from a tall gentleman with plump, pink cheeks and a red-gold wig. He stood, twisting a horsewhip in his hands, while behind him, his manservant staggered under the weight of a loaded cart, and scowled.

"Forgive me—*hem!*—for remarking your distress."

The gentleman leaned in over Susannah and smiled, showing large white teeth. "You appear to be lost—*hem!* If I may be so bold . . ."

Susannah nodded warily. Already so many strange men had tried to "assist" her. But she was tired, and it was growing dark; the gentleman was taming his smile and backing away. "I misdoubt you can help, sir," she said. "I've lost my—friend, who came with me. And now I must get to Surrey."

"Surrey! Well, what good fortune!" Susannah wondered at that, but now the man went on, asking what "great house" she was going to.

"The Marches!" he exclaimed, rejoicing, or so it seemed, in her answer. "The Marches, well!" He repeated this several times in a low, gruff voice that seemed to cough up half his words and bury half deep in his throat. His sword bounced and clattered in its gold sheath at his side. "Why—*hem!*—I shall take you there!" he cried. "For I am—Jonas Hench." He gave a bow. "And a passing acquaintance—though I would it were better—of your good Lady Warrington."

Susannah did not know whether to believe him. It seemed to her London was full of all sorts of impostors. But then, night was falling, and she had little choice. It occurred to her to test this man: to see if his account of the Warringtons matched her father's.

"Then do you know the family?" she said.

Hench gave a snort. "Sure I do! The Lady—her son, m'lord Henry, your master—" Hench broke off. A small, black-faced boy was hopping up and down beside Susannah. Hench harrumphed. "It seems, my dear, you have a message."

Susannah leaned down toward the breathless sweep.

"Miss Bry? Miss Susan Bry?"

She nodded.

" *'Ere.*" Proudly he displayed Anne Bry's box, with its silver lid.

Susannah smiled suddenly—she was so glad to see it again—and said, "Thank you kindly! Where did you get it?"

The boy hesitated. "A lady. A dark lady, an' she said give you this." He drew a grubby parcel of paper from his pocket, which Susannah unfolded quickly and read.

I hear we are free when we gets the shores of England, so I am setting myself free & returne you this. Don't look for me. Wyth Wishes for your Fortune in England,

Yr Sister CLAUDINE *her Mark—X*
Roderick Farquhar Scripsit.

That was all. Susannah folded the note and saw Hench hand the boy a penny.

"Come," he said. "Let us not tarry. We are tiring my good man." He moved past the servant, who was shifting on his feet and grimacing, and led Susannah up the river stairs. Susannah stared in wonderment at the gilt-trimmed, great-bellied red coach.

"We'll be pushed together summat, with my affairs," Hench chortled, ushering her inside. Half the coach's velvet cushions were covered with boxes. "But I like," he said, shifting onto the seat beside her, "to see my wares in harbor, 'fore I pays 'em. Tell me, dovey. D'you go to The Marches as chambermaid—or kitchen maid?"

Chapter 2

———— ✹ ————

A miniature woman in flowing golden robes swung around and struck a silver gong, gently chiming the hour inside the clock of The Marches' Chinese bedroom. The sound was high and trilling, meant not to trouble ladies who had sat up too late at cards the night before; but it woke Susannah, who had slept little. The ride from London had left her wakeful, for she had spent most of it fending off the embraces of Mr. Hench, who persisted in thinking she was a maid on her way to a new post.

"Please," she had gasped, and "Leave me, sir—" to no avail. Snaking one plump arm around her, breathing hard, he had reached for her breasts. They were alone; the dim lights of London, outside the coach windows, had vanished, and the driver's back, up front, was turned. She inched away from Hench until there was no more room on the seat; finally, she tumbled off onto the floor. His arms suddenly empty, Hench gaped and fell after her.

"Mr. Hench, you must know—" she had gasped, "I am not a maid. I'm—Lady Warrington's niece."

"Lady Warrington—" Hench spluttered, and rose to his knees. "Lady—well! I—"

They passed the rest of the four hours' journey in silence.

The coach slowed and turned in beside a gatehouse. This she had taken for The Marches itself, so huge and white it appeared in the torchlight; but after the gate-keeper had examined them, they moved on, to a house so vast she could not even see it all: two broad stair-cases leading up to a door twice the height of her companion, who bellowed, "Hench here!" to the maid who swung it open at last. "Show us in."

The maid gave him a suspicious look in the torch-light, but curtsied. Then she led them across a wide hall of which Susannah could see little but the squares of black and white marble that formed its floor; and then into a parlor lit by twenty or thirty candles. Everything in the room seemed to shine in Susannah's eyes, at once: the sky-blue silk on the walls, the white-and-gilt woodwork of the doors and ceilings and furniture; the jewels on the bare necks of the ladies, as they turned, in unison, to look at her. For a moment, she searched these many faces, in the faint hope that one would appear, somehow, familiar. But none did.

In one corner, a freckled, fair-headed man, and another with a high cockscomb of black hair, played at cards. On a sofa, a plump girl fixed curious eyes on Susannah, a book dangling, neglected, from her hand. Not far away sat a couple, holding hands as they looked up, their faces languid and still as marble sculptures: the lady, with arrow-straight brows and raven hair; the gentleman, velvet-clad, flexing his high-heeled feet. And there was one lady who moved forward, at last, to greet the visitors: a dark-haired lady of perhaps forty-five.

She was only a few inches taller than Susannah, but her lofty walk, nose high and chest thrust forward, gave an impression of far greater height. She was handsome, Susannah thought, rather than pretty, with a long, thin face and a nose tipped by a bead of flesh, which quivered, now, as she smiled.

"Who are you?" she said. Her voice was loud and seemed to strain in her throat to rise to even greater heights.

Susannah looked up at Hench, and then back at this woman, who must be her aunt. "Susannah Bry. From—from America."

Her aunt said nothing. If the news surprised her, she showed it only in a widening of the eyes and an unsmiling, unbroken silence.

"My father sent me. There is a letter—" Susannah felt desperately in the pocket of her cloak, regretting more with every second that her father had not sent a message ahead of her.

In the corner the two gentlemen at cards resumed a low conversation; and still the seconds passed, in ominous silence, while Susannah offered her father's rumpled missive, and while Maria Warrington—her eyes and nose wrinkling—accepted it. She broke its seal, and the paper crackled. "I cannot read this," she said.

Susannah felt her face flush red; and when her voice came, it sounded distant, outside herself, ringing in her ears. She thought of her father's struggle to produce even the spidery, illegible hand there on the page. "It says—" she stammered, "who I am, and why I am come. . . ."

"Very well," said Maria. But it did not sound very well at all. Folding the letter up again, she gave Susannah a long look. Her eyes were dark brown and lifeless. "I do not know why you are here, Miss Bry, but I have no inclination to examine the matter now." Her eyes narrowed, and her mouth began to stretch wide; and Susannah realized that her aunt was, in fact, smiling, as she turned past her and toward Mr. Hench. "Sir, forgive me. I have been uncivil. You *will* stay the night with us, I take it? . . . Augusta!" She turned to the group behind her, beckoning, and the small, plump girl on the sofa stood up. "Take—" Maria's long nose twitched. "Take your *cousin* to the Chinese bedroom, in the west wing. After that, you may go to bed."

Now, as if given some unspoken permission, the other guests in the room began to move, and talk more loudly. The momentary drama of a new arrival so quickly begun and ended, the card players reshuffled, the raven-haired lady and her small gentleman renewed their gossip, and Maria, Lady Warrington, now turned her attention to Hench, whom she seated by the fire and handed a brimming glass of wine.

The plump, short girl came up close to Susannah's side. "Susannah?" she said in a warbling voice, friendlier than Maria's. "I am sure I had never *heard* of you before . . ." Her eyes, a pale blue, looked oddly ready to spill over with tears. They did not spill over, however, and Augusta smiled as she took Susannah's arm and ushered her out of the room and into the dark hall.

"How do you find your way?" said Susannah as they moved down the hall—not the one through which they had entered the house, but a longer, bare corridor leading to a stair.

"Find my way?" said Augusta, puzzled.

"I mean . . . there are so many passages."

Augusta gave her a moment's perturbed blue gaze, then let the matter pass. She asked Susannah where she came from. And with little trouble, Susannah soon found herself telling her. At the tale of the fire, Augusta's eyes widened, but she made no comment; she moved along briskly, a pair of leather-framed spectacles bobbing on her chest. At the door to a chamber she stopped, giving a yawn which ended in a squeak. "Forgive me! These late evenings do not suit my constitution."

"What time is it?" said Susannah.

"Midnight! I will have them send up supper." Augusta walked off as briskly as she had come, leaving Susannah to wonder if midnight was the usual hour for supping here. *And who were all those people?*

Now, in the morning sun, she saw the "Chinese" bedroom properly for the first time: the clock, with

its narrow-eyed figurine chiming the hour—eight—
and the spindly black chairs aligned against the yellow walls. There was so much other furniture in the
chamber that when Susannah rose from bed she found
she had to pick a path through black-and-gilt tables,
pillars, stands, and stools. There was enough here, she
thought, for three rooms, all delicately carved and in-
laid; but it looked disused.

And it was dusty. The porcelain ladies on a shelf,
the brass candlesnuffers shaped like gnarled trees, the
rows of miniature plates and cups on the mantel—
everything her curious eyes lit on, and which she dared
not touch, was covered with a gray film of dust. The
gold velvet curtains sent out clouds of it when she
pulled them open. But, as she sniffed and almost
sneezed, she admonished herself for noticing. *Why,
the Warringtons are rich.* They had so many rooms,
they must not have time to clean them all.

And out, beyond the wavy panes of glass, lay a
world nearly as mysterious and nearly as full of wonders. Beyond the round, trimmed trees of an orchard,
the splayed vines on their trellises, and a row of
whitewashed outbuildings rose hills so green and
smoothly mown that Susannah wondered where the
rich farmland could possibly end. Where was the wilderness? If the Warringtons actually farmed all this
land—why, their wealth must be endless. She felt
giddy, looking out at it: as if she had seen her father's
dreams of plantation and prosperity come true.

Still half-dizzy, with the bright sun in her eyes, she
dressed. She had only the white, bedraggled gown of
yesterday. And as she saw her face, for the first time,
in the washstand mirror, she blinked in dismay. "Holy
ghost," she whispered.

The oath, which had long earned scoldings from
Adela, worked no changes. She saw hair, brown and
matted; a face, greenish and gaunt. What must her
aunt Maria have thought when she saw her? Never
before had she been thin—but on the ship all appetite
had left her. The broth, and the strange, airy white

bread that had come to her room last night had been
the first meal she had enjoyed in weeks.

Thinking, with growing hunger, of bacon and por-
ridge and cornbread, she plunged her face into the
basin of water on the tabletop. The water was cold
and deliciously fresh. She blew bubbles in it, raised
her head, and let the water drip down her neck. She
scrubbed her hands and face with the linen towel and
ran wet hands through her hair. There was no hope
of untangling it, now, but luckily it was so thick, it
did not look as dirty as it felt. Tying it back in its blue
ribbon, she galloped down the two flights of stairs
outside her room.

On the ground floor she heard no voices, no sounds
of breakfast. The long corridor she had traversed last
night was silent; it ended, finally, at a closed door,
which she opened, coming upon a high-ceilinged parlor with dark-green walls. It was quite a different
chamber from the blue one she had seen last night,
yet just as grand. For a moment the pictures of horses
on the walls intrigued her. She read the animals'
names on the frames: Jupiter, Invincible, Hotspur. If
her relations liked horses, they must be kinder and
better than they first seemed—perhaps even Aunt Maria. She left through another door and found herself
in the house's vast entrance hall, two stories high. Here
was the floor of checkered black and white marble
that she had crossed before. All that rose above it was
black, gray, or white, giving the place a chilly stark-
ness in the morning light. Twin staircases rose along
its side walls, which were lined with niches filled with
statues. Now that she had arrived here, she began to
know where she was; though her wonderment was no
less, she lost her fear. She explored further: she followed the light under the stairs, to the picture gallery.

At once she liked this room, with its long bright
wall of windows, and facing wall of paintings and
portraits. She walked along, regarding these faces,
which must be her ancestors': some of them wore high
ruffs and feathered hats, some boots and military uniform. She did not know their names—these ancient

Warringtons and Skowlands—but she knew now that they were grand. She gave a quick, excited spin on the parquetry. *Gracious Lord! But how grand.* Her father had not even told her. And she moved past the portraits of two spaniels, and a bay stallion, toward the figures in modern dress. Here was George II, the old king, and his queen; here were a dark-haired, knob-nosed "Amelia Blackpole," whom she knew to be her aunt, eight years dead; a young and serene Aunt Maria, and—the last— her mother, Anne. Her heart leapt, for she knew her at once. It was the face, not of the miniature but of life: pale cheeks and straw-colored hair, with a rose trailing from her hand. She looked no older than she, Susannah, was right now.

Suddenly she turned from the wall. She had felt a sadness, a foolish notion. *Why have you come back?* the picture seemed to say. *You do not belong.* Her mother was well-dressed, coiffed, refined. And she . . .

One of the windows of the gallery, she saw, was a door, and it was open. And longing, suddenly, for air—to be free of here—she pulled it further, its frame rattling, and ran.

Her feet sank into damp grass and sprang easily up again, and she did not stop to look back until she had come to a patch of forest and some outbuildings.

"Oh, Father," she breathed, staring back, astonished. *This is too grand for me.* What would he think of this place—if he only knew? The Marches stretched across the meadow behind: bestriding it, possessing its land with a lordly complacency. The house was rectangular, of an exact symmetry, casting out identical wings to east and west, and sinking a terrace into the mild downward slope of its lawn. Its three stories of windows were marked by four long, flat-stone pilasters; its only exuberance the flourish of scrolls and leaves that topped each restrained Grecian column. The whole of it, whitewashed to a high gleam, seemed to Susannah to sparkle in the sunlight; and if The Marches had imperfections—a certain dull conformity, for all its splendor—she did not see it. She thought, as she backed away from it, still staring, that she had never seen a house so glorious.

Her feet crunched on gravel, and she turned to see where she was. At the edge of the lawn, here, were stables and a field. In the field was a lone horse, tied to a post. And forgetting the house now—with a kind of relief—she moved toward it.

The chestnut mare started and whinnied. "Now, there! You're a shy creature," admonished Susannah. The mare's eyes were wide and wary. She tossed her head as Susannah stroked her; she sniffed Susannah's hand suspiciously. But at last she whinnied and grew calm again; and, somehow, not thinking, not quite knowing what she meant to do, Susannah found herself untying her: holding her reins and murmuring soothing words, seeing her hard-muscled legs quiver, taking hold of the saddle and climbing up. *Only*, she told herself, *to see how it feels.* . . . Her skirts flew up and settled down around her. She had always ridden man-fashion at home, and no one had tried to stop her.

It was lucky, now, that she did: for the horse bolted away under her with such speed that she was nearly unseated. And before Susannah could worry, now, about riding away with no one's permission, it was all she could manage to pull in on the reins and control the horse. Before she knew it, the mare had leapt the far fence and shot across the meadows beyond.

Susannah's hair blew loose from its ribbon, rising and falling in the wind like a heavy curtain. She knew now that she wouldn't fall. "Go, go on," she murmured in the mare's ear, and rode on, feeling blissfully free.

They ran past the edge of a forest, and a lake, through a daisy-covered meadow, and past a miniature house on a hill. She thought she saw a man there, and a horse, but she had no time to look again; the mare's hooves drummed and thundered. They jumped a high hedge and galloped on, not breaking rhythm, and as they crossed a second field Susannah thought— then she was sure—that she heard hooves drumming behind her. She could not think why she heard them, but she turned her head warily. And, to her astonishment, there was another horse following: mounted by a young man with light hair and a terrified expression. Had he come from behind—from that small house?

As she brought her horse round the edge of the field, he still followed; and as she came back to the hedge, and jumped, he jumped after her. His horse leapt early, and landed with a thud. She reined in at the sound, hoping he had not fallen.

He was still mounted, though his saddle was leaning to one side. He stared at Susannah, wide-eyed, and she heard his rasping breath.

"Are you"—the young man gasped—"all right?" His horse trotted closer, catching up.

"Yes! Of course," she said. "But are you?"

The man had caught his breath and resumed something like a normal expression, though he still looked pale and harrowed from the chase. "I—I—w-was worried—about you," he said. "I—I—th-thought your horse had run away with—with you." He had blue eyes and an eager, slightly pockmarked face. His sand-colored hair, blown loose from a ponytail, hung in tendrils over his forehead.

"No!" Susannah laughed. "This horse is overwillful. She mustn't have had a real ride in days."

The man looked abashed. "You see, I—I thought I would catch up with—you, and save you."

"Save me? Why should you? You probably don't even know who I am." Susannah smiled again at the man, who was keeping pace with her now that her mare had slowed, trotting along beside her.

"Are you—another of my mother's v-visitors?" he said.

He reminded her, when she looked at him again, of Augusta. *Of course,* she thought to herself: *my cousin.* For his shyness, like Augusta's, had an odd way of putting her at her ease. She was breathless from the ride, and somehow the words poured from her. She told him who she was: of the plantation, America.

"And did you learn to ride there?" the man said

now, beginning to lose his stutter. He gave a nod at her legs straddling the horse.

"Is it unladylike?" Susannah's brow wrinkled. "It must be. Anything I truly like to do always turns out to be."

The young man almost laughed. "No! No. Why—I think it is—most brave."

"Brave?" Susannah let out a ripple of laughter at the word. He smiled, looking puzzled. "I—" She started to explain but couldn't. They rode onto a path along the lake she had seen earlier. "What is your name?" she said at last.

"I am Henry. But my family c-c-calls me Harry." Harry was smiling, in his tentative way, but now, as he looked farther ahead, his face fell. He looked at Susannah as if about to speak; but he did not, and around the next bend tripped Maria. She marched along the path, her arms looped through those of two gentlemen: a freckled one and a dour-looking one with a black cockscomb of hair. Susannah recognized them from last night.

Maria's eyes passed over Harry and fixed on Susannah and her mount, chill and unblinking.

"That—that is my mother," said Harry, unnecessarily, when they passed on. "You know—you are riding Cythera. Her horse. No one else—ever rides her." He looked over at Susannah with an odd, apologetic smile.

They returned their mounts to the stables: Susannah with a growing dread, which Harry's reassurances did nothing to lighten. *My aunt's horse.* How could she, she wondered, have been so foolish as to take her? Now, when her aunt hardly knew her: scarcely seemed to like her. . . .

She returned to her room, wondering if some summons, some reprimand, would come. But the only message that did come, around noontime, was a maid's: "Miss? Your bath is ready."

She had not asked for one: they were too much

trouble. But she was glad to follow the maid to the bathing room below, without wondering more at where the order had come from. Every time she opened her eyes, a different maid seemed to appear: the first to soap her, the second to wash her hair, the third to wrap her in towels, by the fire.

"Do you do this for . . . all the ladies here?" Susannah said wonderingly to the third maid.

"Yes'm," said the girl, reproving, "but I be but a cook-maid. Not a lady's maid, miss."

"Then how many servants do you have here?" asked Susannah. The maid had taken her to her cousin Augusta's chamber, which was far grander than her own, with an immense bed with fringed curtains of blue damask. Augusta's separate blue-and-white dressing room was nearly as large as Susannah's bedroom.

"Heavens! I've no notion, they come and go so. . . ." Augusta, munching a sugared chestnut, offered Susannah the dish. "Why, perhaps we've fifty or sixty. But one doesn't *count.*"

Susannah, wondering why in the world one *shouldn't* "count," gladly took a chestnut. Her stomach, by now, was growling. "Is there a maid for every person in the house?"

"Well, yes. And then there are the parlor-maids, the cook-maids . . . the footmen, the coachmen, the grooms, the gardeners—oh, don't trouble yourself to remember them all!"

A maid in a ruffled cap knocked at the door.

"Oh, good! Mary. You're to see to Miss Bry's wardrobe."

Susannah swallowed, and gave a tongue-tied smile. She had no wardrobe: Claudine had taken it all. And she dreaded explaining.

Augusta gave her an astute, kind look. "Would you like to borrow something of mine, dear?" she said.

"Yes, please, I—" Susannah babbled, with relief. "I—had things, but the girl who was my maid—"

"Maids! Oh, I *know*, say no more," clucked Augusta. Together, they heaped her bed high with clothes from the dressing room next door. Though the dress she wore was of plain dark blue, relieved only by the white fichu round her neck, everything else she possessed looked light and brilliant. Susannah had never seen such silks and fine cottons—or worn anything like them herself. All of her dresses had been of calico or plain woolen.

"You needn't trouble," she said shyly, when they had chosen a tan striped frock, the longest there; the maid was fetching scissors and pins from her bag. "I could sew . . ."

Augusta gaped, and Mary looked affronted. "Nonsense!" pronounced Augusta. "We shouldn't *let* you."

After a half hour of Mary's needlework, Susannah's new, English garment was complete. Though it was too short and showed her ankles, it still felt heavy and strange: so much silk went into the complicated tucks that made the back of the skirt swell out. Underneath, she wore three petticoats and a cushion on her rump. All of the women here, Susannah had noticed, puffed out at front and back, the abundant ruffles at their necks surmounted by even frothier curls. How unfashionable her own, square-necked, straight-falling gowns must have been.

Augusta fitted her spectacles to her nose and gave a tug to Susannah's fichu. "Politics and more politics!" she said. "That's all we'll hear at dinner. Mr. Argothlyn on the doom of man, Mr. Sheldon on Progress . . . How I should rejoice, my dear, were we, together, to advance the conversation to . . . literature." Susannah liked her cousin too much, already, to disappoint her by telling her how little she knew of books.

At four o'clock the two cousins lingered beneath the great staircase, examining the guests as they circled hungrily in the dining room.

"Mr. Sheldon," murmured Augusta, nodding toward Maria's freckled companion from the lakeside that morning. His dark-haired and glowering opposite, energetically pacing the room, was Mr. Argothlyn. "Mother likes to keep her politicians about her," whispered Augusta, "and at each other's throats! Though in fact, both gentlemen are Whigs. . . ."

"Wigs?" said Susannah, staring at Mr. Sheldon's thinning head of light hair.

Augusta went blithely on. *"There* are the Framers. Lord Silvius and Lady Caroline." Susannah recognized the pair that the night before had seemed cast in marble: the lady with the black hair and hard, straight brows and the gentleman, still velvet-suited and high-heeled, though the color and trimmings of this apparel, she noticed, had changed overnight.

A dark-suited gentleman with slicked-back hair who beamed and bowed as Maria entered the room, was her secretary, Knole; and the plump-cheeked curate talking to Harry in the corner was his old tutor, Bayliss. "Dear Mr. Bayliss," murmured Augusta. "Such accomplishments! He has Hebrew, Latin, and Greek. . . . Why, he is almost as learned as Harry!"

Footmen in red livery were lining up by the mahogany sideboard, and Susannah and Augusta hurried in to take their places, at the bottom of the table, by Harry, Bayliss, and Knole. Maria presided at the other end, beckoning servants and tossing jibes at her two politicians. From time to time she speared a morsel of meat, waving it in the air for emphasis.

"How do you rate Mr. Hastings's chances?" she called down the table to Jonas Hench. While her guest cleared his throat, she explained, in admiring tones, to the table at large, "Mr. Hench served our East India Company for twelve years."

"Well," growled the politician Argothlyn, "was Hastings the tyrant they're trying him for? Not that one may expect less than tyranny of the mere brute human beast. . . ."

"Hem! Done no wrong!" managed Hench, through a mouthful of beef. "Law, you know. No import to these natives. Keep a firm hand. . . ."

Susannah understood little of this talk. The hurrying footmen, the silver platters, the enormous roasts and pies—all of them seemed so wondrously abundant that she forgot the conversation for staring as they passed. At her end of the table Harry and Bayliss were conferring, on—the cheery, plump-cheeked curate informed her—"the inaccuracies of Hebraic translation." She nodded silently. Across from her, Knole the secretary was craning his neck toward the head of the table.

"He won't understand," Augusta whispered to her, "that he is a *servant*."

The footmen glided from sideboard to table with the second course, much similar to the first. Pigeon pies were replaced by rabbit pies; a roast ham by a leg of lamb. There were boiled potatoes and curious pointed stalks, which Susannah ate, in imitation of the others: biting off their green tips and discarding the rest. Heaps of pink-streaked meat still remained on the platters, and there were baskets of airy white rolls, instead of the leaden cornbread she was used to. The quivering lumps in seashells she passed up, like most of the other guests. She knew she was gaping, unladylike, at each passing platter and wielding the outsize knives and forks clumsily. But she realized she did not stand out. Her aunt gulped her wine a glass at a time, and Mr. Argothlyn, expounding, "No trust to the French!" ate his meat off the end of his knife. Mr. Hench ate with his fingers and a lump of bread.

"Yes! Do tell us your thoughts, Mr. Bayliss," Augusta was twittering. By now, the desserts were being passed: cheese, biscuits, and gooseberry pies.

The plump curate wiped his mouth. "I must admit to finding an admirable seriousness in that work *Paradise Lost*—"

"*Paradise Lost*?" echoed Susannah. Bayliss, Harry, and Augusta all turned to look at her.

"Have you read it?" chirped Augusta. "What, is *that* dire volume still favored in America? Forgive me, Mr. Bayliss—"

"Dire?" said Susannah. "It was better, I thought, than the others. . . ."

"Have you read any of the *newer* poets?" Augusta's

voice rose higher, and her eyes grew watery with excitement. "Crabbe, or Gray, or Stephen Duck-the-Thresher-Poet? What pleasure lies before you, then! . . . *Harry* writes poetry, too, you know."

Three pairs of eyes turned on Harry, who flushed pink. "That is, I . . . F-forgive my sister, S-Susannah. I no—no longer attempt that art."

"Why not?" said Susannah innocently.

"The t-time is past," said Harry. "The p-p-poetic art reached its—zenith with Dryden and Pope, so that—I find—lately our endeavors are l-locked in futility."

"Indeed," said Bayliss approvingly. "There is far more to be achieved, Lord Harry, in your new pursuit of history."

"But he has *published* a book of verse," said Augusta importantly. "*Speciosa Miracula.* Highly regarded, I am told. . . ."

"What sort of verse?" said Susannah. Harry's eyes met hers, eager, and he was opening his mouth to reply when a loud clatter near the head of the table startled the company into silence.

Lady Caroline Framer stood, her chair overturned on the floor behind her. "I shall not *hear* of it," she hissed across the table at her husband; and her black brows seemed to join in a straight line. She spun and stalked from the room, the gray frizz of her powdered black hair flying behind her.

In the ensuing silence, Maria stood. "I think"—she forced a gracious smile—"it is time we ladies left the gentlemen to their port."

As soon as all the ladies had removed themselves, however, Maria excused herself from drinking tea in the music room. "I have matters to see to," she announced. "Susannah, you shall come to my study in half an hour." With that, she swept back to the dining room door and called loudly, "Knole!"

She is angry with me, thought Susannah, as she sat uneasily sipping tea with Augusta. She only half-heard her cousin's speculations on the cause of Lord and Lady Framer's dramatic row. *It must be about the horse—Cythera*, she thought, watching the hands of the clock on the mantel.

When the thirty minutes had elapsed, she made her way up the great black-and-white stair with a sinking feeling. She needed no directions to the study, for her aunt's rich laughter rang out into the hall. She followed the sound and the glow of candlelight to a crimson-walled chamber where her aunt and her secretary were busy conferring.

"Lord Silvius *confessed* it? The actress—Mrs. Fitzgilbert?" Maria let out a loud, incredulous laugh. She did not seem to see Susannah in the doorway. "Ha! He'll be *her* cuckold quicker than he was his wife's. At least Caroline used some discretion. . . ."

Her gaze passed over the door and rested affectionately upon the slick-haired secretary at the desk. "Dear Knole. I vow, you are my eyes and ears. I simply *must* find some way to reward you. . . ."

Knole bowed his oiled, dark head over his stack of correspondence; looking up, he caught sight of Susannah, and gave a cough. But Maria seemed in no hurry to acknowledge her niece. She looked at her blankly, then let out an annoyed sigh. "Knole. Do find that letter now. . . . Come in, Susannah. And sit."

Susannah took a place on the sofa, and had what seemed like several minutes to study the fire and the rose-patterned rug while her aunt stared at the rumpled sheet Knole had procured: her father's letter.

"I can't make out a word of this abominable scrawl."

Susannah looked up. Her heart was pounding.

"I think," said Maria slowly, "that if we are *ever* to know why you have been shipped to us here, without so much as a decent set of clothes or a word of warning—*you*, my dear, shall have to read this." Unblinking, she extended a bony hand, from which the letter dangled. "It quite exceeds my patience."

Susannah knew then what her aunt meant to do. Her father's awkward words, his apologies could only humiliate her. She took a deep breath. "I would rather tell you—myself, why I am come."

Maria, leaning back in her chair, gave a nod.

Knole looked up from his writing. "There has been, er," he said helpfully, "some accident to your family?"

"Our house took fire," said Susannah quickly. "My father thought it best—to send me away, as for some months we would have no place to live, and—"

"It surprises me," broke in Maria, "that he didn't go bankrupt sooner—and send his whole household back for me to support!"

Susannah felt her face redden. *I am the only one*, she thought, but the fact could little help her case now.

"Whatever led him to believe he had a *right* to send you?" Maria waited for no answer. Her voice rose higher. "Well? Did he ever care a shilling for our family? For your mother? Did he ever have an ounce of regard for anything but his own wastrel ways?" Maria half rose in her seat, and now she leaned forward, her dark eyes mean and narrowed. "Never! Never in his life, till it came time to send his daughter begging. . . ."

"My lady. The girl is distressed." In a soft voice Knole tried to intervene. Susannah felt the blood beating at her skin, the tears of humiliation rising in her eyes. She turned her face from her aunt and Knole.

"Well!" Maria turned, glaring, on the secretary. "I am glad you possess such a fine degree of sympathy. For perhaps you might extend it to *me*, in *my* difficulties. Not only has the girl come uninvited, but at a most inconvenient time. *All* my energies must be devoted to the estate—Lord knows Henry's are not! And then there is Augusta's marriage. . . ."

"Now, my lady," tried Knole, stroking at his quill, "there is surely time . . ."

"Little enough!" spat Maria. "She grows no younger."

But she was not to be soothed, despite Knole's efforts, or drawn long away from the subject of Susannah.

"I suppose," she said, standing up and beginning to

pace, "that George Bry expects me to find his daughter a husband. Nay!" She gave a dry, sarcastic laugh. "Why not a dowry, too?. . . Well!" She turned on Susannah. "I can assure you, I will not."

A silence fell. Knole said bravely, "Why, Miss Susannah might marry—even without a portion."

Susannah, catching sight of his admiring look, again reddened.

"Let her, then!" snapped Maria. "But that drunkard Bry cannot expect me to pay for it."

"He isn't a drunkard!" cried Susannah. She looked straight at her aunt, now, defiant.

"Well, child!" Maria looked down on her with a mocking smile. "I will not disabuse you of your innocence. But mark, whatever I do give you, 'tis on my sister's—your mother's—account." She paused. "You shall live with us here until we find you a suitable place. There are ever elderly ladies in the neighborhood, needing companions. . . ."

"Lady Chathenham," murmured Knole.

"Why, yes," said Maria. "Lady Chathenham. Knole, I shall trust you to investigate. In the meantime, Susannah, you shall be of what use you can, here. I trust you are able to write. . . ."

Susannah looked up, astonished, then away from her aunt. She could not bring herself to answer such an insult.

"Can you sew?" demanded Maria. "Can you do sums, and make a neat copy?"

Susannah nodded. She did not trust her voice.

"Well! I can expect no more of one raised in the wilderness, I am sure, in the way of French, japanning . . . the *refinements* of education. But that's of little account to me. There is still work you can do here." She gave Susannah a brief nod. "Well! You may go." She turned, with a sweep of her skirts, and did not see Susannah leave: instead, her eye was suddenly drawn to a gold-bordered invitation card lying on the desk.

"Knole!" She lifted the card in the light, admiring. "You rascal. You didn't *tell* me. The rout at the Dev-

onshires'." She beamed down on her secretary. "At
last."

Making her way through the corridor, the tallow
candle Knole had given her sparking and sputtering,
Susannah sent up a prayer. *Please don't let my aunt
hate me.* She had not asked to come here. But now
she was here, and alone, and there was nowhere else
to go. She *would* work hard—she vowed it now—and
try to please her aunt, and change her mind. Then,
perhaps, she would be allowed to stay here. Perhaps,
even, in time, she would find a husband. . . .

She gulped, and took a deep, straining breath. She
felt as if she were a child again, walking a high fence,
with nothing to either side but a great fall.

Chapter 3

------- 🐚 -------

In the next few days, Susannah strove to be good. She would not run or hitch her skirts up high climbing the stairs or wolf her dinner. She smoothed her wayward hair every time she passed a mirror; when anyone addressed her, she spoke quietly and little. When she and her aunt chanced to meet, Maria nodded at her with an impersonal smile; Susannah thought herself reprieved until, on her third morning at the house, she was summoned to the upstairs study.

"Susannah! At last." Maria blew on the drying ink of a letter and scattered it with sand. She gestured toward a chair, and pen and ink. "Show me your writing."

"What shall I write?"

"What shall you write? Oh—" Maria let out a hissing breath. "Here. I shall dictate." She sounded impatient. "Don't mind the address, it doesn't signify. . . . Then—'I have received with great regret the news of your departure, though naturally wish the best consequences—' Do you take me?"

"Wait, please," breathed Susannah, scribbling desperately. The quill slid through her fingers, casting her letters awry.

"You've taken far too much ink. I shall go on. '—consequences of the journey you undertake. I shall inform you, of course, of the celebrations at Devonshire House. . . .' " Maria went on; she smiled as she paced and dictated; she seemed to be enjoying the tale she was spinning. But Susannah was too far behind to keep track of her words. She handed over the sheet at last, and looked on apprehensively as Maria read: "I have racived with grate regrette . . ."

"What is this?" she said, and tapped her foot. "Well?"

"It is—what you said." Susannah looked down. "I tried—"

"Evidently." Maria began, again, to pace the floor, as was her habit. "I had no expectation"—her voice grew louder—"that with your upbringing you should possess an intimate knowledge of Dr. Johnson's *Dictionary*, or the spelling of *every* word therein." Her breath hissed out again, and her voice suddenly lowered. "But I did expect the simple accomplishment of literacy."

Her gaze ran up and down Susannah, who studied her own ink-stained hands and did not answer. For, if it would be a lie to say she had labored at books all her childhood, neither would she bow to her aunt's accusations. *I did try. . . .*

"Well!" said Maria now. "I shall improve you, as much as I can. I shall have to. For you are no use writing for me"—she batted at Susannah's page, still in her hand—"if *this* is what you produce. Now." She picked up a folded note from her desk. "Take this down to the kitchen, to Mrs. Barnes. It is time you learnt your way about."

When the girl was dispatched—the whole business, Maria reflected to her satisfaction, concluded in a quarter hour—she shouted, "Knole!"

The shiny head of the secretary appeared in the

doorway. She had not wished him in the room while the girl was there—mooning about and interfering.

"Knole." She gave a thin-lipped smile. "I have been thinking. What do you know of Jonas Hench?"

"The—India gentleman?" Knole's mouth opened and closed.

"Would you trouble to find out for me, Knole, what manner of man he is? I am thinking of . . . inviting him here, again."

"The gentleman," Knole could be heard to murmur, "m'lady, is in *trade.*" But Maria was deep in her own thoughts and ignored him.

Augusta was her third and last unmarried daughter, and the most difficult to dispose of. Not that she bore any especial burden of looks or brains—indeed she compared well with Helena and Agnes, and was certainly cleverer. Acquaintances, long nurtured with an eye to her daughters' eventual maturity, had complaisantly taken the hands of the two elder girls: a City banker, Stillwell, for Helena, now twenty-two; and a Somerset squire, Burleigh, for Agnes, a year younger. Their wealth, though not enormous, was respectable: and without the vulgar, new tint of India gold. . . .

Of course Maria did not consult Augusta on the suitability of Jonas Hench—or any other husband. It was her creed that girls must be married young. Age marred a girl's looks long before it gave her wisdom; nor could a daughter's advancing years cast a flattering light upon her mother. . . .

"What do you think," she mused to Knole, "of holding a hunt here, come October? With a ball and a picnic lunch—Lady Framer says they're all the fashion."

"Would"—Knole sniffed—"the India gentleman come?"

Susannah, who was as far from Maria's thoughts now as if she had not existed, struggled through the first pages of her cousin's French grammar. It had

been her own notion—enthusiastically encouraged by
Augusta—though, confronted by long pages of verbs,
she was beginning to have second thoughts. Her aunt
thought her ignorant; and she was determined, in
time, to prove her wrong. Augusta and Harry were
educated and certainly eager to help.

Pondering over the book, she remembered odd
words that Adela had interspersed with her English—
cochon, le bon Dieu, très chère—and wondered if
these strange-looking words could be the same language she had spoken. She remembered Adela's warm,
sweaty scent; her bold laugh, which was like Claudine's. She wondered, sometimes, where Claudine
was; but she was glad, in a way, to be kept so busy
here. There was little time to think, or miss home.
Already it was receding from her. When she wrote to
her father, she could not think how to describe this
life. It was luxurious, leisurely, compared to the one
they led at home: and yet, as the weeks passed, here,
she began to forget that at first it had seemed so
strange.

Though her aunt still professed dissatisfaction with
her—her uncontrollable hair, her loud footsteps, her
sprawling writing—she seemed also to find more and
more uses for her.

"Susannah! Fetch Celeste for me," she would demand, when her proud Belgian lady's maid failed to
waken. Or, "Lyme is taking the coach to Bothwell
village. Will you go too and fetch me a yard-length
of blue ribbon? I *would* send Celeste, dear, but I know
she would take a yard, too, for herself. . . ."

It seemed curious, then, to Susannah, that her aunt
was so wary of servants' pilfering. For earlier, when
Maria had made her practice her penmanship, copying some old house accounts, she had noticed:

27th Jan. *Mrs Barnes, for tea & coffee*
....£4 12s. 7d.
31st Jan. *Mrs. Barnes, for coffee*.......£1 6s. -

And, after only a few more lines, for "fodder," "fishmonger," and the like, again:

10th Feb. *Mrs. Barnes, tea & coffee*......£3 11s. 5d.

Susannah looked up at her aunt, who was inspecting her writing. Luckily on this page she had not made any blots. "Isn't that" she said hesitantly, "very much money for coffee and tea?"

"Yes, dear. But they are expensive," said Maria.

"But—four pounds twelve shillings, another pound sixpence, then again near four pounds—why, even in America tea wasn't but five pennies the ounce, and *that* was China tea, not Indian—"

"What a great deal you know," said Maria witheringly.

"I only meant . . ."

Maria moved away from the table. "Of course Mrs. Barnes buys in extra, dear, and sells it. I wouldn't meddle with custom, to be thought a penny-pincher."

With that Maria seemed to regard the subject as closed. The more Susannah looked at the accounts she copied, the more she noticed the enormous sums being spent on other items: great sums, even for a house this size, that surely were being filtered to that iron-haired harridan, Barnes. Susannah had seen the cook beating kitchen maids about the ears. *If I ran this house, I would change things,* she thought, indignant; but she didn't dare raise the subject again.

"Augusta," she asked her cousin one day, "what should I read now?" She had found her cousin in the downstairs library, scribbling. Augusta spent a good deal of her time composing sonnets, and long epics, and what she called "reveries."

Augusta looked up, startled. "You have finished *Rasselas* and the French?"

"The French, not quite—" admitted Susannah.

"Never mind, dear." The spectacles dropped from Augusta's nose as she stood. "You have borne with

Milton—so which of our modern authors could fail to please you? Here!" Eyes alight, she plundered the shelves, handing Susannah *King Lear*, *The Man of Feeling*, *The Castle of Otranto*, and a fat volume of *The Odyssey*. "In translation."

"Thank you," said Susannah, taken aback.

"Oh, but there are more! You must have Miss Burney's *Evelina*. Such a heartening story of virtue! You know"—she leaned close to Susannah, confiding—"I should like to write novels myself, like Miss Burney's. Do you think that too proud of me?"

"No! Of course you are not proud." Augusta, her eyes bright and her nose twitching, mouselike, seemed to Susannah anything but that.

"Then you must read my *Pastoral* when it is finished." Augusta bowed her head. "And tell me if I overrate myself. Mother always says I do."

"Why—I imagine she says that of everyone."

Susannah had not thought when she spoke, and she realized only too late that she should be more careful. But her cousin smiled up at her. "Do you think so? How encouraging! I had never tried thinking upon it that way."

Susannah ran quickly through *Rasselas* and neglected French for *The Castle of Otranto*. She began on Mr. Pope's *Odyssey* as well but could not get as far as she liked, for her aunt's interruptions. In a few weeks, by running so many errands, she had learned her way around the estate. She knew its ruling personages: the fearsome Mrs. Barnes; the twinkling-eyed butler, Warwick; the head groom, Amos; and the gardener, Clive. Augusta had told her how these sloping hills had been christened The Marches by the first Viscount Warrington, who had traveled in that part of Italy. His son Edmund, Maria's husband, had imposed his own classical notions on the gardens: the round and flat great lawn, backed by two symmetrical lakes. He had seen a pond dug and lined with black rock, to match the real lake already on his land. The Fool's Lake, Augusta called it when she showed it to Susannah; from a distance the two looked of the

same depth. "For they say a fool might dive in it and
break his neck! Though no one has. And there—" She
pointed further, across the real lake. "There are the
temples of Apollo and Athena. Oh, but our follies are
poor! Not like Lady Framer's. She has a hut in her
garden, where she keeps a hermit. See? There is our
Grotto of Venus. . . ."

"Grotto of Venus," Susannah had repeated. *Hermits, grottoes.* There was so much to learn. She looked
across at the mossy cave, wondering, momentarily,
What does it do? But she did not ask the question. She
was beginning to learn how often, here, it had no
answer.

On a cool, clear Saturday morning Susannah rode
out around the "real lake" toward the gazebo. After
she had made two trips into Bothwell today, Maria
had given her permission to take a horse: not her own
treasured, high-strung Cythera but a calmer bay mare
called Livia. Livia cantered sedately under the weight
of the heavy sidesaddle.

"Come *on*, lazy thing!" Susannah kicked the horse
hard as she moved past the lake. Just because she rode
sideways, like an Englishwoman, she didn't want to
be slowed to a dull plod. Livia quickened to a trot,
and Susannah felt her hair blowing, tumbling loose
under Augusta's tricorne hat. She passed the gazebo
and waved at Harry, inside. Then, on impulse, she
turned.

"Wh—I—" Harry stood, reddening. A stack of papers tumbled to the floor.

"May I call on you?" Susannah smiled and let out
a giggle as Harry bent to clear a path. She felt merry
and breathless from her ride; and perhaps her cousin's
shyness made her feel more daring. "What a deal of
writing you've done, cousin!" she laughed. "What is
it you are hiding?"

" 'Tis the p-preliminary work upon—'pon my 'His-

tory.' " Harry stood again, running a hand through
his tousled hair. His eyes, in the sunlight, were a clear
light blue, too much hidden—Susannah thought—by
his shy downward looks and by the bones of his face.

"Your 'History'."

" 'Tis of—" Harry's lips quivered, and he shook his
head with a laugh. " 'Tis of the conquest of the Normans. But I sh-shall not—bore you with it."

"No, please do," said Susannah, who flushed at her
own blunder. She raised her head; she and her cousin
had stopped laughing at once. "No—I mean it," she
said, feeling awkward. "I ought to learn some history.
Tell me of it."

And before long he was: pacing the gazebo's dusty
floor, his eyes flitting from one windowed wall to the
next. He told her of his studies with Bayliss and at
Cambridge: of Roman Latin and medieval Latin, of
books and historians of whom she had never heard.
"Have you heard of Mr. Gibbon's *Decline and Fall?*"
he said.

"No." Susannah puzzled. "His . . . decline?"

"Of course it isn't yet finished," said Harry. His
words came out swiftly now. He talked of ancient
Britain, now, and the poems of the Scots bard Ossian.
"*That,*" he said, rushing on, "is the sort of m-myth
that passes for history." He paced more quickly now,
his face growing heated. "The first *true* work on our
past is being done only now, by—by men like Mr.
Gibbon. If in some measure, I can do the same . . .
shake off ancient myth and aim at truth . . ."

"How it puts you under a spell!" Susannah laughed;
somehow she could not resist it. Harry had suddenly
grown so passionate: so intent.

He looked back, stricken, as if she had betrayed
him. "I am sorry. I meant—I meant not to bore you."

"I am not bored," said Susannah gently. But he did
not hear her.

For a few weeks, he had hoped—thought her different from the others—and now he felt a pang of
disappointment. Ever since he returned from Cambridge, Harry had been pursued by young ladies. He

had observed them—well schooled by their mothers with the words *the young viscount, yes, in his own right*—brighten, relieved, at the sight of a tall figure and a not-unpleasing face. He had begun, many times, hesitantly to talk, as they smiled and nodded— untroubled, at first, by a misplaced, fey giggle—until, in time, their smiles grew thin, and they sighed. Or laughed—as Susannah had—with a look that seemed to say, *Can't you tell me more amusing things?*

Perhaps appearances had deceived him. For he had thought Susannah, with her foreignness, and her own edge of shyness, might understand something of him that none of the others had. He was frightened. He wanted to talk—of history, and far more—without the bars of politeness and obligatory wit. He wanted to love a woman—and it almost did not matter that she might not care for poems or Latin or history. There was a life in Susannah's voice and in her quick stride, untamed by lessons in deportment. Her body was small—no more than the middle size—and that made her physical bravery, as she rode and jumped on horseback, more striking. He knew well that she was no beauty, but there was a lush femininity about her that drew him: in her red-brown mane of hair, in her full bosom, in the generous lips and small nose, more round than classically sculpted; in the dark clear blue of the eyes, below brows a vainer woman would pluck thin.

"What is it, Harry?" He felt her beside him now, and smelled her scent of horsehair and faint flower water. She tugged harder at his sleeve.

"I was not laughing at *you*," she said. "Don't you understand?"

He could feel her sea gaze on him, and he did not dare return it. *Don't*, came the inner admonishment: illogical. He would drown in those eyes. If he buried his head in that long hair, he might never waken. He would end like the madmen in Bedlam, tormented by the flesh. . . .

"Come, Harry," she said. "What troubles you?"

"N-nothing," he said, smiling as best he could. "Nothing. A mere fancy."

Soon she left him, to go on with her ride. And thinking of Bayliss, of Bedlam—of the long work before him—he tried to put her out of his mind.

May turned to June; in the gardens alongside the house the roses opened in exotic variety. Mr. Argothlyn came, alone this time, to stay at the house, and spent many evenings in close political discussion with Maria. Augusta and Susannah would eavesdrop and giggle as, through the closed doors of the card room there would issue a characteristically gloomy growl: "Man, the brute beast . . . No less, Lady Maria. . . . I warrant you . . . hellish merchandising of souls . . ."

On the tenth of June Susannah turned seventeen, and got a needle case from Augusta and a book on Rome from Harry.

Also in June came Mr. Pantafoglio.

He was a small dandy in pink satin, with black hedgehog-style hair. Maria had hired him to teach Augusta dancing in preparation for the Devonshire rout: the grand London ball that would mark the end of the Season, in August.

"You will stay with me for the lesson, won't you, Susannah? I shall need a partner." Augusta had clung to Susannah's hand when they heard Mr. Pantafoglio announced. And as Maria had set her no tasks that afternoon, Susannah accepted.

Mr. Pantafoglio sprang up from the piano bench and clapped his hands twice as the two girls entered.

"Shall we pro-zeed then, ladies?" Susannah and Augusta looked sideways at each other, already struggling to suppress their laughter. Toes twitching, Mr. Pantafoglio struck a note on the piano. "Oh, la! So sharp. And now they are like to tell me that they want to learn the waltz. . . ."

"The waltz?" said Susannah.

The little man looked at her, surprised. "You do not

know? Well, you shall not learn it! Already the shopgirls are dancing it, it has no steps. . . ."

"No steps?" said Augusta hopefully. Her last three
courses of dance lessons had all defeated her.

Mr. Pantafoglio ignored her, striking more chords
and grumbling about the absence of *chentlemen.* Susannah wondered why Harry had not appeared: for
the dancing seemed great fun to her, once they started.
The dancing master ran from the piano to the floor,
demonstrating figures, then playing the fragments of
minuet that accompanied them. *"Phroz the first!"* he
would shout. "Phroz two!" There seemed to Susannah
to be an astonishing number of phrases—usually leading her right back to where she began. Yet once she
had repeated them, they fixed themselves in her feet
and limbs; she waited eagerly to go on. Poor Augusta,
though. The dancing master kept scolding her.

Once she tried to protest: "I thought, *signor,* since
it appeared so in the book—" All week, in preparation, Augusta had puzzled over a volume of black
footprints.

"Aiee!" cried Pantafoglio. "You do not learn the
dance from books!" With the black spikes of his hair
drooping, he ran back to the piano.

They danced on for another hour, but Augusta
made little progress. Susannah tried to draw her now-
tearful gaze, mimicking Pantafoglio's tones in whisper. *"Phroz the first! Phroz two!"* She wished Augusta
could enjoy dancing, the way she was beginning to:
the clip of her heels and the sway of her skirts, and
the music. . . .

"Why doesn't Harry dance?" she asked her cousin
as they walked outside after the lesson.

Augusta heaved a sigh, which set her fichu to fluttering in the wind. "Harry's constitution has e'er been
fragile . . . in the lungs, you know. He used to suffer
such fits of the rheum!" She shook her head. "And
when he was five, and we were inoculated for small-

pox—he caught the malady itself. You have seen—he has the scars."

"They are not very bad," Susannah said mildly.

"Well." Augusta nodded and seemed to concede the point. "He is four-and-twenty now. . . . At least, if he mayn't box, and fence"—her voice was disapproving, at the words—"he has his studies. Dr. Johnson *himself*, and his Literary Club, were good enough to encourage him. . . . Oh, he is most devoted to his work."

"Work?" Susannah repeated. "But he doesn't need to." She couldn't imagine why anyone should work when he was rich; and besides, *work* seemed an odd word for her cousin's occupations.

"Yes, he does!" said Augusta, reproving. "So do I, else we should be unhappy."

Susannah puzzled this over as they came past the stables. "Perhaps 'tis true of Harry," she said. "But I thought—we women had no heavier task than getting ourselves married."

Laughter bubbled up in Augusta's throat, and she turned her nearsighted gaze up toward Susannah. "Oh! It *is* a heavy task, is it not?"

"But I suppose—it must not be, if you fall in love."

"You speak as an innocent," murmured Augusta.

"But—isn't it true that when a man . . . offers for your hand, you must come to love him?" That was what Adela had said. She had learned nothing yet to make her doubt it.

"*I* shan't marry for love," said Augusta simply. "We don't, here."

"But can't you make it come? By thinking on it and—" Susannah was not sure what came next.

"Oh, I *shall* marry, to be sure!" Augusta gave a small laugh, and tossed away the stick she had been twisting in her hands. "I shall have to, to be left in peace."

"But not for some time, surely."

"I am nineteen," said Augusta, in a queer, dry voice. "My mother wishes it this year."

"But—"

They went on talking in low tones until they rounded the edge of the lake and saw Harry approaching on horseback. With some circling and tugging of reins, he brought his horse up alongside them.

"Harry!" said Augusta coyly, lowering her eyes. "Susan and I have made a resolution. A quite solemn one."

Susannah smiled up and moved closer to Harry, rubbing her nose against his horse's velvety one.

"We have resolved, announced Augusta, "not to marry until we are quite old. At least five-and-twenty!"

"F-five and twenty?" repeated Harry. He flushed red and went pale again, and stared down at Susannah. But she did not see him; her nose was still buried near the horse's, whose noises she answered with whirrs and clucks of her own.

"15th July. Orange trees for orchard. . . . . .£10 5s.," wrote Susannah in the account book, copying slowly but neatly from Maria's notes. Her aunt passed overhead, trailing a fox fur. "Improved," she said dryly. "Which is fortunate, as when we return from London, you are to go to Lady Chathenham to see if she can take you as companion."

Susannah looked up, expecting, somehow, to see a smile on her aunt's face, but she was disappointed. "You leave tomorrow?" she said. Augusta had spoken of the trip to London: long delayed, to the annoyance of Maria, who normally spent most of the Season—January to August—in town.

"You, too. You are going." Maria did not offer any explanation. For the truth was that Augusta had whined and begged her mother into it. And once she had given way, Maria had seen the sense of the arrangement. Susannah's services were both cheaper and more biddable than those of the extra lady's maid she had considered hiring to help dress Augusta.

Startled, Susannah could only say, "Thank you, Aunt Maria."

"You may thank me by being a help to Augusta. She and I shall have a great many visits to make in London. Once we are returned here, in August, I shall take you to see Lady Chathenham."

So what had sounded, for a moment, like a kind reprieve, was not. She was to leave The Marches for good, quite soon.

"*Oh,*" was all Augusta said when Susannah told her both pieces of news.

"Do you know Lady Chathenham? Tell me, please—what is she like?"

"Quite old, I believe. And a very—*decided* character. Ah, well!" Augusta gave an uncertain smile. "At least she lives close by here, and we shall see you often."

For the moment, Susannah had to be satisfied with that answer, because it was time for their dancing lesson: the last.

Mr. Pantafoglio's hair slid down over his forehead as the summer heat melted his pomade. The music-room windows had been opened for air, and his greasy odor was attracting flies.

"Two-and-three-and-*yes*, back to me—" he counted. Augusta played on stolidly at the pianoforte, relieved to be excused from the dance. Susannah stepped and turned, more mechanically than usual, trying not to think about leaving The Marches. For, in a surprisingly short time, she had grown fond of it. She dreaded leaving it—leaving her two new friends, her cousins.

If I were to ask my aunt—she thought, and missed a turning. The dance master scowled; and just then there was a tap at the door.

"A chentleman!" exulted Pantafoglio, turning; and Susannah smiled and beckoned him in. It was Harry.

He looked sideways, as if he wanted to escape, but did not move away.

"Well, come, zen, Mister Lord!" Impatient, the dance master motioned Harry to take his place.

The figure was a difficult one, and Mr. Pantafoglio stamped and puffed, with increasing frustration, as Susannah and Harry danced. Not only were the two dancers failing in their duties to the other three, imaginary couples in the dance, but Augusta was adding unwarranted notes, and "Mister Lord" did not know the steps at all. But the young people were deaf to his admonishments.

"Why did you come?" said Susannah, but Harry gave no answer. As Augusta trilled, she spun twice under his arm.

"You are—going to London, tomorrow?" he said.

So somehow, she thought, he must have known the news before she did. Perhaps everyone knew, before her aunt had bothered to tell her! "Yes."

Already one coach full of servants had left; she had seen it go this morning. Now, outside, she could hear the footmen running to and fro on the gravel, loading two more coaches with trunks and crates.

Susannah wondered why, at her answer, Harry seized suddenly at her hand. He was not going; he seemed to have no wish to. She stepped forward beside him, wishing—as often—that the music were faster, more demanding. Drops of moisture glistened on her skin, above the ruffled neckline of her blue, too-short gown. Harry looked down at his feet, trying to follow her; he was tall and thin but not quite ungraceful, and a smile curled at the corners of his mouth. Susannah curtsied to the other, imaginary couples. He bowed hastily, and the last chords hung suspended in the air.

Chapter 4

The two Warrington coaches moved sedately up George Street, past the close ranks of London houses: through coal dust and builders' brick dust, past blank, high facades of red brick and black. They turned, and drew to a halt at a corner: more red brick and black brick. Hanover Square.

Susannah climbed out and breathed the city air again, and winced. It had not changed. Even here in the West End it carried the scents of the harbor: of smoke and sewage. A few yards ahead she saw her aunt and Mr. Argothlyn squabbling, as if in a dumb-show. His pomaded cockscomb had flopped in the heat, as had the white feathers of Maria's straw hat.

"What do you suppose—" breathed Augusta beside her. She had spent most of the ride from Surrey speculating upon her mother's decision to ride in a separate coach with the saturnine Whig. Now an enormous maidservant—"Ernestine," whispered Augusta—came out of the house and joined the pair. Another argument ensued, of which Susannah could hear little. "Sent a letter weeks ago! . . . House should be ready," she heard her aunt cry, and as no one seemed to be paying any attention to her or Augusta, she stepped back on the cobblestones to look at the buildings surrounding her. They were tall and symmetrical, surrounding a square of grass; behind her was George Street, wide and straight. And so much cleaner and more tranquil did it look here than the city she had seen before from the harbor that she felt less that she was in London than in some outlying new town, ordered and modern.

The Warringtons' house was a five-story stack of red brick, smaller and less spectacular than The Marches. Its tiny, white-columned hall, when at last they entered, was swarming with servants, so that Maria had to shout above the din.

"Is the green bedchamber ready? Ernestine, I warned you—"

The housekeeper nodded, her jaws working at some eternal, invisible mouthful.

"Yes, m'lady!" answered the butler, Warwick, in her place, and led the procession up the blue-carpeted stair. Susannah saw now how the house's compact size belied its space; on each floor there were a parlor and two bedrooms. Maria's white-and-gold suite was on the second floor, Mr. Argothlyn's green guest room on the third. Susannah and Augusta slept on the next floor still, behind a disused nursery, with its hobbyhorse and cradle.

Panting from the climb, Augusta collapsed into the featherbed that filled most of the back room. Susannah stood at the nursery window. From here she could see past the squares to the north, to the green meadow at the edge of the city.

She felt unnaturally high, as if the whole crowded edifice might give way beneath her. She saw people running like ants in the street, and even thought she heard voices through the floorboards and walls. People could not be meant to live so, she thought: all jammed together. . . .

The maid, Mary, was rapping at the door. "M'lady wants to see you, Miss Augusta, in her parlor."

*   *   *

Maria had summoned her daughter to tell her of
that night's round of visits. They were to dine with
the Derveys and sup at Mr. Sheldon's rooms; and,
when they came back that night, to write out some
thirty invitations to tea. Annoyed that various acci-
dents—her niece's arrival, estate business, the pro-
longed visits of her politicians—had kept her weeks
longer in the country than she had intended, Maria
was not going to allow any of her time in London to
slip by in solitude. There was much, in a brief few
weeks' society, to be accomplished: possible suitors for
Augusta to be found out, useful acquaintanceships to
be maintained.

"She wants," Augusta reported to Susannah, "to introduce me to all London! As if, but two months since,
I had not *met* all London, with no great love discovered on either side! At least, my dear, you shall come,
too, to everything. I insisted."

"Insisted?" said Susannah, wondering how anyone
could make Maria do as he or she wished.

"To think, she had meant to leave you at home! I
told her I shouldn't speak a word to *anyone* unless you
came. You see," said Augusta, in more confidential
tones, "she *very* badly wants me married."

The next morning they drove to the mercers' shops
in Pall Mall, where beribboned shop assistants rattled
off the names of the fabrics: "Garden silk, Italian silk,
Mantua silk, and velvet . . . Geneva velvet, English
velvet, Norwich crepe, and plain crepe . . ."

They dazzled Susannah, who was beginning to feel
all too conscious of her short, made-over clothes. Why,
even the maids in London dressed fashionably, with
their hair in white caps and their chins buried in ruffles.

At the dressmaker's she felt her own dowdiness even
more. The walls of Mrs. Shields's workroom were
plastered with French fashion plates: *robes à la tur-*

que, à la circassienne, à la chinoise. The last was what Augusta would have for the ball: Maria had determined it.

"Lady Caroline Framer wore that very gown to the Russells'," she pronounced, looking from Augusta to the lady in the print, who wore a full-skirted dress of blue and green stripes, haphazardly draped with sashes, poufs, and tassels.

"Oh, no, Mother." Augusta stared at the picture, her mouth drooping. Susannah, coming up to look at the print, shook her head along with her cousin, though she knew to keep silent.

"I would say," offered the dressmaker—herself gray-haired and practical in an apron stuck with needles— "I would say, that perhaps you desire a pattern, straighter—plainer, if you will, of effect—"

"No, no!" said Maria. "It shall be this." For such a profusion of finery, she reasoned, would overwhelm her daughter's looks. "Lady Framer wore it, and *she* is ever at the height of fashion."

"In her parrymours as well," murmured the dressmaker. Maria gave her a sharp look. She relied on the seamstress's gossip; that, and her reasonable prices, were what brought Maria the length of London to the muddy alley behind St. Paul's where Mrs. Shields kept shop. But she preferred the more interesting items of news kept from her daughter's ears as yet.

As the seamstress was pinching and measuring her for her "Chinese dress," Augusta smiled innocently. "What shall Susannah have?" she said.

"Susannah?" Maria's eyebrows lifted, as if she had misheard.

"She needs a dress," said Augusta slowly, "for the ball. . . . Ouch!" Mrs. Shields's pin had disturbed her composure, but she had achieved the effect she desired. Her mother's expression had darkened, and she said nothing.

"Is . . . Miss Susannah—" The seamstress looked up eagerly. "A relation? I could fit her with a very nice gown, indeed. And—" she offered hastily, watching Maria, "I would be honored, m'lady, to consider half price." Her eyes were already measuring her new, prospective customer—who was wearing, she noticed, a rather short and faded costume. "But only if you wish, Lady Maria. 'Twould be a pleasure."

So Maria, cornered, conceded. For she knew full well what would result, if she refused. *And she brought her poor cousin in*—she could hear Mrs. Shields's voice recount, to the duchesses and ladies-in-waiting who were her customers—*looking so very shabby, and wouldn't buy her a single gown!* Augusta, Maria vowed, would repent of her insolence. "Yes," she said magnanimously. "Susannah must have new clothes. You shall see her after you've done with me."

When the two girls were exiled from the dressing room, for Maria's fitting, Susannah thanked her cousin, delighted. "I only wish," said Augusta wryly, "I had managed as well for myself."

So, under her aunt's beady eye, Susannah was measured for what seemed to her an immeasurable wealth of clothing: chemises, petticoats, stockings, ribbon garters, two day dresses, a pink evening gown, and (what she most desired) a riding habit. Maria insisted, though, that it must be black.

"I have a lovely crimson wool—" ventured the seamstress. Susannah thought hopefully of the redingote pictured on the wall: dark red with wide lapels.

"Too showy," said Maria.

"With silver buttons?"

"Cloth ones." Maria tapped her foot. "And that will be all."

Susannah did not mind, though. She had never owned so many fine dresses. Exultant, she walked out of the dressing room to join Augusta, and as they waited for Maria she could not help looking curiously at Mrs. Shields's next customer, waiting at the far side of the room.

She was tall and black-haired, the high neck of her riding coat setting off a white face with tiny, almost Oriental features. She nodded, smiling, at the girls but did not speak until Maria came through the dressing room door.

"Lady Warrington!" she called, in a throaty, accented voice. Maria stared back at her. "But do you not remember me? We met at tea, in the place of . . . Valerie. . . ." The stranger's voice trailed off, for Maria's features were still cast in stone.

"Of course," the stranger said now, inexplicably—watching Maria lead the two girls past her, out the door.

"Who was she?" whispered Augusta, once they were outside.

"I scarce know her," said Maria curtly. "I know, rather, her poor repute."

Lady Warrington and her charges trundled, in their great black berlin coach, to as many entertainments as the dwindling Season could offer. They went to Gallini's music rooms, and Almack's Assembly to dance. They went for tea with Augusta's eldest sister, in her high, gabled house inside the old City of London.

"Such a queer, ancient place," said Maria, as Helena Stillwell ushered them into her sloping parlor. "Don't you intend moving?"

From Helena's weary reply, Susannah guessed that this was not the first such exchange. "Everett," said Helena, "says as 'twas his grandparents' house, he is loath to leave it."

The room was cold, the tea pale yellow; and Susannah began to guess that Helena's banker husband must be something of a miser. Helena was not coming to the Devonshire ball. "I haven't a new gown," she said, suppressing a sigh.

"Edmund! My little darling." The conversation stopped short as Maria's oldest grandchild, a plump boy of nearly two, waddled into the room with his nurse. Maria took little Edmund into her lap and fed him almonds and seedcakes. "He *is* a clever boy," she said, though Edmund had not uttered a word, yet, in evidence of it. "You must get a tutor for him soon."

Helena looked discomfited. Her thin face, much like

Maria's, seemed to narrow further. "Everett," she said, "wishes to send him to the Merchants' School."

"Nonsense!" said Maria. "My little dear shall have a tutor."

Helena largely ignored her cousin, and even her youngest sister. She and her mother seemed to form a pair: especially so when they held a hushed conference in the hallway, which ended in a trickle of gold coins to Helena's palm.

"Poor Helena," sighed Augusta. But Susannah, somehow, could not summon as much sympathy. Helena sighed a great deal, she thought, for someone so well removed from poverty.

Usually, after supper, the two girls were sent to their room, while Maria might go out again, or join the card parties in Mr. Argothlyn's chamber. At nine o'clock the sun would still linger outside the fourth-floor windows, and as raucous laughter drifted up the stairs, Susannah and Augusta tossed in bed, restless. They shifted and talked: most often, of love.

"Do you ever think," Augusta said once, "of the man you are going to marry? That is—the man you *would* marry, if you chose. . . ."

"Oh, yes!" said Susannah, sitting up, the better to picture him. "He would be dark, and with a—liveliness to his eyes. Not over big—for a tall man would tower over me so. . . ." She did not know where this picture came from. There was some of her father in it, perhaps, and the hero of the *Arabian Tales* she had so often read.

"Oh," said Augusta. She sounded disappointed.

"And you? Do you ever imagine someone?"

"Yes," said Augusta quietly. "Someone who—would be kind."

"That is all?" Susannah watched her cousin nod; she had grown strangely pensive. Trying to distract her, she said, "Do you suppose I shall meet any men at Chathenham House?"

"No. I don't imagine so. . . . But you will come and see us. *Harry,*" said Augusta, with a delicate stress, "will always be glad to see you."

"Oh, I hope so. I am fond of him. Almost as fond

as I am of you! Do you think—we shall either of us
find husbands here in London?"

"No," said Augusta hollowly. "But that is not what
my mother thinks."

"Anyway, there is our promise! Five-and-twenty."

"Yes," said Augusta doubtfully. "Five-and-twenty."

Jonas Hench was building a house at the edge of
London, in the middle of a muddy field off Baker
Street. The section of it so far completed was ringed
by a colonnade of twisting columns and topped by
three onion-shaped domes. As the Warrington coach
drew up there at teatime, even Maria looked in awe.

Hench received them in his drawing room, wearing
a cap and a yellow silk robe. "Welcome! Most welcome, indeed!" he cried. And they drank tea sitting
amid the objects of his collection: bright caged birds,
lacquered cabinets, and a glass-eyed stuffed leopard
from Bengal.

"I acquired my tastes in the East," Hench explained. "Have you seen my clock?" He pointed to an
enormous Buddha on the mantelpiece, with a clock-
face implanted in its belly. At three o'clock the Buddha chimed, lifting his gold eyelids.

Choosing from their host's array of seedcakes and
candies, the ladies talked inconsequentially of London
and the heat. Hench grew restless. At last he leapt up,
throwing the crumbs from his lap. "Why, none of you
has seen my observatory!" he cried. " 'Tis but a small
one, at t'summit of the house. Come, Miss Susannah.
Will you be my guest?"

Susannah looked up at him, and then her aunt. She
had finished her tea before the others, it was true, but
still it was strange of him, inviting her first. Her aunt
gave a thin smile and shrugged. "Yes, Susannah, do go."

She did not look back at Hench as she climbed the five
flights of stairs. She was too nervous. She told herself
that that first coach journey was long past. She had
nothing to fear. Behind, she heard his steady breathing.

" 'Long here!" Hench said in a cheery voice when

they came to the top of the house. Susannah walked
warily beside him, until, halfway down the corridor,
he seized her arm. "D'you remember our ride from
the docks?" His voice growled. "I shan't forget—"

He grabbed her other shoulder and pushed her up
against the wall. She felt his belly crushing her and
cried, "Please! Let me go." But it was no good. He
pressed harder against her. She saw the harsh red face
bulging above his cravat and robe.

"My passion"—Hench's voice caught, and spurted
out—"betters me, betimes. Hear me out."

She twisted against him but could not get free.

"I'll make you an offer. A house. Five hundred a
year—"

"I don't understand you! Let me go—"

"An offer!" The red face darkened. "Such as any
girl'd know the worth of. Such—"

"No. I do not want it." She felt him backing away,
at last: beginning to release her. Regretting her rudeness a little, she tried to call up the words a novel or
Augusta would use at such a time. "I am sorry," she
said with dignity, "that I cannot imagine any—near
relationship between us."

Hench let out a loud noise, almost a laugh. And for
a second he loosed hold of her. She ducked beneath
his arm and ran headlong down the corridor.

"Wait!" Hench called in a muffled voice. "Wait!"

She ran down the five flights of stairs, not looking
back.

That night Maria scolded her niece for being rude
to Mr. Hench. "What did you say to him?" she demanded. She paced back and forth on her white-and-
gold carpet.

"I did not mean—" Susannah tried. But she could
not finish.

"Whatever you *did* say must have been exceedingly
rude. For when he came to take us upstairs, he could
barely speak." Maria turned by the fireplace, brown
eyes glinting. "Perhaps you are too simple to under-

stand that Mr. Hench, whatever his—roughnesses—
may prove a valuable friend. I need not remind you
of his considerable fortune—"

"I'll not marry him!" Susannah blurted out, and
looked up apologetically at her aunt. The words had
escaped before she could stop them.

"What?" Maria's eyelids lifted in surprise. "I am
sure he has no thought of marrying *you*. That would
be absurd for a man in his position."

Susannah tried again, haltingly, to explain, but
found she could not, without telling her aunt all that
had happened. And that, she was too afraid—and too
ashamed, somehow—to do.

Piccadilly was ablaze with lights and clattered with
the hoofbeats of horses. All noble London was making
its way to the Devonshire rout. Linkboys bore torches
ahead of the carriages that lined up at the gates, while
inside, the duke's footmen guided them to the front
doors. The stern classical front of Devonshire House
shone silver in the moonlight: tranquil, unmoved by
the patter of heels on its steps, or the moist excitement
of a hundred matronly faces.

Court robes, *robes à l'indienne*, transparent frocks,
and *robes à la turque* made their way through the
Devonshire doors. Capes, towering hats, and wigs
tumbled in the heat, as the low babble of the entrance
hall gave way to the candlelit din of the ballroom.

Augusta Warrington, squeezed into her *robe à la
chinoise*, stepped into the great chamber beside her
mother. Her stays pinched, and tassels bobbed and
swayed around her with every step she took. Maria,
in a garnet dress, tugged her forward, smiling broadly.

Susannah, in her pink gauze gown, remained behind. Maria did not need to remind her that she was
only here on sufferance: *a companion to Augusta*, that
was all. As if to underscore the point, Maria had spent
all afternoon directing the dressing and coiffing of Augusta, commanding Susannah's assistance along with
that of the maid, Celeste, so that Susannah had barely

had half an hour to prepare herself. Her hair, unlike
Augusta's and her aunt's, was unpowdered; her dress,
with its blue satin sash, looked plain amid so many
shining silks, ornamented with pearls and lace. Her
own unpainted face, she thought, could not give the
more mature and rouged ones here much contest. But
she could not see how her hair, frizzed by the summer
damp, glowed red in the light—or how the candlelight which stung her eyes, also set them glittering.

Hundred-flamed candelabra cast their glow on the
white-and-gilt walls, and on the nymphs and carved
wreaths of the ceiling. The crowd milled and circled,
and through the noise, even Maria's loud, "Look!"
could barely be heard, as the robust, dark figure of
George, Prince of Wales, moved through the doorway
with his entourage. A red blaze of hair passing by,
above a slim figure in a frock coat, soon distracted
her.

"Mr. Cheveril?" she said. Her eyes had taken on an
uncharacteristic, warm gleam.

Almost, the red-haired figure passed; for the music
and noise in the room nearly drowned Maria's voice.
But now he turned, revealing green eyes and a chin
firm and dimpled at once.

"Maria!" He smiled and slid a step closer. "Why, I
find myself torn, here. Whom must I ask to dance,
among three such lovely creatures. . . ?"

Cheveril was from Devon, a Tory: a member of
that party which had for three years clung to control
of the Commons. Like the prime minister, Pitt, he
was young—but twenty-five. And though Maria had
always declared herself a Whig, he sorely tempted her
to change allegiance. A tremor of displeasure crossed
her face as his gaze lingered on her daughter and,
longer, on Susannah.

"Why, with you, of course, Maria," he said, turning swiftly back to her. He led the Warrington party
to his own, which was seated—three men and two
ladies—in an alcove nearby. Augusta promptly joined
the ladies, and a young man—Cheveril's brother—
leapt up to ask Susannah to dance.

"Are you at university?" she asked him, as they took their places in the *cotillon*.

"At Eton," he said brightly. "I go up to Oxford in three years—"

He was only a boy, she knew then: for Harry had talked of going to university at sixteen. But she enjoyed the dance, all the same. She smiled back at her partner's beardless face, wondering if the dark man of her dreams might yet appear.

Owen Argothlyn and William Sheldon surveyed the dancers from the doorway of the card room, keeping their distance from the pursuing legions of matrons with unmarried daughters. The first, because he suffered a congenital distaste for bright-eyed and hopeful young females; the second, for fear of the reproaches of the matron he yet hoped to make his wife.

"There she is." Argothlyn pointed glumly, glass in hand. "The fickleness and rank deceit of the human female knows no bounds." Across the floor the lady in question was dancing and talking, with lively looks, with the red-haired member from Devon.

"Cheveril!" Sheldon's habitually sunny face drooped, in the nearest it could come to a frown. "Why it is, man. A Tory! Hang me, how'd he get in here?"

For even had Maria Warrington not been a firm Whig—their hosts, the Duke and Duchess of Devonshire, were. At the last election, the Duchess had campaigned among the butchers and bakers of London on behalf of her pet Whig, Charles James Fox.

Argothlyn's black brows descended as he peered again at the dancing couple. But at last he said, "Take heart, Shelly. Our Maria's no giddy girl. She'll leave off Cheveril—soon's she learns he's got no money. Parents' only property's a crumbling heap on the Channel."

"And if she doesn't?"

Argothlyn shook his head. "The native greed of the female will out."

Sheldon stared at him, his mild, freckled face puzzled. "Why, you talk as if you don't *like* Lady Maria!

When you—" His voice shook with emotion. "When you've—been staying at her house, and—" Rapidly he swallowed the remains of his wine, for courage. "Why, if you have—no *honorable* intent towards the lady—I should order you from her house! I should challenge you—"

Argothlyn only gave a low chuckle. "My friend—I revere the lady. Although I should not be fool enough to show it, as you do."

The air was hot now, the music louder, and in the ballroom there were but few souls left who refused to dance. Augusta had a partner now, a stout married man from Cheveril's party; and Susannah had been asked for this dance by a soldier. He was handsome in his red uniform, and courteous, even if he did talk of nothing but the 48th Lancers.

Silks and satins, plain and embroidered, paraded around her; pearls glowed on perspiring bosoms, and sweat trickled down the edges of frizzed wigs. The orchestra launched into the next dance, a rondo. This Susannah had only begun to learn in her lessons with Mr. Pantafoglio.

"Where—" she gasped to her partner, as the other couples spun and churned around them.

"Here, m'love!" cried the Lancer, red-faced. He grabbed her by the elbows and whirled her vigorously round.

All at once it went to her head—the bright lights, the glass of wine she had drunk, and the music. She saw the others' spinning stop, and felt her partner let go of her hands. But she could not stop, she kept on turning. She whirled away from the Lancer, into space. The walls of the room spun round her, and she did not know where she was until a man in the next line of dancers stopped her.

Dry, warm hands fastened on hers. "Come, my whirligig," said the man, in a low mocking voice. "Serves the buffoon there right, to lose you." He glanced back at the partnerless Lancer across the floor, and Susannah had time to take in his face. Twinkling brown eyes, and a nose slightly aslant; black hair in loose curls, and white teeth, as he said—in that strange, guttural voice—"Will you dance again?"

Their line was proceeding forward, the music steadily slowing. The couples ahead were bowing to the Duke and Duchess at the end of the room, and retiring.

There was something familiar, compelling in this man: something that made Susannah want to look on him for a long time. And she had opened her mouth to say *yes*, before realizing she was too late. She had come up before the Duke and Duchess.

The silver-haired Duchess, seeing a new face before her, clasped Susannah's hand and murmured a welcome as she rose from her curtsy.

"Thank you, my lady," Susannah breathed back, in awe. The Duchess's narrow eyes gave a twinkle. She was near middle age, more gracious than lovely; still, there was a warmth to her that the stiffly handsome Duke lacked. Curious, and dazzled, for a moment, by them both, Susannah lost sight of her partner. And when she turned to find him, he was not there.

She moved toward the wall and saw him: but far away and half hidden from her by the milling crowd. She saw his dark head and his suit of purple velvet; a lady in green and gold was tugging at his hand. *I know her*, she thought for a moment, but was not sure. Wasn't she the foreign lady her aunt had cut so decidedly at the dressmaker's? She saw the pair laughing, moving ever farther away. And she could not explain to herself why her heart sank. She did not even know the man's name. Now he moved through the door, and out of sight.

Later she toured the public rooms of the house with her aunt, Augusta, and Cheveril. In a long painted parlor, they watched a burly figure stagger past, clutching his mouth.

"His Highness the Prince," chuckled James Cheveril, "has drunk above his limit."

But neither this, nor the rest of the evening, made much impression on Susannah. Mr. Cheveril introduced their party to enough politicians and scribes to please Maria and Augusta both. Later Susannah danced again, with two soldiers and a curate. She talked to them but later could not recall what she had said. To them all, she looked starry-eyed: they supposed at the honor of meeting the Duchess.

Outside, Jonas Hench rolled down Piccadilly in his coach, discontented. The ball was on at Devonshire House. Everyone who counted in London, except for a handful of rabid Tories, was invited. He had just passed a lifeless evening at his club, Drake's—he would have preferred it to be Boodle's or Brooks's—and had spent five guineas on an unsatisfactory poke at a whore near Covent Garden. He felt something like burning, and it was not in his stomach or even in his genitals—though often enough those burned, too, after such encounters. No, the burning that aggrieved him was that of the torches of Devonshire House. All of London was inside there, except for him. He could not put up with this state of things much longer.

By the card-room doorway, Nicholas Carrick and Valerie d'Aubusson watched the crowd in the ballroom dwindle. Her gown was a shining assembly of green and gold; his suit was of purple cut velvet. For a moment their eyes met in friendly complicity. They were of nearly the same dark brown, glinting with lights.

A waiter lurched across the floor, draining the dregs from a tray of glasses. The orchestra played on, but the dancing had ended long ago, and nearly all those who remained were couples, whispering in corners, negotiating the evening's end.

"Are you not heated in all that finery, Valerie? Here, let me fan you." Carrick loosened the tortoise-shell fan from his partner's hand and waved cool air across her neck and bosom.

"Stop," she protested feebly, watching him out of the corners of her eyes.

He surveyed the room, still fanning. "Who was that girl in pink? Do you know her?"

"Your little—partner, for which you left me to dance alone?" Valerie's voice took on a sharp edge. She let out a forced laugh. "No, *chéri!* Why should I know her? She is come with the lady Warrington."

"Her daughter?"

"No! All her daughters are extreme-plain."

Carrick studied the Frenchwoman's face, which had suddenly grown hard. "Valerie! What has put you so out of countenance?"

Valerie glared. "She is so rude, Lady Warrington! She thinks she is so much better than me, when all she does is throw her rotten guineas on the floor for the Parliament dogs to pick up—"

"Calm, my dear." Carrick fanned. "My sweet, stay calm. . . ." His gaze swept across the dance floor again. "If she *isn't* Lady Warrington's daughter, then who do you suppose—"

"You Scotch! All the same! Running after the women, *sans cesse*, without end—" Valerie broke into a torrent of angry French, which she made no effort to translate piecemeal into English as was her usual habit.

"*Vous—Français.*" Folding up her fan, Carrick rapped her shoulder with it lightly, smiling. "You French! I can't understand a word of your scurvy language."

Susannah and Augusta were sent up to bed after the ball, but they both knew that for many hours they would not sleep. Grumbled oaths and shrieks of laughter rose up from downstairs, where Maria and Argothlyn were attempting to play chess.

"I *didn't* hate it so utterly as . . . sometimes." Augusta sounded tearful. She worked at the knot of her stays, which fell open with a creak. "After all! *You* were there, dear. I talked to—men of character! Mr. Fox, and Mr. Walpole, and . . . Oh, Susan! If it weren't for Mother—"

Marriage, thought Susannah, running up to put her

arms around her cousin. What a curse it was, here in England! Maria had scolded her daughter on the ride home: for dancing too little, wasting her talk upon women and old, or married, men. . . . Augusta's curls were knotted, and her face was damp with tears. "Shh," said Susannah. "You mustn't believe her."

The maid, Mary, came now to help them undress; and when they were in their nightshifts, in bed, Susannah tried, "Can you not tell Harry all this? Couldn't *he* stop your mother from her plans?"

"No." Augusta buried herself further under the bed-clothes. "*He* doesn't wish me to marry yet. But he is too gentle. He will not do a thing against our mother's will."

London was slowly emptying, like the Devonshire ball in the early morning. "Society" returned dutifully to the country that gave it prosperity, until only the poor, the single men in lodgings, the shopkeepers, and the illicit lovers remained. Maria Warrington stayed on as long as she could, buying new clothes and new ornaments for The Marches. But when the invitations—except from Sheldon and a few cousins—ceased, she realized it was time to go back to the country. Somewhat to her relief, Mr. Argothlyn stayed behind, at lodgings he had taken near Parliament.

Back at The Marches, she ordered a thorough cleaning. The whole house needed turning inside out: the statuary a dusting, the carpets a beating and shaking. She sifted hurriedly through the letters on her desk. Bills, a few invitations, something from an address in Virginia. *Virginia?*

"Knole!" she called sharply. "Knole. Where are you? What is this?"

The secretary emerged, apologetic, from the privy closet. "Virginia? Ah, yes, m'lady." His face fell. "As regards that—I fear you will have to send for Miss Bry."

Chapter 5

Susannah stood frozen in the center of the study. She had no one to run to. Tears swelling in her eyes, she looked at Knole, then at her aunt. The furs on her aunt's bosom rose and fell, but she knew she could not go, could not lay her head there. *He was well when I left him. Perfectly well . . .*

Nathaniel Jackson, their neighbor, had written, because there was no one else who could. "Your father died in the early morning of June the twenty-first. Lately he had been stricken with a great distress of the internal organs. . . ."

He had not been ill, not spoken of it: And even when she had had no letters, she had not feared, knowing how little inclined he was to writing. She stared at the sheet and read the last words, in the unfamiliar Jackson hand.

He died tended by the woman Adela, whom he ordered in his will to be made free. This we have sent to you . . .

But for that, she did not care. "Is there no more?" she said, the tears falling, the paper shaking in her hand.

"No, Miss Bry, that is all," said Knole. And though another voice called after her, her aunt's, she did not heed it but ran through dim halls to her room and closed the door.

She knew now she should never have come. If her father was ill, she would have tended him. A fragment of memory—her father in the cart, clutching his belly, swearing—came to her and as quickly passed. *If I had known . . .*

She lay on the bed unmoving, curled against herself.

The day passed. Augusta came to see her, and later Harry tapped softly at her door. "I—I brought you these," he said.

Susannah opened her eyes—it was still day—and saw him in the light of the hallway. He shifted, his face in shadow, and came toward her now, his arms full of books. Slips of paper marked places in two of them. "I—wh-when my father died, I f-found them—found them comfort." She pulled herself up in the bed to answer, but no words would come; and, leaving the volumes by her bedside, he turned his face from her and was gone.

She looked at them and at first did not see what he meant. One volume was of sermons by a man called Donne; another of old poems, from the last century. So much about death and the grave, the extinguishing of life. But she came to one, at last, that Harry had marked by a man called Herbert, and thought, *He understands.*

Who would have thought my shriveled heart
Could have recovered greenness? It was gone
Quite underground . . .

She thought she had died a little, too. Gone underground, where she could care for no one with her whole heart again.

The next afternoon, in the study, they read her the will. It had come along with Jackson's letter. Knole sat, subdued, behind the desk, Maria looking over his shoulder. Augusta put a comforting hand round Susannah's as the secretary drew a nervous breath, and began.

" 'I, George Williston Bry, bequeath to my daughter, Susannah Margaret, all land and worldly goods belonging unto me . . .' "

"Is that all he put?" whispered Maria. "Is it legal?"

Susannah could only stare, the stream of her father's words stopped, violated. Knole's eyes met hers for a moment, then guiltily fell.

" 'And order,' " he murmured.

"Louder, Knole," said Maria.

" 'And—order—all my debts to be paid from that remaining, viz. . . .' "

The will went on to describe the Virginia farm. Maria shook her head and looked impatient.

" '. . . Besides which, ten acres, unknown to me, in the city of Manhattan, state of New York—' "

"What?" said Maria.

" '. . . in that place known as Lispenard's Meadows. Boundaries, viz.: to the south, the continuity of the southern border of Collect Pond; to the east, the continuity of the street known as Broad Way. . . .' "

"What is this place?" broke in Maria.

Susannah shook her head, bewildered. She did not understand what Knole was talking of: only that her feelings were numb to it. Some few acres of land: a bad bargain of her father's, most likely. For he had always taken strange payments in kind, when he would have been better off insisting on money. Susannah had listened, and inwardly cringed, while he bartered away hard-grown tobacco for wood or whisky or tools they didn't need. He had never talked of this

land: but then there was so much he never told
her. . . .

"That is all, Miss Susannah." Knole's voice interrupted her thoughts: then her aunt's.

"What do you know of this land?"

"Nothing, Aunt Maria." Susannah's own voice
seemed to ring loudly in her ears. And somehow
now, as Maria spoke, even more loudly, the faces
around her seemed to blur, and grow large and con-
torted. Her head ached; and when Augusta drew
her against her shoulder, to comfort her, Susannah
was surprised to feel the cloth of her cousin's dress
grow wet with tears.

"You must cry, it is all right," whispered Augusta.

"We have business to finish. Augusta! Will you explain—"

Susannah lifted her head at the sound of her aunt's
voice. Through her tears, she saw Maria's sharp, dark
eyes; she saw Knole's head, bent low, hiding his face.

"No. No—I can't explain," came the words, and
somehow she was rising: pulling free from her cousin's
hand, leaving the room. She heard her aunt calling
her name. And she ran. She ran downstairs, not
knowing where she meant to go, except that she could
bear that room, that harsh and thoughtless voice, no
longer. She ran across the gallery and outside: along
the edge of the lawn, toward the lakes.

Her aunt asked questions. Could she not see? *There
is nothing left.* Nothing: no lands, no house, no family. Her father was all her family, and long before the
house burned—even years ago, she had begun to
guess—he had lost the rest. Even had Jackson cared
to protect her inheritance—which he would not—she
would lose it. She would lose it all. The debtors would
swarm in; they would sell the farm, the slaves. *If only
it had not burned,* she thought suddenly, fiercely. For
now other people would come to live on the land, and
their house would be new; and the woods would bear
no trace of the Brys' struggle. Their work and their
lives would be swallowed up in the wilderness.

Still running, she tore a path through the forest, by the lakes.

"Susan!"

She heard a faint cry behind her but did not turn; and only when she heard footsteps and a rasping breath, and knew it was Harry, did she stop.

He clutched his chest. "Susan. I saw you run out. I was afraid—"

"I am sorry"—Susannah struggled for a voice—"if—I troubled you."

"Are you all right?"

Susannah's face was blank and pale above her black riding habit. She forced her eyes wide open, to keep off tears. "Yes, I am—well. I only needed to come away." *Leave me,* she willed her cousin; but, almost as soon, she wished him, *Stay.* For, while he talked to her, the worst thoughts must keep away. She could only think the worst thoughts alone.

Harry did not leave. Still short of breath, he took her arm, leading her gently across the high knoll between the lakes. "I—shall take you to a place I like. There you may feel better."

Susannah doubted it, but she said nothing: tried not to think, as she watched the grass shift under her feet.

"I remember—" said Harry hesitantly. "I remember it myself. When m—my father died, they tried to make us think so—quickly of estates, and affairs. . . ."

They were moving up an unkempt path, on the far side of the lake, toward the stone Temple of Apollo. Susannah felt the branches and thorns catching at her skirts. "At least—you had an estate left," she said roughly. Her mouth trembled. "I'm—sorry, Harry."

" 'Tis easily f—forgiven." Harry gave a small smile. "I understand." He followed her across the dusty floor of the temple. For a few minutes she did not speak, but perched on the low wall, kicking at dry leaves.

"It is wrong of me even to care," she said slowly. "Father is gone. Everything grows dull beside that, and yet—" She stopped; but Harry was nodding, listening, and she knew she must go on. "I am—so afraid, because I know—I can never go back. I have nothing. I know it is covetous, and wrong—" She turned toward him, her eyes searching. "Do you think it wrong, Harry? That I mind losing it—so much?"

Harry furrowed his brow in puzzlement. He owned more land than he could see from the Temple of Apollo, and it had never caused him particular joy or sorrow.

"Perhaps you think it foolish." Susannah stood up and began to pace, her clenched fists digging into her ribs. "But the farm was all we had. All that was mine."

"Everything here is—yours, if you'll have it," Harry's voice was so low that Susannah could not make out his words.

"I am sorry. What did you say?"

Harry's face reddened: it was long, lean, nearly handsome above his rumpled neckcloth and coat. Susannah turned to him, her faint smile lightening his heart, but all he could say this time was, "Of c-course I should like you—to keep all that is yours."

By the end of September the muddled affairs of George Bry were no longer his sister-in-law's concern. Maria had made her views known to Susannah: that the land in New York should be sold as quickly as possible, with whatever capital it raised invested to provide a small income. And she did not understand why Susannah refused this clearheaded advice. Land in America was of no use to her now. Still, Susannah insisted on writing to Nathaniel Jackson, and then to the factor he named in New York, to find out more. As such matters could never be resolved immediately, Maria let her write. "At least," she concluded, dismissive, "the practice of penmanship cannot hurt you."

And now October's hunt began to occupy Maria in earnest. She added to her guest list; she had Mary sew new fox-fur trim onto her best riding habit. Every day she patrolled the stables to check that the empty stalls were swept, the riding tack polished; every day, too, she walked her flighty mare, Cythera, round the yard, fidgeting in the saddle and grumbling at Amos, who held the reins.

In the kitchen gardens, in the orchards and fields, workmen were tidying, clearing dead leaves and burying the flower beds in straw. The hedges and fences on the estate were made to present obstacles: but surmountable ones. Trees and branches were clipped, fences lowered a plank or two. There were those critics of Lady Warrington's "hunts" who said she made the sport too easy, too artificial. But she paid them no heed. There was scarce any beauty, she said, in nature, without artifice.

Susannah strained to see Chathenham House as the coach made its way up the rutted drive. Behind a dense crowd of oaks, she glimpsed the red bricks of its front, the three sharp peaks of its gables. As she climbed out behind her aunt and crossed the bridge over a dried-out moat, her every sense told her this was too soon. A week had passed since the reading of her father's will, and still she felt shaky and unsure: as if any distress, however small, could upset her and make her blurt out the wrong words.

A forlorn-looking maid hauled open the front door and led Maria and Susannah down a stone-floored hall.

"Lady Warring-*ton!*" A loud female cry assailed them. "Lady Warrington! Here I am. . . ."

When they had wound their way to the voice's source, Susannah was surprised to see that it was a tiny, white-haired woman buried in crepe, in an oaken chair.

"Susannah," said Maria in warning tones, "Go and meet Lady Chathenham." Susannah made a low curtsy.

The maid had vanished, and there was no sign that tea or anything else would be served. Maria and Su-

sannah took seats on the hard wooden settle by the
fire.

"So! You wish to be my companion," said Lady
Chathenham with a piercing look. Her eyes, a brilliant blue, seemed to bore into Susannah, so that, for
a second, she was unable to move her lips in reply.

"Yes—yes, my lady. If you please." Susannah
breathed out, now, relieved. Her voice had not betrayed her.

"You'll have to *work*, you know. I don't keep anyone for free. Can't afford to. Now that Clement is
away . . ."

There followed a digression—clearly meant for Maria rather than her niece—upon the intellect of Clement, Lady Chathenham's son, who had departed at
the late age of twenty-one to study the classics at Oxford. This, complained Lady Chathenham, left her
with few able hands about the house. "But, my dear,"
she said, "you shall remedy that. Can she keep track
of figures?" The old lady directed her question at Maria.

"Well, I suppose. I have tried my best. I cannot
vouch for—"

"Yes," said Susannah more decidedly. "I can."

This caused both older ladies to stare at her. Lady
Chathenham, whose stare seemed to grow more
hawklike every minute, said: "Mind you, we do not
deal in *large* sums here. We have two maids and a
gardener. That is all."

Susannah knew, looking around at the bare room,
the polished settle and stone floor, that this did not
augur well. Two maids, in such a large house . . . But
though, for a moment, she felt sorry for them, she did
not think to feel sorry for herself. For, if she was to
come here, the time must be far off yet. . . .

"In three weeks?" Lady Chathenham's voice pierced
her thoughts.

"A month, perhaps . . ." Maria was thinking, cal-
culating. "Let us say in a month's time. Then I shall
have Susannah's help with my hunt-ball. I do hope

you shall be part of the company, Lady Chathenham."

"Oh, yes. Though . . . I *am* fragile, you know. I
shall need much assistance." Lady Chathenham's
cheeks creased, as she offered Susannah a thin smile.
"Perhaps you should like to make a start to your duties
by assisting me at your aunt's great fete, Miss Bry."

Susannah nodded, though she felt only dread at the
prospect.

"I expect you should like to hear of your *other* duties, too."

"Yes, my lady."

"To be sure, you shall not want for occupation!"
The old lady's bright eyes gleamed. "Well. For a start,
I like to be read to—five hours a day, at least. A worthy, inspirational tale is what I require. You should
have to take my books to the lending library and write
out my house accounts. And rub my joints for the
rheum, dear, and walk to town for tea and coffee. . . ."

Walk to town? Susannah wondered at it. Bothwell
was a good five miles away. At The Marches the
coachman always took her. Perhaps Lady Chathenham did not even keep horses. At this thought, Susannah's mind sank into a sudden gloom. She reproved
herself for such selfishness, but it did no good. Words
of her aunt, from sometime after her father's death,
echoed in her memory. *No one owes you a fortune*,
her aunt had said, *just because your father has lost
one.*

I am lucky, she tried to tell herself, as the older
women talked on, negotiating her transplantation in
October. But she could not help thinking, wishfully,
If only I could stay at The Marches. She had grown
used to its luxuries: its friendly servants, its books, and
stables full of horses. And there, though she had
known her loneliness, she had not felt it so completely. There, she had her friends: her cousins. . . .

Finally they were shown again through the creaking front doors. The coach horses kicked up the loose
stones in the drive, as if even they were eager to be

away. *At least,* thought Susannah, *I shall not go for
a month's time.* But that month, she knew, would not
be long. She heard an imagined clock, ticking.

"*My dear Miss Bry,*" Susannah read eagerly. The
letter had been sent over a month ago by packet boat.

> *Your enquiries as to your Property at Lispenard's
> Meadows have been treated with our fullest At-
> tention. . . . Tho' the Land is damp and in need
> of drainage, it is pleasingly situated at the edge
> of the City and with plenty open Country to the
> North. It is possess'd of a House most comfitable
> of white Board, in three Storeys, & of extensive
> Stabling. As such we deem it tenantable at the
> sum of (in English pounds Sterling) £60 per an-
> num & we seek yr. leave in assigning it to a Mr.
> Mowbray, of New York. . . .*

Susannah hopped on the marble of the entrance
hall, and ran to tell her cousins. *My own house!* She
truly did possess a house, and land—even if, as Jackson had warned her, all her father's Virginia estate
had gone to pay his debts. But Jackson, at least, had
been her protector in one sense: he had kept the exis-
tence of the New York land hidden from Bry's creditors.
This—Lispenard's Meadows—would be Susannah's
own, despite them. Already she could picture the
white house, with its bright windows: perhaps a col-
umned terrace to the front. She found her cousins at
last, in the library.

"Sixty pounds a year . . ." Augusta scanned the letter through her spectacles. "Well! My dear. No doubt
. . . why . . . For New *York* I suppose that must be
quite a fortune!"

She kissed Susannah, and said more kind things
about the white house, so that, whatever unconscious
slight there was in her earlier words, Susannah for-
gave it. Harry's congratulations were more grave.

"I am—g-glad," he said, meeting Susannah's eyes, "that you shall have somewhere of your own."

"What does it mean—sixty pounds?" asked Susannah. Truly, she did not know. She could calculate only, from her account-book experience, that it would keep the cook here about six months in tea and coffee.

"Why—" said Augusta carefully, "I believe Lady Framer has a companion with fifty pounds a year who buys her own clothes and is reckoned quite in the fashion."

"Many a p-poor farmer's family lives on less," said Harry.

"Oh, Harry!" said Augusta impatiently. "What use is *that*? Susannah does not intend to be a farmer." She smiled suddenly at her brother. "But tell her your news!"

For it seemed Harry had had an important letter, in the same post.

"L-L—Lord Exon's written," he said. "From Northumberland. He says—" He looked down at the letter still in his hand. "He says, 'The Exon manuscripts are at your disposition.'"

"But what are—" Susannah began.

" 'Tis for my 'History,' " Harry said eagerly. "The Norman invasion. T-till now, one source remains, that no one has yet consulted. The papers of—of—W-W-William de Warenne!" He jumped from the couch and began to run his free hand through his hair, and pace. "I—I knew they were kept at Exon Castle, in the North. There are—maps and records and even a sort of diary. And now—now I shall see them. I shall be able to write my 'History' after all!"

Later, in her room, Susannah opened up the silver-lidded box that held all her possessions from home: her mother's spoon and rose-shaped pin and portrait. She tore a strip of paper from a sheet on the table, wet a quill, and wrote out LISPENARD'S MEADOWS. She recalled the boundaries of the ten acres there as closely as she could, and wrote them down, too. North of Collect Pond. West of Broad Way.

My own land, she thought. *I am not so very poor, after all.* For, even when she read to the end of the factor, Brown's, letter, and found that, after fees, only £45 a year would come to her—*Still, I shall not have to depend on Lady Chathenham for everything.* And now, when her aunt called her penniless, she would know—she could say—it was not true.

October came, and after a week of fitful storms, the sky cleared to a bleak, changeless white. Now Maria could hope for a dry hunt day. A full week before the great event, Mr. Argothlyn came out on the mail coach from London. Mr. Sheldon came galloping down the drive on horseback, barely an hour behind his rival. Maria's daughter Helena and her family arrived. And, resplendent in his red-and-gold coach—accompanied by two horses, five hounds, and three riding habits—came the well-pleased Indiaman, Hench.

Maria welcomed him warmly. She gave him the green suite of rooms, on the first floor, and sent the prettiest of the maids up to tend them. Knole's researches had uncovered nothing untoward in Hench: nothing but an excess of wealth and an obscure London background. *Nothing*, thought Maria, *that marriage cannot mend*.

On the eve of her hunt, as the sun was dimming, Maria looped her arm through her guest's as they stood together on the terrace. Beyond the lawn and the fringe of trees, the sky was pink and golden.

"Ah! The Marches," said Maria, with a trembling sigh. " 'Tis a sight that will ever give me pleasure."

"Err . . . is that so!" Hench turned, taking cognizance of his companion. "Aye, yes, Lady Maria. A fine view. 'Minds me of the one out o' my own place along the road. Henshawe."

"Does it?"

With delicate prodding, Maria was able to extract

a few particulars. *Eight hundred acres. A house of forty rooms.*

"And have you any—other properties?" she said. Hench happily obliged her with a park in Scotland and a plantation in Barbados.

"Well!" she said. "You put us to shame, with our one poor patch of land." Maria looked up; her face, in the evening light, grew youthful, and there seemed to be a gleam of admiration in her eyes.

"But Lady Maria!" Hench grew gallant. "Now I won't hear that! Not a word of it. Why, the Warringtons—*hem!*—you're an *old* family hereabouts. Why, you"—Hench's forehead shone with the sweat of inspiration—"you, here, have summat—can't be bought!"

Maria gave a gentle sigh. "I daresay you're right, Mr. Hench. The first Warrington knights—so I am told—possessed these lands even six hundred years ago." She went on dreamily. "You know, Edmund—my late husband—was ever attached to the land. How he grew to loathe the specter of London! Of course, here—with the living of Bothwell, and the tenants—he did command such loyalty."

Hench listened, more and more attentively, while Maria rhapsodized: apparently to no purpose. She talked of her long acquaintance with the neighboring landowners, the Chathenhams and Northfords. She talked of London and of her elder daughters' splendid marriages. She touched, ever so delicately, on the Devonshire rout. Loosening her arm from Hench's, she backed away, as if to study him. "Do you ever think, Mr. Hench," she said, "of standing for Parliament?"

Hench puffed visibly. His pride was touched.

"Are you a Whig, Mr. Hench, or a Tory?"

Hench racked his brain for an answer. It was a difficult question. He knew the Warringtons were traditionally Whigs; yet hadn't Maria lately taken up some upstart Tory from Devon? "A *Tory*," he said, sounding more certain than he felt.

"Splendid! I admire a man who stands by his prin-

ciples." Maria paused. "You probably know our man
from Bothwell is—of the elder sort. A matter of a few
years . . ."

"Indeed?"

"There *is* a contest. A small one. But we in the
neighborhood do what we can." Maria smiled. "I can
see that a certain—position—has its appeal for you,
as any man." Hench puffed again. And at the same
time—almost as he was beginning to apprehend, and
even to expect—Maria offered, "What a shame you
have no wife."

"Well, I—"

"What think you, sir, of my daughter Augusta?"

"She's—" Hench did not seem to recall her.

"She is inside the gallery now—just at that window."

Hench turned cautiously, at that soft-voiced hint,
to look. *"Hem!"* he coughed. "Well! Lady Maria.
I . . ."

In truth, he had not thought on it before. Augusta,
round and motherly in a plain blue gown and white
fichu, caught sight of him, though she did not seem
to recognize him, and gave a nod, before moving away
inside.

"Her dowry," said Maria regretfully, "would be
small. My husband's will, you see . . ."

Hench displayed an unquivering profile.

"Four thousand."

"Well!" said Hench, with a benevolent nod. "You
know, sums are no matter to me!"

"Shall we go indoors, Mr. Hench? It grows cold."
Maria's button eyes shone, and she displayed her fine
teeth.

*At four thousand and the Commons, I'd marry the
Lady Maria herself,* thought Hench. The thought
rather surprised him. Triumphant, he took Maria's
arm and strolled into the house.

Chapter 6

The morning of the hunt dawned clear and cold. On the great lawn and the gravel paths horses danced and snorted, waiting for the start. Some fifty guests had come to The Marches: Derveys, Ackerleys, and all manner of London acquaintances; neighbors, like the large family of Sir Nestor Northford; rich Warrington relations, and poor and distant ones. Their costumes ranged from Sir Nestor's twenty-year-old green frock coat to Lord Silvius Framer's cutaway jacket and sparkling new spurs. Battered beaver tricorns and round riding caps bobbed in the air. A team of footmen held fast to the hounds' collars, springing back, relieved, at the horn's first echoing notes.

The hunters plunged forward, a tangled mass: squinting, hunching low, flapping reins. A few fell. At the edge of the first wood, the pack thinned, some falling to the end, some to the middle of the chase. Susannah, on the slow mare Livia, was one of these. Behind her, a wall of Derveys and Ackerleys pressed ahead; to the front, her aunt Maria was taking the lead, just ahead of Sheldon and Argothlyn, whose blond and soot-black heads strained forward, like their horses', neck and neck. Uncertain of a scent, the dogs had dispersed into fields and coppices. Some of the hunters did so, too.

Everett Stillwell and Lord Silvius Framer rounded back together toward the mirror lakes and their concealing shrubbery. Lord Silvius slowed his horse and took a pinch of snuff.

"Your difficulty," he drawled, offering the snuffbox, "is that you are scrupulous on account of your wife."

"Well!" Stillwell's face was dour. "You would be, too, if your wife had Helena's temper."

"She does, my friend, she does. I must simply disregard it." Despite his small size, Lord Silvius was able to look down on his companion from his tall horse.

"Ah." Helena's husband pursed his lips. If he harbored any unchivalrous thoughts on the morals of Lady Caroline Framer, he concealed them. "Yes. You do have a point. The upper hand . . ."

"To be sure." Silvius gave his reins a lazy flick. "After all, what can they do but throw fits? When Caroline starts at that, I simply go out to my club. I suppose *you* have a club—" The drawling Lord winced, hearing a horse crash through the trees behind him. Everett Stillwell sighed, through gritted teeth.

"Ho! Have they caught a scent this way?" Jonas Hench grinned, coming up alongside them.

Harry Warrington shifted from one group of riders to another. He had lost hope of catching up with Susannah. Far ahead, across the field, the white plumes of her hat fluttered in the breeze as if to taunt him. Her small arms, her black-clothed back clenched and loosened; she moved with Livia's rippling leaps, as if they were but one creature. Harry kicked his horse, only now remembering to loosen his reins; and at last he thought he saw his cousin looking behind, and slowing.

*   *   *

In fact, Susannah had not seen him but her cousin Augusta. There, trailing one side of the pack—past Sir Nestor Northford's bouncing belly and five hungry-looking Derveys—rode Augusta, without her spectacles, looking terrified. She had not wanted to come out at all, but her mother had made her; now she rode blindly up to the obstacles in her path, clutching at her horse's neck as it jumped and landed. Gradually Susannah let herself fall back, until she was alongside her. They rode together, breathless, for a time. In the distance she saw the tightly buttoned figure of Mr. Hench heading toward them, waving.

"Fence," she called, as one loomed toward them.

"Where?" cried Augusta, wide-eyed.

"Up there . . . about—about *there*!"

Augusta bent forward, clinging to her horse for dear life, as it cleared the fence and trundled down on the other side. Catching her breath at the nearness of the escape, Susannah decided to give up on reaching the head of the pack and stay with her cousin.

"There's a hedge," she called. "Shall we slow down—"

"Pity! I was just getting in me stride—" Jonas Hench's bark arrived before him. "Splendid hunt weather, eh?" he said, catching up. Augusta gave him a terrified nod, and a gurgle of assent.

"I see you're a game little trotter," Hench said warmly.

Harry was in a miserable position: trapped between two female Derveys.

"History!" one of them was gushing, showing great buck teeth, in response to his terse answer to the other's question.

He looked behind and spotted a gap. No one was following. Sharply he reined his mount in, and while the two sisters stared, his horse whinnied, reared, and turned.

Harry's heart thumped and he closed his eyes. He had never attempted such feats before. Now he steered right, steadily right, approaching the trio to the side of the field.

"Harry!" Susannah turned first and gave him a friendly wave. "Hedge, Augusta!"

Hench and Augusta jumped, and she jumped, and Harry followed after. At last he was beside her, near her. She was still calling out obstacles, as Mr. Hench had not taken up the task. And the snatches of conversation she threw Harry's way—"There *was* a fox in those woods there, I'm sure I saw it—*Fence!*"—fell to him like so many garlands. He could not think of words he would treasure more.

Jumping a hedge and emerging onto a clear field, James Cheveril bent forward and prepared to ride with the wind. He had kept behind, mingled with the pack, till now. But he saw the gap widening ahead: those two Whigs, the light and the dark one, were tiring. Lady Maria, misusing her horse no doubt, still galloped ahead of the whole field, unstoppable. And nothing but a flat expanse of stubble lay between them.

He let his bay stallion have all its head, and determined to catch her.

"Damn me if it isn't the rank conceit of the Tories." Argothlyn cast a dour look sideways at his companion: his rival. Even before the words were out, the blaze of red hair had shot past both of them, the bay stallion taking the length of the field in a burst of speed. Maria, in her fox furs, was turning her head: giving her pursuer a taunting smile, even as she urged her own horse on, faster.

"Cheveril," gasped William Sheldon, his freckled face flushed. Panting, he bounced in his saddle, in a vain attempt to speed his horse.

"There are times," Argothlyn said slowly, "that youth, in the human beast, cannot but prevail."

"I'll not hear of it!" Sheldon's high voice rose in a

frustrated whine. "Why—I'm young yet! I'm not forty!"

They were even now, up ahead: the young Tory and Maria. The bay's rump rose and fell in tandem with the lively chestnut's, the red hair with the coils of graying dark brown.

"A Tory," growled Argothlyn. "Damn him!"

"You've made a fine tableau of a hunt, Maria." Cheveril's tones were warm, almost intimate, despite the several feet that lay between them.

"Tableau?" Maria frowned; then, looking at her companion, she seemed to remember good humor and let out a brittle laugh. "No doubt, Mr. Cheveril, you mean some slight to the morning's sport."

"I mean only—" Cheveril broke off to steer his horse sharply right. To his satisfaction, Maria followed, just as sharply. In that direction lay a coppice: the chance, he knew, to slow and find shelter.

"Do you see something that way?" called Maria.

Cheveril smiled back. "What, in this sham charade of a fox hunt?"

They slowed, coming to the scrubby fringe of the woods.

"Firstly, Maria," he said casually, "your hounds are well-fed to the point of obesity. 'Tis no surprise they don't hunger for blood. And . . ." But now he stopped, his gaze tracing the length of her figure, in russet wool and fox fur. He smiled. "No matter, is it? Whether the hunters chase the fox—or each other."

"I see," said Maria with asperity, shaking her reins. "Then I must keep well ahead."

Cheveril answered, courtly, "Your duty as hostess commands it. But," he added, as Maria moved ahead, "you should be safer in company."

"Not yours, Mr. Cheveril—"

"Indeed," continued Cheveril, smiling, "you *need* a companion, to ride alongside you—and warn you when you are about to tumble over one of the obstacles you have created."

*   *   *

Through the small wood, again in fields, across
fences, the riders went on chasing each other, but the
fox—if ever there was one—continued to evade them.
The hounds panted ahead, and in the middle of the
pack, Ackerleys and Derveys shook their heads and
mopped their brows. But there was consolation. At
the farthest point in the chase, Maria and her red-
haired companion swung round, leading the hunters
back toward the picnic. As they rode past the others,
motioning, calling out directions, Maria observed her
train of guests, mostly with satisfaction. All the
Northfords, jolly, red-faced, breathless; the two
Framers, their costumes still immaculate, rejoining
each other with all semblance of goodwill; Jonas
Hench, exerting himself in conversation with Augusta; Harry, riding next to Susannah, talking eagerly. *Still?* . . .

He had spent, thought Maria, more than enough
time with her already.

In a sheltered grove a half mile from The Marches,
the oak branches, as Maria had ordered, were fes-
tooned with bright autumn leaves. From their
branches hung silver candelabra. Every now and then,
a few of the oaks' natural brown leaves would drift
down, to be brushed hurriedly by the servants from
the tables covered in green cloth. The footmen helped
the hungry riders off their horses and to their seats.
For though this was but a picnic, no comfort was neglected; the tables were set with bone china and silver, and the oaken serving table was laid with pies,
capons, and legs of lamb. Lady Dervey poked her
daughters in the ribs and ordered them to stop gawp-
ing. Jonas Hench, less inhibited, raised his glass to
cheer the hostess.

*   *   *

Augusta sat at Hench's table, flushed, scarcely believing she had survived the morning's ride. And now Mr. Hench kept telling her what a success she had made of it: why, he was a mite close-sighted himself, he said. He topped her glass up with wine, and she flushed redder, casting a desperate glance around for Susannah.

Flushed, her forehead damp with sweat, Susannah was tugging Lady Chathenham's chair back an inch farther from the table.

"No, dear. Too far."

For the last quarter hour, since she had ridden back to the house to see Lady Chathenham arranged in a comfortable gig from the stables and carried, not too slowly, not too quickly, to the feast, she had been learning the true nature of her future employment. "Companion" was the least of it. Already she felt exhausted.

"Well! I need to see my food to eat, do I not? Where are my spectacles? Go on, fetch them. Be quick!"

In the end, Susannah had to run back to search for them in the gig, which had been moved well out of sight of the picnic. When, at last, she had delivered them into Lady Chathenham's lap, she moved, panting, to her own place, down the table. Harry turned as she passed and caught her eye with a crooked smile half of amusement, half of sympathy.

The rest of the places at their table were filled by the large family of the rotund Sir Nestor Northford, who, with Lady Chathenham, took charge of the conversation. From time to time, as they ate, Harry caught Susannah's eye and smiled; the talk moved, as he had earlier predicted, from sunken fences to wheat yields to the divine service at Bothwell.

"I'm not one for these low-church—"

"No, nor I. Quite right."

"Affectations!" Lady Chathenham broke in shrilly, wiping her nose with a napkin. "Half these new churchmen think they've a calling to the people, like that Wesley. Sedition, I say!"

"I suppose they do *feel* that calling, though—don't they?" Susannah whispered to Harry, sure that the others, deep in argument, would not hear her.

"Yes! Wh-what of their work with the people, Lady Mary?" Harry spoke out, with a gleam in his eye. "Miss Bry herself w-wondered—"

"*Did* she," said Lady Chathenham, peering at Susannah down her beaklike nose.

"As—as it is," said Harry, "half the church sleeps through the service of a Sunday."

Sir Nestor gave a disgruntled snort, through his food. Lady Chathenham widened her eyes. "Well! In my day, I—"

"What are you trying at?" whispered Susannah to Harry. Several of Sir Nestor Northford's daughters were now busy soothing the old lady. But Susannah could not resist a smile. "Will you have me tossed out of her house before I begin my employment?"

"What?" Harry gasped. He seemed to be growing red, from the wine.

"Well? You knew why I went to visit there. Didn't you?"

"No. I—What do you mean? You are to go—"

Susannah nodded, and tried to speak cheerily of her post. "Come! I'm sure I shall be a splendid maid-of-all-work. You cannot say I oughtn't—earn my keep." She smiled, and wished she could feel as lighthearted as she sounded. Harry now looked more worried than aghast. "Come, cousin, I shall be well enough there," she said, and reached, in a moment of pity, to pat his hand.

As the afternoon light began to dim, the servants lit the candles, and the torches beyond the grove. Lady Chathenham let out a loud yawn, and Susannah, gleeful in the hope that the older woman might be returned to the house in time for her to ride back for the afternoon's chase, offered, "Shall I take you back indoors, now, my lady?"

By the time Lady Chathenham was safely settled in a bedchamber at The Marches, her various complaints satisfied, and Susannah returned, full speed on

Livia, to the picnic site, the afternoon hunters had almost departed, and Susannah was damp with sweat and breathless.

The group setting out was smaller than in the morning, Sir Nestor and most of the ladies having headed back for the house. The rest, unsteady from their picnic, rode out toward the darkening sky.

"One more round!" Maria called out, lifting an imaginary glass in salute. She tottered in her sidesaddle as Cythera bolted forward.

"Aye, this time we'll catch him!" someone answered, in a fainter voice—William Sheldon or James Cheveril, perhaps. Susannah rode at the back of the crowd, with Harry beside her.

Some of the dogs howled; the hunters headed through a wood. Beyond it, hills and hollows waited to trap them. But Maria kicked her horse on, unafraid, with Cheveril, Argothlyn, and Sheldon close behind her.

The light was dim, and the three men heard the noise of hooves splintering wood. They galloped ahead, for they could not stop; then, from behind, at the fence, they heard a moan.

Maria had fallen. She lay sprawled in a patch of underbrush, half on her side, her back twisted. As the next group of hunters approached, she waved feebly; and ahead, they saw her horse running loose. Some leapt the fence, for they were too late to stop; but the rest slowed, climbed down, gathered round. And now, the politicians, too, returned.

Susannah, with Harry at the back of the crowd, heard only the uncomprehending calls.

"Lady Maria?"

"What is it?"

There was a loud moan, from the ground.

Scarcely thinking, moved only by instinct and alarm, Susannah handed her cousin her reins. "Hold these, Harry, I shall go see."

She pushed through the horses, the standing riders, to the front of the crowd. Maria's three politicians were kneeling round her. Now, she could see, Maria breathed and moved. Cheveril clasped and slapped one of her hands. As she looked up with a dazed, mud-stained face, the three men, above her head, began to argue.

" 'Tis nightfall soon!" came Sheldon's high, fright-ened voice. "We must take her away! We must move her—"

"Don't be a ninny," said Argothlyn.

"We must—think clearly," said Cheveril, rapidly, flustered. "First of all, we must *not* move her—"

"But she must come away from here!"

"You fool—"

Susannah stood at Maria's feet. She tried to smile down at her aunt, to reassure her; but she was not sure Maria understood, yet, what had happened. Kneeling down, she smoothed her aunt's skirts and crept up next to Cheveril to speak to her.

" 'Twill be all right," she said. "Can you move your legs, Aunt Maria? Can you try?"

For that, her father had taught her, was the signal danger on horseback—broken limbs. Speaking to her aunt again, she found that Maria could move her arms and lift her head.

"What are they doing?" said Maria, in a small voice. She looked up at the three men with lost eyes.

"There. Lift your head again, Aunt." Unbuttoning her jacket, Susannah rolled it in a ball and stuffed it beneath Maria's head, as a cushion. Gently, she tried to straighten her aunt's legs. Maria winced.

"It is her leg," said Susannah to James Cheveril, who, arguing loudly now with the others over which of them was responsible for the fall, did not hear a word.

She stood. Still the men scarcely seemed to see her. "*It is her leg,*" she said again and, as they still argued, felt her frustration grow into anger. "Don't you un-derstand?" she cried. "She is *hurt*, she will grow ill if she lies here longer! There is no time to lose. We must each of us *do* something."

As the politicians looked up, more startled than comprehending, she went on: "All of you must see she is kept warm and quiet. I shall ride to the surgery at Bothwell, and—on the way I shall send a cart from the house. Only stay here till it comes."

She ran back, through the horses, to Harry. "Come with me," she said, reaching for her reins and hoisting herself up into the saddle. Quickly she explained what she had told the men. "I think they should never have done *any*thing," she said, with growing puzzlement. For when she looked back, the three politicians were still arguing.

Livia stirred her tired haunches to a trot, and the hooves of Harry's horse drummed on the road, close behind.

"Will she be all right?" Harry called.

"Yes—" Susannah had no breath to answer more. She hoped she had done right. Later, she knew, the others might accuse her of forcing herself—acting too quickly. She hoped they would understand: Aunt Maria must, surely. Perhaps her aunt would even thank her.

When Dr. Wallace had bandaged Maria's knee and given her a sleeping draught, various people came in to consult her wishes about the ball.

"It *must* go on!" Maria croaked from the depths of her featherbed, at her son and Susannah. "Would you have me pay eight musicians for not playing? And the food, Henry . . . the waste!"

Both young people looked damp and bedraggled—and the girl, Maria noticed, looked oddly expectant. *Well!* She must dampen any expectations *she* had. Maria coughed. "You two may leave me. Henry, you are looking peaked. Have your hair dressed."

Her son and niece left her, looking subdued, and other visitors, more essential to her happiness, lifted the tentlike draperies of her bed *à la polonaise*. After Maria had a few doses of the doctor's potation, their faces began rather to blend together.

"My dearest Maria!" William Sheldon clasped her hand. "It was unspeakable, the fright I felt at seeing you. . . . My faith in human happiness, I thought, that minute, dissolved. . . ."

"Tch," Maria clucked pleasantly. "Say no more."

"But I must! Or perhaps—have you an idea of my devotion?" Sheldon, his freckled forehead bright pink, went on this way for some time. "Maria," he said at last. "Marry me."

Maria smiled, and her dark head rocked on the pillow. *No.*

Downstairs, a few guests already milled in the dining room. Most of them were dressed for the ball, but Augusta, taking advantage of her mother's absence, had kept to the comfortable guise of her heavy brown riding habit. She dodged around the tables, sampling the pastries, pursued by Hench.

" 'Tis a rare girl, Miss Augusta," he was saying, "what has *your* sensibility for lit'rature! How do I know it? *Hem!* I can *see* it with m'own eyes. Why, most girls your age talk of nought but follies and romances—"

"Why, Mr. Hench. You demean us." Augusta looked down demurely.

"I vow I do not! Why, you're by far and away an—ex*emp*lifier to your fair sex." Hench took a few swallows of sherry, winding up for the next round. "Why, you've a *quantity* of learning, Miss Augusta, such as to make you quite exceptional. Not many a female nowadays reads Greek!" Hench waved his empty glass at a footman. Flattery, he thought, was damned thirsty work.

The musicians folded back their black silk coat sleeves, and Lord and Lady Framer presented themselves before them. Lady Caroline had exchanged her riding habit for a gown of bold cherry stripes, and the tamed raven locks of the morning for a gray, powdered frizz. Lord Framer, too, was heavily powdered, with a hint of black pencil around the eyes. The viols and clarinets tuned and struck up a minuet; and now, like two automatons, the Framers began to circle and spin.

One by one, the wanderers in the gallery turned to watch. All of them—or nearly all—longed to create such an effect. For it did not matter, just now, that the couple had fought like cat and dog last night or ignored each other for most of the morning. Lady Framer's cool gaze, beneath arrow-straight brows, clashed and locked with her husband's, with a charge that any scientist in the chamber might have called—electricity. Helena Stillwell, who was no scientist, patted her two-year-old ball gown, and sighed.

Susannah stood in the dining room doorway, watching the Framers dance, without much interest. She did not understand her aunt. Why, Maria had looked almost angry, when she came to her room with Harry; and she had not thanked either of them for riding for the doctor. *Why?*

"Will—you dance with me, Susan?"

Harry had come up beside her. He took her hand in his and bent his head to hear her answer.

"No. I shouldn't." But no sooner had she answered than her sense of duty, to mourning, was eclipsed by regret. The dancers now joining the Framers on the floor all looked light and carefree. *Why not?* she thought. What use had George Bry ever had for dutiful scruples, such as kept mourners from the joys in life? "Can I—change my mind?" she said.

She danced shyly at first, looking down: half in fear of some mysterious punishment. But no sudden silence ensued, no heaven-sent darkness or scolding. No one seemed even to notice her black skirt and black bodice, borrowed from Augusta. She lifted her head now and took her next turn, in large, quick steps, her skirt swirling.

"Maria. I have never asked this of a woman before. It has always seemed to me the most miserable of states—designed only to further the suffering of the hapless beast that is man. But—Maria, I find myself

wishing against all sense . . . Damn me, Maria! I wish
you would marry me." Argothlyn's eyes glittered behind his black brows.

"My dear Argothlyn—no!" Maria threw her head
back on the pillow, letting out a series of irrepressible
giggles.

The music went on: light, flirtatious, without sub-
stance. It hurtled from a trio into a rapid rondo.

Susannah skipped and leapt, pulling Harry with
her. And still, this obstinacy of Maria's made her
wonder, so that when he smiled at her, she looked
back, momentarily, with dark, anxious eyes.

"Why does—your mother hate me so?" she said as,
a slower tune starting, they took hands and moved
into a line.

"She—she doesn't dislike you," said Harry, his eyes
shifting nervously. "There is—much in her mind, of
late, I think. Like all of us, she has her—her secrets."

As Susannah's turn came to step forward and twirl,
she felt a little happier. "All of us?" she said playfully.
"I don't believe it. You don't have secrets, Harry, do
you?"

Harry's face clouded, and he missed the next step
forward. Smiling, tugging him toward her, Susannah
said, "Come, tell me. What's your secret? It can't be
anything very bad."

"I—" Harry began, and, "No." And he looked
thoughtful for all the rest of the dance and scarcely
spoke.

When it was over, as Susannah rose from her low
curtsy, he took her hand again. "Come—come away,"
he said. "I have s—something to tell you."

He drew her quickly ahead through the crowd, out
the end of the gallery, through the music room, the
parlor; and everywhere there were guests, talking,
drinking, playing cards; and nowhere would he stop
and speak, and tell her this thing that so weighed on
his mind.

They came to the marble entrance hall, which was

cool and empty. Susannah could barely see Harry's face. It looked gaunt in the light of the high candelabrum, the eyes shadowed, hooded, afraid.

"Come—" She tried to tease him. "No secret of yours can be so terrible!"

"I am afraid," he said simply, "to speak it."

"But you may be easy with me. I am your friend."

"But do you see"—Harry's voice was urgent—"I can never be easy with you. I can never bear—but to be your *friend*. Because I love you."

Susannah stared, silent, for at first she could not believe the words. And then, as quickly, she knew they explained all. Harry's attention to her; his sympathy for her troubles; his shyness. "Oh, Harry," she said, with a rush of regret.

She saw Harry's face—kind, ardent, nearly handsome—as he took her hands up in his and bent to kiss them. And she felt the heat of his skin, as he kissed, and kissed again. How good it would be, she thought, to be able to say she loved him in return. But it was not true. How much pleasanter to see that face every day, than Lady Chathenham's . . .

A thought had come to her, which made her fearful of herself, and she jerked her hands back, away, afraid. *If he truly loves me, I should not have to leave.* If he loved her, enough to marry her . . .

"You are—too kind," she said. "I know I—do not deserve it." Slowly, again, she extended her hands, and clasped Harry's, which were cold, within them. The candles flickered, casting their orange light in the hollows of Harry's face. "I have a wish," she said, now. "I know it is selfish—but I wish that I could stay here, at The Marches, with you."

"S-selfish? But you are not selfish, Susan. You are—b-brave—I have seen it. And good."

"Oh, no." And now the guilt at what she meant to do pressed upon her, more than before. "Do not think me good, Harry! You are wrong."

"But you are good, and I love you, and I want—"

"And I—" The great hall seemed suddenly to have

gone silent, all noise beyond died away. The candle flickered. "I want it, too, Harry."

I am a liar, she thought. *And I am wrong. This is wrong.* But she had come too far now, she knew, and could not speak the truth. She had chosen this way; and in it lay her security, her freedom. Perhaps, her happiness. *Lord, forgive me,* she thought. *I will make him a good wife. He shall never know I do not love, as he does. I shall try so hard—he shall never regret it.*

She saw her cousin, bending his head close to hers, his eyes shy, tentative, deep-buried beneath the bones of his lean face. "I wish—I could stay with you, Harry. I wish I were not to leave tomorrow. I know I must—"

"No!" Harry spoke fiercely. His eyes glittered in the light. "You shall not—leave here. Nothing shall take you away, I—I love you too much. Will you marry me?"

"Yes."

Her face was solemn; and her still mouth, her eyes dark with fear at what she had done, Harry took as signs of her own faith: a love as deep as his. And his heart triumphed.

In the gallery the party went on as before. After six dances, Lady Caroline Framer abandoned her husband in the middle of the floor; he gave a dramatic shrug and stalked off to the card room, where already Sheldon and Argothlyn were getting very drunk. In dressing gown and furs, Maria made a grand entrance, balanced on the arms of two footmen. Jonas Hench led off a round of applause for the hostess. She then seated herself in fitting majesty by the fire and listened to her third proposal of marriage. Or, if it was not quite one, it struck her as nearly as good.

"My compliments on your fete," whispered James Cheveril, kissing her hand. A dark-red lock fell rakishly across his eye. "You have grown very dear to me," he said. Maria felt a strange thrill run through her body, and shivered.

All in all, the hunt ball was a grand success. The money flowed at the card tables, and the orchestra played on with scarcely a break. Augusta danced with Jonas Hench for most of the evening. Unlike most other men she had danced with, he only laughed good-naturedly when she bumped into him.

Susannah and Harry returned to the room, both smiling and quiet, as if they guarded a secret. But by now even Augusta was too preoccupied to notice.

When most of the guests had gone, Harry accompanied his mother to her room. She leaned hard on his arm as she walked, wincing, every few steps, with sudden pain. Silently they threaded the long way down the corridor. The room was dim. Harry bent to light a taper from the fire.

"Mother," he began, drawing breath, trying to keep his voice steady. "There is something—I—m-must tell you."

Maria only grunted, jabbing a hand at the bed-clothes where she sat. Harry came, set his candle down, and began to loosen her furs.

"My maid will do that."

Harry stood again. "Mother—I must speak to you, about S-Susannah. She—she shall not leave here. She shall not go to Lady Chathenham's."

"What?" Maria looked up, squinting. "Ring for my maid, Harry. I want to be put to bed." She looked at him, again. "What is this whim of yours, about Susannah?"

"It is—no whim, Mother." Harry stopped, and the words came slowly. "Susannah—is to be m—my wife."

"Your wife?" Maria's voice rose. She thumped a hand on the covers of the bed. "I need to be put to bed, Henry! What nonsense is this you talk? Go away and forget it. And send for my maid!"

"I am s-serious, Mother. I mean what I say."

"Absurdity." Squinting, Maria craned her neck to look at her son. "You know it is impossible. For a thousand reasons."

"What reasons?" Harry demanded, bending down beside her.

"She is quite unsuitable! A penniless chit, raised in a swamp by a drunkard. She has not the least education, nor manner—"

"She has," said Harry quietly, "a generous nature, wh-which—is all that concerns me."

Maria snorted. Jabbing the bedclothes, she struggled ineffectually to rise. "Whatever *nature* the girl has," she said contemptuously, "she remains Bry's daughter. He is a soldier of fortune and a spendthrift. And blood will out."

Backing away from his mother, shaking his head in impatience, Harry stood. "I shall ignore your words," he said, "as they are unworthy of any ch-charitable disposition. Susannah is your own—sister's daughter. Is that not blood?"

"You shall stop this, Henry. You shall stop this caviling. I vow you shall not go through with it!"

Looking, still, steadily at her, Harry took a deep, shaking breath. "You—m-misunderstand me, Mother. I shall."

Maria snorted. "The girl is no more than a schemer. I will teach you the truth, however long it takes me! Think! How long has she been here? And how long, till she ensnared you? She is no more than a vile little slut, and a schemer—"

Harry grew pale, and his voice trembled. "She is not a—s-s-schemer."

"How can you treat me with such treachery?" Maria's shout echoed in the air. "I cannot—countenance this marriage. I will not hear of it! I forbid it!"

"You c-cannot forbid me, Mother. I am of age." Harry took a step, turning his back on Maria. She saw his chest shaking.

"There. You are unwell, Henry," she began to taunt. "Soon you shall suffer. You shan't be able to breathe. And why? Just as when you were a child, Henry. You try to disobey me . . ."

"No." Straightening, taking a long, deep breath, Harry turned. "I am—not ill, you see, Mother. And— I shall do as I wish."

Maria looked up with steady, steely eyes. "Now— when I am injured—bedridden—only now do you confess this plan of yours. When I have my—" She stopped. "*Augusta's* marriage to think of. . . . And when I am quite helpless"—her eyes grew wetter— "and can see to nothing at all. . . ."

Harry gave the shadow of a smile. "You are far from—helpless, Mother." He leaned closer to Maria. "I *will* marry Susannah. Soon. You shall have nothing to arrange, because for *once* I shall manage it all."

In the gallery, as the last guests were departing, Augusta seized on the chance to speak to Susannah; she tugged on her sleeve, whispering, "I have had an offer!"

"An offer?" Susannah could only repeat. So much had happened tonight, and so quickly, that this new happening only stunned her. Augusta was pulling her into the hall.

"An offer of marriage! What shall I do?"

"Why—tell me of it!" said Susannah. But scarcely had she spoken when she knew who the offerer was. The hall was cold, the candles in their stand burned to stumps; once again, the room and statues held their silence.

Augusta's words rang out against the stone-clad walls. "Mr. Hench!" She drew breath. "Why, I—I never expected it. But he said such kind things. He said I had lovely eyes, and—evident intelligence."

Susannah swallowed, not knowing what to say. "Then do you—think you love him?" She heard her own voice, as if at a distance, echoing. She thought of Hench, in his carriage; Hench, in a corridor, pressing her to the wall. She knew she could never speak

of these things. For that would destroy all the hope
she saw welling in her cousin's eyes.

"I cannot think him quite *handsome*," Augusta was
saying now, her voice—almost pleading at first—
gaining certainty. "However, I—think I should be
able to grow fond of him. He wishes to marry soon,
he says. And travel to Rome for the winter."

"Then what," said Susannah, in a light, faint voice,
"will become of our resolution?"

"Then have you had an offer, too, Susan? Is it—"

Susannah could not speak but only nodded. She
knew, from her cousin's sudden bright smile, whom
she meant. "I am sure"—she struggled for words—
"we shall both be very happy."

But she did not know. She was no more certain of
it now than when she had stood here an hour before.
Still I do not love him, she thought: that magic,
promised in her childhood, had not worked. Still he
was only Harry: kind and stammering, a friend. She
knew what honor there was in this marriage, which,
in a few moments' certainty, she herself had so surely
desired: had brought about. She would be a viscountess. Mistress of The Marches. The rest would come: it
must. Slowly, in time. *Love will come.*

Chapter 7

———— ❧ ————

As she settled the hat and veil on Susannah's head, Mary's face was pinched with concentration. The bride stood still as a doll, which Mary dressed and powdered and pinned; and the maid saw nothing amiss in that. She would be content, were all brides so obedient. . . .

Susannah had been bathed, and had her hair rinsed in orange-scented water. Mary had toweled her and rubbed her from head to toe with orange perfume; she had dressed her in petticoats and a satin gown, the white of the January snow. The bouquet she trimmed gave off the scent of rosemary.

Rosemary, thought Susannah. *For happy weddings.* She remembered that childhood tale of Adela's: and perhaps, like the other, it was not true.

Mary held a dangling pair of pearls up to her ears, and Susannah nodded, distracted. *I do not know him.* All day, the thought had drummed in her ears, until it stopped all other sound. *I do not know him.*

She had tried to speak: to delay the wedding a little. "Sometimes I think—" she had said carefully to Harry,

"I have much to learn here. This house is still new to me—"

But he had looked hurt. And she knew then, there was no stopping what she had set in motion. Maria had not been pleased at the engagement, she knew; she scarcely acknowledged it. And yet Harry had prevailed.

"I want—" he had said, "t-to be together with you. Alone. Only—us. S-say when it shall be."

A feeling of dread had filled Susannah, which she could not confess: a fear of the marriage bed, of the solitude he spoke of. But she knew no reason to prolong their engagement, except for her mourning, which was now nearly over. Augusta's wedding was set for early December, in London; and Harry had already suggested that theirs be here, at the church in the neighboring village of Bothwell.

Slowly, to reassure him, she pronounced a month. "January?"

Then, it had seemed an eternity away.

"If you would stand, please, Miss Susannah. . . . There!"

Mary smiled at last, satisfied with her handiwork. Susannah blinked and looked again in the tall mirror. The pale skin of her throat seemed to fade into the ruffles at her neck, which frothed like sea foam above her bodice, with its buttons of mother-of-pearl. The veil of her straw hat was drawn up over its brim, containing a cascade of ribbons and white silk flowers. Her face glowed now with rouge, which was the only paint Mary had applied; her lips were white, and she bit them, to give them color.

"Are you happy, miss?" said Mary.

Susannah was surprised to hear the question. Then she realized that Mary must mean . . . happy with her appearance. "Yes, Mary," she said. "Could you— leave me, a moment?" Susannah hurried to add, as Mary departed, "Thank you!" She looked in the mirror again, trying to accustom herself to the reflection.

Her body looked firm and solid: strange, how she felt her heart thumping inside her so, as if she were hollow and thin. She slid on the carpet in her kid slippers, and tried to smile.

She remembered how Augusta had glowed on her own wedding day, beneath the high roof of St. George's, Hanover Square. Her pearl-embroidered train had stretched half the length of the aisle. All of Hench's business associates and Maria's London acquaintances had attended; there was much stamping of feet and clanking of foot-warming boxes in the pews. It had snowed that morning, and the service droned on, unconscionably long. But afterward, at the great party at Hench House, the guests had warmed themselves with rum punch and reveled until dawn. The bride and groom themselves escaped after dinner, for an inn at Gravesend, from whence, the next morning, they would sail for the Continent. Augusta had talked eagerly of the trip for weeks: they were to stop in Paris, then make a leisurely route to Rome. At last she was to see the monuments of which she had read for years. *Rome!* she had exclaimed, once, merrily. *Why, no marriage can be fearsome when it begins in Rome!*

Susannah turned from the mirror and tried to walk steadily to the window. The soles of her shoes slid on the Chinese carpet. Outside, the land she had first seen so green was brown and bare, with a dusting of frost. And it seemed the cold there was within her, too. Soon she would be married; she would share her cousin's bed. She felt nothing—not delight, not even fear—at the thought of it. When Harry had kissed her—as he always seemed so eager to do, catching her alone in hallways, or outside, on their walks—it had not seemed pleasant. And the hunger it seemed to rouse in him, as he pressed his warm mouth against hers, found no equal in herself. Sometimes he would kiss her hands, full of affection; or try to pull her close, stroking the curve of her back, her waist, toward her breasts. . . .

She would pull away. Sometimes he said, "You

are—right. Soon enough we shall be married. Forgive me."

She could not explain that it seemed to her unnatural: that he, so like a brother, should kiss her, press against her. But now she was numb. Her hands, her cheeks and breasts, were chill, prepared. When the time came, she would not feel it.

She felt eyes on her, though she did not turn. Now she heard her aunt's voice.

"Susannah."

Maria clutched her gold-headed cane, in the doorway. She had taken to walking with it, since her back pained her from her fall. Her hair was blackened and showed no gray; her mouth was tight, her cheeks, thickly powdered, settling into grim folds around it. "Henry has gone ahead," she said, her mouth tightening and the folds deepening. "Come, Susannah. Everyone will be waiting."

The stone walls of the little church glowed golden in the sun. Four heads turned in the pew, expectant. Maria's long face showed no expression; and Mr. Cheveril's, next to her, showed one of vague amusement. She had not wished him to stay, but he insisted. "Why, Maria, you've so few guests, you *must* have me. After your daughter's ceremony, with near two hundred . . ." Cheveril had smiled good-naturedly; but Maria was not to be drawn on the subject. "Very well, James," she had said in a voice only barely agreeable. "Then, come."

Next to Cheveril sat Maria's second daughter, Agnes, bright-eyed and plump, like Augusta, but more placid. For this month of weddings—first Augusta's, then Harry's—she and her husband, John Burleigh, had made one of their rare trips from Somerset.

Harry had not cared to invite a great number of guests; it was his old tutor and friend, Bayliss, who was to take Susannah to the altar.

She saw his pink face only in hazy outline through her veil. But, through the gap between the veil and her gown, cast across the flagstone floor she could see the thin leaves of rosemary. *For happy weddings.* She walked—the organ's notes were slow—and yet she seemed not to move at all. The walls around went gray as the sun vanished behind a cloud. Ahead, the three figures were still distant, indistinct: Everett and Helena Stillwell—the eldest cousins, the witnesses. And in the middle, beside an empty place—Harry. Of course he did not turn; and his blurred figure, nearer now, could have been almost any man's. His hair was tied in a black ribbon, and his thin legs held uncharacteristically still.

They reached the altar at last, but Susannah imagined herself still walking: ahead, forever, up a stone path that would not end. She did not even hear the vicar's first words.

". . . A prayer of thanksgiving. O mighty Lord our God, who hath given us the fruits of thy forest, the flowers of thy field, the grace of thy everlasting mercy . . ."

The thin, quailing voice rose above her. She tilted her head and stole a glance at Harry. His head was bent low, his face closed and still. For a moment he looked—again—a stranger. But the feeling passed. His hand was cold when it joined hers.

Now, just as the time before had slowed, the questions, the vows, came unnaturally quickly. She could not hear the words she repeated, for the hum in her ears; she scarcely breathed, and now they were clasping hands, turning, making their way back down the aisle toward the door. Outside in the yard, the others gathered round them. Maria opened her arms to her son, with an oddly sorrowful look, and pressed him to her. Then she lifted Susannah's veil, her cheek brushing past her new daughter-in-law's as she made the sound of a kiss. Momentarily drawn apart by the others' congratulations, then pushed together again, Susannah and Harry found themselves alone in the berlin, the coach horses hurtling them back toward The Marches.

Susannah said nothing. Every time she began to

speak, the words in her throat seemed stupid or wrong. Harry looked down at her, and away. Suddenly he took her hand and bent toward her, fastening his mouth on hers. Startled, she tried to escape him. She gasped and backed away. But his mouth followed, persistent, his lips soft, hungry, warm against hers. She kept her mouth tightly closed, and her eyes; the hoofbeats of the horses drummed in her ears.

When at last he released her, she turned away, facing the window. Harry still did not speak. He clutched her hand tightly in his.

At the house there was a wedding dinner: rabbit stew, pigeon pie, jellies, and roast beef. Susannah would usually have tried them all, but today she could barely manage a mouthful of each. Harry, at her side, did not eat much either. His brother-in-law, Burleigh, with a round-faced grin, tried to make sport of this.

"All 'er appetite's caught up in anticipation, I'll wager!" he said, topping up Harry's glass. "Drink up, Harry. Gives strength—"

Harry only flushed and backed away; and Agnes, at her husband's elbow, clucked. At the head of the table Maria was murmuring with James Cheveril, disregarding it all.

And so the afternoon wore on, until the early winter twilight. Burleigh's few attempts at joviality were silenced; Maria sat glumly, dispatching quantities of port; the sisters, Agnes and Helena, gossiped at a corner of the table. To Susannah it seemed interminable.

Harry's friend Bayliss stood and raised his glass in a solemn toast. "May all the fruits and happiness of marriage be yours," he pronounced; and slowly, one at a time, the others stood and joined him.

"To Harry and Susannah," offered Cheveril, smiling. Maria, at his side, did not respond. Her eyes were glassy and wandered across the scene, and Cheveril had to tug at her arm to get her to drink the toast.

"Many children!" bawled Burleigh. But now there was an uneasy shifting. And Susannah found that the

women—Harry's sisters—were surrounding her, and
the men surrounding Harry likewise, until they were
being borne out of the room into the great entrance
hall. Jostled and propelled by the company, they
mounted the separate stairs; and now a loud cheer
broke out, below. A crowd of maids and footmen had
assembled, and called out their good wishes, whistling
and clapping, as the bride and groom reached the top.
For the young viscount's wedding day was a feast day
for all the house, and once the married couple was
dispatched, the servants could set to their own eating
and drinking belowstairs.

Susannah and Harry were led down a hall and
pushed through high, unfamiliar double doors.

As the doors slammed behind them, Susannah heard
Burleigh's voice raised in one last toast.

"To—"

But she heard only a chastising rumble of voices,
then silence. She turned to Harry; now she saw the
maid, Mary, and the manservant waiting stiffly on
either side of the great bed. This bed was like none
she had seen before: as big as a room in itself, with
thick square pillars and worn, green-embroidered
curtains.

"M'lady?" said Mary now, with a faint, knowing
smile. And in an officious, dutiful silence, the servants
led the bride and bridegroom to their separate dressing rooms.

The two small chambers were on either side of the
bed, behind it; at the same moment, in their white
nightclothes, Susannah and Harry emerged. Mary
turned back the bedclothes, and ran the iron warmer
between the sheets. Just as on any other night, Susannah hopped from one foot to the other, waiting. The
marble floor was so cold she thought her feet would
freeze to it. The quiet fire in the chimney gave scant
warmth to the old-fashioned room, with its bare
floors and paneled walls, painted in black and gray
marbling. A faded tapestry, in the green of the bed-
curtains, hung in a frame above the fire. Sliding under the covers, Susannah fixed her gaze on it. She did

not look at Harry. Mary and the manservant left, and
now the deep chill of the bed wrapped round her.

In the silence, she could hear the room's tiniest
sounds: the wind whistling through the shutters, outside, and the crackling of timber in the fireplace. She
heard Harry's breathing, steady and slow. "Are you
awake?" she said.

"Yes . . ."

He was so far away, she did not even feel his
warmth. She trembled from the effort of lying straight
and still. She wanted to talk to Harry—to ask what
he had thought of this strange day. To break the silence. She felt the skin of her legs and arms shrink
into goose bumps.

A hand slid through the sheets toward her; it ran
up against her stomach, and retreated. Susannah
heard the rustle of covers. Now a bare, furry leg slid
over hers and, reaching and groping, her cousin—her
husband—pulled her down toward him. She felt his
sticky hair beneath her chin, and a quick hand seizing
her breast.

She let out a cry, trying to move away; but this only
sent the hand into frenzies of affection. It stroked and
circled; now he reached down, with his wet mouth,
through her nightgown. Susannah lay motionless and
squeezed her eyes shut. She had a vague notion of
what he was going to do, and that in it there was little
pleasure for a woman. Panting now, covering her face
and neck with kisses, he struggled with the yards of
fabric that enveloped her. The cold had stiffened her
limbs so, that she could not move to help him, even
had she wished to. His hands poked her sex, prodded
it, pulling inadvertently at the hair, so that she let out
muffled cries of resistance. Sometimes something long
and warm thrust itself at her, forcing itself against the
tender skin there, that was closed to it.

"What—where—" murmured Harry above her.

"I don't know. Please, stop."

"B-but we must!" And Harry went on, stammering
other words she could not understand. "We must," he
said again.

"No, not now." The fleshy member below pushed at her; and, growing more frightened as it went on, she thought that if it entered her it could do so only by making a wound. "Please—" she breathed, and tried to writhe away from it. "No . . ."

And by some miracle, Harry retreated. She heard him coughing, far away. The fire cracked, and all seemed peaceful. And then she heard his coughs come again: faster, harder.

"Harry? Are you unwell?"

"I—" The voice seemed to shrivel in his throat. "I—" His voice died again, and he seized her hand, from across the wide bed, and, as he coughed and began to wheeze, his fingers dug into her wrist.

"Harry?" she said, kneeling, crawling closer. In the darkness of the curtained bed, she could see nothing. "Harry?" She grabbed the arm that seized at hers: shook it, and shook his body, afraid. "What is wrong, Harry? Speak to me!"

She heard the high whistle of his breaths and felt his shoulders strain and shudder. Crawling around his feet, now, heedless, she pulled back the curtains and knelt beside the bed, in the firelight.

"It—is—" Harry struggled, and pulled himself up to sit. His forehead was pale, glistening with sweat. "It—will be—" he said at last, but no more words would come. His shoulders hunched, and the muscles of his neck jutted out as he fought for breath.

"Tell me what to do," she said in fear, knowing that he could not. Only now did the memory of Augusta's words come back to her. Harry had a trouble of the lungs, she had said. . . .

Harry's wide eyes seemed to plead, but she knew not for what. And in fear, at last, she left his side, lighting a candle, wrapping a shawl around herself, stroking his cold forehead and saying she would return. She ran down the broad stairs, and when she penetrated the kitchens below, all the servants, gathered round their feast table, turned and stared.

But when she found Mary and told her what had

happened, Mary began to fetch supplies, without a word.

They ran upstairs, with the cloths, the jars, the kettle of water. As Mary startled the kettle boiling, Susannah said, "Shall I send for a doctor?"

"No—" managed Harry, in one wheezing breath. " 'Tis—"

" 'Tis all right," said Mary. "We've managed before. . . ."

Before? thought Susannah, stunned. She held Harry's hand as he knelt by the boiling water, breathing in the herb-scented steam. Mary covered his back and arms in warm cloths; and gradually he began to cough, and breathe again.

Mary left them then; and so they spent the remainder of their wedding eve huddled by the fire in the steamy room, until at last Harry could breathe easily, and talk.

"I—suppose you got a bad bargain," he said with a wry smile as they made their way back to the bed.

Susannah smiled weakly. She felt uneasy, somehow, at his pleasantry. "Does that happen—often?" she said, as she drew the covers up over them both.

"No. Scarce—ever, anymore. I do not know—what brings it on." His fingers reached over and touched her hand. "Do you know," he said now, "this is—my family's wedding bed? I was born in this bed, and my father before me."

Susannah let his hand lie still, in hers. She wondered at this sudden, queer access of words. It was almost as if that seizure, that fight for breath, had renewed him. For he went on talking strangely, hurriedly: about his grandfather, the first Viscount, who had chosen the pattern of roses and fleurs-de-lis on the bed-curtains, intending a peace between England and France which had never come.

He talked about his great-uncle, who, unusually, had married for love.

"What? Has no one else?" said Susannah.

Harry smiled sleepily and held fast to her hand. "No. The rest of the family had made—eminently p-practical marriages. They all—opposed him, for what he did. He m-married a Scotchwoman, who s-spoke no English. He had met her—m-marching through the Highlands with his regiment. They thought here, that she must have—put a spell on him. For she was poor. But I think they were wrong, and she was only—beautiful." He looked over at Susannah, his eyes gleaming in the light.

She stroked his cheek. "You should sleep," she said.

"Come near?" he said. Already he was drifting off to sleep. "I think," he murmured, "we are like them. We shall be happy. . . ."

But while he slept, now, Susannah lay awake, watching the charcoal of the fire deaden to darkness. The scenes of the evening coursed through her mind: the awkwardness, the shame that made her want to curl in on herself. *The next time,* she thought, *I must give way.* She knew she must not chance making Harry so ill again.

James Cheveril woke with a start. The tent-shaped pink bed looked familiar; the body leaning over him, shaking his shoulder, a little less so: tall, well-preserved but for a slackness in the stomach. He gave his most dazzling smile and pulled at the ribbons of the nightdress. "Maria? Awake so early?"

"Don't be a ninny, James. You must go."

"What? On the wedding morn? Am I to be tossed from bed at whatever god-awful hour this is and—"

"Seven, James. The sun's nearly up. Now, go."

"No." He gave a boyish pout. "Don't want to. Besides—" He threw off the sheets, smiling, to reveal an enormous erection.

"James." Maria averted her eyes; they seemed to wander back again, of their own will. She turned and walked stiffly to the dressing table. Taking a brush to her coal-colored hair, she slowly adjusted her features. At last, with wide, sad eyes, she turned to Cheveril. "Oh, James! I was a terrible fool last night. Do not torment me with my weakness. . . ."

Cheveril looked puzzled.

"Well?" said Maria more sharply. "You *knew* I was in distress, because of the girl. . . . Not what I had hoped for my son. And you—" Her voice quavered again now, hinting at tears about to break through. "You took the gain of me! A mere widow, alone in the world . . ."

"Ma-ria." Cheveril's tongue rolled over the syllables of her name. He sat up slowly. "Maria, Maria. Spare me the theatrics. You are not such a clever actress as all that."

Maria blinked. The tears receded. "I am not acting," she said haughtily. "I am resolved. You shall not find me—weak again. I cannot afford to be so foolish." Coming forward, her gaze softer, she added: "You know the risks we women take, James. There may always be a child."

"What? I thought you were past that." Cheveril spoke coolly as he searched the floor for his breeches. So he was unprepared for the hairbrush that struck him, hard, on the neck, narrowly missing his head.

Maria backed away, distraught, as he stood and approached her. There was a tolerant smile on his mouth but a hint of menace in his eyes. He rubbed his neck. " 'Tis mighty hard, Maria, to rouse you in defense of your virtue. But I see you'll well-nigh murder for your vanity."

"Stop it, James." Maria's wet eyes wandered to his face, and down again. "You are being shameful. And childish—"

He seized her by the shoulders and stopped her with his mouth. In the space of a few seconds, she turned pliant, then limp in his arms. He maneuvered them both toward the bed.

"There," he said. "Isn't *this* better than anger?"

Chapter 8

———— ❧ ————

The tall clock ticked in the library of The Marches, a room furnished in green leather and walnut, beginning to overflow with volumes. A fire crackled behind the hearth screen, and two candles burned on Harry's desk, eking out the feeble light of the winter afternoon. A quarto volume of Tacitus was open before him, while Susannah, curled on the sofa, leafed through a picture book on Venice. He looked up at her now and again: she was remarkably still now, like a picture, and he knew it would not last.

He looked down again, quickly, as she shifted in her chair: but not quickly enough, for she caught his eye and said, "Are you weary of that? Will you come out?"

She was always wanting to go out these days; somehow the reading that had once occupied her seemed not to hold her attention for more than an hour or two, now that they were alone. Harry did not understand this. He himself grew ever more immersed in Saxon times.

"Out?" he said hazily. "Right—right now?"

"Oh, never mind," said Susannah, not trying to hide

the sound of impatience. "Anyway, we should be frozen." She twisted, planting her feet on the floor, and stood to warm herself at the fire. " 'Tis a lucky thing you're not as nearsighted as Augusta, reading so much! What is it about—that book?"

"It is—about Britain under the Romans." Harry looked distracted. Locks of his hair had come loose by his face, and a spot of ink had landed on his nose.

"Oh," said Susannah, not quite comprehending. Another episode of history had confounded her expectations. The Romans in Britain? Rather than asking Harry about it, and getting, inevitably, a long explanation, she pointed at the page he was reading. "What does it say?"

Harry pulled the book closer and, bending down, began to translate. " 'When Caesar arrived at . . . the field of battle, he drew up his army in four lines. The enemy . . .' " He looked up. Susannah's eyes were darting around the room.

"What does this mean?" Susannah sounded out a name from the shelf before her. *"La Foi-blesse de l'Esprit Humain."*

"Wh—" Henry pulled back from his translation. "Th—that?" He looked up at the title. *"The Weakness of the Human Spirit.* Are—are you intending to take up French again?"

"Perhaps," said Susannah carefully. Augusta's grammar book had not given her a taste for it. She would rather, if it came to it, have more dance lessons with Mr. Pantafoglio or a morning with the cook, Mrs. Barnes, discussing recipes. If only the woman had not urged her—virtually ordered her—to have a few weeks' leisure before taking charge of house matters. . . .

"Or," said Harry brightly, "if you wish to know more of the Romans . . ." Stumbling on a chair leg, he moved to the shelves. "Here! S-see this."

He handed her a green volume: *A Short History of Rome.*

"Thank you," she said politely, retreating to the sofa. The print was very large, she noticed: interspersed with rough engravings. It was a child's book; and she did not know why she felt suddenly hurt at being given it. *Oh, well.* "*The Foundation of Rome. . . . Rome began, as the myth relates, on seven hills . . .*" She tried, but she could not concentrate. *What is the use of it?* She knew she could never know as much as Harry. She might read French grammars and children's histories from dawn to dusk—still, she would never have his memory. That infuriating memory, which lost hold of nothing: not history, not foreign words, not even the childhood tales she told. . . .

"What?" she said abruptly, looking up. "Why do you stare at me?"

"Will you—come away to bed with me?"

Not again. Slowly she said, "I thought you were working."

Since their wedding night, again and again, he had tried. Though he never forced her; and she never had, explicitly, to refuse. *It will come,* he said always, hopefully, kissing her. He never seemed ashamed of this failure. "As it is," he would whisper, sometimes, as he stroked her, "it is greater than—any bliss I have known." He would touch her back, her ears, her arms, and bend to lick her breasts with a kind of glee. He would press her tightly to him; and then, at her whimper of distress, let go. "In time," he would whisper.

Now he stood watching her, his hair loose and the wrinkled folds of his shirt drooping sadly, like his mouth.

"Come, then," she said tonelessly. She would lie still and bear it. *All, except . . .* She shrank inside at the thought. Without looking back for Harry, she walked out, and across the gallery, to the stairs.

The house was still and quiet, the fields outside hard with frost. The walls echoed Susannah's footsteps, and the formal rooms now left empty languished: swirls of dust rose when she opened the front parlor door. No callers came but the Northfords and the vicar. By

the end of February Susannah was almost as over-
joyed by letters as she would have been by visitors, so
when two letters came together one day, she tore at
them with eager excitement. She ran to find her husband, her steps ringing on the marble stairs. The first
letter was on golden, thick paper, covered with the
curlicues of Augusta's writing; the second came from
Tunbridge Wells, where Maria had gone to take the
waters after the exhaustion of two weddings. Naturally, she turned first to Augusta's.

> *We have visited the Tivoli, and the ruins of the
> Forum, which fill'd my heart with a shiv'ring
> wonder. . . .*

"Harry?" Susannah called. Her feet clattered on the
hallway floor, and she found him at last, in the distant third-floor chamber that had been Bayliss's study.
He looked up from the dusty volumes on the bed with
a dazed expression. "Listen!" she said, hugging herself
against the cold. "Augusta's been to no end of famous
places. She says . . ." She read on, from where she
had left off: of the Contessa Ceccherini with whom
Augusta passed the time, of Jonas's loathing of foreign
food and his efforts to buy Venetian glass and art.
"'Soon,'" Susannah read aloud, "'we shall be a
veritable gallery at Hench House. We have bought a
Hercules Fighting the Lion by Carracci, a *Crucifixion*
by Tintoretto, a *Judith and Holo-fernes* . . .'" Susannah struggled with a few of the names, but Harry did
not, as was sometimes his way, correct her.
"I hope she is content," he said absently. He had
worried, before, at his youngest sister's abrupt and
worldly marriage. Now it seemed to him an age ago;
and a nearer fear, a need, came over him as he
watched Susannah pace the room, in silent commu-
nication with her cousin. Her auburn curls hung loose
down her back, and she hugged herself, and laughed.
Once again he wanted her; he wanted to run up
behind her and embrace her. To touch her hair—but
she would shake him off, like a cat peevish at being

stroked. It was always the same. He loved her more
than ever, and now that he had her, he still could not
be content.

"Oh! Harry." Susannah had turned at the doorway,
her face bright with excitement. "You shan't ever
guess. Augusta says . . . your mother is getting married!" She paused, and watched Harry blink, startled:
but he said nothing. "To Mr. Cheveril! Holy—" She
bit her tongue before an unwanted oath could come
out. "How can she have heard it, in Rome? What will
your mother—" She handed Harry Augusta's letter
and quickly tore open Maria's.

"Yes," she said at last. "It is true. They were married two days ago—"

"What?"

"—at the Church of King Charles the Martyr. They
go to London next month."

Harry stared at Susannah in disbelief; now his gaze
wandered to the walls, the window.

"At least," said Susannah merrily, "she will *have* to
like Mr. Cheveril. She chose him!"

But at Harry's angry look the smile fell from her
face.

"What is it?" she said.

"She—might have told me. She might—at least—"
Harry shook his head, and broke off.

Two weeks passed: the time ordained by Mrs.
Barnes in which Susannah was to "settle" to the house
and its ways. Susannah decided she had waited long
enough. For everything, as far as she could see, was
still done according to Maria's old orders. Though Susannah had requested breakfast in the bedroom at
eight, it seldom appeared before ten-thirty. She would
ring the handbell by the bed, first abashed, then gradually growing angry. She had not *asked* to be waited
on; but Mrs. Barnes kept the larder keys, and all the
maids, like co-conspirators, held fast the secrets of the
kitchens. Every time she went belowstairs, she came
up against stony-faced disapproval from the scullery

maids, laundry maids, and parlor maids. Asked where this food or that implement was, they would curtsy and dumbly shake their heads.

"I don't *like* pigeon," Harry would grumble at dinner, or: "Another almond pudding?" And that, too, took getting used to. Harry was so used to seeing what he liked to eat or drink simply appear, that it was impossible to explain to him that perhaps he should be grateful it appeared at all.

"But I don't like almonds," he would say pettishly, and, after a glance at yesterday's newssheet or a letter from London, he would look up regretfully at Susannah and half apologize. "F-forgive me, my dear. But I don't. It—it is very simple."

So Susannah could see that she must begin to take charge. She retreated to Maria's upstairs study, to arm herself with information. Knole, the secretary, was no longer here to assist her, for he had followed Maria to Tunbridge Wells.

She opened the account book to its latest page.

Mrs. Barnes, gen'l
Expenses till April .... £400 8s. 2d.

Four hundred pounds! It astonished her. This was Knole's writing. It seemed the old practice of listing items had been abandoned. Had Knole and Maria given the cook four hundred pounds to last till April? For she remembered quite well how the cook had come to Harry at the end of February: "Um so very sorry to ask ye, m'lud. But the housekeeping money . . ." She claimed it had run out, and Harry, in a hurry to be done with the business, had written out notes of credit for the town merchants, and handed her coins: in all, nearly two hundred pounds.

Susannah marched down to the kitchens with the heavy volume under her arm. "Mrs. Barnes?"

The cook turned, red-faced, from the pot she was stirring.

"Well, Mrs. Barnes?" Susannah held the open book out before her.

The heads of kitchen- and laundry-maids turned, up and down the whitewashed room. In truth the old cook still intimidated Susannah, but she tried not to show it.

"What, pray, have you spent six hundred pound on between January and now?" She felt her voice shake a little; but she thought of her aunt—of how *she* would sound—and held firm.

Mrs. Barnes, grown somewhat redder, puffed: "I dun't huv to 'count for my 'xpenses to *you*, m'm. 'Twas m'lady Maria und m'lud thut guv me the money."

"And I'm asking you now where it went."

"Ut didn't went, madam. I've a hundurd remaining." Mrs. Barnes gave a nod, as if to affirm this, to each pair of eyes that turned to her from above cutting boards and basins. The eyes moved to Susannah, who drew back a little.

"Perhaps you should come upstairs, to explain."

"I can't, when thur's a ragout fixing, m'm."

Why, Susannah wondered, *does she not call me "m'lady," like Maria?*

But, as it turned out, she had no chance to ask. For when she at last appeared upstairs, Mrs. Barnes immediately gave her notice. Or, Susannah gave *her* her notice: She was not sure which.

The cook planted herself in the doorway. "I dun't like to be treated mistrustful-like," she announced.

"I don't mistrust—" Susannah lied, stepping forward.

"An establishment like this in't a *farm* the likes you come from, madam. It costs a deal to keep! I maught tell you, i'faith, thut you haven't the custom o' the place—"

"But I know what things cost," said Susannah, her certainty fed by her rising anger. Even when she had run errands here, she had not liked or trusted this bulky, shifty-eyed head cook. "I've looked at all last year's books," she said. "I think, if you wish to stay here, Mrs. Barnes—"

'Well, mebbe I dun't wish to stay on, wi'out Her Ladyship."

Maria. Susannah clenched her teeth and tried not to show that the words had had any effect. "Perhaps—you had best leave then."

"Thut I will!" Mrs. Barnes's voice rose shrilly, as she turned, without curtsying, toward the hall. "Thut I will! Hap'ly! There's better places as want me—"

"And I want the last hundred pound back."

The woman turned, smiling contemptuously. "Mebbe." She paused, and gave a knowing nod. "I'll need a letter of rufference, fer me next place."

Bribery, Susannah thought. The old bird was not going to relinquish the money, without the guarantee of another job. "I don't know," she said at last, "what I could say, to recommend you."

"Huh—"

"And," Susannah braved her way further, "if that hundred pounds is not left here on this desk, I shall go straight to Bothwell and have you arrested for theft."

After Mrs. Barnes's departure early the next morning—leaving some sixty pounds on the desk, which was better than Susannah had expected—Susannah set to making new arrangements. She asked Warwick, the butler, whom she felt instinctively she could trust, to supervise accounts and purchases. The under-cook maid, Em, would take charge of the kitchens and the larder-keys. Susannah set about writing letters to the storekeepers in Bothwell, checking their charges. It was a lot of work: to Harry's mind, tedious work. "Why do you trouble yourself with such small matter?" he asked one day, after Susannah had told him the details of her search for a cook. She had finally decided to give Em the post. Em was young and agreeable; her food was plain, but she never served almond puddings.

"Trouble myself?" Susannah repeated. "Why— *some*one should."

"But—but the servants can manage on their own.

Can't they? They're hardly likely to spend the—m-money we have in a year."

"How much money *do* we have in a year?" If it was enough to afford £600 every few months, Susannah thought, then it must be a great deal indeed.

"*I* don't know," said Harry. His tone suggested that the knowledge was dull, ungentlemanly. "Ten thousand? Twelve thousand? I suppose someone must know. Knole, or my mother."

Ten thousand pounds? It was a dizzying sum. Where, Susannah wondered, did it come from? She had heard Maria mention "rents": and there was a steward, she knew, who collected them from the family's tenants in Surrey. And they held stocks in trading companies, she thought. They must hold piles of certificates, and of gold—somewhere. *Where?* When she next saw Maria and her secretary, she decided, she would ask.

Now, with Warwick and Em in charge, she felt more the mistress of the house and its rituals. Hot chocolate and rolls began to appear in the mornings, and tea at four to fill the long interval till dinner. The laundress consulted Susannah about the days for changing sheets and beating carpets. Perhaps it was all small matter, as Harry said. But for Susannah, it was familiar ground: something she understood.

She still did not understand marriage: the relations between husband and wife, which, six weeks since the wedding, she still knew nothing of.

What Adela and *The Lady's Book of Devotions* had hinted to her in childhood, she had begun to guess was true: this horrible, physical side of marriage benefited only husbands. For all her discouragement, Harry had not given it up. Often his explorations lasted for hours. She felt her body was being invaded; she could not explain the fear. When once she had tried, "Perhaps we should live—simply as friends, Harry," he had turned away, curling up on his side of the bed, still and silent. His breathing, to her relief, had stayed steady, but he refused to answer. And she had felt so alone, suddenly, that she had tried to take back her words. There was no response: and for almost a week after that, he left her in peace. But now, again, in the vast, chill bed, his old hunger for her returned.

He blew out the candle by the bedside, his eyes searching her face for a sign. She pretended to sleep, watching warily through her lashes as he climbed in beside her, drawing the curtains.

He pulled her closer, kissing, sucking on the side of her neck, moving his mouth over her collarbone, her left breast. His voice was muffled against her skin.

". . . adore you," he was saying. "Susan . . . I am—so lucky." He sucked greedily on her nipple. Susannah felt it grow tight and hard, and squirmed away. His teeth hurt her. His hands groped, more hesitant, below.

"Don't," said Susannah, by habit now. She did not like that part of her body. It was ugly, hairy.

"Only hold me," Harry whispered in the dark, pulling her hand downward. *It* was as alive as ever, springing up beneath her fingers. She did not mind touching it, if he asked for no more.

"I don't want—" Harry breathed, "to hurt you. Or force you, if you don't wish. But I—"

Susannah's body went rigid in the dark.

"No?" Harry said; and then, anticipating her answer: "No."

Susannah went on stroking his member, without paying much attention. As often, she was thinking of other things. "What if we should go to London?" she said suddenly.

"Why?" Harry went on, carefully: "There—it should be different?"

"Oh, yes!" said Susannah, yawning. She let her hand drop. "There, we could go out. It is so cold here. . . ." She wriggled further under the sheets, thinking of what seemed, all of a sudden, to be the positive delights of London. The coach rides down the teeming Strand, the dressmaker's, Gallini's concert rooms . . .

She guessed what Harry had meant to ask. But she put off thinking of that till another time.

They made the trip at the beginning of March, a dank and misty month in London. The city's smoke pall hung thicker than ever in the air, and the house, lazily tended by Ernestine, smelled of dust. Still, to Susannah it seemed less oppressively empty than The Marches; and the sight of life around her in the house, and in the streets, cheered her. But the hopes the city raised in her as quickly died: for of course she knew no one here, and was invited nowhere. No balls, no dancing: and Harry started immediately to work on the books he had brought with him. When, after a few days, the change he had hinted at did not come about, he grew distant, absentminded.

A few invitations did come, from the Ackerleys, the Framers, and Derveys—Susannah suspected, out of courtesy to her aunt. Sometimes she brought them, hopefully, to table.

"The Derveys?" Harry would repeat the name, whichever it was, without enthusiasm. "Go. Go, if you like, Susan. . . ."

It was not that he refused to go out. Sometimes he did leave the house—alone—to meet other scholars and authors, at a coffeehouse. He said the talk, at these dark dens by the Strand, was serious. It would not interest her.

Susannah knew she might go out on her own. Many married women did. But the prospect frightened her. She was not sure where Maria's friends lived, or what to wear. She told herself: *the next time* . . . And she wandered about the house in search of entertainment.

She read *Henry IV, Part I*, at random, from a volume of Shakespeare. But many things in it perplexed her, and she laid the book aside until her husband came back from taking coffee with Mr. Boswell. She asked him at supper, "Why was Bolingbroke called a traitor?"

"Who? Good heavens, Susan. Where—where did you come at that?" Harry stared, perturbed, at his knife. He was trying, not very adeptly, to butter a piece of pound cake. Susannah reached silently for the knife and the cake and told him about the play.

Carefully, perhaps unnaturally slowly, Harry explained the divine right of kings.

"Oh," said Susannah, her forehead wrinkling.

"Do—do you see now?"

"No. . . . Kings aren't divine, we know that. Why should anyone believe they are?"

"Many people still do," said Harry seriously. "M-many more kings should topple did their peoples *not* believe it."

"But they aren't—"

Harry went on, dreamy-eyed, caught up in the subject. "Though in—in America, you have established a far more ideal nation. A land of self-governing city-states, in which each man may be citizen . . ." Harry went on in this way for a time, speaking of "utopias," of "newfound lands."

Susannah was surprised to hear him speak so reverently of her country. Before, he had only talked of its evil—slavery. Often, it was true, he talked of liberty, of democracy: but only as distant and, to Susannah, rather tedious notions. She tried now to break into his reverie. "You know—life in America is surely not so perfect as you think! Why, you might find the people—coarse. They haven't your education. . . ."

"But—but I do not speak of appearances! I have read Mr. Jefferson's persuasions. I have a—faith in America." Harry's voice lowered. "Some day, m-my dear, I should like to go there with you."

Harry, go to America! To cross the seas, with his weak chest—forgo all the comforts he took for granted . . . Susannah laughed and said, "What a romance you make of it! Whyever d'you fancy it so?"

She laughed again, rather pleased at Harry's sudden

adventurousness; and she did not notice the hurt in his eyes.

At the end of March, an invitation came that was not from any of Maria's acquaintances. Susannah studied it over Harry's shoulder as he bent by the light to read it.

"Carolus Potter!" he said, sounding pleased.

"Who is Careless Potter?" Susannah giggled at the name.

"A p-poet. He used to write of—s-sheep and farm-yards, but it seems he's Latinized his name. I wonder," Harry mused, now, "if Bayliss is coming."

"Is it a dinner party?" said Susannah, excited. This Latinized poet sounded an interesting character at least. "What should I wear?" She did not expect an answer to the last, from her unworldly husband. But she did not expect, either,

"Oh, but—you cannot come."

"Whyever not?" She folded her arms, resistant, and waited for Harry's reasons, none of which seemed very good. The poet's rooms were cramped, he said. Other ladies would not attend.

"I should *like* to be the only lady," she said. She wheedled and pleaded. Harry flushed, discomfited; but he would not come round.

On the night of the party—a mild, moonlit night at the end of March—she stood by in near silence as Bayliss called, and the coach bore the two men away. She knew her upset was foolish, unfounded. Harry was an admirable husband in this way: never before had he gone out, of an evening, on his own. *But neither have I*, said an inner voice, rebellious. *I never go out—we never go out, anywhere.*

She tried to put the annoyance from her mind: to occupy herself, as she had on many another evening. For a while she tried to stitch initials onto a handker-chief; then she searched the bookshelves for an unread Gothic romance.

At midnight, when Harry had not come in, she

sighed and took her light upstairs. Mary, the maid, unpinned her hair and helped her out of her clothes; as she was about to blow out her candle, she heard her husband's steps on the stairs.

He smiled, and stumbled in the bedroom doorway.

"Did you have a good night?" she said coolly.

Harry's tongue lolled and tripped over itself as he answered. He had drunk more, evidently, than was his habit. He tugged his coat and cravat loose. "Oh, yes! A—a splendid evening. The conversation was general, and, and—"

"Long?" she suggested, annoyed, and rose to brush out her hair again, while he talked on.

Harry's face glowed. "Mr. Gibbon was there! And—and George Crabbe, the parson-poet. For an age I talked to Boswell, he goes on so, when he drinks—"

"Does he," said Susannah; and she wondered why she could not resist this carping pettishness.

"I talked to Gibbon the longest. Oh, he's not at all what—what you'd fancy from his—p-prose. He's quite fat, and red-haired. A—v-very gnome! We agreed to correspond. . . . Oh, and Killburn, the actor, was there. And Mrs. Montagu—"

"Mrs. Montagu?" Susannah spun round. "A *lady*?"

Harry saw her expression and tried to soothe her. "Yes. I know, S-S-Susan. She *is* a lady. But a v-very old one. And intellectually—exceptional . . ."

"I see." Susannah could feel the tears rising to her eyes, and she turned to the mirror to hide them. "Were there other ladies, then? *Cleverer* ladies than me?"

"No! Susan. I—" Harry, in his shirt and breeches, slid down and knelt beside her. "Susan, you are crying. I—" He reached to put his arms around her.

"No!" She threw him off. "Go away."

Harry backed away, silent. She did not look up at him.

"You were too proud to take me," she said. "That is it! A wife of so little learning"—she gulped and bowed her head—"would not credit you! 'Twould spoil you for their admiration. . . ." She did not know why she spoke so—what drove her on—or if it were even true. At once the frustration of so many quiet nights, the clock ticking, Harry's pawing, his superiority—or it surely seemed that—boiled up in her, and she could not stop. "Everyone," she said bitterly, "*admires* you so. Your mother, Augusta. Those men . . ."

Harry stood still, his face shifting—though she could not see it—from bewildered hurt, to anger. He moved closer to the mirror, to her. "The only admiration I wish is—is yours."

"Admiration?" Susannah's voice was high and brittle. "From your wife? But that is the wrong word."

He bent down and seized her arms. His grip was stronger than she had expected. "Then maybe the right word—is love." He pressed into her from behind, his arms wrapped tightly round her. His hands squeezed her breasts, too hard, so that she let out a sound of protest. "Or," he said now, in a low, even voice, "if you don't love me, you might—pretend. As other wives do."

"It isn't true," Susannah protested: But all at once, she knew it was. *I cannot love him*. If she did, she might have borne the pain, the awkwardness, to give him what he wished. . . .

He rose, lifting her with him, covering her neck with urgent kisses. "I want you to love me," he mumbled. "You—you must. Now." He pulled her down on the bed beside him. His breeches and stockings tumbled to the floor.

"The light," she said, faltering. "Put it out."

"No. I have never seen you in the light." Harry's voice was steady and certain. He was pulling at the hem of her shift, raising it up above her breasts. Quickly, viciously, he reached for her private parts; he thrust his fingers into the flesh: there, where always she had stopped him going.

"No." Susannah squirmed and tried to free herself.

With his other hand, Harry was working her shift higher, free from her body. He pushed at it clumsily, afraid to lose hold below, so that at last she was uncovered but her arms were caught up over her head, in the fabric. "Why." He said tonelessly, holding them

fast there. His mouth groped at her neck. "You always say—no. Has it not been long enough?" His
words were muffled. "When are you to be my wife?
P-properly my wife? When?"

Susannah opened her eyes and looked down. All
their nakedness lay exposed in the light. Her own
white body with its ugly dark fur; his sex jutting out,
red and engorged, beneath his shirt. *Why does he
want this?* His fingers fixed themselves between her
legs, seeking, forcing an opening. At last he had let
go of her arms, but they were stiff, and she did not
try to move. His rod was pushing at her, forcing her,
as if her flesh were a wall to be battered down.

"Where does it go? Where?" Harry gasped.

"I don't know." She held back tears. Through half-
closed eyes she saw the two bodies below: two bare
creatures, fumbling. She closed her eyes and thought
she would take herself far away. To home, to the sea,
to Venice. To anywhere but here . . . A sudden, tearing pain brought her back. She cried out, but Harry
was oblivious, flailing away, his flesh rubbing against
the aching skin of the opening he had made. It went
on and on, and she cried out, *stop*, to no avail. She
turned her face to the wall, refusing his kisses: refusing to see.

He groaned, and collapsed on top of her, exhausted.
When he rolled away and looked at her face, search-
ing, her teeth were still clenched, and her eyes closed.
He was too afraid to rouse her, or try to speak.

Sun slid in through the cracks in the bed-curtains.
Harry sat up, staring at his wife for a second, but she
still slept, turned away. He rose quietly and went to
his dressing room.

He has gone. Susannah turned very quietly, to make
sure. The other side of the bed was empty; and
through the dressing room doorway, she could see
Harry standing, naked, his thin body pale and smooth
as marble.

Trying to be silent, she wrapped her gown around

her and ran into her own dressing room. The place
between her legs ached when she moved. She wondered if there was blood there, but she did not want
to look. Her face in the mirror was puffy, and the
place between her thighs was sticky and damp. She
felt hideous and dirty, and when Harry came near,
behind her, she turned, alarmed, as if attacked.

He laid a hand on her shoulder. His voice was
hoarse.

"Do you—" he said. "Will you—"

"You brute," she blurted out, backing away. "Why
can't you leave me? Leave me alone!"

In an instant his hand dropped. "I—*will*," he said
slowly. "I shall not—trouble you again. Perhaps"—
he blinked quickly—"I have been a fool, to think your
attractions so great, that—I should come to beg for
them."

Susannah turned. For an instant she thought, *He
cannot mean that.* But then she knew he did. For his
head snapped away when she looked at him. He
turned, and as he moved through the closet, the parlor, the hallway, she heard a row of doors snap shut
behind him.

Susannah knew that such difficulties would mend
themselves. Why, they must. She and Harry had no
choice but to live with each other. So they must be
friends again. She did not make too much of Harry's
silence at breakfast or his disappearance from the
house that afternoon. Of course she had spoken rashly:
but he must see that. At least he might cease his demands on her body for a time. Perhaps they would
agree . . . to a *Platonic* marriage. She had just recently learned the word.

But Harry did not speak to her that afternoon, or
that night. At dinner, Ernestine fixed a beady stare
on the master, then on his wife. And that night Mary
made a fuss over Susannah's bath, rinsing her hair
with lavender water and asking if she felt well. Earlier that evening Susannah had heard Harry asking

Ernestine to ready the small guest chamber on the
third floor. So she knew that news of a rift must have
spread quickly through the servants' hall.

Then, he will not forget it, she thought, as she lay
alone in the big green bedroom. And she knew she
must take some step, herself. She went upstairs and
knocked on his door.

"Come in," answered a stifled voice. Harry fixed his
eyes on the fire in the grate.

She took a deep breath. "Will you forgive me? For
this morning."

"No—there is nothing t-to—to forgive. You are—
quite right. I was a brute. I shall—not risk being so,
again."

The bed in the green room that night seemed wider
and colder, even, than the great marriage bed at The
Marches. Susannah had not realized how she had
grown used to sharing it.

They began to pass their days separately, meeting
only for silent suppers—and Harry was not always at
these, as often he spent the evenings out with his
friends: Bayliss, Carolus Potter, Mr. Gibbon. He went
out without telling her and would return at nine or
ten o'clock. Sometimes, hearing him pass the front
parlor, Susannah would try, "Where did you go tonight, Harry? How was it?"

"G-g-good night, Susan. I am g-going to bed." He
would not answer her questions. Even at those few
words his jaw tightened, his stammer increasing.

"Won't you have supper?" she would plead. "We've
had letters from your mother and Augusta. . . ."

"T-tomorrow, I shall—I shall see. . . ." Hunched,
his hands in his pockets, Harry hurried up the stairs.
Susannah's news, of which she had had so much
hope, waited, unuttered: that Maria was hiring the
sought-after architect, Robert Adam, to make alter-
ations to the Cheverils' house in Devon. That the
Henches, and their cartloads of Venetian glass and
paintings, were coming home.

Mr. Brown from New York had written too: someone wanted to buy Lispenard's Meadows. He advised Susannah to accept; the price was good. But she felt somehow attached to the place and did not know what to do. She wanted to write, *no*, but whenever she lifted her pen to do it, a fatigue would come over her, and she did not know whether it was reluctance—or sadness. Harry had always taken a small interest, for her sake, in this, her property. But now, when she asked his advice, he had nothing to say.

When the warm weather came in April, she sometimes took a horse from the mews and rode out into St. James's Park. She would admire the fine array of costumes there and curiously watch the courting couples on the promenades. It seemed to her that she had gone from childhood to wifehood in a matter of months: never learned to flirt, as these ladies did, or ridden out with suitors. She had married before she could fall in love—and now she thought, with a strange desolation, *I never will*.

Some of the ladies here were bold and daring. In extravagantly plumed hats and low-cut gowns, they smiled broadly at the men: let them paw and pinch them. Sometimes they even retreated behind clumps of trees with their suitors. Susannah did not know what to make of that—or how to answer the men who called to her, tipping their hats, as they rode past. The men smiled, and the women *quizzed* her, as was the way in public places: examining her from head to toe, with an air of finding her wanting. She trotted quickly past them and tried to ignore all these games and motions, which she so little understood.

The days followed one another, tense and nearly empty of conversation. Then one evening, Harry announced he would be going north: to Exon Castle.

"To—where?" said Susannah. She remembered that there was some cache of manuscripts there: that last fall Harry had received from this place some letter that tremendously excited him.

"Exon Castle. In—in Northumberland."

It was the far north, just south of Scotland. *The other end of England.* Susannah's heart seemed to flutter. She watched her husband's face as he stood by the parlor fire. "Am I—am I to come with you?"

"No," said Harry slowly. " 'Twould not be wise. I am told the—the castle is—c-cold. And damp."

She heard the refusal and did not press again. "For how long?"

"I do not know."

"Then—are you leaving me here?" Susannah's voice, which she had tried to keep calm, rose, despite her. "But—surely you will want to see Augusta, and your mother? They are coming to London soon. What will I tell them?"

"S—say what you like." Harry reddened, and for a moment he looked at her. His eyes flitted up and down her. He turned again, quickly, and moved out of the parlor, up the stairs.

She thought she could not move; then, somehow, she found herself running after. Calling, in a high voice that was not like hers, "Wait! Don't! I am sorry." But at the last words, the voice dwindled and died. She stood on the second-floor landing and heard no answer from his room, above.

She began, then, to tell herself the journey was not what she had thought. *Of course he must see the papers. For a long time, he has said so.* Perhaps the castle *was* cold and damp. Perhaps he was not going—only to be away from her.

In two days he was ready to leave. The weather was wet this time of year, the traveling difficult. "Would it not be better to wait?" Susannah asked. But he shook his head; and she knew then that all she had suspected was true. *He would be away from me.* Early in the morning a driver came to the front of the house with the hired chaise that would take him through the muddy roads: the week-long journey.

Standing on the cobbles, he embraced Susannah

quickly, kissing her cheek, for the benefit of the servants who stood by. The unaccustomed warmth of his skin brought her close to tears. For a second she wanted to cry out, *Stop! We can give it another chance. We must.*

But everyone was there, watching: Ernestine, Warwick, Mary, the new maid Peg. They all waved Harry off, happy and smiling in their motley costumes, and Susannah could only wave, too, and pretend that the man departing was her fond husband, who would send for her soon. But he would not. He had promised only to write her when he had arrived.

When she went back inside the house and saw its empty rooms, she wanted to run after the coach and tell him. Only she had told him so many times before, and he never seemed to believe it. *I am sorry.*

Chapter 9

———— ❧ ————

Augusta Hench descended from her purple sedan chair with its gilt nails and handles, and smiled, a little ill at ease, at each of its carriers. Ravi was from Calcutta and Mohammed from darkest Africa, and to tell the truth she did not know what to make of them—or her husband's other exotic servants.

"I may be a few hours," she said, enunciating, not sure if they understood English, thumped the knocker, and waited under the portico, beaming and still pink from the Roman sun. As the butler opened the door, Susannah rushed forward, embracing her.

"Oh, Augusta! I've missed you." She sounded warbly, almost tearful. "But—you're different. Are you—?" She stood back, and when Warwick took Augusta's wraps, saw the swelling at her waist.

"Yes." Augusta beamed even more. "A few months, only. Where is Harry?"

"Harry is . . . Harry is . . ."

Augusta's eyes widened, curious, while Susannah, still not answering, led her into the parlor, which smelled stale and dusty.

"Harry is . . ." Susannah took a breath. "Harry is in Northumberland."

"North*um*berland?" Augusta echoed. "Already?"

"Yes. He—was in a great hurry to begin there."

"That can't be, Susannah. Surely not so soon after . . ."

"Harry is most devoted to his work." Susannah tried to sound both cheerful and protective: in fact, as Augusta used to sound when talking of her brother.

"Hm." Augusta frowned and set to arranging the ribbons of her bonnet on the table in front of her.

"You see, he didn't wish me to come yet, as the castle is cold and damp."

"Cold and damp! And Harry to stay there alone, with his chest!" Augusta shook her head; but in the few seconds Susannah permitted herself to study her cousin's face, she saw no signs of suspicion at the truth.

Tea arrived, and Susannah was glad to busy herself with saucers and strainers. Augusta reached for a seedcake. Neither spoke to break the silence, and once the tea was poured the quiet grew more palpable. At last Susannah said, in a high, thin voice, "Will you tell me of Italy?"

To her relief, Augusta was easily diverted from the puzzle of Harry. She glowed with the memory of monuments; of dinners in Venetian palazzi. She mused upon the strange, bereft court of the Stuart Pretender, who had just died in Rome. But now she bit into a lemon tart and frowned. Her knobbed nose trembled. "You know I have *learnt*," she said, low and earnestly, "of a great number of things on this journey. Of"—she sniffed—"worldly ways. We live, Susannah—in an age of most shocking license."

Susannah had no notion what she meant. She answered, as evenly as she could, " 'Tis what—people say."

Tears hovered now, as was their wont, in Augusta's eyes. "I never should have thought—why, the scandals ladies would talk of! The freedoms they permit, in their own houses!"

"Freedoms?" Susannah repeated.

Augusta babbled on, tearful and almost merry, in turns. "The married women . . . they keep what they call *cavalieri*. They meet them at night, for their husbands are never home. They do things that . . . Why, even my dear friend the Contessa . . ."

Susannah tried to soothe her, reaching for her hand. "That is all in Italy. Not here. A different country . . ."

"That is the worst—" Augusta's words came in a rush, and stopped. "For I am sure, Jonas—" Her plump, bejeweled fingers scrabbled against Susannah's palm. "You know—" she sobbed, "I have no secret from you, darling Susan."

"Yes," said Susannah, "I know." And she wished she could say more. Tears were in her eyes, too, and she reached her arms round her cousin. She had not touched, or really talked to anyone, for longer than she could remember.

Maria and James Cheveril kept a stony silence as their coach rattled along the Tyburn Road.

"I still," said Maria abruptly, "think we should buy the house in Kensington." No answer came, and she looked inquiringly out at her husband through the folds of her traveling mantle.

He answered at last. "Maria, dear. You did say you would be happy to live in Devon."

She let out a hissing sigh. "James. I said that before I *saw* it. And a month or two in the country with your family is one matter, but—"

"Then why would you have Mr. Adam in to rebuild their house? At a cost of God only knows how many thousand pound—"

"We couldn't possibly attempt to live there as it *is*, James. I must have *some* comforts. And I said I would pay."

Cheveril glanced out the side windows to see how near they were to Hanover Square. He ran a hand through his thick hair, as was his habit, and said patiently, "*Who* would pay, Maria? You cannot afford all you take on. Nor can I, with an election coming."

"Move to a cheaper borough, then! Hang it, James, what good is it standing for that seat if your family can't even get you in it?"

Cheveril looked around uncomfortably.

"Or why don't you get in the Lords, if the Commons is too expensive?" said Maria. "Obviously you haven't *known* the right people. And you shan't, unless we live in London."

"Or Kensington?" Cheveril raised his eyebrows, skeptical. For that village, despite its royal palace, was still more country than city—a full two miles from Piccadilly.

"Yes," said Maria placidly. " 'Twill be the next fashion to live there, you shall see."

Cheveril gave up, with a shrug. Hanover Square, and release, were approaching. "Fine, then," he said. "*You* find the money for Kensington. You know full well what I've got."

Maria gave a dry laugh. "Would I did before the wedding!" She paused. "I can manage the matter, James. A word with Henry . . . Leave it to me." The coachman unlatched the door and she stepped down. "Come along, then!" James looked strangely reluctant. "I swear it," she said. "You shan't have to say a word."

He stepped down at last, with a doubtful glance at the puddled pavement.

"Exon Castle!" cried Maria, a short time later. "Left two weeks ago? But—how very inconvenient." She exchanged glances with her husband. "I needed to *talk* to Henry."

"What about, Aunt?" said Susannah innocently.

Cheveril and Maria exchanged glances again. "Oh, I'll not trouble you with it," said Maria; and just then the tea came, sparing her more explanations.

Maria surveyed the room. The plume of her hat,

flattened by her cape, fluttered feebly in the breeze. "The corner card table has moved," she observed.

"Yes. I've rearranged the rooms." Susannah felt her hand shaking as she raised her teacup. With Augusta, she had managed to hide the truth. But would a decorous silence hold up to Maria's inspection?

"And *that* footman is new." Maria tilted her head back toward the door and the man who attended outside.

"Yes."

"I must say they are well-behaved—your people. Wouldn't you say so, James? Why, Ernestine even took my cape without my demanding it." Maria raised her eyebrows, turning toward her niece. "Pray tell me, what have you done with them, Susannah? They were never so good in *my* day."

"Done?" puzzled Susannah. "Oh! I have given them a rise in wages, that is all."

Maria's mouth hung open for a second, then closed in disapproval. "A rise, my dear? In their station they will only throw it to waste, upon drink, and . . ."

"They were paid little enough," said Susannah. Two weeks ago she had learned, from questioning Mary, that three servants were thinking of leaving. Wages across London were rising steadily. Her mind working over the problem of replacing them, Susannah had begun to wonder what would happen if they went. Servants knew more of their masters' doings, she had begun to realize, than the closest friends. Word of Harry's and her trouble would spread to the kitchens of Ackerleys and Derveys, Henches and Stillwells. . . . And she did not know how she could bear the shame and continue to pretend. Aloud, she said, "I should not have kept them at what they were getting."

Maria looked disapprovingly at Cheveril, who shrugged. Susannah offered a dish of cakes to her visitors.

"When will Henry be back?" said Maria suddenly. She wrinkled her nose, examining the dregs in her cup.

Much as she had to Augusta, Susannah explained

Harry's manuscripts, the cold castle, his eagerness to work. . . .

Maria, however, seemed to guess at the truth. "What a poorly state of affairs," she said at last, with a narrow smile. "I always suspected my son was not quite fit for *la vie à deux*. Oh, pardon me, Susan—you have no French, of course. 'Married life.' " As Susannah and Cheveril both looked tongue-tied, Maria took an expansive breath and went on. "Though my son has had no ear for my counsel of late—I am sure *I* did not neglect to impress upon him the duties of marriage." She gave a little, formal cough. "I hope you, my dear, were not remiss in those duties."

Susannah felt her face reddening. She had no answer for her aunt. She stared into her teacup and was thankful when Cheveril broke in.

"Come, Maria. Let us not meddle in your children's affairs." His voice, slow and sententious, seemed half consciously to mock his wife's. His eyes flitted across to Susannah, at last catching her anxious glance. "I am sure Susannah has made an admirable wife."

"Has she?" said Maria.

A silence hung in the air. Maria stared at Susannah, and Susannah stared at her teacup. James Cheveril, combing his hair with his fingers, at last came out with: "This Mr. Adam! He is truly a marvel, Susannah. He's planning some splendid works for my parents' house. *Grecian* in style."

"Ah, but perhaps we can't afford it," said Maria. Cheveril ignored her. And in this way, talking steadily and sipping, he managed to steer them all through tea. Susannah nodded eagerly at his descriptions of Cheveril Wye, and only noticed once the Cheverils had left the room that her fingertips, fastened on the edge of her cup, were white.

She waited until she heard the Cheverils' door close, upstairs, and then, clutching her arms round her, ran up the two flights to her room. She fell on the green bedclothes, burying her face, drawing in heaving sobs. But somehow no tears came. She sobbed, but could not cry.

*   *   *

Whatever her criticism of Susannah's management, Maria found the house comfortable enough to stay in for three weeks. She also felt free to take charge of the servants, so that when Susannah summoned Em, the cook, in the mornings, it was often to hear that "Lady Maria's ordered dinner already, m'lady." Wanting above all to avoid Maria's questioning, Susannah did not venture to change any of these orders. The Ackerleys, the Derveys, Lady Framer in a leopard-lined cloak—all swept in to dinner at Maria's invitation.

In the days Maria and Cheveril spent at the house, Susannah saw more of "society" than she had since her marriage, and though she remained wary at having to fend off questions about her husband, she did feel more cheerful now than she had been. Before the Cheverils came, time had weighed on her here, with little to do but read and take rides out in St. James's Park. She had almost decided to go back to The Marches; but now she thought she would stay a while longer. After all, she had seen little yet of London.

Maria made no more mention of Harry's journey to Northumberland—perhaps because Cheveril's agile tongue silenced her. Whatever criticisms Maria had to offer she reserved for Susannah's dresses, hats, and hair. She was also busy making plans—although she did not speak of Kensington until near the end of her and her husband's stay.

"I have some business to discuss with you," she said, appearing one morning in the study where Susannah was updating the house accounts. She glanced over Susannah's shoulder, but if she noticed the sprawling penmanship, or its improvement in the last year, she made no remark on it.

"As my son is not here," she said, "I am sure you will take up the matter for me. James and I intend to purchase a house. The house we propose is in Kensington village, and is on offer for . . ." Maria hesitated and coughed. "Seven thousand pounds."

"Oh," was all Susannah said. It still seemed a great
deal of money to her, even though, since coming to
London, she had met the family's banker, Mr. Chilliam, and learned that they had some £10,000 a year.
Out of that, Maria was annually paid her widow's
jointure of £2,000, and, Susannah knew, was not le-
gally entitled to any more.

As her aunt still stood, twisting the knob of her
walking stick, Susannah said, "Please—sit down,
Aunt." She wiped her pen and put it down, turning
to face Maria.

"Perhaps," said Maria, sitting, "Henry has not given
you permission for . . ." She paused.

"Yes, he did. Months ago . . . He so little likes to
be bothered with money!" The words came out in a
rush. Susannah smiled, and Maria compressed her lips
in reply. "You know I cannot—do as you wish,
straightaway." Susannah took in a quick breath and
tried to sound composed. "I will go to Mr. Chilliam
and ask. It seems a great deal of money to me."

"A great deal of money! But what do you know
of—" Maria sputtered, then restrained herself.

"I will go today, if that is all right," said Susannah;
and Maria—a surprisingly meek Maria—retreated.

Later that afternoon Susannah came to her in her
upstairs parlor. "Mr. Chilliam has agreed," she said.
"But he should like to see the house. And also"—
Susannah took a deep breath—"he has advised me to
ask for—a demand note."

"A demand note," Maria repeated, with frigid calm.

A demand note was simply a promise to return a
sum at the lender's request: Mr. Chilliam, within the
dark and solid walls of Coutts' Bank, had explained it
all to Susannah. The seven thousand pounds, he said,
were a rightful portion of the Warrington estate. If,
in some emergency, it was needed, she and Harry
could reclaim it.

Maria, of course, understood the reasoning of it,
and she had no choice, in the circumstances, but to
accept. But "Demand note!" she shrieked that night
as her coach rattled toward the Framer mansion.

"Who is *she* to speak of them? She came to England penniless, and now—*demand* notes!"

Cheveril edged along the cushioned seat, away from the full blast of his wife's voice. "All the same, my dear. It was a reasonable enough request."

"But who is she to make it of me? *Who is she?*"

Susannah and the banker drove out to Kensington to inspect the house. It was, Susannah noted, probably the largest residence in the area, the royal palace excepted: brick-built, square-fronted, surrounded by lawn. It had something of the country in its gardens and something of the city in its high facade; though in the village, the country seemed to prevail. Cowherds led their flocks through the streets, and London's market gardeners grew their wares in the nearby fields.

The demand note was signed and witnessed; Maria pursed her lips and scratched her name violently onto the page. She nodded a curt farewell to Susannah the next day, when she and Cheveril departed for the Framers' fashionable Gothic-style mansion in Oxfordshire. There they would wait, until the painters and furnishers had readied their new house.

Not long after they left, Susannah took her aunt's advice, though she did not think of it as such, and rode to Mrs. Shields's workshop to have new dresses made. She leaned forward to peer out the carriage window, with some of her old, fearful excitement at entering the busy heart of the city. The street vendors waved to her and some of the passersby on the pavement snarled and cursed, for the coach had to force its way through thick crowds, the horses balking, the wheels rolling over feet as well as stones. But the people on the streets were Londoners, and their expressions changed as quickly again to smiles, to boastful cries. *I am a Londoner, too* . . . thought Susannah, experimentally. But she knew she was not; in a few weeks she would likely go back to the country, where she belonged.

Mrs. Shields was overworked and harried, as ever, but she remembered Susannah. "The new viscountess!" she beamed. "You should send a boy ahead, you should—not the least ready. Never mind! T'other lady's just finishing."

Susannah walked through to the seamstress's workroom, and was surprised to see that she knew the "other lady." For wasn't she . . . Susannah tried for a moment to remember, and the vision became clear. The dark lady Aunt Maria had snubbed: the lady in green and gold at the Devonshire ball. And the gentleman . . .

But now the lady's smile, her words, pushed memory back. "I think I remember you," she said. "I do not know why." Her voice was low and guttural, rasping on its *r*'s.

"I—I do, too," said Susannah. Her face, somehow, had fixed itself in Susannah's memory: a long oval, with the porcelain complexion of an Oriental princess. She had the black hair, too, and the dark, narrow eyes. Susannah ventured, "You knew my aunt?"

The lady did not answer. She smiled obliquely, and the swatch of pale satin that she had been smoothing across her chest she took up, suddenly, and pressed to Susannah's arm. "*This* would go well on you. It is a delicious color!"

Only then did Susannah notice the peculiarity of her phrases; her English accent, otherwise, was close to impeccable. Bare now but for her shift, the dark lady stood back, examining. The satin was of a pale rose shade. Mrs. Shields, who had been busying herself with a pincushion, looked up and nodded. "Oh, yes," she murmured. "Perhaps a stripe . . ."

"No, that exactly! As it is," cried the dark lady. "With your hair and eyes—" She indicated both with a wave of the hand, and smiled. "It is the very shade of your skin. . . . If I may ask it, where are you come from?"

Susannah smiled back, hesitant. "America."

"*C'est ça*. I ask because your voice is . . . different."

"Is it? No one has ever said so."

"It needs another stranger—I mean, *foreigner*—to hear it." The woman touched a finger to one delicately sculptured ear.

Mrs. Shields gave a cough now and asked what Susannah might be needing. Susannah told her: a few dresses for the day and perhaps a new riding habit, in a brighter color than black.

The seamstress placed a maternal, bony hand on her shoulder. "Do sit down, m'lady. Er . . . will that be all, Madame d'Aubusson?"

Susannah strained to catch the dark-haired lady's name but could only pick out a succession of vowels.

The other woman half answered, seemingly absorbed in the fashion plates on the wall. "Mm. I suppose. May I think? There might be something . . ."

As Mrs. Shields showed Susannah different drawings, different fabrics, the Frenchwoman hovered around, curious, throwing in the odd comment. Susannah, feeling lost beneath a growing heap of cloth, felt grateful for her advice. Did she look fat in this? she asked her, as Mrs. Shields gathered a flowery print around her waist. Did the pink satin really suit her best?

She reached for the flesh-colored cloth again; the sheen, the warmth of it, appealed to her. And yet, she thought, there was something sleek and brazen in it: something her aunt would never have approved. She laid it over her own shoulder. "Isn't it—" she said baldly, at last, "like being naked?"

"But that is why it is good!" The Frenchwoman broke out into a merry laugh. Susannah looked back at her, puzzled. "The fashion—" said the dark lady, approaching, "is not for being like all the others. It is for bringing out your *qualités*. It is . . ." She set to work with Mrs. Shields, draping the satin over Susannah's shoulders, drawing it tight at her waist, then testing its fall from her hips. All the while she decried the fashions of the year: the graceless puffs and bustles all the women of London were wearing. Mrs. Shields, always ready to agree with a customer, nodded assent; and as the two women conferred, Susannah was surprised to find the trouble of decisions taken out of her hands. Her new evening dress was to be low cut, lower in the waist than was the fashion, and falling, uncushioned, in generous folds to the floor.

When they were done, the dark-haired woman moved away and at last began to dress: first in extravagantly lacy petticoats and garters, then in a close-wrapped coat with wide, falling sleeves, which reminded Susannah of the costumes of the Chinese figurines at The Marches.

"Are you in London long?" she said to Susannah, smiling up as she worked her foot into a pointed red shoe.

"Not much longer, I think. Soon I will be going back to the country."

"Oh, don't do *that*!" the woman cried out impulsively. "You will perish there! Come to Vauxhall with me instead."

And Susannah, abandoning propriety just as this lady had, said she would be happy to. She had heard of the Vauxhall pleasure gardens, with their pagodas and bright lights. Quickly they exchanged names, and Valerie d'Aubusson slipped away, leaving a faint scent of orange in her wake.

"Quite lovely, she is," commented Mrs. Shields. "Though"—she sniffed—"a *bit* outside the conventions. Foreigners!" She leaned close to Susannah, confiding. "You know, she's *really* the natural daughter of a French count."

Susannah nodded and listened to more of the seamstress's gossip (though there was no more about Valerie d'Aubusson). Only when she was halfway home did she realize, with regret, that the woman who had talked of Vauxhall had never asked her address.

Not many people walked about London after dark, even in moonlight. It was a pity, Valerie declared, that they were all so afraid of cutpurses. A gray-green light bathed the roofs, the cobblestones, and chimney pots. *"Mon chéri!"* she cried, "Say! Is not this England full of wonders?"

Martin Fellsacre, her companion, was eager to agree. "Most certainly," he said in a singsong voice. "And you, my French rose, are lovelier still." He reached and squeezed her hips as they marched along, but Valerie would not be distracted. They both walked quickly toward Hanover Square, keeping an eye out for moving figures in the shadows.

"But what do you—" Martin panted, keeping up. "What d'you want with this Lady What's-her-name? Since when was you friends with Ladies, anyway?"

"Sale singe!" Valerie swatted him with her folded-up fan. "Dirty monkey . . . I know much more about 'ladies' than you."

It was true: Martin, the son of a brewer only recently knighted, could not boast the knowledge of any nobler lady than Valerie. He was not sure whether she was teasing, and backed away from the slashes of her fan. Valerie giggled and patted his arm affectionately, finding his obtuseness, this time, rather endearing. If he was a bit dense—she thought to herself—he did have the profile of a Greek statue. And he was rich. If they walked in the dark instead of riding, it was only because he was at the end of his month's allowance. Surely Lady Warrington would have a carriage to take them to the Thames.

"She is lovely. But unfinishèd," murmured Valerie. She tried to picture Susannah's face and could not, quite, though she could remember her pink-and-auburn coloring. Only last week had she managed to ferret out the American viscountess's address and call on her. "Her husband," she told Martin now, "has left her for his studies. Imagine, she must be bored! *We* will see to changing that, no?" Martin's attention seemed to be drifting, and Valerie gave him another touch of the fan.

They called at Susannah's house, and the Warrington carriage, as she had hoped, took them to the river. There, Valerie insisted, they must not cross a bridge but take a boat. " 'Tis the only *façon*—fashion!" she cried, and set to haggling with the boatman who would take them across.

But Valerie was right, after all. The white moonlight shone on the rippling water, the oars splashed, and, but for the dull shouts of passing rowers, all on the river was silent. Even the Thames's earthy stench, to Susannah, seemed magical. When the boat bumped up against the south bank, they could see the lights of Vauxhall already, shining above a wall in the distance. They ran toward the lights, Martin panting and Valerie giggling. Martin paid three shillings at the gate; and then they were inside, in the midst of it. All around them, fantastical constructions—white towers, pavilions, and pagodas—stretched up into the night, lit by hundreds of oil lamps and torches.

"But—" said Susannah, blinking in the light, "what do you *do* here?"

"Why," Valerie giggled, "whatever you dare not, in day! What a question! Come!" She tugged at Martin, whose gaze had fixed on a frothy blonde in shepherdess costume, and they left the central pavilion, with its loud orchestra music, for the long, wooded paths behind. Never, even riding in St. James's Park, had Susannah seen so much finery in one place: such an assembly of feathers, paste jewelry, and lace. But Valerie's practiced eye was not so easily dazzled.

"Mercer, or master weaver." She nodded at a passing man in a striking lavender wig, and his companion. "And that, *Suzanne*, is not his wife. . . . What think you of Martin, *chérie*? Should I marry him?"

"What?" Startled, Susannah looked over at her friend. Martin Fellsacre was loping not far ahead.

Valerie laughed and whispered, "Pretty but dull, no? Perhaps the horns would suit him."

Susannah was puzzled, and grew more so when they drew up near a pagoda painted as—so she called it— a grotto of Venus. When she spoke the words, Valerie started, inexplicably, to laugh. One hand, with its neat, circular nails, rose to her mouth. "Forgive me!"

gurgled Valerie. "But do you know what a grotto of Venus *is*?"

Martin strode between them, interrupting. "Valerie!" he said, with a severe look. "Don't talk filth to Lady Susan." But Valerie soon cajoled him into a better humor, begging him, at last, to take them for supper.

They ate in the open air, under the roof of a rotunda, watching the endless, bright-colored, circling crowd. Supper came: a tray ordered by Valerie, full of sweet cakes and confections. Susannah sipped a glass of sweet wine and ate a cherry tart, feeling dizzy. Valerie whispered steadily in her ear, despite the presence of her beau.

"In a husband"—Valerie chewed her cake and looked grave—"I think zere are three virtues. The first—" She paused to aim an annihilating glance at a redhead Martin was eyeing. "The first is the fortune, the second, if possible, old age . . . and the third, absence!" She took a gleeful swallow of Monbazillac. "At least, *chérie*, you have the last!"

Susannah's eyes darkened, and she did not know whether she felt scandalized or merely confused. Or even—tickled and pleased, in a strange way, by Valerie's irreverence.

Valerie licked a knob of cream off her finger. "*I* think you are in a position to be envied. Tell me, does your husband have a mistress?"

"No!" said Susannah, astonished. "Why, he couldn't."

"Don't be a monkey, *chérie*. All men have mistresses."

"Harry doesn't! I'm sure of it."

"All wives are so sure—for a time. 'Tis bliss to hear you speak. Such faith!"

"But I *know* it," said Susannah.

Valerie seemed not to hear. She took Susannah's hand, touched her nibbled fingernails, and clucked. "*Chérie*. You are not to worry. There is no time!" She reached forward and pulled at Martin's pigtail of blond curls. "We shall amuse ourselves so, you will forget that you ever had a tedious husband . . . Martin! *Dis donc!* Take Lady Susan and dance."

She danced, and wondered at Valerie's words. Did all men have mistresses, and bold women—like Valerie—lovers?

"Lady Susan?" said Martin Fellsacre, leading her through a turn. "You are serious! 'Tis most forbidden here."

She shook her head. All around her, bright gowns, patched with buttons and lace, collided with drab frock coats and red soldiers' uniforms. Everyone here seemed so merry: old and young, Martin, Valerie . . . Were they in love, or part in love? Or was it all more complicated than she had ever thought . . . ?

Valerie and Martin staggered up the stairs of the lodging house off Covent Garden where Susannah's coach had left them. At the top of the third flight, they stood outside the door, panting.

"Look," gasped Martin. He pulled out the linings of his coat pockets. "Nothing."

"Ha! You have something left, surely. You always do."

Valerie gave him a playful clap on the stomach and turned her key. Inside, there was one large room, which served her as salon and bedroom. Its walls were covered in tattered cut velvet, their worst gashes plastered over with print-shop engravings. Dirty bedsheets and bills covered the floorboards; and in the middle of it all, two men lay sprawled out on the sofa, coats and shoes discarded at their feet.

"Anthony. Carrick!" Valerie kicked the couch leg to wake them. "What do you do here at this hour?"

The blond man's eyes opened first. "We paid your rent," he answered groggily.

Valerie looked startled. "Thank you," she said crisply, regaining composure. "You had no need. Carrick!" She kicked the couch again, waking the second man. He was dark-haired and handsome, though his eyes now were puffy with sleep.

"What? Isn't she grateful?" Carrick turned to his companion. "See? I told you she wouldn't be. Ungrateful French bitch."

Then his eyes met Valerie's. They exchanged a look of friendship, and of endless contention, and at last Valerie gave in, spreading her arms in surrender.

"I am grateful. Men!" she sputtered. "You bastards. I am grateful."

So the evening did not end with Vauxhall but went on into the next day. Valerie poured out brandy for her visitors and dealt out cards for her favorite game, piquet. Anthony Ogilvie, the blond man, was curious about her new friend.

" 'Lady Warrington'? Whatever can you want with her?" He brushed his straight, sandy hair out of his face, which was boyish, with pouting lips. "I've heard nothing of her. I shouldn't have expected Warrington to marry any lady of . . . interest." He sorted his cards, discarded two, and drew.

"Bookish fellow, I hear," said Martin Fellsacre sagely.

"Anyway," drawled Carrick, "what can a Lady want with the likes of you?" His voice was low, rasping, betraying his Scots origins.

"*Protection*," countered Valerie, "from the like of you. Anthony? Declare." She frowned, with seeming absorption, at her winning hand. "And besides. Do you remember how the old Lady Warrington has refused to speak to me?"

Nicholas Carrick nodded and shrugged.

"Well! This is her son's wife. Her—how do you say—her daughter-in-law." Valerie giggled, the merriment in her eyes dimming to a mischievous gleam. "She is very young. And she pleases me. I should like to show her some things, which the old lady would not approve. *Declare*, Anthony!"

She giggled wildly as Anthony Ogilvie tossed a mismatched jumble of cards to the floor.

Chapter 10

❧

A second letter came from Harry, longer than his first, curt notice of safe arrival. Now he covered nearly a page in tall, narrow script, describing Exon, his neighbors, and his work.

> *I can envision no situation more conducive to tranquility and calm historical Reflection, than this—atop windy Rises no more inhabited than in the England of King Harald.*

Harry wrote very like the authors of history books. There was a chill, a studied air to his words, which Susannah saw; and she did not know how to reply in the same way. So she lingered and postponed it until, a month later, she set to the task. *"October is cold,"* she wrote. A blot fell from her pen. *"I am stile in London."* She had no idea what Harry would like to hear. News of his family? City gossip? Valerie had warned her most strongly against writing in detail of *their* activities.

"I should not like to think," she had said, giving Susannah a black look, "that I should appear in any word you sent your husband. You know, a woman does not properly tell a *husband* of her doings. For that, there are friends. . . ."

Valerie had sounded so decided that Susannah thought, now, that she must take her advice. She turned to Court gossip, of which her friend was an ever-flowing font.

Do you know Mr Hastings India-tryal is still going? Can you imagine, a tryal thus to last near a year? Mr Burke in the House has call'd him an Oppressor & Tyrrant. Also the King was at Cheltenham this Summer for Madnesse, for he had begun talking to Trees. . . .

She paused, but soon set to scribbling again. Writing was easier than she had thought. Why, all she had to do was keep from telling of herself.

Mr. Cheveril & Yr Mother you know have bought exceedingly splendid furnishings for their new House. In August they held a Rout in its Honour, but I did not go.

She had gone with Valerie and Martin to Ranelagh Gardens that night, having only been told of Maria's rout that very day—by an abashed James Cheveril, who gave every appearance of having sneaked out to Hanover Square to invite her.

I was ill that night in the Nose, but I am better. Of late there is strange news of that Kens'gton house, that its Decoracion was over-expensive— but perhaps it is not my Affair to write upon that, your Mother may tell you soon otherwise. I know, tho', she has let some people go, Mr Knole her Secretary came to me one day looking for Work, & appear'd so pitiful & appeasing that I took him.

Expecting a servant or messenger, she had turned, surprised, to see Knole bowing low in her parlor doorway.

"Pardon me, madam," he murmured. She noticed that his black hair, once shining, was now greasy, and one of his stockings was torn.

"What—what brings you here?" she said, fearing yet another request for money from Maria. For the seven thousand pounds toward the house in Kensington had not been enough; there were furnishers' and, it seemed, previous tradesmen's debts to pay, for which sums Maria had been writing repeated demands in the last few months. Susannah, so far, had paid them, but she did not know how much further even the large income of the Warringtons would go.

Knole looked down at the battered hat in his hands. "I beg leave, my lady, to ask if you require some person to take charge of your affairs—"

"Are you no longer with Aunt Maria? I mean—Mrs. Cheveril?"

Knole shook his head. "Alas, no."

"But what has happened, Mr. Knole?"

"Mrs. Cheveril has needed to make . . . economies." Knole's face, controlled until now, began to twitch. "Had you but seen it—m'lady! 'Twas such a day. She called us in—one by one. The undercooks, the seamstress, the grooms . . ."

"But how long—" Susannah began.

"Two months since, m'lady," Knole said humbly. "Without a reference."

"Without—" Susannah repeated, astonished. She thought of Knole's dogged devotion at The Marches. "But that's shameful!"

Knole coughed. "She reasoned, my lady, that if she appeared to let us go by reason of dissatisfaction—the news of her economies would not get abroad, as it might. . . ."

He told a tale, then, that surprised her: of unpaid painters and upholsterers besieging the house; of loud shouting, from the masters' rooms, and ornaments flying. The younger servants, he said, had found work again quickly enough by pretending that they were new to London. But he had not.

"Of course, you will come here," Susannah said, in answer to his pleading look. "Why, I should have needed help anyway."

It was true: Knole lightened the burden of bankers' statements and documents, which sometimes perplexed her. They had settled into happy partnership, helped by the fact (she suspected) that Knole was growing slightly in love with her. . . . *"I have new Clothes,"* she set down at last.

> *I hope you will not think me extravegent, but remember I am seeing to the ex-chequer now! With the help of Mr. Chilliam & Mr. Knole. And does that not deserve a small Reward? I am*
>
> > *yrs Affect'ly, Susannah*
> > *Hanover Square, 9 October, 1788.*

Affectionately, she thought. It was true enough. Even though he had left her, she could not begrudge him that. For, after a fashion, he had given her . . . freedom. She scattered sand over the page, folded and sealed it. A footman would take it to the post office; and the daily post coach, the two hundred and fifty miles north to Exon Castle.

"No! Lower down, *chérie.*" Valerie tugged at the pink bodice of Susannah's gown. *"N'faut pas être pudique . . ."* she said in French and explained, " 'Not to be—prudish!' " She pulled at the laces that closed the back.

Susannah sucked in her breath, for the boned bodice had grown tight, pressing her breasts up against the satin that furled about her shoulders, like a petal. It was the color of her skin, only slightly darker, and she loved the sheen and the feel of it. *But still . . .* She looked down. Her shoulders were bare, her breasts nearly so as well.

"Don't you fret for that!" said Valerie gaily. "I fix. . . ." She draped a length of gauze around Susannah's shoulders, deftly twirling the ends round the stem of a hothouse rose, which she tucked into the bodice. "Voilà! You are covered." The gauze was nearly transparent, so Susannah could not see that it made much difference. But then, most London ladies seemed to dress to show as much of themselves as possible. The world was hard to shock, said Valerie; and in such things, she was usually right. She had overseen the making of Susannah's new clothes, and certainly the plain fabrics and straight, swirling skirts she counseled suited Susannah better than the short waists and boxy hips of fashion. "No! Never brown! Never spots!" she had cried at the sight of some of Susannah's old dresses; and Susannah had watched a more glowing, sinuous figure than she expected appear in her mirror, dressed always in blues, pinks, and lavenders.

Valerie made her sit down now and opened up the china pots that held different shades of face paint.

"Where is the party to be?" said Susannah, watching her friend's hands dart over her face, in the mirror.

"At Golden Square. Ogilvie's rooms, or else he has rent them . . . I am not sure."

"Ogilvie?"

"Anthony Ogilvie. A man of charm. He gives all the *fêtes*."

Susannah's face and neck were now pinkish-white. She made an experimental grimace, wondering if the paint would crack.

"Little monkey! Keep still." Valerie dabbed a darker pink on her cheeks.

"And *your* house," Susannah said suddenly. "When shall I see it?" For she never had. Valerie always said that it was dirty or being redecorated.

"Hm?" Valerie squinted at her handiwork. "My house? Oh . . . but I shall soon move! Have I tell you?"

"Where to?"

Valerie smiled. "Berkeley Square. At last I give in.

Fellsacre has *beg* me to live in this place he has furnish
for me. . . ."

"Do you mean Martin?"

The Frenchwoman laughed, and tiny lines showed
at the corners of her eyes. Susannah wondered for a
moment how old she was: twenty-five? Thirty?

"Phou!" said Valerie. "Where would Martin come
at the money? Put your head back. . . . It is his *father.*"

"Do you mean . . ." said Susannah, wondering, "he
is buying you the house—so that you will marry Martin after all?"

"Yes, something like that." Valerie laughed again
and told Susannah to close her eyes. She dabbed something moist on her eyelids. "But I am not sure I will
get married. I think I will wait for something extraordinary. Maybe a real English *duke.*" She smiled se-
renely.

She blackened Susannah's lashes with charcoal; finally she dabbed pink rouge on her lips and made her
turn toward the mirror. *"Voilà!"*

Susannah saw pale, even-toned skin and eyes which
stood out from the mask, a bright blue. *"Oh,"* she
said. It would take getting used to. Perhaps Valerie
would take her surprise as a compliment.

"Now! The hair." Valerie had already washed and
colored it, with a red paste that she said gave it lights.
She worked her fingers gently through it, untwining
the tangles.

Susannah watched for a while; then, thinking back
to their earlier conversation, she said, "Have you never
been married?"

"No! I have never want to be." Valerie was busy
now with ribbons and wires and pins. She wound most
of Susannah's hair into a coil at the top of her head,
letting a few long curls fall down her neck.

Susannah persisted. "Then, how did you come to
England?"

"Oh, I was come here with a man," Valerie answered, without interest. "He had many estates, and
terrible—how do you say—before-thoughts, that his

people would rise and take them. So! We have put his
money in jewels and come here."

"What has happened to him?" said Susannah, curious.

"Oh! I do not know." Valerie twisted a curl around
her finger. "But I think he was right, you know—
when I see what arrives in France."

"What do you mean?"

"Oh! *Politique* . . ." Valerie's enthusiasm for the
subject seemed to have waned. She stood back, examining the effect of Susannah's curls, and bent to
apply more coal pencil to the corners of her eyes. "My
friends in France," she said, with a shrug, "are not
content with their assemblies. They want more—like
here, you see. But! That is nothing to me. Shall we
go?"

The rooms at Golden Square were dim and warm
with candlelight. Sweat trickled down most of the
faces around the table: the women, whose painted
cheeks and foreheads shone; the men, who caressed
the women's thighs as they drank port and joined
loudly in the general talk, of the theater. Valerie
d'Aubusson squeezed her lover Martin's knee with one
slim hand and licked the chocolate from the fingers of
the other. She leaned forward, toward the dark man
at the head of the table, as he spoke; and Susannah,
at that same moment, drew back, afraid.

She had seen him before.

"Beauty's the least thing in an actress!" he declared.
His voice, low and clear but for a residual Scots growl,
carried down the table, toward her.

She had heard that voice, long ago at the Devonshire ball. She had spun wildly across the floor, and
he had caught her: with the same mocking look he
wore now, and she had thought . . .

But it did not matter, what she had thought. That
was over a year past; now she was married. By rights
she should not even remember it.

"Take Mrs. Barry," he said now. "The first great

actress of our stage." His brown eyes, sparkling in candlelight, flitted about the audience. For a second they seemed to bore into Susannah's, in her hiding place. "Now, they called her no beauty. She was a hook-nosed, dun-colored creature—but she'd the passions in her. All that counted. She'd the air of quitting one man's bed and readying for another."

He reached across the table for an apple, and sank his teeth into it as he sat back. His gaze flitted, triumphant, satisfied, across his audience; and then it seemed, to Susannah, to fix on her. His eyes lingered as he bit into the fruit again, and the sound of that crisp skin breaking seemed to her to echo in a long silence.

But no one else in the hot, rented rooms felt it so. A red-faced man was moving around the table, pouring brandy; the straw-haired girl beside Susannah tugged at her sleeve.

"Where'th Anthony?" she whispered. Her name was Sarah Hutchings, and she was a friend of Valerie's.

"Anthony?" Susannah broke from her reverie. At once, the room became noisy and busy. The voice of the dark man was only one among many. She had not seen Anthony Ogilvie, their host, since the meal began. She told Sarah so.

"Oh!" Sarah's blue eyes had a lost look, and her upper lip caught against her teeth as she talked. "He has dithappeared. Why do you think, Lady—"

"Let us outdoors!"

Once again, the low Scottish voice cut through the air. Susannah looked up and saw the dark man standing by the door to a terrace, which he opened and, bowing low, beckoned some of the ladies through.

"Fool! We shall freeze," whispered Valerie to him, pinching his arm as she passed. But the guests trickled steadily outwards, behind her.

"Anthony'th gone," murmured Sarah, studying the carpet.

Susannah answered mechanically, "I'm sure he has not. Not from his own supper . . ." But even while she talked to the other girl—who seemed to her a

rather lost creature, craving sympathy—she studied
the Scotsman. His face, she told herself, after all, was
not perfect. As he turned his head again to both sides,
she could see how the long, straight nose leaned
slightly to the left, cramping the features beside it. He
wore his hair strangely, too—cut short, as if to fit beneath a wig, though he had not troubled to wear one.

"Aye, you're right, Carrick. Let us outside!" A
bright-faced Anthony Ogilvie issued in from the far
door. He rushed toward his friends, an unnatural
gleam in his blue eyes.

Susannah looked over at Sarah Hutchings, beside
her, whose features had melted into a smile of relief.
"There! Do you see?" she said. Sarah wandered past
her to the terrace, as if drawn by an invisible thread.

And as the door closed she was the only one inside.
She had determined it: she would not follow him,
moping after him, just because, by chance, she had
once danced with him. *Carrick.* "Damn!" she whispered, scraping wax from the table with her nails; she
did not know why. She looked around at the green-
walled dining chamber with its smoking sconces; at
the rose-colored closet to one side and the row of doors
leading to empty rooms on the other. For all their
luxury—their gilt furniture, their wall panels painted
with cherubs—the rooms had a dusty, neglected air,
all the more marked when they were empty.

The others had been outdoors, it seemed, an age.
Curiosity overcame her. She stood and walked to the
door, and half opened it.

"You don't mean to deny," a mild-voiced man, a
barrister, was saying, "that the institution of marriage
has its practical *uses.* . . ."

"Ha!" A big, square-built, red-faced man threw
back his head, laughing, and while some of the ladies
tittered, the barrister queried, "Would you not agree,
Mr. Carrick, with Dr. Johnson's words: that 'Marriage has many pains, but celibacy has no pleasures'?"

At the sound of his name again, *Carrick*, Susannah
felt her heart begin to pound. *Why should I care?* she
thought. A cold wind grazed her shoulders. *What*

should I care what he thinks on marriage? The door
beside her creaked, and at the sound Carrick's gaze
moved up and found her.

"Why, I'm no enemy of marriage," he said, with a
lazy nod at the barrister. Again, almost insolently, he
stared up, across the terrace. "Why, a happy marriage must be perfection. A rose without thorns.
And"—he began to move through the crowd—"you're
just as likely of finding it."

Now he faced Susannah. Quickly, before she was
able to speak, he reached up to the bosom of her dress
and tugged the rose, on its thin stem, free. Her scarf
drifted loose, and he caught it.

She felt the cold air on her skin, yet still could not
move as, smiling, he wound the scarf around his wrist
and tucked the rose into his buttonhole. Her heart-
beats sounded in her ears. As she slid back through
the door, she forced a smile to her lips. For a second
she watched Carrick and the others; then, as the
crowd began to stream in again, she ran for the safety
of the empty closet.

She hid in that chamber, with its mirrors and pink
walls, trying to pull her dress higher, feeling her face
go alternately hot and pale. Outside she had been so
tongue-tied and foolish. *Because of him?* She heard
the chatter in the other rooms growing louder. She
leaned against the window frame, watching her reflection in the mirror opposite. For a moment she felt
at peace. Then something moved in the smoky light
of the doorway.

She looked over, and her heart began to pound
again. Carrick was standing there. She could see only
a silhouette: a compact body some inches taller than
hers, which he held taut, his arms folded, one foot
posed before the other. He seemed to consider her,
and slowly walked closer.

If he is come to apologize, Susannah thought, *I will
be dignified.* She bit her lip, preparing herself.

But she had no time to remember how. Suddenly
Carrick was behind her, his body barely, but decidedly, touching hers. He reached for her hands, then

took quick hold of them, sweeping them back behind her. He held them there, his fingers tickling, lightly stroking her palms.

"Where is it you come from?" he said, smiling at their twin reflections in the mirror.

The question surprised her. "Here," she said defensively. "And before that—America."

Her heart beat quickly. Because her dress squeezed her waist in so tightly, all the blood surging through her seemed to rush to what was above and below. Her chest rose and fell quickly with her breathing, and she saw Carrick was looking down at her breasts, at the swell of them. She twisted her hands in his. She knew she ought to escape, for she did not know what she was feeling. The embroidery of his waistcoat grazed the bare skin of her shoulders.

He let go of her hands, and smiled as he stepped easily round to face her. "I did not think they grew such wildflowers in America as you. I had thought the place inhabited by—drab little Puritans, and savages."

"No. I—" She knew he must expect a witty rebuke. But she had none. She knew also that she was free to escape now, for he held no part of her. But she did not want to escape. He looked into her eyes—his were black pits, lost to her sight—and, with one hand, then the other, he reached below the curling edge of her dress. He lifted her breasts above the cloth, stroking their high curves, and the valley between. The lower half of his body moved against hers. And all the blood that had rushed down there, inside her, was set coursing again as he stroked the tips of her breasts. He tilted his head away, watching her. With a questioning glance, then curiously, deliberately, he stepped back, bending to take the tip of her left breast in his mouth. His tongue worked over it, teasing it, and it felt so good, and yet was such torture, that she had to squirm free. She let out a little cry. He pulled away then but returned his hands, teasing her nipples, even pinching them until it seemed to her that there was no feeling in her body but exactly there: there, and in that place between her legs where the flesh was moist and swol-

len, and finally seemed to have a heartbeat of its own.
The blood pulsed and seemed to flow upward, spreading, warming her. She let out deep breath.

She realized now that her eyes had been closed, and
when she opened them she saw Carrick smiling, his
teeth glinting in the dark. She let out a low sound of
fear, not quite a word, and in answer he kissed her
quickly on the forehead. He reached inside his frock
coat and pulled out her wrinkled scarf, and as she
took it, he plucked the rose, too, from his collar and
offered it to her. She shook her head, on a sudden
impulse.

He said, "A token?" and smiled back, tucking the
rose back into his collar as he left her.

She did not know how long it took for her breathing
to slow, for the color to leave her face. When she had
stopped trembling, and righted her scarf and gown,
she emerged into the dining chamber, now empty.
She knew that her skin was damp, that the paint must
be running down her face; but when she saw the others
in the next room, she knew they would not notice.

She saw the barrister settling one of the women—
bold, dimpled Mrs. Ashby—on his knee, while sweat
trickled from her neck down into her cleavage. Another gentleman was conferring with a blowsy lady
called Diana, while Carrick, Anthony Ogilvie, and
their red-faced friend played a loud game of cards by
the fire. Pipe ashes and the odd card dropped onto the
hearth.

Valerie and Sarah Hutchings played at piquet under a pair of dripping candles, and Susannah, seeing
an empty place, slid gratefully onto the sofa beside
them.

"You amuse yourself well, my dear?" said Valerie
absently, sorting her cards. Susannah was glad that
Valerie did not look up to examine her.

"Oh, yes. It is different from—other parties," she
said.

Valerie thoughtfully laid down a card. "You should
be careful of Nicholas."

Susannah's heart thumped. "Nicholas?"

Valerie threw a glance at Carrick, in the corner, then at her friend. "We have all seen your little . . . conversation, on the terrace."

"But—"

"No, *chérie!* 'Tis not what you think. I am not jealous." Valerie glared at Sarah, who was shifting in her chair, impatient for the game to go on. "But he has only interest in—cheap women. Whores. Not ladies." She looked Susannah smilingly up and down.

"Why, that's nothing to me. Why should I mind him—or what he likes?" Susannah spoke rapidly, pleased with the certitude she thought she was showing Valerie.

Valerie shrugged, her white shoulders working loose from her gown. She picked up a card from the table, then returned it. "Such a famous writer—he could have whatever lady he wants! I do not know why he chooses cheap women—and stays with none of them."

"Then, is he really famous?" said Susannah.

"Oh, yes," said Valerie. Sarah, puzzling at her hand, breathed the same words in echo.

"Have you not heard of the *Cyberion?*" said Valerie.

Sarah hurriedly discarded five cards. She looked up, pink-faced. Wisps of straw-colored hair hung loose around her eyes. "*Thyberion,*" she said, "is a motht thelebrated poem!"

Valerie stared impatiently at Sarah, who, at last catching her meaning, studied her cards and declared, "Five, Valerie . . . a point of five. Thyberion," she went on, "is a young printh who ventures to the Holy Land—"

"Or," interrupted Valerie, "some say, a poor but well-looking Scot who designs to make his fortune in London!" She gave a nod at the hands of cards. "Point of five? Yes, I suppose, Sarah . . . *good.*"

"Oh, 'tith vathtly adventurouth," Sarah went on. "Thyberion is theeking vengeance, for hith father, who wath murdered. . . . Oh, and 'tith greatly funny! The second canto thpecially . . . Oh. I thcore five, Valerie. And—and a quart."

"How high?"

"Queen."

"Queen? Not good, Sarah . . . She forgets to mention," added Valerie to Susannah, "that there *exist* but two cantos. And I think there will only be another if the Baron Blackcroft cuts him off."

"Baron Blackcroft—cuts him off?" puzzled Susannah.

"His grandfather. He has support him these seven years. What should become of Nicholas without?" She laughed.

Sarah looked about to protest but said only, "A trio of . . . of kingth."

"*Not good*. You know, *Suzanne*, Ogilvie"—she nodded at the party's host—"is the son of an earl and more steady. . . . If you seek a lover—"

"But I don't seek any such thing!" Susannah felt her face growing hot as she protested.

"Fie, *Suzanne*. Do not be so timid. So, you wish a lover. Everyone does. What of it?. . . *Declare*, Sarah, dear."

"I thtart with . . ." Sarah's brows lowered over watery blue eyes. "I thtart with thix." She looked up at Susannah. "Mr. Carrick ith an actor, too," she said enthusiastically, giving no indication that she had heard what just passed. "He appearth in hith very own playth. Like *The Good Huthband* . . ."

"Yes," said Valerie, with a sniff, "though he takes a second or third role, not the lead. Some might call it a modesty beyond all . . . *vraisemblance*. A quart to the ace. Also a tierce—seven. A *quatorze* of queens . . . Fourteen. I start with twenty-one." She smiled, victorious, at Sarah and gathered the cards for the next stage of the game. Piquet looked exceedingly complicated to Susannah, who wished, right now, that she could divert the conversation to any topic other than Nicholas Carrick. But Sarah seemed intent on pursuing the subject.

"Mr. Carrick, immodetht?" she said. "Why, what cauthe have you to rate him tho poor?"

"No cause at all! Except that he is my friend," Valerie said.

"If he *is* your friend—" Susannah began to join in, but stopped. She saw Nicholas Carrick swallowing the last of his port and moving toward them.

Now he stood above them. "Valerie, dear," he said loudly, "will you not introduce me to your new friend?"

Valerie fixed her eyes on the cards she was shuffling. "I believe," she said steadily, "that you have introduce yourself. And you are quite drunk."

Sarah looked up, wide-eyed, at Carrick, who had turned from Valerie and was gazing down on Susannah.

"So," he said. "You are the Lady Warrington. And an American! What a motley company Valerie keeps." He paused but, hearing no reply, rallied on. "An American viscountess! Why, the very notion . . . Why, next they'll be creating monkeys dukes and earls and our Indian-savages Princes Regent! I vow, that would serve the king. . . ."

"I beg your pardon?" Susannah looked up at him, for the first time now. She wondered if all this was pleasantry, and gave a faint smile, which vanished from her face as he went on, "An American viscountess! Why, what qualifies you? A noble birth, I suppose, in the fine city of Boston, or Philahymnia—"

"Virginia," said Susannah in a low voice.

"Ah. Virginity! 'Tis a rare commodity here, sure enough. Yes, let us speak of your virginity. . . ."

At that, Susannah made a sudden, half-intended move back. She did not understand. *How can he rail at me so? How, after* . . . She felt the sofa beginning to tip backward, and at the same time, with an angry shout—"Carrick!"—Ogilvie, the party's host, stepped in to right it.

His dark-blue eyes narrowed under a sandy fringe of hair. "Carrick, behave!" he said, but his voice was amiable now. "What are you about, discommoding these ladies? Go back where you belong."

"I was in jest!" protested Carrick, his voice weakening. "Why—the lady didn't take it ill."

But Ogilvie's skeptical look dismissed him. "If she did take it ill, she'd be more courteous than to say so."

Frowning, Carrick bowed, and retreated to the card table. Ogilvie knelt down to speak to Susannah. "Pray, don't take him amiss. He can be—inexcusable. But he is my friend."

"A fine friend!" snorted Valerie.

"Do *you* believe me, Lady Susan?" said Ogilvie.

Susannah smiled and nodded, wondering briefly how he had come to know her name.

"There is," Ogilvie said in a low voice, "much passion in him. Too much. I do hope, dear lady, that you be not driven from my house by—"

"No! I have been—most pleased here, Mr. Ogilvie. Thank you." Susannah was vaguely conscious of having named her host wrongly. *The son of a earl*, she mused. *Then he is Your Grace, or "The Honorable"*. . . .

"Anthony." Ogilvie stood, bending to kiss her hand. "And I hope you will come again."

They did not stay much longer. Soon Valerie, bored with Sarah's card playing and the neglect of Martin Fellsacre, who slumbered in a corner, got up to lead the way home. Most of the other ladies followed.

The gentlemen remained, except for the barrister, who had taken a woman away with him, and Martin Fellsacre—who, waking to find Valerie gone, had run out the door to catch her. They gathered around the fire, a trio of long habit: Ogilvie, Carrick, and red-faced Tom Gant.

"Bath! You want to go to Bath?" Tom Gant chortled, and spat a lump of brown phlegm out onto the carpet. "What do you, my good fellow, care for resorts?" He stared at Ogilvie.

"I speak only of making a change this summer," said Ogilvie. "If not Bath, perhaps Cheltenham. I hear much of the waters."

"And of the waters of Maidenhead!" came Nicholas Carrick's hoarse interruption. "Were they not so difficult of access."

Tom Gant snorted, his red face flushing darker. "Why, what's a lack of maidenheads to you, old Nichol? Since you'd rather prod the gaping holes of—"

"Tom!" Carrick cut him off. His brows and eyes grew dark and thunderous. "So! You think you know my tastes in women. What if I told you I have simply not *met* any woman who accords with my desires?"

"Don't talk nonsense," said Ogilvie dismissively. "They all do." He twirled an empty glass in his hand, looking around despondently at the ash-strewn remains of his party.

"Innocent women bore me," fumed Carrick. He stood up and started to pace the room. "Most ladies," he went on, "are prudes and will never be otherwise: they are taught so. And whores are never taught at all—so they keep you almighty dull company."

The other men nodded, as though these seemed fair-enough assumptions.

Carrick spun and faced them. "Now, suppose you could *find* a lady who'd be taught. So, you see, the perfect lady'd become the perfect whore. . . ."

"Huh!" snorted Gant. "A fine story, for one of your plays."

"Besides," said Ogilvie mildly, still meditating on his glass. "There are ladies, such as you describe, who might . . ."

"Ach, it's a tedious business," said Carrick, starting to pace again. "The Lady Marys or Henriettas, with all their little pruderies . . . who'll not disrobe but in the dark, and *giggle* when you touch them and, God forbid, won't move . . ."

" 'Heavens, sir, I mustn't let you,' " mimicked Tom Gant in a falsetto.

" 'Eel' " Carrick squealed, sinking to his knees, rolling his eyes. " 'My honor . . .' "

Ogilvie glanced down at his friends and sighed. As they went on giggling and squealing, he reached again for the decanter.

"What ails you, Ant'ny?" said Carrick.

Ogilvie shook his head, and his face lapsed into a smile. "You," he said tiredly. "You fools. *You* ail me. Do you know what I think, Carrick? You should content yourself with Valerie."

"I . . . haven't had Valerie," said Carrick slowly, deliberately. This set Tom Gant off into peals of laughter.

"Haven't—" Gant spluttered. "Haven't had—"

"No!" Carrick turned, glowering. " 'Tis her friend I intend for myself."

"Her friend? Lady Susan?" Ogilvie's forehead, below his fringe of hair, wrinkled in puzzlement—or reproof. But Carrick did not see it.

He smiled, staring past his friends, as if at a vision. "Why, yes. The little Warrington, from Virginia . . . I shall have to make amends."

"Gd'zounds!" Gant's puffy lips opened into a circle. "You'll not have her. Twenty guineas says you shan't."

"Tommy. Nicholas." Ogilvie turned his head from one to the other. "Come, leave off. 'Tisn't a betting matter."

"Ach! You and your petty snobbery. Were she no 'Lady,' you'd not be so fine!" Carrick turned sharply from the fire, toward Gant. "Twenty guineas," he urged. "Are we on?"

"A petty sum!" cried Gant. "Agreed." As he leapt to take Carrick's hand, a glass, knocked from the table, fell tinkling among the playing cards and ashes of the hearth.

Chapter 11

———— ❧ ————

"M'lady—a gentleman called."

Susannah turned, startled, to look at the maid. Peg was the shiest of the house servants and, she thought, her favorite: perhaps because she lacked Mary's sauciness or Ernestine's immovable bulk.

"A gentleman?" Susannah repeated. "Who?"

The maid stared at her with bright, frightened eyes. "A dark gen'leman. Says he'll come again. And he said give you this." She thrust out a paper-wrapped package, which Susannah tore open with fingers still numb from a walk in the park. Inside was a book in a cheap red binding: *Gromby's Theatrical Poses, 1788.* On its pages were engravings of scenes, and lines from plays. She read the words in black ink inside the cover: "In hopeful repentance, Nicholas Carrick. 2 Jan. 1789."

"Is that all he said?" she called to Peg. "Nothing more?"

Peg shook her head, looking as bewildered as her mistress, and escaped down the kitchen stairs.

* * *

Nicholas Carrick. The name had echoed in her mind
for a long while—a throaty Scots voice, a breath, a
whisper—but she had not seen him again. It was not
likely, she told herself, that she would.

She had thought of his caresses by the window at
Golden Square, until she had grown numb to them,
and thought they had lost all their power. A strange
thing had happened to her body. Like a cat, she
longed to be stroked and touched, not in her husband's clumsy fashion, but in that distant, lingering
way of Nicholas Carrick's. She remembered his later,
crude words sometimes: but far less often. Somehow
she put them from her mind. She found herself weighing her own breasts in her hands, fingering the tips of
them, remembering. Sometimes she woke in bed with
a throbbing between her legs at the remnant of a
dream she could never call back. She did not understand it, but still the name came to her. *Nicholas Carrick.*

Valerie, with her passion for piquet and new gowns,
surely could not know what it was like to have such
longings. Stretched along the white-and-gold sofa, in
the new apartments she had at last accepted from
Fellsacre, she would pour Susannah dark coffee and
invite her confidences: *So, you wish a lover* . . . But
Susannah could not bring herself, yet, to say it.

Nor could she speak of such things to Augusta. She
had spent Christmas in the country, at Henshawe,
among her cousin's spinster friends and dark-skinned
servants and squalling new baby, Jonas. For all their
numbers, it was a gloomy time. Augusta was indignant at Harry's having remained in the North so long
without visiting; and she could not understand why
Susannah was so loath to visit The Marches. Susannah
told her that she would hate to see it empty, covered
in dust cloths and tended by a few servants. But that
was only half the truth. She knew the house could call
back only unsettling memories.

No, her life was in London now. The morning after
visiting Vauxhall with Valerie, she had decided it. She
had glimpsed a new life here, of amusements, excite-

ments, new friends; and she did not want to retreat from it until she had learned all it held. The house at Hanover Square had become her home: cozy, nearly warm from the fires that blazed on its small hearths. In the afternoons and evenings she would visit with Valerie and Sarah; mornings, she would gossip in the study with Knole. The secretary kept her informed of price rises and share sales; also of goings-on in the Cheveril household. Maria, he said, had cast off all her old Whiggish friends and was becoming a Tory, like her husband. But Susannah was seldom troubled by visits from her aunt. And that—her gradual estrangement from that family—she no longer much regretted.

Two days passed after the *Theatrical Poses* arrived, and Susannah began to give up hope that Nicholas Carrick would come again. He was a vain, tormenting man, she decided. If he did come after all—she resolved—she would not ask him to stay.

But at eight the next morning he appeared on her doorstep with two horses. Susannah saw him holding the reins, as they stamped and blew steam on the pavement behind him.

"Well?" he said. "Are you ready for a ride?"

"Yes! I mean . . . No, not yet. I . . ." *Damn*, thought Susannah. The refusal she knew he deserved would not come. Carrick's eyes twinkled and played over her face and body, and she shivered in her thin morning gown, suddenly conscious of her bare face and uncombed hair.

"Go on, get ready! I've a deal to show you of London." Carrick bounced on his heels as he spoke, the muscles of his legs, beneath his thin breeches, tightening. In the daylight his brown eyes looked narrower, merrier.

Show you London! she thought. *His arrogance!* She had been here nearly a year. "I'll—I'll be back in a moment," she stammered, fleeing upstairs.

"Now, no fancy dress, Lady Susan!" Nicholas called. "We'll be upon the river today. . . ."

Susannah wondered what he meant—*upon the river*—as she hurried into her oldest black habit and cloak. But she felt too proud to ask. Nicholas handed her into her saddle, and they rode out in the cold. This year's frost was so severe it had chased all but the hardiest peddlers indoors. The cold had suppressed the usual stench in the air; even the dung heaps were buried in snow. The streets were eerily deserted.

"Where are we going?" Susannah called.

Nicholas flicked his reins, and did not trouble to answer. They wound through narrow lanes into the piazza of Covent Garden, where a few of the market women, bundled in layers of clothes, called and waved at Nicholas. A pretty one tossed him a holly sprig.

"They know you?" said Susannah. She could not keep a note of jealousy from her voice. Of course she had always thought Nicholas handsome—ever since the Devonshire ball. But if a score of other women did, too . . . *What chance have I then?*

What chance do you think of? she admonished herself. At the same time, Nicholas said lightly, "Aye. They're pretty girls. A pity they've to wear themselves out working."

And if he threw a mocking glance at her—her old but well-made costume, her cape and long black gloves—she was not sure of it. She let it pass, and—as the damp walls of houses narrowed in on them—she called, again, "Where are we going?"

"London!"

"But we're *in* London! Hanover Square's in London."

Nicholas's eyes danced. "My, but you're persistent. We're going to a *different* London. Does that satisfy?"

Susannah tilted her head and gave him a quizzical look. "I suppose it must. . . . Are there still more houses back there?" She nodded her head at the nearest alley.

"Why, yes. Through all the old part of town. When

good Elizabeth forbad building—thought to keep this city down—all these hidden courts and closes went up. Like Jack Ketch's Warren, where they brick up the windows to hide the corpses. . . . Well! Would you pay your respects to St. Paul?"

Susannah was looking warily at the bricked-up windows above her. *Jack Ketch's Warren* . . . She had not heard of the window tax, and it did not occur to her that Nicholas might regale her with less than the truth. At the mention of St. Paul's she cried out eagerly, "Oh, yes!"

As they wound down Fleet Street, the bulk of the great cathedral rose up above the highest dormers and roofs. Outside its doors, Nicholas took her reins and bade her go in. He murmured that there was no safe place to leave the horses. "Besides, I'd scarce be welcome, disbeliever that I am."

"What? You don't believe in—"

"Go *on*, little one," said Nicholas, with a look of resignation. She wondered at the nickname. Did he think of her as a mere child, then? *And how can he not believe in God?*

She walked the length of the broad, quiet nave. Her steps echoed the hushed ones of the lone verger who crossed the transept with a candle. Gold glinted on the columns, the walls, the high ceiling. She wondered at the work of men, the years, that had gone into this place, and when she was outside again she asked Nicholas, "How can you disbelieve in—that?"

"What?" He gave a dry laugh and helped her onto her horse. "Wealth and worldly power? That is what the church advances, you know."

"No! . . ." The lone word flew from Susannah's lips. "But what of . . . God?"

"Do not look so horror-struck, Lady Susan! I do quite well without him." Nicholas's mouth twisted at one corner, and he kicked his horse ahead, bearing right now, toward the Thames.

"But you know you must . . ." Susannah's voice trailed away. *He must believe.* She had heard, from Harry, of Deists and Platonists—of strange European

varieties of faith. Of failing faith, perhaps, but never
the complete lack of it. She said, now, with decision,
"You've need of God's grace. Nought good happens
without it."

Nicholas made no answer, and she was afraid she
had angered him. *Why should I care?* she reminded
herself. But it was too late. She did care. Her eyes
darkened, as she rode behind, although he did not see.
The horses' hooves clipped on the cobbles of the narrow street where he led; and she saw that where it
came to an end, below the gray line of the sky, all
was white. Nicholas pulled his horse up. His lip
curled, and he let out a breath of steam. "I haven't
God to thank for anything," he said in a low voice.

"To be sure you do. You—"

"Nay, Susan." He tossed his black curls, and made
no excuse for the familiarity. "There you sit, healthy
and clothed—you have never feared hunger, have
you?"

Susannah shook her head.

"P'raps you haven't lived in a garret, like that one—
there!" He pointed up at a dormer window, with a
pane missing and the high wind whistling around it.
"But I have."

He had dismounted, and now he gathered the reins,
leading the horses into the near yard of an inn. Susannah studied him. She tried to imagine him meeker,
younger, in shabbier clothes. "No," she said. "I do not
believe you. You jest."

"Nay, I do not." Nicholas waved for a hostler. "I
wrote *Cyberion* the First in that room there. Aye,
I know Father Thames! In all its moods and seasons . . ."

As she was wondering at his words—for she heard
no rushing river here, nor saw one ahead, but only a
snowy field—Nicholas turned away to settle the
horses' stabling. When he reached up to help Susannah dismount, he smiled, almost as if, a moment ago,
there had been no talk of God or poverty; then, when
she was on the ground beside him, his look darkened
and he went on. " 'Twas my folly to leave Scotland,

you might say, without profession or friends here or inheritance. In the end—in brief, a cousin died, my grandfather owned me, and—Lord, stop me, Lady Susan! I shall drone on and bore you."

"Why, talk of what you like," said Susannah, gently. "I understand. . . ."

"No!" Nicholas broke in, with a sharp laugh. "I'll wager you don't." He lent her his arm, and they walked out of the inn yard and down stone steps. And now, to her surprise, they stepped out onto the white expanse she had seen before. It was not snow but thick, slippery ice; and it stretched for miles to either side. It was the Thames, after all—frozen solid, all the way across to Lambeth. At the docks downriver, ships were trapped in port, their masts swaying in the air like bare trees.

Somehow she resented Nicholas—for getting the advantage of her, surprising her. So instead of showing the girlish delight he must expect, she walked on calmly. Small figures were crossing the ice, most heading for the cluster of booths and stalls in the middle of the river.

Nicholas seemed to study her; then went on casually, where he had left off. "You are rich, Lady Susan. Why should you know toil and trouble? You were born well, I'll wager, in your country, and married better. . . . Some rich husband you'll soon enough make cuckold—"

"Stop!" Susannah pulled her arm free. "How dare you speak to me so? I was not rich! You know nothing of me."

"Aha! A woman of honor, then." Nicholas was unperturbed. "The fair's this way, my lady. There're a number of goodly spectacles. If you care to—"

"No! I don't want to come anymore." Susannah's voice sounded small and, even to her, childish.

Nicholas shrugged and smiled and walked ahead, his footsteps silent on the ice of the river. She thought, *I hate him.*

He moved farther, his hands in his pockets, coattails swinging. Still he did not look back. She did not know what to do; in a moment she would be stranded here. She followed.

She could see the fair now, up ahead: the smoke of fires on ice, the vendors' stands, the crowds gathering up near the wooden puppet theaters. At least when he promised this, Nicholas was not jesting! She could hear the music of horns and drums—and was the tall brown creature on the ice a dancing bear?

Nicholas glanced back and took her arm, as if they had never been parted. "What'll you have?" he murmured. As they walked from one stand to another, sampling the wares, she felt the warmth of his body through her cloak. It was a curious warmth that tickled and set her spine tingling: like the gingerbread he bought her from an old woman's stall, delicious and overpowering at once. The crowd pushed past her and Nicholas, crying wares or singing, or swaying, drunk; dressed in dark, well-worn cloaks or in ragged shawls and torn stockings; trailing ballads in hand, and small children. Dogs and pigeons followed the path of crumbs it left behind.

"Hot mutton pies, hot!" cried the peddlers.

"Come buy my singing birds!"

"Ballads of the fair! Puppets and ballads. Puppet, sir? Ballads of the fair!"

"Will you have one?" asked Nicholas, and before she could say yes or no he was spilling coins into the vendor's hand. The puppet had carroty string for hair, and legs and arms that jumped when Susannah pulled the cord in his head. She played with him surreptitiously, suppressing a childish glee. They came to the dancing bear, which turned out to be no more than a pelt hoisted on a stick, and to the horse that could mind read. Or so proclaimed the wizened man who held its bridle.

"And this young lady 'ere!" he called, his eyes lighting on Nicholas and Susannah. "How many husbands will *she* 'ave?"

The horse whinnied and stamped. One, two, three times—four. *Four!* Susannah drew her cloak closer round her face, in embarrassment. Nicholas was laughing, and threw the man some coppers. "Ask another!" he cried. "Another!"

" 'Ow many times . . ." the man pondered. " 'Ow many times she been kissed?"

At that, the black horse whinnied and went riot. He shuffled and stamped, and all the crowd around started shouting out questions. Nicholas clapped and called, "Again!"

But the wizened man had moved on to other customers. Still hiding her face, Susannah slid away along the ice.

"How many, Lady Susan?" sounded Nicholas's far-off voice. She moved faster, gliding, enjoying the feel of the slippery floor beneath her.

" 'Twas you paid him!" she called back. " 'Twas mostlike *your* mind he read, Mr. Carrick!"

Here the ice was smooth and empty, and above it the sunless sky, darkening. Susannah's toes were numb, but she slid farther. It was such fun. In this last year, with its lies and worry, she had near forgotten . . .

She slid so fast that at last her feet escaped her. She sprawled backward, and Nicholas, panting, bent down to pick her up. Their arms locked together as she stumbled for a footing. She laughed, afraid, and Nicholas's lips, curling in laughter, too, came close and almost met hers. He pulled away. "Come!" he said. "Home!" And he drew her up to her feet.

They rode back in the chill, smoky air, and, before she expected it, she found herself deposited on her own doorstep, with her puppet and a ballad book. Nicholas vanished across Hanover Square with the horses. That night, she fell exhausted into bed and slept too deeply and soundly to dream.

A week passed, and Susannah heard no more from Nicholas Carrick. She thought of the day she had spent with him, and was embarrassed at what seemed her own childishness: questioning him about God so and taking offense at his flippancy. Why, men of the world behaved so; she must learn, and be like Valerie. *He will not come again,* she thought, and blamed herself.

But then he did: taking her by surprise, just as he first had. He strode into her parlor, another morning, a few days later, his breath steaming and his hair dusted with snow.

"What? Not ready?" he said, with a flickering glance at her undress; and their round of excursions through London began in earnest.

They went to Dr. Clark's Waxworks, the House of Commons, and the Tower menagerie; and all along the way Nicholas bought Susannah presents: fancy-dress masks, a doll, a harlequinade book of nonsensical scenes. They ran up the steps of the needlelike London Monument and stood high above the city, both terrified.

"I don't like—" Susannah clung to the railing and shut her eyes.

"Don't you like high places, little one?"

" 'Little one'!" Susannah reeled but tried to answer back. "I am eighteen. And not very much smaller than you, sir!"

"Full eighteen!" said Nicholas mockingly; but Susannah noticed that by now he, too, was looking dizzy and backing up against a wall. "Then how old am I?"

"I don't know!" Susannah's words vanished in the wind. "Twenty-five? Or—"

"Nay. A veritable Methuselah! Thirty-six." With a quailing look out at the river and dwarfed church spires, Nicholas reached for her hand. "Man—" he gasped, "was not meant for such unnatural heights. Come!"

With a hurry and relief as great as his, she followed down the steps.

Another afternoon he took her to the Three Georges to dine. It was his favorite tavern, near Covent Garden and the theaters. In its cozy, dark-paneled warmth, filled up with mulled wine and roast beef, Susannah found herself telling Nicholas things she would never, before, have expected him to understand: of her father and the farm in Virginia, of Adela and her proverbs. Of the ways of suitors, and courting there, that she had missed: the long calls and riding out.

"Are you courting me?" she said suddenly, giggling, her tongue loosened by the wine.

" 'Courting' you?" Nicholas's gaze grew serious, and his smile dropped. "In the antique sense, perhaps, Lady Susan. I seek your regard—perhaps to amuse you. No more."

Susannah looked up, silent, wondering why she felt such a keen disappointment.

"What? Does that displease you?"

"No, of course—of course not."

Nicholas tipped his hat to her, courtier fashion, across the broad table. "For one does not seek to disappoint . . . *madame*." He drew out his words in his best imitation of a Frenchman, his bowed head concealing a smile.

Come to Wray's *Love's Perfidy* at Drury Lane—
Take a box, giving my name. I will find you—
N.C.

Susannah stared at the note, which had come to her house by footman. *Drury Lane?* She smiled, as a flush of excitement rose to her skin. She had never been to the theater before. Nor did she know when to go, or what to wear there—so she threw on a cloak and ran to Berkeley Square, to consult with Valerie.

Behind the door to her friend's apartments she heard shuffling and giggling, and a masculine growl.

Valerie issued forth at last. "Well! *Suzanne!* Come in!" She pressed both cheeks to hers, with a noise like kissing. "*Georges!* Do you know who is here?" she called. "Do you like?" she said to Susannah, spinning to display her narrow red robe. "*Georges* says it comes from China." She gestured toward a graying head poking cautiously out of a doorway.

Georges—whom Susannah guessed to be the elder

Fellsacre, the brewer—had a heavy, careworn brow. He looked rather ludicrously the dandy in his own Oriental dressing gown, like Valerie's, and an ill-fitting gray wig. He bent forward to kiss Susannah's hand, muttering her name. This, then, was the provider of these apartments—who last autumn had banished his golden-haired son to a long term in His Majesty's Navy.

"*Love's Per-fiddy!*" Valerie exclaimed, examining Nicholas Carrick's note. "What a delight! But we are late. We must go, *Georges*, immediately."

Late? Susannah wondered. It was only just past three. While Fellsacre struggled into a suit, Valerie, for lack of time to change, draped herself and Susannah with pearls. She hurried them outside and into a hackney cab.

In the crush outside Drury Lane Theatre, George Fellsacre became agitated. Two or three men seemed to hail him, but he lifted his hat to hide his face. "Come along," he grumbled, "if you *would* bring me . . ." He tugged Valerie past the ballad sellers and guardsmen at the door.

"Poor *Georges*," murmured Valerie, into Susannah's ear. "He does not see he is not the only man to go out with a woman not his wife!" She opened and slammed a row of doors, searching for an empty box. At last, near the end of a row, she found one. The seats inside were green-covered benches with no backs; but it did not seem to matter, as everyone in the boxes leaned sharply forward, peering out. Valerie took her place, crying out, "Look! There is Lady Chislemere. And there is Killburn—but that must mean he is not acting. . . . Is that Fox?"

Susannah perched, too, and bent forward to look. Below in the pit, all was noisy chaos. Men leapt over seats and tossed coins at the girls selling oranges. Tall men, loud men, fat men . . . but nowhere could she see Nicholas. The theater was dim and hot; the smoke-stained gilt of its carvings glimmered. Her skin grew damp under her blue velvet gown, and as she waited, the hubbub of the crowd dimmed, in her ears, to a murmur of anticipation.

"Where is he?" she said.

But Valerie did not seem to hear. "Oh, 'twill begin soon!" she cried. "Be patient. Now is the First Music. . . ."

Susannah tried to distract herself, studying the place where, twice, Nicholas Carrick's plays had quieted these hundreds. Its three tiers of boxes; its stage, above a struggling orchestra, rimmed with tall spikes.

"What are those?" She pointed at them, looking at Valerie.

"To keep the people off the stage!" her friend shouted. "Against riots . . ."

Susannah nodded at the answer, already forgetting her question. Soon he must come to join them. He would burst through the box door, exuberant, laughing. . . .

The Third Music began, and Valerie cast an appraising look over her friend. *Comme tu veux*, "as you want," was a favorite phrase of hers; and she had spoken no more to Susannah of Nicholas since the night of Ogilvie's party. She could see now that there was no reaching her and turned, instead, to her lover. She lit on George Fellsacre's lap, and stroked the gray tendrils poking out from beneath his wig. The footmen in the uppermost gallery roared for the play to begin.

"Perdita! My excellent love. Do not go—"

As the play's hero, in a broad yellow wig, dropped to his knees onstage, the dark, sprightly heroine cartwheeled away, showing the tops of her stockings beneath her flying skirts.

"Hurrah!" came the shouts from pit and gallery. "Again!"

Susannah rubbed her sore back and shifted on her seat. The play was well into its third act, and third hour. Still, its yellow-haired swain, Percy, dogged the path of the fickle Perdita. George Fellsacre, in his corner of the box, was snoring. And again Susannah was about to nudge Valerie and ask, *Where is Nicholas?* when a loud crash of drums echoed from the pit. A new player, black-haired and brandishing a sword, strode forward. His low voice, with its rolling consonants, cut through the restless babble of the hall.

"Perdita. My angel. My undoing . . ."

The crowd stilled. The figure, in his long black wig, turned, and as he swept Perdita up in his arms, Susannah heard Nicholas Carrick's voice ring out again.

"Thy hatred of my sex—I call it a ruse! And I shall have thee."

Susannah's skin tingled. The voice was at once so strong, so assured and intimate, that it sounded as if he had spoken directly to her. *And yet he will not even know I am here.* . . . She saw Perdita collapse in Nicholas's arms, and a fierce, unwanted jealousy seized her. Then, as quickly as he had embraced Perdita, Nicholas dropped her. She fell back, her hooped skirt gaping. Nicholas swaggered offstage, to loud whistling and stamping from the pit.

The play went on, but none of the actors following commanded the attention Carrick had. Like most of the audience, Susannah and Valerie began again to whisper, to stand and move about the box. "We will walk," Valerie announced. And as Susannah was leading the way out the door, she ran nearly head-on into Nicholas.

"Don't walk out now," he urged, in the mesmeric tones she had just heard: as if he were still onstage. But now he was far, far closer: speaking in her ear. "In sympathy," he said, "for the playwright, who is my friend, Susan—stay."

Now he was leading her back to her seat; drawing, as if by magic, a bottle and even glass goblets from the deep pockets of his crimson costume-coat. He had left off the black wig; the curls of his own hair, and his face, were damp with sweat.

The golden wine fizzed as he poured it. "Tomorrow," he said, grinning, "all concerned in this ill-starred production shall fall under the ax of the pamphleteer critics. But tonight . . ." His eyes searched for Susannah's and finally found them: wide and dark as the night-blue velvet of her dress. "Tonight, we shall forget our shame—and rejoice!" His voice rose, exuberant. "For I have done."

"Will you not be in the play again?" Susannah said.

"No. Not tonight." Nicholas's fingers played idly on her back, above the lace ruffles of her dress. "You see, I was a mere diversion. Perdita must marry her stumbling suitor."

The bubbles in the wine stung Susannah's throat and blurred her thoughts. "But what if—what if she doesn't?"

Nicholas laughed. "What else can she do?"

"Why—go looking for you again." She flushed, realizing what she had said, and tossed her head in embarrassment. "I mean—your part. What is its name?"

"Malefoglio." Nicholas's finger traced steady lines at the nape of her neck. "What? In her place, should you take to the chase?"

Susannah's hands trembled in her lap as she smiled and said, "I am sure . . . I do not know any man worth it!"

Nicholas chuckled. As onstage the yellow-wigged actor renewed his pleas, Nicholas reached and nudged Valerie, who was dozing on Fellsacre's shoulder. "Shall we go home?" he said. "Lady Susan's fast becoming my harshest critic."

And though it puzzled her—leaving before the Turkish pashas' dance and the final Music—Susannah agreed. Nicholas tucked his wig and champagne bottle under his arm, and they wandered down the empty stair and to the street.

"To Grandfather's!" cried Nicholas to the hackney coachman who took them aboard.

"No, Nichol—" said Valerie, sleepy.

"Swallow Street, Berkeley Square," growled Fellsacre.

"*Then* to Great Russell Street," said Nicholas, with an offended shrug, to the coachman. "As they wish—"

He smiled at Susannah. "But you will meet Grandfather, will you not?"

"At eleven o'clock?"

"Why, that's the time he's most wakeful!"

The house of the fourth Baron Blackcroft was high and gloomy, built of soot-stained brick.

"Are you sure—" Susannah whispered, at the front door. No light gleamed from within.

"Of course he'll want to see us." Nicholas slammed the knocker again. "In any case, *I* live here, too. Though the confounded servants seem to forget it."

A pale butler came at last and ushered them in.

"My son? Is that you?" called a distant voice, as they followed the butler's candle up the narrow, dark stair.

"Yes, Grandfather," Nicholas answered. They came to a great room whose size was revealed only gradually, as the butler lit a row of tapers on the wall.

At one end sat the Baron, rigid and unmoving. He was lean and white-haired, and did not start at the light. A worn red-and-gilt tapestry covered his lap, and another the back of his tall chair. In the corners behind him Susannah could see five or six oniondomed cages of gold wire, whose inhabitants, wakened, trilled dispiritedly within.

"You have brought someone," said the Baron. His eyes, an icy blue, seemed to look through Susannah, and beyond.

"Why does he call you his son?" she whispered to Nicholas.

"He never had a son, so it pleases him. Go up," Nicholas urged, "and take his hand."

She obeyed. The Baron clasped her hand in his leaf-dry, thin one.

"Tell me. Are you a pretty girl?" The Baron smiled faintly.

"Of course she is, Grandfather," said Nicholas, bounding forward. "What is more, she is a Lady."

Baron Blackcroft's laugh was slow but gleeful. "Ah!

But they're all ladies. Are they not, my son?. . . What is your name?" he said to Susannah. She told him. "My dear," he said, his face wrinkling with concern, "are you recently widowed?"

"What?"

Nicholas broke in. "She's no widow, Grandfather. You've read her wrong."

Susannah looked at Nicholas, mystified.

"My grandfather reads the human qualities through touch." Nicholas spoke loudly, so that they both could hear. His grandfather smiled. "What else can you tell of her?"

The Baron frowned in thought and stroked the lines of Susannah's palm. "You are but young. Eighteen, yes?"

Susannah nodded, then remembered to speak. "Yes."

"Why, you have worked with these hands!" The Baron's eyes wrinkled. "But that is well. You'll not grow spoilt. . . . Nicholas never brings me girls. You must come again. Have you seen my orrery?" He thumped the arm of his chair. "Nicholas! Show it her. I would get up, my dear. You must excuse me. I grow old." He let her hand go, and his face grew composed and vacant.

Nicholas, cowed as Susannah had never seen him before, followed his grandfather's instructions. He led her to the back of the room, through a maze of tables and dusty books, with titles like *The Mesmerist* and *A Scientifick Theory of Gravity*. In a far corner sat an assembly of metal weights and balances: hoops for orbits, and knobs for the seven planets and moon.

Nicholas took her hand, and at the same time lifted one of the orrery's lead weights. "Once set in motion," he said, "it will not stop." He gave the weight a push now and reached for her other hand. The planets began their clockwork circling. Susannah moved closer in the cold air. She looked back at the Baron, and his blue eyes continued to pierce her.

"Do not be afraid," said Nicholas. "He does not see."

Their bodies touched through wool and fur and velvet, a slow warmth spreading through her, connecting them. Nicholas's hands dropped to Susannah's waist, and she shied, looking back at the old man. "He does," she said. "Else—how can he know so much?"

"He cannot know all. Let me show you." Nicholas pressed a finger to her cheek, until she turned her head toward him. Then he caught her in a swift embrace and held her. His arms held her immobile, fluttering uselessly, like one of the birds in the cages. He bent over her, for all the world like black-haired Malefoglio in the play: except that his mouth was not still but moved over hers, devouring hers. The Baron stared on.

Chapter 12

———— ❧ ————

Maria Cheveril bent close to her writing desk, in her large but bare study in Kensington. Her pen picked up speed.

How have you heart to ignore a Mother's concern? Twice I write you—no reply—but is it not just, near a year pass't, to consider—

Her dark eyes narrowed. For there was, indeed, so much to consider, though Henry refused. . . .

that Susannah has not proved a fit wife, that she nor stays by you, as is fitting, nor has given you Heirs—that she lives in London the year long, where she comports herself with loud and Loose company—

Here Maria stopped. A lack of proof seldom dampened her assertions; but now it did. For Henry was factual to a fault. And should he ask, how could she answer but, "Lady Framer said that Lady Chislemere

saw . . . at the theatre . . . a Frenchwoman of poor
repute . . ." *No.* Best to change approach.

> —*that you are not bound under* all *Circum-*
> *stances permanently to accept of such a wife.*
> *There are means . . .*

Here, the matter was delicate. Maria was far from
defeated by her son's marriage; indeed, only a few
months after it she had started her search for a means
of declaring it invalid. She had begun her investiga-
tions with the Church.

"Isn't it against the law for first cousins to marry?"
she asked her friend the Canon.

The Canon had not proved helpful. "The marriage
of cousins in England is quite legal," he said. "We are
not the Church of Rome."

One solution yet remained.

> *A Bill of Divorcement in Parl.*—*with James's*
> *help, should you consent to it*—*might yet free you*
> *to marry, in time, a* loving *wife who would bear*
> *you children. There must needs be Evidence, and*
> *Expense*—

But these—like the help of James Cheveril—were but
minor mechanical necessities. True, she had not yet
consulted James; but she could easily bring him round,
when the time came.

"Maria, pet, have you done yet? The Ackerleys are
here."

Her husband was calling from downstairs: her good-
hearted, mild, vain husband, who would do anything
to preserve his own peace. She opened the door and
heard the clatter of china and silver below. The
house's sole footman lounged, half asleep, in her
doorway.

"James, dearest. See to them but for a minute?" she
called down sweetly. She coughed—for such dulcet
tones put a strain on her voice—and threw the top of

her inkwell at the footman's leg, where it left a black trail. "Wake up, you!"

She sat again, and scribbled the last few, requisite lines, ending upon

the constant devotion of your loving,

MOTHER

and tossed the missive, folded and sealed, at the footman. "There! For the post. And there's work to be done in the sitting room, you know! . . . Will I never have a moment's peace in this benighted house?"

Glimpsing the first few words, Harry turned his mother's letter on its face. He did not want to look at it: to see that hateful message repeated yet again.

"Lord and Lady Exon are below, sir." His waiting man, a sullen, gravel-voiced Irishman, seemed, uncharacteristically, to smile. "And another lady. A Mrs. Hallward."

"Thank you, Fermanagh." Before he went downstairs, Harry picked up the letter again. *Divorce*—he thought it a brutal and ugly word. He bent over the hearth, and watched the efficient swoop of his mother's hand crumple into blackness. *So many letters*, he thought, *and we write them to no purpose*. He looked down at the sheet that still lay on his desk, half covered in neat writing. Another one of his tedious missives to Hanover Square: descriptive, bare, dry of feeling. To which his wife would make a belated, equally empty reply, telling him of the king's reported health or the cold weather. Wasn't it—

"Enough!" he said aloud. Startled at himself, he glanced around. His voice still rang against the gray stone walls. He would not obey a word of his mother's letter. No—on the contrary—he would call an end to this separation. Even if there were difficulties, matters unresolved . . .

He had been at fault too, he knew. She was very young—he had not had enough patience. He would tear up this latest letter and write the truth. He loved her no less for all the year past. And he would see how she answered.

Chapter 13

———— ✺ ————

"Well," said Sarah Hutchings, shifting to an easier position on the sofa, "you could go ath a fairy! Or in Grethian style, or hithtorical . . ."

The invitation had come a week ago, for St. Valentine's night:

BAL MASQUÉ
11, the Evening—No. 10, Swallow Street.

It was scented orange and inscribed in Valerie's spidery hand. But Susannah had not confided to her—or to Sarah, who sat in her bedroom now—how much this masked ball might bring about.

Sarah was still talking. "—or maid or shepherdeth . . ."

One might go as queen, or naiad in thin draperies; or as a madwoman in rags. (That, it was said, excused any outrageous acts "one" expected to commit.) One might go in motley finery and call it fancy dress. But none of these sounded right to Susannah. "Shepherdess?" she said, considering the heap of rejected articles of clothing on her bed.

"A fanthy-*dreth* sheperdeth, of courth," said Sarah. She leapt up, pointing at a white satin gown. "What of *that?*"

But *that*, Susannah realized with a start, was her wedding dress. "No," she murmured, shaking her head to toss off a solemn thought.

Hadn't Nicholas said once that his favorite shade was blue? *Yes, blue*, she thought, and reached deeper in the heap of clothing on her bed. Here was an old dress of Augusta's, of sapphire satin, short and fraying at the seams. "This," she said, with decision. "And how do you think, Sarah—I could go, and not be known?"

Sarah gave her a puzzled look. "Not be known?" For that was seldom the aim at masked balls. "Why should you—"

"To play a game. A game upon someone."

He has only interest in cheap women. Whores. Was it true? Had he already lost interest in her?

Last week she had called on the Baron Blackcroft, as he had invited her to visit; and Nicholas had met her by surprise on the stair. "You are kind, Lady Susan," he had said, with a bow. They stood near the place where, a week before, they had embraced. Yet quickly he moved past. . . .

"A *game*," said Sarah. But she did not seem to guess. With Susannah, she hunted for a mask and veil; and when Susannah tried it on, she shook her head. "You'd need a wig," Sarah said, "to be thertain. P'raps a blond one. If you thtay in the dark . . ."

"I will. And the dress?" said Susannah.

"Too short." Frowning with concentration, Sarah tugged at the bodice, until its round neckline fell below Susannah's shoulders. She draped a lacy petticoat round her waist: a scrap of that could make an apron. A shepherdess's crook and wig they had yet to find, but they might search the shops around the theaters.

"Then why not—even shorter?" said Susannah suddenly, tugging her skirts a foot off the ground. That would free her for dancing; and it was said that the sight of ankles and high heels was a great attraction to men. . . .

"Why, Thusan. You do aim to *provoke!*" giggled Sarah.

"To be sure!" said Susannah. Her face showed strangely white and wide-eyed in the mirror.

So? She heard Valerie's whisper in her ears. *You seek a lover. . . . So does everyone.* By now Susannah almost believed it. All around her she heard the rumors: the Prince, the Devonshires, Lady Caroline Framer and Lord Asprey. . . . Yet Susannah knew she was less worldly than they. What must be a small step to them looked a great and frightening one to her. Her stomach grew hollow and empty at the thought of it. *But I do love him.*

There was a knock at the door, and Peg came in. She bobbed her head, abashed, at the letter on her silver tray.

Susannah took it, and looked at the writing. "Oh. From Harry," she said, half to herself, as she broke the seal. Peg remained, tray in hand, and at last got out the words: "There's a gentleman in the hall for you, m'lady."

"Gentleman?" Susannah's voice rose, hopeful.

"From Mr. Garnett, the shoemaker, m'lady."

"Bother!" exclaimed Susannah, hurrying downstairs. Once again, she supposed, Knole had carried his principle of paying bills late to extremes.

When she had gone, Sarah's eyes lit on the letter cast down on the table. She made her way, mouselike, across the carpet, and with many darting glances at the door, picked up the single sheet and carried it to the sofa.

Her blue eyes grew round and wide as she mouthed the words; and as she came to the middle of the page she gave a sudden shudder of emotion. "Susan, I loved you then. I would love you still. Might we put past wrongs behind us, and—"

But she could read no more, for steps sounded now, running up the stairs. Sarah glanced frantically around the room. The table looked all too distant. Hastily she

folded up the letter and shoved it deep in the uphol-
stered fold at the corner of the sofa where she sat.

Susannah entered, smiling. "Finished! Eight months'
account past due. What can Knole have been about?"
She did not seem to notice her guest's wide, guilty grin.

They went to work together, cutting away at the
hem of the sapphire gown, and the neckline.

"Here?" said Sarah.

"No. Lower." Susannah tossed her curls, suddenly
resolute. *Comme tu veux*—she echoed Valerie's phrase
in her mind. No—it could not be wrong to try for
what she truly wished.

Some hours later, when Sarah had gone, Susannah
wondered what had become of Harry's letter. No doubt
it was much the same as his others, full of the Exons and
the Norman Conquest. She looked on all the tables and
shelves in her room but had to suppose, when she could
not find it, that one of the maids had cleared it away.

"Bother!" she exclaimed to herself again. Then,
knowing that Harry's letters had a way of hanging over
her till she answered them, she took out her ink case,
and improvised a reply. *"Dearest Harry,"* she began.

*I am glad your work is coming on so well. Fancy,
soon it shall be Spring even here in murky London! I suppose all sorts of extreaordinary
Mountain-Flowers are shewing themselves at your
Castle. You must forgive me a dull letter, for
nothing new seems to happen here . . .*

It was St. Valentine's night, at last. Susannah looked
down at her costume, through the eye slits of her
mask: at the round hills of her breasts, edged in blue,
and the swirling satin of her skirts. She had tied a sash
of dark blue silk close round her waist, and there and
in the brim of her straw hat, had tucked pink and
blue silk flowers. She glimpsed the white stockings
and beribboned, high white shoes; and perhaps, with

luck, below the mask and false blond curls, the blue of her eyes might still show, too. Peg handed her her shepherdess's crook. Her skin tingled with cold as the coach made its way to Swallow Street.

A masked footman opened the door for her, onto a green, bright garden. In the dead of winter, Valerie's rooms had been transformed into a miniature Vauxhall, with bright candles and orange trees and ivy-covered trellises. Green-paper leaves were wound around the curtains and pillars, and in the next room, where the guests paraded, strings screeched a minuet.

A few heads turned as she entered; they had the faces of phantoms, of painted players, of exotic insects. And though Susannah recognized here a mouth, there a sweep of the arm, she could not place them. Nor did these people seem to know her. They summed her up and turned back to their partners, or their friends. At last, in a corner, she recognized Sarah, in her diaphanous robes as Diana. She gave her a secret nod while the flutes lingered on a low, entrancing note. She searched the room again as the music rose. *He is not here.*

A group passed by her, shouting for drink, for "War on France!" A shower of wine fell on her. She gasped, indignant, and the culprit turned. He still held his glass high. "Here, lovey!" he bellowed. "Let me dry you—"

She thought she knew him. *Folly,* she thought. But it was true. The red-gold wig and pink jowls beneath the mask: the plump hand reaching toward her, with a handkerchief. *Jonas Hench.* She spun away, struggling with the veil in her hat that she knew, in the last resort, would hide her; but as she did, another man clasped her arm and drew her away.

"Madam. You are not for *him.*"

Her savior's voice was soft and foreign; he wore a dark ponytail and a suit of crimson velvet. Now he seemed to stare at her; and behind his mask, a laugh rippled from low to high.

"Valerie?"

"Whisht!" Valerie touched a finger to Susannah's lips. "Would you have the whole world to know where

I am?" She pulled Susannah down onto a bench between two orange trees.

"What is—" Susannah began. *What is Hench doing here?* she almost asked; but she knew that if no one was to know her, she must be sparing with her voice. "Where is Nicholas?"

"Nicholas?" Valerie echoed. "I do not know. Do you expect him?"

Susannah shook her head, disappointed. Valerie stroked her cheek with her long fingers. "There are other men here. Besides me!" She giggled. "Do you see? There is Ogilvie—" She pointed at a slender man in an owl mask and purple domino. "There is Tom Gant, there are—"

"But *he* is not here," said Susannah, petulant.

"Pssh." Valerie sighed. "Will you insist, so? There are many good men in the world—all there for your pleasure."

Susannah smiled weakly.

"You are yet young!" said Valerie. "Take my counsel. Many men can please you, if you let them." She traced a curve along the edge of Susannah's gown, smiling as Susannah jumped back, surprised. "Do not forget!" she said, laughing. "I am a gentleman making love. . . ." And feigning the smile of a satisfied lover, she vanished.

Now Susannah did not know what to do. She wandered through the rooms, watching herself in the looking glasses: practicing boldness. She watched the other women pass, painted and unafraid, matching the men glance for glance—and the men, strutting, in slashed doublets or sweeping, bright dominos. She tried smiling at them—perhaps one was Nicholas, she could not tell—and felt invisible. They glanced her way, but all had their partners; and only one man pursued her, glass in hand, and that was Hench. He charged down the length of the drawing room toward her; and she was glad, then, that she knew the doors and passages of Valerie's rooms. She ran out into the dark corridor and, feeling the walls, found a hidden door. She pushed through the ranks of robes that blocked her way, and emerged, on the other side, in Valerie's dressing room. At first she thought she heard the clatter of a door somewhere, and footsteps; but she looked warily around in the dark, and there was no one. Panting, she leaned against a cupboard door; all around her, tall mirrors of smoky glass shot back her pale reflection. She stood motionless, hearing no sound but her own quick breaths. And yet she felt someone was watching.

Cautiously she stepped forward, toward a mirror. No one was here. *Look*, she told herself. *Nothing*. She saw only herself: her mask and white ankles, her shepherdess's crook. She saw the shadow behind her and spun to face it, but by the time she did, it had moved forward and taken hold of her.

She heard a low laugh. "You—" he said, and his arms gripped hers. His dark cloak swung round her, enveloped her. It was warm, inside. "I had *seen* you," he said, and she smelled Nicholas's own scent, his sweat, the powder and musk fragrance of his hair. She knew him. And she felt her limbs go loose. Her skin was warm, and she feared nothing. The time had come.

He held her so fast in his arms that she could not move; but his mouth waited, and only brushed her skin, touching on her lips, then on the soft skin behind her ear. His breath fell warm on her neck as his lips moved down past the stiff curls of her wig, crossing, recrossing the wide, low neckline of her dress. Feeling her nipples grow hard, as his chin barely, accidentally, brushed them, she twisted in his arms, resisting, and felt his hands only fasten around her arms, behind her, harder. For a moment the whole, taut length of his body pressed against hers. She felt his hardness, and her own aching soreness where it bulged against her. And then he let go.

With a smile that in the thin moonlight was only a confusion of shadows, Nicholas lifted his cape in his hands and bowed away.

Wait, she almost said, but stifled the voice in her throat. She must not be heard. She must not be known. Nicholas, with a last playful nod at her, was turning. . . .

His hand was on the door to the next chamber. She ran toward him, her high heels slipping on the rug, and reached for his hand.

"Yes?" he said; and seemed to smile. But he did not move to touch her.

She did not know what to do. She felt helpless, foolish; and yet something drew her on. She held his hand fast where it lay against the door; she raised her other hand to touch the smooth, shaven skin of his face. Her finger traced the full lips, the deep curve beneath the slanting nose. Standing on tiptoes, she raised her own lips up to his. But he did not move. Only a lazy arm curled around to stroke her back as she pressed her lips to his, searching their surface for a reaction, a response. And slowly they opened to her questing tongue, his head bending lower as she curled her hands round his neck. *I will not lose him.* She held fast to him, exploring his mouth, the one part of him she dared, with all her love and hunger. Slowly his lips began to move with her own.

And she did not know when it became no longer her own venture but his, no longer her own hunger and longing but his quick lust for her, his skill, which drew her away from the door and into the room again; which lifted her up against him, where again she felt his hardness, and laid her down on the narrow sofa in the silver paling moonlight.

He tugged her gown low, below her breasts, and now adored them, each in turn, longer than he had at Golden Square; until all her being was drawn to the places where his tongue played, where his teeth brushed and nipped; and then he would raise his head, and she saw those same white teeth, gleaming. He fell on top of her, as she kissed him, and his long rod, now clothed, now a second later, naked, pressed against the place between her legs, which ached with wanting. It slid between the wet lips there, and there was no time now to undress, but Nicholas did not stop, and she did not care, and they rose and fell together in the tangle of their clothing. He slid in and out of her, sometimes drawing far away, only to drive

into her faster, harder. Now he moved rapidly, fiercely
against her. She moved to meet him, and there was no
pain, no shame, only this need to go on, harder, deeper,
to have him delve farther into her, until there was no
secret, no space he had not reached—this hunger, that
overtook her at last, and cast all else in darkness.

He sat beside her now, her stockinged legs draped
over his lap. He twitched a lock of her dark hair, for
the straw-colored wig had long ago fallen away.
"Well? Did it please you, little one?" he said.

She could not answer. She felt her face flush red,
and was thankful for the cool concealment of the
moonlight. She tried to tug her skirts down, to cover
herself. "I know it—was too bold. I . . ."

"No!" Nicholas tossed her skirts away, laying his
hand back where it had been before. "It was surely
not, Lady Susan."

Susannah flinched.

Nicholas reached up, stroking the curves of her
breasts, her waist, her hips. "I think I shall want you,
and want you again."

"We must leave," she said, and wished she had not
said it. The noises outside, muted for a time, had
started up again: the shouts, the laughs, the violins,
more raucous than ever. She wanted to lock this room
against them all: to stay, and keep Nicholas with her.
For he would leave her, now. She knew it. All would
be at an end. . . .

Her eyes grew dark, and she turned her head away.

"I should not give you up"—Nicholas touched her
chin lightly—"after such a beginning. Our delights,
when we meet longer—can be only the greater." At
last she returned his gaze. He drew up a lock of her
hair and kissed it. "Well? Will you be mine?"

She answered, confused, her voice trembling. "Of
course."

"And belong to no one else—unless I wish it?"

She nodded.

"And . . . do anything I might want?"

"Yes," she whispered, and thought, *what a strange question*. But as they crept away through the bedroom, into the corridor, Nicholas embraced her again, as if to reassure her. All lovers must make such vows, she decided; and thought no more upon it.

Jonas Hench stood in the hall, nursing his indigestion. *He* had enjoyed no dalliance tonight and was more than ready to quit this overheated madhouse. Indeed, he thought, were it not for that blue shepherdess—with her generous figure, of the sort he favored, and her strange, familiar air. . . .

He heard a shuffle behind him, and instinctively pulled himself straight. As he turned and saw the couple emerging from the bedroom, his back seemed to lock in place.

He did not know the dark fellow; but he recognized *her*. As the man pulled at her hand, she shot a frightened glance back along the corridor. Her dress was blue, but her hair now was brown—and her face, smiling sleepily, was Susannah's.

He had begun to think her virtuous: believed it, when she ended by marrying the scholarly Viscount. If he felt an envious lust for her now, he did not acknowledge it. Nor would he admit to injured pride. But something in him was affronted, offended. He did not quite know why.

The next morning Susannah woke late and dressed slowly, her mind in a haze. Somehow she had lost Nicholas, once they returned to the party. She had found Valerie nibbling at cold chicken from her table; and she knew her look of preoccupied hunger well enough not to try to confide in her. She had the masked footman summon her coach then, and, her thoughts in confusion, returned home.

It was true, he had said *I shall want you again*. But perhaps he had said such things only to please her. She had entered a strange, bleak terrain, where she knew not what to look forward to, or hope. All she knew was that she could not leave off thinking of last night. She stared at her reflection as she brushed her hair, disappointed at how little changed she seemed. No woman of experience, no wise eyes or knowing smile reflected back, but only her own face, still like a girl's, puffy with sleep above the ruffles of her muslin dress. She paced her room, and the dining room where she ate breakfast. And then she heard the familiar hoofbeats in the square. She looked out the window, and her heart leapt.

Nicholas had not come alone this time, but in Anthony Ogilvie's open carriage.

"Come, Lady Susan!" He stood, as they halted. "We're off to Bridewell!"

She climbed in beside him; she knew almost all the others in the company. Ogilvie, who drove, and Sarah, and red-faced Tom Gant and his mistress, called Lydia. They welcomed her in, and perhaps only she was struck by the thought that there were, here, three couples. *Nicholas and I are the third.* The notion pleased her.

The carriage rattled over cobbles as Anthony whipped the horses on.

"Anthony! Pray tame your horses!" cried Lydia. Tom Gant's arm was fastened round her plump waist.

"What, lost your courage, have you?" called Nicholas, winding his own arm around Susannah. Tom Gant caught his eye, and winked.

"Say," he addressed Nicholas. "For that twenty guineas I owe you—"

"Pay it no mind!" said Nicholas, flashing Gant a look of annoyance.

"What twenty guineas?" said Susannah.

"For the filly!" Gant tossed a sack of coins across to Nicholas. "Yesterday's races! I always honor my debts. . . ."

The coach thumped suddenly into a ditch, and Sarah Hutchings, on Nicholas's other side, let out a forlorn cry: "He thall have us run down!"

Ogilvie, up on the driver's seat, was oblivious.

*   *   *

Susannah did not realize till they got there, that Bridewell was a prison, and they meant to go into it. She looked up apprehensively at its vast, nail-studded door. "We aren't—" she said to Nicholas.

"Come along! 'Tis viewing hour."

"But I can't—" she began.

Nicholas let out an exasperated sigh. "The cutpurses aren't here for their own amusement, you know." Seeing no change in Susannah's face, he tried another tack. "Why, a prison's a world! Filled with every human type. . . . They gape at us, and we at them. . . . Come, Susan! Don't look so serious."

He paid the gatekeeper and pulled her in. Ahead, the other couples whispered and shivered in mock horror. The hall was dark and had a sewage scent, subdued by whitewash and the reek of ale. In truth, it was not so horrible as Susannah feared. The jailor led them to a courtyard, where twenty women or so yawned and stretched their arms in the sunlight. Some of them sat at benches, sewing; others paced around drinking from mugs, talking in shrill voices to their neighbors. Some of them were ragged, but nearly as many, Susannah noticed, wore finery such as filled the boxes of Drury Lane.

"Why are they all here?" she whispered to Nicholas.

With a gleam in his eye, he began, "They are ladies who—"

"They're harlots!" Tom Gant bellowed. "Whores!" Some of the women looked up sullenly from the barred court. "Why," he chortled, "they treat these damsels like princesses, they do! Beef and three pints of ale a day, they get. In the old days, the keepers thrashed 'em into beating hemp. But *now* . . ."

"Look!" squealed Lydia, pointing to a thin girl. "*She* mustn't be more than fourteen."

Just then a different girl detached herself from the crowd, moving gracefully forward in a brown silk dress that matched the color of her complexion. She smoothed her thick, reddish hair as she strolled, and would not take her eyes from Susannah.

Chapter 14

———— ❧ ————

"Claudine."

Susannah stood before this dark reflection of herself. She had never seen it before, as she did now: how much Claudine was like her.

Gant and Ogilvie were looking over curiously by now. Nicholas stared at Susannah. "Come, what is it?"

"Nothing. I—Nicholas, I know her."

"*Know* her," he repeated.

"How did you come here?" Claudine's voice was slow and dignified. She had changed little. She was still tall, still slender; her face, perhaps, had grown paler, whitened by the English climate or an herb vendor's fading creams. Her clothes were still surprisingly fresh, and her almond-shaped eyes were clear, unblinking.

"I came for a visit. I never knew . . . I never knew you'd be here. Why?" At Claudine's refusing stare, Susannah rushed on. "Never mind! Don't speak of it. There's no need."

"Susannah," Nicholas interrupted: for by now not

only his friends but all the women prisoners were looking on with unconcealed curiosity. "What is all this?"

"*Debt,*" pronounced Claudine suddenly, ignoring both Nicholas and her fellow prisoners, one of whom let out a hoot of derision.

"What? How much do you owe?" said Susannah. "We'll pay it, won't we, Nicholas?"

"Wha—" Nicholas began, backing away.

"Oh, but we must. Please. I swear I'll explain. How much, Claudine?"

"Well—" Claudine spoke with seeming reluctance, giving a nod toward the sullen jailor. "I owe 'im here thirteen pound."

"Thirteen pound! That's nothing. Nicholas—" Susannah turned to him with pleading eyes. "Please. Talk to the man. Give him what he wants. We cannot leave her."

"I don't understand. What is she to you? Is she a runaway servant, or—"

"Please. I promise I will explain. But not now. Please . . ."

Nicholas shrugged, and sent his friends on to explore the further reaches of the prison. The jailor gave Claudine a nasty look and came forward to make the exchange: not without some show of reluctance and a few shillings over the price. Then he shoved Claudine through the barred gate toward her redeemers. She stood for a moment, surveying both of them, but said nothing. Then she walked closer to Susannah. Her gaze took in the fine muslin of her dress and her blue cashmere cloak. Susannah seized her hands.

"What good fortune I came!" she said. "I almost did not. I couldn't bear . . . But at least you are quit of it!" She raised a hand to touch Claudine's hair, but the other woman drew back. "If you were in difficulties," said Susannah, letting go of her hands now, "you should have sent me word. Surely you knew where to find me. . . ."

Claudine looked at Susannah quizzically. " 'Twas no

trouble of yours," she said. "Leastways, I've the *gentleman* to thank."

And as Susannah stood, stunned into silence, Claudine glided over to Nicholas, who stood farther off, by a wall. She studied his coat and the new, tall riding boots he wore, hunting fashion, over trousers. She smiled. "I am indebted to you, sir. I do not wish to be. Tell me your address, and I will render you the money."

As she spoke, Susannah was reminded of Adela: of her lilting West Indian voice, of her herbs and lessons. For a moment she could almost smell the warm air of the Virginia kitchen. Then it was gone.

"Claudine," she interrupted. "Do you have a place to stay? You know, you might . . . come and live with me."

Claudine turned. "What, as your servant?"

"No. But in my house. It shouldn't matter, no one would notice." Stopping, knowing she had blurted out the wrong thing, she tried to repair her words. "I live alone, so there are a score of empty rooms. . . ."

"What? I thought you was married." Claudine tilted her head, glancing at Nicholas, and then back at her. For the first time, she looked curious.

"Yes. But I . . ." Susannah fumbled for words to explain.

"But you know 'twould not arrange well." Claudine smiled. "You remember how we fought, when we were children. . . ."

"Then where will you go?"

"I've a place with friends, at Covent Garden."

Covent Garden: the district of theaters, of gaming houses and cheap lodgings. Susannah wondered how Claudine had come there. And what—she wondered, as Claudine moved away—what had happened to Farquhar? The blond, grinning second mate of the *Rosaline* . . .

Nicholas was smiling at the dark girl with a kind of complicity, saying, "—Blackcroft House, in Great Russell Street. Will you ride along with us?"

"No. No, thank you." Her eyes wary, Claudine

backed away from Susannah and Nicholas. "I must gather my things from here first. I do"—she gave a half smile—"have a few things to my name." She turned her back and started down the corridor.

"Claudine!" Susannah called. Suddenly there were so many things she wanted to know of her. What had happened to Farquhar? And did she ever miss home?

Without answering, Claudine moved around a corner and out of sight.

"Well?"

Nicholas pulled Susannah closer on the seat of the open coach. Tom Gant, Lydia, and Sarah had just descended. Up front, Anthony drove the horses on at his habitual, ferocious speed.

They were alone. Lifting Susannah's hand up in his, Nicholas kissed the tip of each finger, one by one. His eyes lingered on her face, and she felt her skin flush, her lips move to meet his, almost of their own accord.

Smiling, Nicholas spoke suddenly, in mock reprimand. "You know what you must tell me."

Susannah looked down.

"Who is this Claudine? And why did I pay thirteen guineas to put her back on the Strand?" He gave her fingers another kiss, and a nip. "My dearest, profligate little one."

Susannah pulled back. "On the Strand? What do you mean?"

Nicholas chuckled and ran a hand across the clothed curve of her breast. "Why, surely you didn't believe her tale of debt."

"Yes. Why, many people are in debt! Valerie and—"

"Susan, dearest. Your Claudine is a street whore."

"But—" Susannah shook her head, unbelieving.

"Of course," he said, "after a few days in Bridewell she owed the jailer."

Still his hands persisted, one stroking her palm, one twirling its thumb about her breast, and she struggled to keep her composure. Anthony, to her relief, did not turn round. "What you say," she protested, "cannot be true! It means—"

Nicholas shrugged. "Honest-enough profession. P'raps she'll move up in the world—like Valerie."

"Valerie!" Susannah protested. Why, Valerie was different. Sir George loved her. Surely he did. . . . "Claudine says she is my sister," she said weakly, at last.

Nicholas was nonplussed. "You must mean your half sister."

She nodded.

"I don't quite understand." Nicholas's voice was placid, deliberate. For a time his hands came to rest, and she told the whole, hateful story: of childhood, the sea voyage, Claudine's revelation.

When she was done, he said only, "I can see why she bears you a grudge."

"But I did nothing to deserve it." Susannah kissed the fingers that lay, now, twined in the curls of her hair. "How am I to blame, if—"

"Shh." He stroked her cheek. "Who said anything of blame? But I *know*, Susan, what 'tis, to be on the wrong side of family favor. When my cousin Rupert was alive, rest his soul, I didn't stand to get a penny from my grandfather. . . . Why, 'tis a shaming thing! To be put out of inheritance . . ."

"But there was nothing to inherit! And I hate the thought so. That Adela"—she fought a tightness in her throat—"was Father's mistress."

"But all men have mistresses." Nicholas smiled. "Which reminds me. Am I to descend here?"

Susannah looked out and around her, as she had not in some minutes. The carriage was crossing Hanover Square. "I wish—" she said, shaking her head. She knew she dared not risk it. Nicholas had come to her house already too often. She did not know how far she could trust her servants, so many of whom had until lately been Maria's.

"It is the same," Nicholas murmured, "at Great Russell Street." The coach had stopped. He looked hard at her. He wanted her, she knew. And there was no place. . . .

Valerie's rooms, perhaps: but Susannah didn't know when she might feel brave enough to ask her. Nicholas had promised to find them a place of their own. But she did not know how long that would take.

He climbed down, and taking her hand, formally, to help her from the coach, he spoke again, in a louder voice—perhaps to amuse himself, or Anthony. She could not tell.

"As to whores," he said, "think no more of them! For dissipation most oft loses them *all* their powers."

Claudine threw back her head and laughed as she stepped outside. She clutched her sides, her hair tumbling forward, and the laughter seized her lungs and would not stop. Far too long, it had been pent up inside her. Far too long, that jailor had taunted her and all the other girls, calling them poxy whores, strumpets, Jezebels. . . .

So now, at last, she had shouted back, as the jail door clanked shut behind her. *You'd not get e'en a whore to bed with you, never!* And she had cursed and shouted, and then she began to laugh. She was free.

Though the Bridewell lay some two miles from Covent Garden, she relished the walk. Her heels sank deep in the mud of Tothill fields. She thought the sky had grown wider, the ground below broader, more generous and capacious since she had last seen the outdoors. For though she had been inside the Bridewell barely a week, it seemed an eternity. Her few months' sentence was of little account to the jailor; it was he who governed all privileges and releases, he who totted up her debts—for blankets, extra food, a few hours' sunshine in the yard. He who had sold her freedom for thirteen guineas.

And cheap, at that, she thought, smiling now at passing waves of boys and peddlers as the mud path turned to Tuthill, and then into Parliament Street. Even the murky Thames to her right seemed to glitter in the sunlight. She sauntered down the middle of the road, her wooden heels clicking on the cobblestones—

sidling away only when she heard hooves drumming behind her. And then she would stand by, looking up at the coach-and-four or coach-and-six as it passed, peering into the windows to seek the faces of its passengers. Sometimes she would spot an old customer; and sometimes a prospective customer would spot her. Her dark skin, she knew, was an advantage in that. She remembered a man in satin shoes who had once run up to her, whispering, "You're the one . . . saw from my coach! You're the one! Must come with me." If they had troubles, perversions, obsessions, she reasoned—it was their own affair. That man had been worth fifteen guineas: she'd spotted it in the shoes.

Of course most of them weren't good for much: a toss and a shilling. And the walking was a bedraggling business. Up all night, out in the cold, in the rain . . . If Rattray'd had his scurvy way, she would never have had two hours' sleep together.

Rattray had followed Sparrow, who had followed Farquhar, after he left her. The memory of it crossed her briefly, like a shadow. And then—what was she to do, with him gone? Be a servant, worn to the bone, like her mother?

No. The only way was whoring. And whores got lucky, too, betimes.

Nicholas Carrick! She mouthed the name as she walked along, her shawl sliding from her shoulders, showing skin the color of milk tea. Her hips swung from side to side. Just past Charing Cross she noticed an apprentice in leathern breeches following at her heels. A customer, but she threw him off. "Varlet! Begone, you mistake yourself."

For today—her day of good fortune—she would bear no trafficking with poor 'prentices. For soon she would be nearing her money. Then, going to Carrick . . .

Scarcely could you hear of Drury Lane without hearing of Carrick. Carrick's *Two in the Game*, his *Good Husband* . . . She wondered briefly how Susannah had come to be with him. Was she his mistress? Claudine giggled, covering her mouth with one hand: her crooked teeth had never been her best feature, and jail could not have done the reek of them any good. Silly goose Susannah, the mistress of a man like that! She didn't deserve him. With all the luck *she* was born to, she probably had a rich husband somewhere, too. . . .

The Good Husband! she thought, with another laugh. *That Carrick ought to know* . . . She could guess from the way he'd looked at her that he appreciated women. And only a fear for the state of her looks had kept her from eyeing him right back. But she knew how she would see him again: his thirteen guineas. Her freedom money. Once she fetched her savings, she'd buy a fine silk dress and new shoes and hire a carriage to take her to Great Russell Street, to repay him. . . .

She would be an actress. Carrick would surely help her to the stage, once she showed him what she could do: why, hadn't the boys all applauded her on the *Rosaline*? And an actress had her pick of keepers. She'd move from officers to knights, to barons and earls. She'd be carried about in a sedan chair or her own velvet-lined carriage. In a year's time her velvet slipper mightn't deign to touch the pavements. . . .

The piazza opened up before her at the end of Henrietta Street—it never changed. There were the fruit and flower sellers, the scrap-tin men, the pickpockets. She could pick *them* out, to be sure: darting through the crowds, their faces black as sweeps'—as sooty as the housefronts of this Covent Garden. Claudine knew better than to pity them: why, she'd worked hard to be better than they. Whenever *she* plucked a sooty hand from her pocket, she showed them. She'd slap the pickpocket's face, with a curse so high and continual that all the street sellers gathered round to hear.

Weaving her way to her side of the piazza, Claudine thought: *what a deal of things I've learnt, here in London.* She moved under a brick archway, through a narrow door, where, inside, an even narrower stair wound through the defunct entrance hall of what had once been a nobleman's house.

She kept away from the walls, for damp trickled

down their rotting paper. It took some courage to climb up by herself: for she knew that Jack Shaddock, Rattray's friend, often waited at the stair turnings to cosh comers in the head for their purses. And she did not know, just now, how she'd stand with Jack. She climbed the third steep flight and came to her door. *Strange.* It stood ajar.

She waited for a moment on the threshold, catching her breath. Usually the room was tight closed: this time of day her friends, Bett and Clary, would be sleeping. But now she could see right through the room to the far windows—where before, curtains and leaning Japanned screens divided it in three. The sun cast stripes across the dusty floor. Claudine pushed the door farther open and stepped, catlike, inside. She would not stay. Something was wrong here. With fleeting steps she crossed the floor and stood before the fireplace, counting.

The walls of the room were covered in squares of dark oaken paneling, divided by raised bars. It had been fifty years since anyone had lived in this place as a house entire, or cared for it, so all the wood had begun to rot with damp, or to dry and crumble in the sunlight.

Claudine fixed her sights on the right-hand corner of the mantel. There was a device, but with the room bare she was no longer sure she remembered it. *Over three and up two . . . Over two and up three . . .*

The square was just level with her head. Digging her nails into the soft wood, she gave the raised bars around it a tug.

The panel fell to the floor with a clatter that made her heart thump. She reached inside the hole in the wall and drew out a leather sack. No one had known her hiding place: not even Bett and Clary. In jail she had not dared send for it, for sure as hellfire it would disappear, while she went on rotting in Bridewell.

Fifty guineas. She worked the top of the sack open, just to make sure they were there. In her hands she had the price of a silken gown and coat—a seat at Drury Lane, and countless coach rides across London.

In the last two years she had cheated Rattray of this much. A gold two-guinea piece gleamed in her hand, plump and beautiful. There was the king, with his double chin and curls. Those strange words, which she mouthed now: *GEORGIUS III DEI GRA . . .*

She heard the steps coming up behind her. But by now it was too late to escape.

"Ha! Claudie Hamilton. G'*day*, Claudie Hamilton."

She didn't need to turn and look. She knew the voice. That had been the name she adopted on coming to London—Hamilton. She had thought it elegant. . . .

Calmly, not turning, not looking, she tipped the sack of coins into her bodice. They landed in a lump below her breasts, where they dug into her skin. Some of them ran through her gown and fell to the ground. She didn't know whether to reach for them or run, and as she spun around, she knew she could do neither. Rattray was there, with a knife.

He smiled and his teeth, of finest African ivory, gleamed brightly. He was a short man, with black hair and a jutting jaw.

"Back with us noo, are ye, Claudie Hamilton?"

She tried to duck to the side, and around him. But with a swift move he grabbed her wrists and pinned them to the wall. The handle of his knife pressed into her palm. Claudine blinked and tried to show no fear. And thought, *He has not enough hands to keep hold of me.*

She spat out, "A fine turn you served me, letting me rot in jail!"

"Ye stole from me—" Rattray's voice was low and menacing.

"Aye, and who wouldn't? We hadn't none of us decent to live on!" Claudine's eyes flickered from Rattray's knife hand to his groin and her knee below. She kept up the stream of words. "You were a bleeding thief, Rattray! Living on the wages of starvin' girls . . . It's no wonder you can't keep hold of 'em, stinking mean cowheep you are! I'd never work for you again, long as I live—"

"Shut yerself, woman." Rattray's bloodshot eyes

widened, and he bared his teeth. "This time ye're going to mind me. An' mind me weel."

"Never!"

"Ye will. And I'll have what ye saved out on me froom befoor." Rattray raised his knife hand and quickly replaced it with his elbow. Claudine twisted her body sideways, ready to break away, but at once felt the knife-point at her chest. It worked a steady line, as if in practice, down the front of her bodice. Towards her fifty guineas: and right now she thought she loved them more than she cared for herself.

"Do what you want!" she cried out. "You're not having 'em!"

"Oh, aye. That I am." Rattray smiled, scraping the knife point over her ribs. The cloth of her dress began to tear, and a shilling piece clinked to the ground. "I'm having yer money," said Rattray, almost pensively, "and I'm having you, back. Ye know, ye were my best money mill exceptin'—" He paused, with a placid look on his face: which gave way only slowly to pain, as, struck down below with all the force Claudine could work into one knee, then the other, he clutched his breeches and crumpled to the ground. His knife fell to the floor, unheeded, and Claudine stepped around him and picked it up. She held it out in front of her with both hands as she backed out of the room. Coins spilled out of the gash in her dress, onto the floor. Rattray was snarling, beginning to stand.

"Don't you come near me!" Claudine's voice rose to a scream. "Or I'll run this through you, I will! I don't know what you did with Bett and Clary—dirty poxmonger! God damn you to hell—you won't do it with me!" She backed out through the doorway, her knuckles rigid around the knife handle. No one could wrest it from her. *Let him try.*

But Rattray was standing. He staggered forward. Claudine knew she had been a fool to stand there, cursing him. She picked up her skirts and fled.

Everywhere she ran, she scattered coins. If she bent to pick them up, the hole in her bodice only gaped wider, casting more of them down on the pavement. She clutched Rattray's knife to her stomach, below her shawl, trying to keep it hidden and stem the flow of coins. But the farther she ran, the more it cut her dress and scraped her hands. Night was falling, the Strand turning to a black, sinister alley. There were streetlamps, watchmen, of course: but the wisest of them stayed indoors and let the poor devils on the streets run their own risks. If a cutpurse spotted her gold, she'd be done in with the knife and forgotten. London was an evil place. No one knew that better than she. What had been her home was gone now, as was all trace of her friends. All the steps she heard behind her she was sure were Rattray's. He might be lurking, waiting. . . . She thought she might cast up at an inn: but she was afraid. If she stopped too near, too soon, he might still find her.

"Miss—" A wheedling voice drifted from a window above her. She jumped sideways, to the middle of the street, nearly knocking over a fishwife. The woman pounded her on the back and let out a curse. Claudine knew it was mad: this running frenzy. The man in the window couldn't be Rattray. But, pressing the knife closer with frozen hands, she ran ahead.

Twice on her way in toward the warren streets of the City, she thought she heard steps following her; and twice she flattened herself against alley walls, praying they would pass. And they did. Ahead, high above the roofs of tenements, gleamed the lantern of St. Paul's. Her sides ached, and she did not know how much farther she could go. Often she had trawled for custom near Blackfriars Bridge; she might go there, except . . . what man she met would give her shelter? What protection, but for five minutes, on the bridge or in an alley corner? At least from the bridge she might cast her eyes about and be sure he wasn't near. Clutching her ribs against their aching—she thought the money had nearly all gone—she wandered down the next lane on her right, toward Paul's Wharf.

"Pssht," a voice called after her. She turned on it, ready to run.

"Pssht!" It came again.

"Who are you? Leave me be."

A thin figure in a cloth cap, a boy, detached himself from a doorway and sauntered up closer.

"Poorly devil you are, too!" said Claudine. "Pestering ladies this hour o' the night. What d'you want?"

The boy touched his cap and gave the beginning of a bow. Claudine noticed now that a limp yellow feather projected from his hat. *Poor cad, he must think himself a dandy*. "Well? Speak up, I can't bide here all night."

" 'Tis a fine evening," said the boy, with more self-command than she expected. He straightened his back and walked ahead of her toward the wharf and lightless Thames. "Ye'll be working for yourself, I suppose."

A *pimp*, thought Claudine. Well, she'd have no more to do with them. "Aye," she said, following warily, "and no other."

"Well, then." The boy stretched both arms out before him, cracking his knuckles and giving Claudine an appraising glance. She noticed him raise his eyebrows but did not think to look down where he had, at her bloody hands and bodice. "Run from the law?" he said. "I could help you. D'ye hear tell of Mrs. Inverness?"

Stunned, Claudine drew to a halt. Mrs. Inverness was the richest madam in the city of London! But before she began to smile with pride, she grew suspicious. "Her!" she said. "What'll a poorly lousebag like you know of *her*?"

"She's me very mother! Mind your mouth, wench."

"The one such as keeps the house?" Claudine's mind was working. If the boy spoke truth—why, this was almost as good luck as meeting Carrick. She'd be safe inside a house—and rich. Rattray wouldn't be able to touch her.

"The one such as keeps the house!" the boy scoffed. Turning back toward the cathedral, he picked a half crown up off the pavement and tossed it casually in the air. "Aye, such a house as there might be room in. Are you coming?"

*   *   *

Mrs. Inverness was not her real name, of course.
She had named herself after that Scotch city because
she liked the sound of it; but she had grown to old
age, and earned her fortune, without setting foot outside London. Her house in Red Lion Square had no
name or number, but a password: at whose sound,
through the keyhole, one of her girls, dressed as a
chambermaid, would leap to the door. When the pa-
tron was admitted to the dining room, the other girls
flocked round to see how they could serve him. Mrs.
Inverness particularly prided herself on her variety.
Her girls ranged from the palest of blondes to a lithe
and scowling Creole (or so she called her). But on
occasion there were gentlemen whom nothing in all
her vast range could tempt.

"G'd help us, man!" spat Tom Gant. "What's your
trouble?"

"Trouble?" Ogilvie's eyes were glassy. "I've no troubles."

"So much the better then! Make a choice."

"In time, my man." Ogilvie tapped the arm of his
sofa. "In time."

The women moved about them, some bold and
cheery in their low-cut, well-bolstered gowns; some
meeker, lowering their eyelashes over consumptive
cheeks transparent as gauze. A girl in a red gown,
with bright red lips, leaned over Ogilvie. For a second
her skin, warm as if with fever, touched his. He pulled
away. "Why—" he began, draining his glass, "—why
did Carrick not come?"

Gant grinned. He stared into the cleavage that appeared above him and hazarded a kiss. "It would seem,"
he said slowly, "that his new mistress sates him."

"What, does she keep him under lock and key?"

"No, man—indeed, he grows unnatural steady."
Gant was staring at the curtained doorway of the par-

lor. His eyes bulged. "Now *there's* something might distract him . . . Say, have we seen her?"

Ogilvie looked up, frowning, and they both puzzled for a moment at the new girl, who, with her wild hair and dusky skin, did look oddly familiar. But if they had seen her before, neither remembered where.

A pale, bug-eyed young man wearing a turban had followed the girl in, and now, as he beat on the drum in his lap, the girl's hips began to sway: at first gently, as if a wind blew them. The gauze that covered her legs turned transparent in the candlelight. She unwound the sash around her waist as the drumbeats gathered speed, looking at once sensual and utterly bored.

"If that don't wake her up, *I* will!" cried Gant, rising in his seat. But the girl with red lips had approached him and nudged him down again on the sofa, with a pout. "Well, what matter," Gant murmured, and hugged the girl in red closer.

Though Ogilvie frowned at the scene, as if in thought, his eyes grew wider. A girl had settled on his knee, but he stared past her; and in time she left him for a boisterous Irishman in the corner. He was content to watch the dancer, whose eyes, for a second, met his. She spun faster to the drumbeats, arms circling, hips twitching. She reached to unfasten her short, gold-embroidered jacket, and now her brown-tipped, girlish breasts were on display. She shed her trousers, and danced naked. At the far end of the room a pale blonde was undressing; the Irishman descended on top of her. Gant was burying his face in the red-gowned woman's bosom. Another couple writhed, still fully dressed, on the floor, and yet another made for the stairs and privacy. Ogilvie only watched the dancer, with the shade of a smile on his lips. But when the drumbeats halted, she picked up her clothing and left.

Claudine stamped down the passage toward the stairs, wiping an arm across her damp forehead. *Over! Thank the Lord.* Just let the old lady try to keep her from her bed.

Mrs. Inverness's son, still in his turban, jumped up to follow her. He was the watchdog of the house, strangely impervious to female charms. "Claudie!" he called, in a pettish voice. "Wait! Me mother'll want a word—"

"Let '*er* find me, then," answered Claudine. She walked on down the brocaded corridor. She had had more than enough of Mrs. Inverness's whims. A pretty penny she'd make, working here! Of the eighteen guineas she'd had left after her flight from Covent Garden, all but five had gone to pay for her food here, and the new clothes the old lady insisted she have. She had to pay board, linen laundry, part share of the wages for the drab who cleaned the house. . . . At this rate she'd never be fit to go and see Nicholas Carrick.

"Wait," the boy's whine followed her; then a more commanding voice joined in.

"Claudine!" Mrs. Inverness did not bother to wheedle. She was an enormous woman, square-faced and iron-haired, and seemed not only to keep a constant eye on the cashboxes in her front room, but on her customers. She clapped a hand on Claudine's shoulder. "A gentlemen wants to see you."

"Lud Christ! I've seen ten today—" Claudine stopped and cast a surly look, through her hair, at her employer.

"A partic'lar gentleman. 'E only wants you."

"Aye, so *you* tell it." Claudine felt Mrs. Inverness's hand digging uncomfortably into her arm. "Please, Mrs. Inver," she said, in a more wheedling voice. "I'm dead tired, so I am. An' with the flux running in the square—"

"Catch the flux or anything else, and you're out of here!" Mrs. Inverness's broad brow set into a grim line amid the ruffles of her cap. "Show 'er back to the parlor, Will."

Grumbling, Claudine went.

Pushing through the curtains again, she surveyed the room before her. It was dim and windowless, lit mainly by a roaring fire. Candle sconces dotted the red velvet walls, dripping their wax on the activities below. A red-faced young libertine and a roaring-drunk Irishman, Claudine saw, were making the most of the house's hospitality. The red-faced man was pumping into one girl, on a sofa, while trying to keep another one standing by, amused with his hand. The Irishman was telling his girl a story as he lay on top of her—or that was what it sounded like—crying out intermittently, "Yo *ho!* Yo, *ho!*" The girl giggled and simpered, feigning merriment. Just as Claudine knew she would, in her place: only better. . . .

The sandy-haired man she had seen watching her, earlier, sat, dazed and motionless, on his sofa. He must be the one Mrs. Inverness meant. But as she approached, he only stared at her, just as he stared at the couplings in front of him. Claudine knelt beside him and took his hands. "What would you have me do?"

"I don't know." But slowly the man pulled himself straighter. A fringe of blond hair fell in front of his eyes, and, not bothering to brush it back, he smiled. "Sit in my lap," he said in a hazy voice.

She sat down, and while her buttocks worked against his still-limp member, she examined his stockings and shoes. Clock-patterned silk and silver buckles. His breeches were of fine, thin brown wool. *A real gentleman.* She smiled as he moved his hands over her hips. And she slid down his legs and knelt on the ground before him.

A few seconds later she looked back, for he had not come to join her. *How queer.* He only leaned forward, staring at her, with an expression of puzzlement. Of terror.

"Well, come then," she said. But he shook his head.

"Then I will!" cried another voice, from the middle of the room. "And come again!"

"Tommy—" The nobleman shook his head, smiling weakly at his red-faced friend, who, rising from his current labors, was approaching. "Tommy, you astound me. You've the powers of an ox."

"All the powers i' the world!" cried the red-faced man, his friend. He dropped to the carpet and took hold of Claudine's hips. "Watch this!" he cried.

And Ogilvie did.

*   *   *

A half hour later, Claudine crept out toward the hall. Some of the gentlemen had gone, some dozed, and the rest lay in a drunken, sated state indistinguishable from sleep, the shrunken worms of their cocks dribbling and drooping.

"Coming up?" another girl whispered to her, collecting her red dress from the floor.

Examining Ogilvie, and his silver shoe buckles, again, Claudine shook her head. "Soon," she whispered. She would be the last to stay behind. She walked around the walls, pinching out all the candle flames but one. She knew that if she were caught, that would be the end of her here. _But how else will I ever get out?_

She had snatched locks of the customers' hair before, for Mrs. Inverness's collection. Dukes' hair, ambassadors' hair—even a prime minister's hair—lay tied and numbered in a box in the front room. But the old lady kept the book that connected the numbers to names locked away. She would divulge nothing: "Till death part me from my secrets," she said.

Aye, till death part me from my secrets, thought Claudine. Kneeling in the near darkness, she felt for the coats of the two men sleeping nearest: her own polite gentleman and his red-faced friend. The red-faced man's yielded up nothing; but the pocket of the nobleman was heavy with coins. Gold coins, some of them; and she counted out five. She had no place to store them away. She was naked, and her Turkish costume was too flimsy to hide them in. And her mouth . . . no, if she needed to speak, it was too uncertain. She knelt again on the floor, stifling laughter, and slid them deep into the one place she could think of. She stood and gave a hop on the carpet. Nothing fell. _Saint George!_ she swore to herself. _A gentleman_ . . . A gentleman in the house, and none too soon. Maybe her luck was changing.

Chapter 15

———— ✿ ————

Susannah climbed the stair to the top of the tall, narrow house. "Southampton Street, 3d House on L., at the top," Nicholas's note had said. For two weeks they had been denied each other, meeting only quickly, chastely at her door, communicating otherwise through messages delivered by servants. Now Nicholas must have found it: their place, which he had promised for so long. But what was it? A garret?

As she went farther up, the steps grew narrower and more treacherous, ending, at last, before a low door. She turned the key that waited in its lock. "What're we to live in?" she called out playfully. "A rooks' nest?"

Then her eyes fixed for the first time on what was before her, and her tongue was stilled. The room so overflowed with mirrors, draperies, and carpets that she could not take it all in at once. Dark red brocade covered the wide bed in the corner and hung over the windows, its warm tones reflected in the Turkey carpets on the floor. She tiptoed across and opened the next door. The tiny dining chamber just held a table

for two. On one wall there was a tall mirror, and on
the others, paintings of cherubs, flowers, feasts of fruit
and wine.

"Nicholas!" She nearly stamped with impatience.
"Come, I know you're here! However did you come
at this?"

But no answer came. She walked back to the first
room, whose two windows looked west across the roofs
of Southampton Street. She stood, watching the
pinkish-gray light of sunset through the flawed glass,
and near-silent steps came up behind her, from the
doorway. Nicholas's arms slid round her waist.

"How did I find it?" he whispered into her ear.
" 'Twas the greatest luck. Mrs. Dartwood, the actress
in *Love's Perfidy*, left not a week since, to go and live
with Killburn."

"May they be happy forever!" Susannah turned,
pressing her cheek against his coat. "For I know *we*
shall be."

"Yes. Yes, of course, my pet." Nicholas slid out of
her embrace and went to lock the door. And if there
had been some hesitancy in his voice, it was gone now,
as he took her hands, dark eyes twinkling. "Now, my
pet, I shall ravish you till you tire of me. Nay—until
you collapse from very exhaustion."

"I don't tire so easily," said Susannah. "Why, once
I used to ride all day without—" Nicholas laughed,
and stopped her words with kisses.

"Come by the fire," he said. The flames, below the
painted Dutch tiles, were roaring. Holding her hands,
he brought her down to her knees, pulling at the ties
at the back of her bodice. It fell to the floor, as did
her skirt. "These"—he pulled her close—"are *our*
rooms. And what we do in them no one will know.
Will you remember that?"

Susannah nodded, wondering why he spoke so, but
still the voice went on, low and hypnotic.

"And you are Mrs. Temple. Remember. Should our
landlady ask, that is the name I have given for us."

She nodded quickly again, understanding the
words, letting them pass, watching the curl of Nicho-

las's lips as he spoke, feeling his hands throw off the
last of her petticoats and close around her waist.

"Here," he said, "we can possess each other when—
how—we wish. Think on that. At last. There is nothing forbidden."

His words coursed into her ear, and down through
her, to a tingling place in her spine. *Nothing forbidden.*

"Let me take off the rest," he said.

They sat on the carpet in the light of the fire, and
he untied the ribbons of her chemise. Leaning down,
he kissed the pink tips of her breasts, as he had that
time before. For a moment she felt shy at her nakedness. But his lips worked against her, not letting her
think, his mouth widening to take in more of her, his
tongue sliding, flickering. And when he drew himself
away, kissing her lightly on the lips, she ached all the
more for his slowness, his remove. She thrust her body
toward him, falling back beneath him to the floor.

He untied her garters and her stockings fell, and
now his kisses lit along the insides of her thighs. He
leaned up on his elbow, his fingers stroking the red-
brown hair of her sex.

"Don't look," she said.

"Why not?" He caught her by the waist before she
could move away. He wet his fingers with his tongue,
and thrust them in between her tight-closed legs. "You
will not stay that way." He laughed with narrowed
eyes. "Before we have done, I shall see it all, I warrant. What do you wager me?"

His fingers stroked and slid. They reached inside
her, and somehow she could not stop him, for their
path had grown slick and moist.

"You want me now." There was a kind of triumph
in his voice. "Now." She felt her legs loosen, and his
member slipped inside her.

She opened her eyes, realizing only now that they
had been screwed tightly shut; and she saw Nicholas's
dark gaze, intent on her face, yet not moving, shifting, as she smiled and tried to speak. He looked down,
a slow, lazy smile spread across his lips, yet she knew,

somehow, it was not because of her. He was in the grip of this act, which possessed him. His body moved ever more quickly against hers, stabbing, sharp and fast, ever faster, and not ceasing. She felt her body push up against his, and her sex fill with a strange throbbing. Then she seemed to melt away. Her skin was hot, and her body below a widening lake. She could scarcely feel his motions anymore; yet still he stayed inside her.

"You have done?" she whispered.

"Nay." He smiled. "I shall go a long time yet." And suddenly he gripped her shoulders and pulled his body, hard, up against hers. And somehow, again, she could feel him inside her, when he began that fierce, quick motion. And she was glad.

She had fallen into a drifting sleep, her body covered by Nicholas's own, in the fire's heat. And she felt a sharp cold on awaking. She looked around. "Where . . . are my clothes?"

"Does the fire not warm you?"

Nicholas sat near her, on the floor, bare-legged, in his white shirt.

Susannah sat up. Her hair fell and half covered her. "Come. Where are they?" She looked around and still did not see her gown or petticoats.

"I have locked them away," said Nicholas with a mischievous look. "You have no need of them. We shall be warm enough here to go naked."

"What?" Susannah giggled. She did not believe him. "What folly! As if we were . . . Amazons." She got up on her knees and began to peer around for her lost garments.

"No! I am quite serious." He stopped her, holding her two hands fast, and as she looked up shyly, caught in his gaze, he went on. "You shall have them back when the time comes. And until then, you shall learn to be at ease with being looked at."

Something in his intent gaze on her made her want to curl away: as if his look had penetrated the red-brown hair that fell across her breasts and barely covered her; as if, should he want them to, his eyes could even penetrate inside her.

"You cannot," she said, grown suddenly ashamed, pulling her hands away from his, curling into a ball. She did not like to be seen so: naked. It reminded her of that cold room at The Marches, of Harry; and even the stifling heat here could not overcome it.

Nicholas stood and pulled her to her feet. "But see yourself," he said. Four mirrors on the walls around them cast back their own reflection: he, in his white shirt, and she, all roundness and dark spaces.

She cowered against him. "I don't like to look. It is ugly."

"Why?" His voice surprised her with its gentleness.

"It isn't . . . white, like the statues."

Nicholas laughed, squeezing her arms in his hands. "Have you ne'er looked at other ladies? They're not like statues. Men shouldn't want them half so much if they were."

"But—I am sure the statues are prettier. All one color."

"All one color! I've a notion. . . . " Taken with an idea, Carrick the dramatist began to search the room. "Mrs. Dartwood must have left something," he murmured, searching the mantelpiece, the cupboards, the dressing table. At last he came upon it: pots of color and powder. "Paint! Now come to me," he said. And when Susannah approached, wondering, he began to work away. He threw powder onto the fur between her legs until it was light brown and the air was filled with dust. Then, with the intent look of a little boy at play, he went to work on her nipples, daubing them till they were nearly as light as the rest of her, and then, laughing, powdering her breasts, her shoulders—her whole body. "There," he said. "Call me Pygmalion."

Susannah looked in the mirrors now; her body was an even whitish-pink. When the strange dark colors of it were covered, she actually liked the shape of her body: it *was* round and generous, like a statue.

"Well"—Nicholas gave a shrug—"I happen to prefer the look of nature. But if you are pleased . . . I'll see to dinner." He pulled on his breeches and turned the key in the door of a wardrobe that Susannah suddenly knew contained her clothing. Leaping at him, she tried to grab his hand. But he pulled his fist away, closed tight. "Surely," he said, "Lady Susan, I've not gone to such trouble for nothing."

"But if we're to eat—" said Susannah, perturbed.

"I shall see to that!" His voice was merry. "Come, love. Trust me. I've made sure you shan't feel the cold."

"But—"

"There are your shoes," he said with a nod of his head toward a dark corner by the bed. "Put them on if you like. They make your legs look longer. And *here*—" He had come upon a wisp of gauze, a chemise left behind by Mrs. Dartwood. "Against the cold."

Susannah tried it on as he left. It was nearly as transparent as glass. And she waited. She felt terribly bare. She was not used to the air against her skin, its every breeze warming or cooling her. She felt aggrieved at Nicholas, for leaving her so: and powerless against him. Once—not two months ago—she had had her defenses: clothing, a fear of the eyes of society, and a wary suspicion. Now all those had gone; she was forgetting that she ever possessed them. The fire shone on her skin, and the mirrors reflected her. And she waited.

He came back with dinner, and would not abandon his own clothes. "Why?" he said, to her question. "Men's bodies scarce bear being looked at." She did not think so, later, when he undressed and the firelight gilded his lean body. She did not think so at all, but she was not bold enough to speak it.

"It shall be delightful to make you wanton," Nicholas murmured, before falling asleep. And his voice seemed to course, low and certain, down her spine. "Then, you shall do anything. There shall be nothing—you will refuse. . . ."

And she did not doubt his words. He laid a hand

on the powdery, damp place between her legs, and, startled at first, she gradually grew used to her nakedness, her limbs easing, nearing sleep. It seemed a strange word: *wanton*. She had never thought it a word of compliment. And yet something in his voice made it seem a quality more desirable than any other. . . .

The next day they remained. They ate, and he would feed her while she closed her eyes: cakes and wine and sour, early oranges. "Look at me," he would say, and he would stare at her naked body and grow almost angry when she shied. *Look*, he said, but she would turn her head at last, lying back or standing as he told her, while his eyes devoured her.

"Try this," he said, now. "Close your eyes." He dipped a finger in wine, and wet her lips. And she sat back on the bed, smiling, for she liked this game better than the other; and now he stroked her hair, and pulled her head toward him.

"What is it?" she said. Her tongue reached something warm and salty, like skin. She could hear Nicholas's breathing, and smell his close scent. His legs grazed hers. "What—" she said. She looked up and let out a strangled, startled sound. "You—"

"Aye, go on."

"No, I—"

Nicholas stroked her hair, and pulled her closer.

"What do you mean? I've never—heard of such a thing."

He backed away, and knelt. Looking into her eyes, he said slowly, "There is more variety to love, Susan, than is dreamt of in your . . . *Lady's Book*."

"Yes." She smiled, at the name: at his remembering.

"Well? Do you want to know how to please a man, the way a grown woman does? Or not."

"Yes?" She stared down: it seemed to have grown bigger, higher.

"Only think: There is always more to be tried in the world than you have heard of."

When there came a knock on the door—Mrs. Hall or a mistaken neighbor—Nicholas would motion Susannah to the bed, where she hid beneath the covers. The interruptions were few and quickly gone. He warmed a basin of water at the fire and bathed her with a cloth; what was left of the powder on her body dripped down and dissolved in the water. She slipped his shirt away and bathed him too; water splashed onto the hearth, and hissed in the fire. The hours of the day blended together, the darkening and lightening of the sky signaling nothing, not even the passing of time: for it was as if they were removed, suspended above it.

As the darkness fell a second time, they faced each other across the spindly gilt table. The dining room had no fire, and Susannah's skin tingled with the unaccustomed cold. They finished the rabbit stew Mrs. Hall had brought, and began on the oranges. Nicholas poured sparkling cider into her glass. It fizzed like champagne as he lifted the table away. Now there was only empty space between them.

Susannah stopped drinking, startled.

"Go on, finish."

"I can't—now. You stare at me."

"Does it matter? I have before."

Susannah at last shook her head. Nicholas, in his silk dressing gown, regarded her, leaning forward, elbows on his knees. His eyes flickered from her hand, which tipped the glass, to her throat as she swallowed, and downward.

"Let your legs part," he whispered.

"Why?"

"Are you eternally asking 'why'?"

Susannah felt a tightness in her throat, and a curious excitement. She wondered what he would want now. He sounded so certain. When he was pleased, Nicholas was lionish, powerful. He seemed ready to embrace the whole world, and her. She longed for the rich sound of pleasure in his voice. To be absorbed in him: in that sureness, in that happiness . . .

She sank back in her chair now and did as he said.

"More." Nicholas knelt, taking her ankles in his hands, then her knees: pushing them farther apart, curling her feet around the chair's front legs.

Susannah felt the beginning of a "why" again, on her lips. Why did he want to look at that ugly redness? She looked to the side, her eyes half closed.

"Because I wish to." It was odd. She had not yet asked him the question. "Let your arms fall. Look at me. Yes. Your eyes. They are so very . . . blue." He moved forward, and his fingers brushed the fur of her sex, then stroked its nub of flesh—lightly, slowly. She felt a tremor, and he stroked faster. More than anything she wanted him inside her. But only his fingers entered her, twisting and flickering. Suddenly it was too much to bear, and she unwound her legs from the chair and wrapped them round him. She drew his body against hers and, not minding anymore that he looked on, so removed, let out a cry.

Other times he did not watch but lost himself in taking part. He would pull her closer, reach inside her until she thought there was no space in her he had not touched. He would fall back, groaning, half joking that she drove him to exhaustion, and return again. Late on the second night, near sleep at last, he lay still beside her.

She curled against him, hugging him. "Nicholas, I'm so happy! I love you so much." Her heart pounded strangely, now that the words were free, open in the air. He did not answer.

"What is wrong? Nicholas?"

"Don't give your heart too freely." He frowned, with his eyes closed. She did not know what to answer. And now he rose in bed, half smiling, kissing her hand. "*Reserve*, Lady Susan, is no bad thing."

"But you speak against it so! You—"

"I abhor *prudery*, my dear. A different thing."

"You don't love me." Susannah's voice was low.

"I have never said that. I . . ." Nicholas's eyes
seemed to search the room for words. "What, do you
have no faith in me?" he said suddenly. "Because I
don't act the City gallant and prate of love from my
first breath to my last?" His words grew quicker, his
tone merrier. "I say, why talk weakheartedly of con-
stancy when no lady'll be convinced? Of late we hear
naught but tedious tales of married love. . . ." Nicholas talked on, of gallants and ladies, stroking her back
and kissing her shoulders and hair. *Why, he must at
least feel a fondness for me,* she thought. And was
there so great a step between fondness and love?

Whatever the reason—their talk of the night before, or exhaustion (which Susannah, too, was beginning to feel)—Nicholas decided the next morning that
the time had come to leave. He opened the window,
which let in a blast of cold, smoky air, and tossed
Susannah's clothing, by now very wrinkled, onto the
bed.

Her dress and cloak felt strangely heavy; still, they
did not prepare her for the chill wind that rushed up
the outside stair. "Will you write me?" Nicholas said.
" 'Tis better I do not write you. We might come
here"—he sounded cautious—"Wednesday next?"

"Wednesday next! A week hence . . ." Susannah
couldn't keep the disappointment from her face.

Nicholas turned and took her hand. "Did we not
agree to be careful?"

"Yes, but—"

"Three days in hiding was scarce careful, little one.
You have appearances to maintain." He flashed her a
devilish smile. "So, you've a week to do it. But, I warrant you, no more!"

He let go of her hand at the door. They hurried up
the street to Covent Garden, where they found a
hackney cab.

During the ride Nicholas grew strangely thoughtful. "Perhaps you are right to talk of love," he mused,
breaking the silence. "I *write* of it such a great deal.

I think I should be grateful—to know quite what it is."

"Why, it is simple! It is—"

"No." He touched her lips. "Speak not of it until you are sure yourself."

The house at Hanover Square had managed to fall into neglect in only three days. Susannah found mail piled high on the hall table, and dust in hills on the stair carpets. There was a stink in the air of chamber pots, and now she learned that the elder housemaid, Mary, had run away (Ernestine vowed it was to elope), taking with her half the kitchen cookware.

Warwick, Ernestine, and the remaining chamber-maid, Peg, stared dolefully at Susannah as she came in the front door. None of them dared ask where she had been. Only Ernestine ventured to speak, while showing Susannah the empty pot hooks and bereft larder. "Oh, 'twon't do, m'lady. 'Twont do at all! her Ladyship gift us those pots just last year. . . . But you know, m'lady, we couldn't speak up—you away these three days, an' us not knowing where. . . . "

Somehow, rather absurdly, Susannah found herself patting Ernestine's calicoed shoulder and promising not to leave again, without warning: even though she knew perfectly well that Ernestine would have stopped Mary's absconding had she been awake and sober enough to do so. She wondered if all ladies found themselves under as much obligation to their servants as their servants were under to them. Heaving a great yawn as she went upstairs, she decided, yes, they must.

So the next days, rather against her will, were filled with business. She longed for Nicholas to visit or write, even though he had warned her he would not. Every bill she scanned seemed to demand a great effort of will. For minutes at a time, she would sit transfixed, staring into the dusty air as the ink dried on her quill. In the mornings a bar of sunlight crept across the room; she would lean back, closing her eyes, feeling it cross her bosom like stealthy hands. She imagined she was back at Southampton Street, by the fire—that the hands were Nicholas's—and felt her nipples grow hard under the cotton of her gown. She wanted to throw off her dress and stand naked in the sun, as she had, sometimes, at the garret windows.

But something would always call her back. Sometimes it would be the ink dripping onto her gown, or Peg or Knole. As the secretary talked to her, in his close-lipped, grinning way, she found her mind wandering again.

"New York?" she would ask, catching a word of his. Or, "Maria?"

And Knole would explain, again, the demands of each. It seemed Mr. Brown had found a new tenant for Susannah's house at Lispenard's Meadows; and Maria Cheveril had presented her with a bill from one Mr. Robert Adam.

Knole handed her the architect's account. "For Restorations Plann'd at Cheveril Wye House, Devon . . ."

"Three thousand, nine hundred and thirty-two pound?" read Susannah. For once, she was shaken completely from her reverie. "What has she done to the house, Knole? Why—does she even intend to live there?"

"I believe she will spend the month of July there, m'lady." Knole gave a dry cough.

"But why is this sent here? What's this to do with us?" Susannah's tone moved slowly from puzzlement to annoyance. "Every time she cannot pay a bill herself, she sends it here!"

"I believe," ventured Knole, "she has not had to live, before, under any constraint of income. . . . "

"She is not poor." Susannah's voice was sharp, but now she sighed and threw up her hands. "Mr. Adam is owed, all the same. What can we do but pay him?" Knole looked back at her, his face blank, shaking his head; then, her eyes brightening suddenly, Susannah said, "Or perhaps not."

"Perhaps not what, madam?"

"She might still pay *part*, out of her two thousand

a year. Say—five hundred pounds. After all, our income isn't endless, either."

Knole was silent, picking at the tip of his quill pen.

"Do you think me too harsh, Knole?" Susannah frowned, confused. For such great sums still swam in her head sometimes: enormous, yet—set against the Warrington wealth—of little importance. "After all," she said slowly, "It is but money."

"Only money! Dear—m'lady. It is the foundation of all decencies in life!"

"Indeed," said Susannah, beginning to laugh. "Then I shall write to my aunt, as I said." The image of Maria, in full spate of wrath, rose in her mind. She resolved to brave it. "I think," she said, "that I shall also write that we will pay *no more* of her debts."

She wrote and, with relief, began to see her pile of papers dwindle. She had sent Ernestine to buy new pots, and hired Peg's younger sister Sally as the new maid; now, she hoped, the house would be at peace again. Once she had done with these letters she would be able to read *Cyberion* at last, and the editions of Mr. Burns and Mr. Crabbe that she had bought. Then she would be able to talk to Nicholas about verse— about his work. Surely he would be pleased at that.

The garden path at the back of the Cheverils' house in Kensington led, among statues of sea nymphs and putti, to a miniature, moss-grown waterfall. Here Maria strolled, a hundred paces morning and night, to ease the soreness in her back.

"Jonas!" she cried out, delighted, one morning in April, as heavy steps sounded behind her on the path.

"Maria." Hench kissed her hand, beaming up like a hopeful puppy.

"Jonas, dear. I have considered. I think—we have serious business to do."

"What, pray?" he answered eagerly. Maria exchanged her walking cane for his arm.

"You remember," she said slowly, moving forward,

"that business in February—of which you informed me."

Hench stared at her.

"You *must* know. Susannah!" she snapped. "At that disreputable St. Valentine's—masque."

Hench drew back, surprised at her sudden ill humor, for he did not know of the letter, in Susannah's sprawling hand, that had accompanied the return of Maria's architect's bill: "I am advis'd that your finances, and Mr. Cheveril's, are wholy separate from ours. With all due respect, & c . . ." Maria heaved a damp sigh and raised one hand to her brow.

"Poor Lady Maria," said Hench, humbly. "How can I—"

"I *was*"—Maria lifted her chin proudly—"on the point of asking you . . . Ah! 'Twould be of no use, I suppose. . . . " She paused at the side of a mossy bench until Hench, with some reluctance, removed his coat to cover it. She sat, and squeezed his hand. "You move in such different *circles*, Jonas, than I. You are a man of the world: that is why I ask. You have greater powers than I of observation. . . . "

She paused delicately, but Hench did not seem to catch on.

"If you could but observe—what *Susannah* does, it would help me greatly. If you knew for instance, that she had formed—some indecent attachment. . . . "

"You mean—" Hench gave an uneasy chuckle. "You want me to be your—*hem!*—your spy? Your fee'd man?"

"I ask but little, Jonas. It would be simple for you."

This, he reflected, was true. To keep an eye alert, an ear open—it was not much. Though, as yet, Maria had given *him* little of what she had promised. The member for Bothwell, now seventy, hung heartily onto his Commons seat. . . .

"Of course you do not understand," Maria went on, in a sad voice. "What it is to be a woman—cut off from all gentlemanly society. . . . We know so little! What is more"—her tone turned elegiac—"James and I are promised to spend the summer in—Devon."

Devon. The name tolled on her lips. The outer counties of England were as the ends of the earth to Maria Cheveril. Bereft of London gossip, bereft of men but for her husband . . .

"Well—*hem!*" said Hench, at last. "Of course—I'd wish you satisfied. I'll do what I—" He coughed again.

"I knew you would understand." Maria's gaze was smooth and placid; she made no move from the mossy seat. Lately she had lost all patience with Susannah—and with her son. Something must be done to rid him of her, for his own good. And to that end, she had begun to make inquiries. She had quizzed her husband on the parliamentary mechanisms for divorce. "What! Are you wanting divorce from me?" Cheveril had answered, with a jocular smile. She had put him off the trail with a concocted tale about the Framers. Her letters to Henry had changed tone; they became sympathetic, conciliatory. For soon she hoped to show him proof: a name, to attach to Hench's lurid tale of the midnight masked ball. For Henry was ever one to insist on proof. But—once he had it, and was convinced . . . *divorce.* That distant quarry, like a fox hidden in woods, drew her on.

Susannah's efforts to talk of poetry with Nicholas did not succeed as she had hoped.

"What think you of Mr. Burns?" she asked him, the second time she came to Southampton Street. The afternoon sunlight streamed through the window where she stood, and Nicholas reached round her, stroking her breasts through the ice-blue silk of her jacket.

"Mr. Burns? Very little, i'fact. Why do you ask?"

"But—he is a Scotchman, like you. Does that not give you some . . . native sympathies?"

Loosing his hold, Nicholas came around to face Susannah, holding her hands. There was a perturbed twist to his mouth. "Have we come here to delight in love? Or merely to talk of my compatriot and his Scotch provincial fripperies?"

Susannah bowed her head. "May it not be both?"

"Dear Susan—no more tedious creature exists than the common bluestocking, who prates on poetics and lectures on high learning! Forgive me if I wish to preserve *you* from becoming one." He pulled her closer, planting kisses in her hair.

"But what is wrong in learning?" she said. "My cousin Augusta's vastly learned, and *she's* not dull. Her reading—'tis not to lecture people, but for her own amusement—"

"Does she amuse herself better than this?" Nicholas's voice was low and rolling. He reached up under Susannah's skirts, unfastening her petticoats. "Well? Does she? Or should she disapprove? . . ." His hand probed, fluttered between her legs. "Can any of that family of yours . . . know our own felicity?"

And she knew they could not. Sometimes it seemed to her that no one else—not even Valerie—could. She was so happy: Nicholas seemed to care so much for her now. He was always telling her what suited her well: which clothes, which expressions, which ways of making love. He must care about her a great deal, she thought, to take such time to make her what he termed his "ideal." And if he troubled so much to rout the disagreeable, the prudish, the serious from her nature—didn't that mean, in fact, that he loved her? *Harry never cared to change me,* she thought. And so she grew, week by week, more content to be instructed by Nicholas. He knew so much about the world that she would never have guessed: even her own repute, he knew how to preserve, for if he took care to withdraw from her in time, that—he said— would keep her from getting with child. It was true, he did not always manage it. And sometimes her own passion overcame caution. She clung to him—*I want his child,* she thought—and all the sense she managed, later, to recover could not rid her of the traces of that primitive urge. Often, though, she was glad she was without child: safe. She loved the meetings with Nicholas at Southampton Street, and writing the notes, twice or thrice weekly, to confirm them. Now that it was spring, she often journeyed there on foot, through Covent Garden. And she loved the swirling crowds there: the ever-changing, stylish, painted and ragged figures. The orange girls, the actors, the darting sweeps, and flower sellers. The cries—"Violets, daisies, pinks!"—and the colors overflowing in their baskets; the country scent of the nosegays she bought, which all too quickly died. Nicholas was always saying what a great number of the poor, and of pickpockets, there were in London. She did not believe it. Claudine, she remembered, had said she lived here, too; and often Susannah looked around, wondering if she would come upon her. But she never did.

One morning she walked to Valerie's house, carrying strawberries and violets from the market. She found her friend, unexpectedly, alone.

"Des fraises!" Valerie exclaimed, jumping up from her sofa and ringing for coffee. "Strawberries! Oh, where did you get them? The Covent Garden?"

Unpainted, with her hair hanging down her back, Valerie looked nearly the ingenue. She toyed with the coffee in its pot when it came, asking Susannah questions that she left her no time to answer. "Nicholas, they say he is vastly improved. Is it true?"

Puzzled, Susannah opened her mouth to answer.

"Oh, for he is a man—known as difficult. You know, I have never think he would be good for you." The Frenchwoman's forehead wrinkled as she floated cream in Susannah's coffee.

"Difficult? No . . ."

"Why, he is known as a man with—many up and downs. *Mélancolique* . . ."

"No! I am sure he is not," Susannah protested. She took a sip and winced at the bitterness of the coffee. "Why, I have known him near a month, and he has always been kind and cheerful. I've known him to be nothing else. Except—" She thought of the one time, long ago, that he had argued with her. But that was

long ago, on their first walk through London. And it
was about religion, which she had not mentioned to
him again. "I know nothing," she said now, more
firmly, "that would make me think ill of him. And
perhaps—you should know him better before you
speak so badly of him."

"You are surely loyal." Valerie gave a wry smile,
dipping the tip of a strawberry in cream. "You may
not think it, but with him you must always be watch-
ful. Other women—"

"I am sure there are none." The coffee burned in
Susannah's throat. She thought she could not swallow.

"Ah, well!" Valerie shrugged. "Per'aps." Sipping
from her cup, she began to pace the room. It was new
and bright, with a marble fireplace and chairs covered in white watered silk. Valerie, though, seemed
heedless of all her expensive new belongings: already
the sofa was coffee-stained, the flowers rotting in their
Chinese vases. She turned, drumming her fingers on
the back of the sofa. "And the *drogues*?"

"What?"

"The drugs, the medicines. Laudanum—"

Susannah looked up, wide-eyed. "What? You don't
mean he is ill."

"No!" Valerie allowed herself a ripple of laughter.
"No. They all take them, though—the drugs. Ogilvie,
the most of them. Opium, laudanum . . . To stir the
imagination."

"Nicholas's imagination needs no stirring!" Susannah stared at her friend, indignant. "Why, he is a
poet! I don't believe you. I don't know why you tell
me such things. I—"

"*Pauvre chérie.*" Valerie ran around the sofa and
sat down beside her. "Then you *are* in love. Oh, these
foolish English!"

"Why?" said Susannah. She stared, with blurred
sight, down at the remains of her coffee. "What is so
foolish in it?"

"You English! You are incapable of a *galanterie.*"
Valerie stroked Susannah's back, and shook her head.

"Sarah is the same, with Ogilvie. . . . But do you not see? You have a good husband. Surely you have no need to play at love! With other things, perhaps, *mais oui*, but—"

Susannah broke in, in a small voice. "I shall never love my husband. I love Nicholas."

Valerie studied her for a moment. Then, without speaking, she drained the cream pot over the last strawberry and offered it to Susannah. "You shall see, in time!" she said. "For me—I may confess you this— there is someone new."

"Oh?" The strawberry tasted sour and galling in Susannah's mouth. She spoke dully, as if by rote. "Who?"

"Have you met a young poet called Cyrius Brown?" As Susannah's head shook, Valerie went on. "I think I have found at last the perfect English gentleman! Oh, he has no money. I think true gentlemen never do. Fellsacre has money, and—" She gave a disinterested shrug.

"You would—leave Sir George?" said Susannah, surprised.

"Yes. If he is not content with it."

"But—the apartments—" Susannah did not know why, but she thought also of Fellsacre. She pitied him.

Valerie laughed. "The apartments! What matter, they are not mine. Nothing is. Every place I have live in has always been—provisory." She tossed her long hair, with a shrug so violent that it threw her ruffled gown off her shoulders. "Cyrius has promise me, he will take me away this summer, to the sea. His cousins are at Brighton, and—oh, so many lovely people!" Valerie stretched back, the sun crossing her forehead. She seemed to have forgotten all of her previous admonitions. "Then where will you go," she said, "this summer? You and Nicholas."

"Take me to one of those places you talk of," said Susannah, impulsively, a few days later. "The places in *Cyberion*. Crete, or Naples, or Seville . . ." The late sunset streaked the sky over the rooftops of Southampton Street. Susannah studied Nicholas's face as he looked out, one arm wrapped around her. The right, flawlessly handsome side of his face was to her; and, search as she might, she could see in that straight nose, that easy curl of the lips, no sign of melancholy: drugs, degeneration. *Whatever can Valerie mean?* she thought.

Nicholas laughed. "Why should you wish to go south? The men there would devour you whole. There are diseases—"

"I'm never ill."

Nicholas kissed her neck, unbuttoning her jacket. "Aye, you're young yet."

"You, too!" she said: for he seemed determined to believe the opposite. He still liked to talk of her as half his age, even though this June she would turn nineteen. "Let us go away, though," she persisted. "Out of London—"

Nicholas slipped the jacket off her arms. "All right, then," he said amiably. "We shall go to Bath."

Chapter 16

———— ❧ ————

The city was small, built of white-golden stone, in the hollow of a valley surrounded by high green hills. Susannah had only to look down, through the window of the post-chaise, to know that they were far indeed from London. From the road, Bath looked a clean, bright place, almost a miniature, shining in the last of the afternoon sun, while all around, farmers and horse carts worked the fertile hills.

"Look!" Susannah whispered to Nicholas, who sat still, his eyes half closed, beside her.

"My bones ache," he grumbled. "Damned rutted roads."

They rolled rapidly downhill and into the streets, and at the inn near Bath Abbey where the chaise stopped, and the other four passengers began to shift and gather their belongings, Nicholas only sat still, little interested in what was around him. When they climbed out, Susannah had barely time to glimpse the square abbey spire above the yellow-stone houses before Nicholas waved down a hackney coach and or-

dered it to The Circus. That was where Anthony
Ogilvie had taken a house for the summer.

Look, Susannah wanted to whisper again, at the
sight of the perfect circle of four-storied houses, all
alike, connected to each other by the long carved
friezes beneath their windows. They climbed the steps
of a house on the north side of The Circus, the driver
following behind with their trunks. In the front hall,
they heard violin music and laughter from a back
room, and the voices of what must be Anthony's other
guests; but they followed the housemaid directly upstairs, without stopping to see who was there. Soon
Anthony joined them for supper in their yellow-
papered bedroom; there seemed to be no more formal
meal planned, and all evening, well past midnight,
they heard voices, laughter, and steps in the corridor.

Susannah wanted to explore, to meet the others; but
Nicholas avowedly did not. They settled into their
bed, with its muslin summer curtains, and he could
not sleep. He paced across the floor, taking draughts
from the green bottle that had sustained him during
the ride.

" 'Tis age, set in, I know it," muttered the playwright.

"You're not old! Come here to me." Susannah
opened her arms and was glad when he nestled next
to her, for now something of affection—even of attachment—seemed to show in him. "There," she
whispered. "Now, sleep. There's naught in the world
to be anxious for. . . . "

Nicholas twitched in her arms and shook free. "Of
course there is. You know I've been a fool to bring
you here. Any day we might be discovered."

"Who'd discover us?" Susannah stroked his back. "I
know no one in Bath."

"Susan! Of a summer, the whole world's in Bath."

"What's the whole world to me?" said Susannah
cheerfully. She was no creature of "society" like her
aunt. . . . "Of course," she added now, "I shouldn't
like to see my aunt Maria. For she dislikes me all out
of reason. I think it's to do with her bills!" She gig-

gled. "Anyway"—she planted a kiss on Nicholas's shoulder—"I am sure she is in Devon."

By the next morning she had forgotten their talk and was eager to discover the city and its diversions: drinking spa water in the Pump Room, strolling the Orange Grove and the Parades, dancing at the evening assemblies, and, of course, soaking in the warm waters of the baths. She laughed at first as Lydia Cram, the red-haired actress who lodged with Tom Gant in the next-door chamber, explained their ritual.

"But whatever do they think it *does* for them?" wondered Susannah at the first sight of ladies and gentlemen bobbing like linen-draped corks in the King's Bath, which was surrounded by walls with sheltered niches but, on top, quite open to the air.

"The waters have powers to *heal*," answered Lydia, affronted. "Why, are you in such good health, child, that you dare laugh at others' infirmities?" Lydia claimed debilitating fainting spells and spent every morning in the Cross Bath. The other guests at Ogilvie's house were less regular in their attendance.

The house lay in one of Bath's newest quarters. The Circus, like the broader Royal Crescent, had been built to the grand outlines of a palace or coliseum: for Bath was a city of new buildings, a vision of classical design. Here, all was clean air and symmetry and splendor, with the dirty closes of London, and their inhabitants, by all appearances banished. The visitors to The Circus certainly could not see them. But when they climbed the spiraling stair of the Ogilvie house, they could see the sky.

Under the glassy cupola, off three tiers of winding steps, there were rooms: so many guest rooms that it took several days for Susannah to come to know their inhabitants. There was a long front salon, suitable for dancing, facing out onto the granite-paved center of The Circus. At the back of the house there was a circular library, its niches filled with marble nudes. There the guests gathered at night, following an assembly; or, failing an assembly, they met there to

while away the hours, the red damask curtains closed
against the darkening evening.

On their second night at the house, Susannah and
Nicholas penetrated this inner chamber. The candles
on the red-papered walls were few, and a dozen faces
seemed to beam out at Susannah in the half-light.
Ogilvie started to stumble toward her, but Tom Gant
took his place, calling out the names of faces she could
barely distinguish. There was a barrister, Beaton,
whose wigless head was bald as an egg; two bright-
painted actresses whose names she couldn't later remember; and a lithe, auburn-haired creature called
Nell Cameron, whose green gaze upon Nicholas put
Susannah instantly on her guard.

Tom Gant puffed and grew pinker in the face; his
woolly hair stood on end as he bellowed, "And now—
gentlemen, strumpets—what shall be our play?"

"Objection!" called Nicholas. "Susannah's no
strumpet but a free-spirited lady!"

Susannah reddened. The other women seemed not
to notice the words at all.

"Free-spirited lady then," shouted Gant, affably.
"What shall we play at? Attitudes?"

All the men applauded. The two actresses giggled.
The game seemed to involve each lady's disrobing,
piece by piece, as the men failed to guess what dramatic role she was playing.

"Bereavement!" a gentleman would call out, or,
"Plotting of vengeance!"

As the ladies wore so many layers of clothes, there
were great numbers of wrong guesses.

"Mourning the death of her lover!" called Nicholas,
once Nell Cameron was standing on the mahogany
table in only her transparent shift. Nell smiled, gazing
steadily at Nicholas, and tore it off, too. Gant clapped
loudly.

"It _wath_ mourning." Sarah Hutchings pouted below the table; she had been assigned the role of Nell's
confidante.

"Ne'er mind, ne'er mind!" said Tom Gant, as Nell,
still naked but for her stockings, jumped from the ta-

ble and wrapped an arm around his waist. Lydia
Cram glared at her. A few minutes later, without
hurry, she put on her clothes again.

Susannah dreaded that her turn would come. She
couldn't help staring as Nell had strutted on the table.
A game! She was only just used to Nicholas's seeing
her naked, and she could not imagine it, before all
these others. . . .

Turning away from the Attitudes, she toyed with a
book in the case behind her: *Metamorphoses*, said its
cover. It seemed stuck fast to the wall. When she
pulled at it harder, the whole row of spines beside it
dislodged, and she saw that there was nothing but
blank board behind them. *Fakes!*

"Miss Bookworm in the corner! We haven't seen you
play!"

The voice was Tom Gant's. She turned from the
wall and looked hesitantly around the room.

"Come on!" said Gant impatiently; and slowly she
climbed up onto the table.

"I shall die straightaway," she whispered to Sarah,
below. " 'Twill be such a certain thing, they'll have
to let me go." Sarah's eyes bulged and she looked
about to protest; but Susannah only took a deep breath
and closed her eyes. *Now.* She clamped both fists to
her heart, sliding down on the smooth wood, and gave
a shudder.

A man called, "She's been to see a play by Wray,
and expired of boredom!"

"Wray," snarled Nicholas, "is my friend, man—"

"Her lover has left her!" called a colder female
voice.

"Take off two!" called Gant.

"Make her stand! Can't see her, if she don't
stand. . . . "

Susannah felt Sarah untying her sash. Her heart
pounded and she kept still.

"She is—dead. Been stabbed." Anthony Ogilvie
spoke, a little groggily, from his corner.

"No, man! Don't guess it—" Susannah heard Gant

whisper; but she lifted her head and shot Ogilvie a grateful smile.

"Stabbed!" said Ogilvie. "Clear as day. Let her go."

Gant glowered, but came forward to help Susannah down off the table. She breathed again at last, freely. The relief was so great, sweat seemed to stream from her pores. She returned dizzily to the couch, where she had been before, and nearly fell into Nell Cameron's lap.

Nicholas looked up. One of his hands slid along Nell's thigh. "Why'd you not give them summat to guess at, pet?"

She stared down. That woman had lost no time in taking her place. *And what is he doing?* She bridled all the more at the sight, as she thought of the trouble she had gone to onstage to keep her nakedness, herself, for him. . . .

He stretched out a hand to her now. "You shall learn," he said obliquely, "to play our games." He pulled her down into his lap, kissing her below the ear. "You promised once to do all I should want. Do you remember?"

"Y-es." His thumb played lazily on her right breast, but she did not protest. The others might see—but Nell had gone. She had left Nicholas's side, disgruntled, to join the lawyer, Beaton.

"What if I should *want* you to take off your clothes before the others? What if that should please me?"

"I do not know—if I could."

Nicholas's hand had stopped for a moment. "In this house we are free, remember. We are no petty shopkeepers, to suffer ordinary rules."

"But what rules do you mean—" began Susannah, feeling her voice beginning to shake.

"Shh, pet." Nicholas touched her lips. "Come to bed, don't look so grave. Our life here will amuse you vastly, in time, I warrant."

So, as the days passed, Susannah tried not to look grave. And perhaps it was not so hard. This was a

frivolous house; these, forgetful rooms. And the men
all drank too much here, and the women—most of
them at least—treated their bodies lightheartedly, like
toys. Toys for the men to play upon. Green-eyed Nell,
especially, invited their casual caresses. Susannah
watched Nicholas, warily, and tried always to inter-
pose herself between him and Nell. Usually she could;
and when she could not, though she was sure their
flirtation went no further than what she saw, she was
stung by jealousy.

In the mornings none of this would trouble her.
Waking in the bright yellow room, she was filled with
contentment. It was delicious to lie here, in the mid-
morning sun, and feel Nicholas beside her. To know
that tomorrow he would be here still, and the morning after. His dark lashes would flutter against his
cheeks as a dream passed; and she would lie on her
side and watch him, absurdly happy.

In the light of morning the memories of the nights
seemed but a dream. The talk, the easy complicity in
the air—they were gone now. She must have imagined them. And if she had read aloud from *Fanny Hill*
or watched Nell and the actor, Curry, perform a
whole scene of it before her—it was not real. If Tom
Gant had kissed her neck, toyed with her breasts—she
had allowed him, because Nicholas wished it. And,
because she played the games, Nicholas stayed by her:
even though the other couples shifted and changed.
Nell Cameron had seduced Beaton, and Lydia Cram
the actor, Curry. Sarah, after pining for months for
Ogilvie, had started to share his chambers.

And into these shifting currents entered Valerie.

She arrived one evening at dinnertime, unan-
nounced. "Mr. *Brown*?" She spat the name back in-
dignantly at all those who tried it upon her. "Mr.
Cyrius Brown? I vow! I shall never be *friends* with a
poet again! He takes me to the house—it is crawling
with 'orrible brats. Eight—ten of them! I say, 'Where
are your friends, your cousins?' And he says, 'These
are my cousins. And my dear, I have tell them we are
married. . . .' 'Married?' says I. 'I shall ne'er be mar-

ried to you!' So, of course I could not stay." Valerie
collapsed into a dining chair, dropping her straw hat
on the floor. "Also, I should not like to stay on that
sea—too close to France."

"What of France, dear?" asked Ogilvie, puzzled.

"You mean you do not know?" Valerie's voice rose.
"There is a revolt! Two weeks since!" Nine forks
dropped onto their plates; only the barrister, Beaton,
went on eating his custard.

Now any of the audience Valerie might have lost
before returned, as she told of the news from Paris:
the mob gathering at the Palais-Royal, the storming
of the Bastille. The faces around her shifted from
boredom to horror or, alternatively, to a fevered excitement.

"Beyond belief!" Ogilvie's face glowed pink, and his
eyes shone.

"The king's very prison, a rubble!" cried Carrick.

Valerie's eyes seemed to catch fire off his. "Now
per'aps some of the *people* will come to rule."

Beaton patted his perspiring forehead with his napkin. "Good gracious! This is very bad."

"Not all lawyers think as you," said Valerie, mischievous. "You know, the mob at the Palais-Royal
was—how do you say—brought to violence by an ad-
vocate!"

"Never, in this country," said a disgruntled Beaton.

"But what will happen to you?" Susannah said,
now, to Valerie. "If your family—your father is . . ."
The comte d'Aubusson. Had Valerie spoken of him
or . . .

"My family?" Valerie looked vague. Then she said
brightly, "Oh, but my dear Susan! In the new regime
we should have *friends*."

"Then your father's high station would do you no
harm." Nicholas gave an inexplicable chuckle.

"*Assez!* What is the news *here*?" Gracefully Valerie
turned the subject. And though, for a few hours perhaps, the company thrilled, or trembled secretly, at
the nearness of revolution, by nightfall it was forgotten. For a few hours Carrick had retreated to his

room, seized by a notion, to scribble some notes; but now he returned, and in the library this night passed like all the others.

"Three pair! I win." Lydia Cram's bare bosom swelled in triumph as she displayed her cards. The candles planted at the corners of the card table shone on her moist, pink face.

"What do you say to two aces, m'dear?" countered Tom Gant.

"Oh . . ." Lydia's voice descended into a whine.

"Come, don't be so hard on her." Nell Cameron, in a dress of shimmering green, left her cards and crossed to Gant's side.

"She in't the only thing I'm hard on." Gant gave her a greedy look. "Time you shared my bed, too, Miss Nell—"

Susannah heard Lydia let out a squawk; and, feeling awkward, she was about to move unobtrusively from the room when she heard Nicholas, beside her, call out, "Come off it, Tommy! You're not man enough for two—"

"Oh, no?"

"Man enough in your own notions, Tom—" Nicholas rose and sneaked up behind Nell Cameron: jesting, still; laughing, slipping an arm around her waist. "But do you wager he is, when it comes to it, Nell?"

Susannah's eyes flashed indigo as she jumped up from her place. How she wished this house rid of Nell Cameron. . . .

But a hand seized her arm before she could move farther.

"Whisht!" The voice was Ogilvie's. She turned and stared: Ogilvie was drunk, and swayed from side to side. But as he still held her arm, looking at her so steadily, she stayed back. "Would you have him think you jealous?" whispered Ogilvie. "That most—fishwifely of conditions?" His gaze wandered to Nicholas and Nell, and back to Susannah. "No! Don't have him know you care. Ignore it. Play the game."

"What game?" Susannah thought of all the previous nights, previous games. Of Nell's posing; of Gant's hands on her skin, inflaming her more than she had expected—making her afraid.

"The game of love," said Ogilvie simply. "Listen . . . listen to me, Susan. I have known Carrick for years. You'll only e'er succeed with him—by being fickle."

When Susannah looked round again for Nicholas and Nell, they had vanished, like most of the others, from the room.

"Why?" was all she could say to Anthony Ogilvie and his strange pronouncements. *Perhaps he has designs on me, too,* she thought; and she wondered what she would do then. *Embrace him, to show I am fickle?* But as Ogilvie talked on, sometimes strangely and abstractedly, she could tell, somehow, that he would not want that. He took draughts, from time to time, from a green bottle, and dashes of whiskey from the decanter beside him.

"Fickle," he mumbled. "All the world's fickle. I think—there is no true friend."

"Why—I'll be your friend, if you like, Anthony. In faith—"

Ogilvie nodded, hazy-eyed, and she did not think he understood her. She looked suspiciously at the green bottle; like Nicholas's, it bore no label. And she wondered, for a moment, if that was what Valerie had meant. . . .

Eventually, holding her hand in friendly fashion, he fell asleep. She went up to her bed alone. When Nicholas came in some hours later, she pretended to be asleep. *Play the game,* she thought to herself, and tried not to think of Nell. For she guessed that, in Ogilvie's mixed-up talk, there was some truth. Nothing had changed. Nicholas was still by her side; in the morning sunlight his lashes still fluttered in his sleep.

She lay back beside Sarah Hutchings against the stone steps of the King's Bath and tried not to think of all the last few days' confusions—Nell and Nicholas, her newfound friendship with Ogilvie. And she half dreaded the questing voice that tried to draw her back.

"Thusan, might I athk you—"

She opened her eyes and saw Sarah's dimpled face pucker with anxiety.

"But of course," she said wearily. "What is it?"

She prepared herself for one of Sarah's long confessions: that she was not so in love as she had thought, or that she was afraid she was getting fat. She submerged herself in the murky green water, leaning her head back against the stone basin. In the open sky above the clouds compacted, threatening rain. But she thought she would wait until it finally came, to leave. Here in the water she felt so clean: almost free of worry. Trails of steam rose up around her.

". . . because, you know, he'th not really my lover—not in the thient*if*ic way. Although . . ."

"What?" Susannah lifted her head. "Do you mean Anthony?"

Sarah nodded, and her voice shrank to a beleaguered whisper. "We thpend the nighth together, but . . ." She shook her head.

"Maybe he . . . wants to wait a time."

"No. Thomehow—he doesn't *want* anything more. I athk him—'What can I do, Anthony?' I thay. But he only . . ."

Across from them in the bath, a young girl, accompanied by her treble-chinned mother, lost her footing, her skirts floating up undecorously. Two gentlemen from opposite ends of the pool rushed to rescue her.

Watching, Susannah wanted to laugh. She knew she shouldn't. "It *will* be all right," she said, and patted Sarah's hand. She wondered at Anthony Ogilvie's strange behavior; but already Sarah, having unburdened herself, seemed to be forgetting it.

"*Here*, Mr. Beaton!" Sarah called out now, eagerly. The bandy-legged barrister, in his green bathing gown, lost his purchase on the steps, in his excitement. He landed on his belly, in front of her.

"Would you," said Nicholas, looking hard into Susannah's eyes. He pulled her close, and drove into her again.

Her legs were wrapped tight around him, and she gasped. "Would I—"

"Have another man."

"No . . ."

"Yes!" He drove once more, farther, kissing her, the roughness of his beard grazing her neck. "I said—*yes*. If I asked it, you would. . . . " He pressed her hair against the pillow.

"Then, yes," she said. Tears rose in her eyes. She no longer understood. There were right answers, wrong answers: times he wished loyalty, times he talked of wantonness. . . . "What of Nell?" she said suddenly. "Then is it the same? Nothing—"

Nicholas lay still now and did not answer. When, at last, he did, his voice was soothing and soft. "I care, little one, only for you."

Now he was apart from her again: that quick closeness, that absorption—she thought ruefully—a deception. She wished she could be part of him—she felt so near to it sometimes, making love. She would wish for what he wished, and know his thoughts. She would know him, be all absorbed in him: and yet it never happened, quite.

"Go on. Do go on," Nicholas said in a hazy voice: the voice of mild drunkenness, of after the ball. They had gone all together to the Assembly Rooms that night, with Nell and Valerie both dressed up as men. They had worn scarlet breeches and waistcoats, parading ever more boldly round the floor as the staid master of ceremonies grew pink with rage. Now the clocks downstairs tolled midnight; in a dozen rooms Ogilvie's guests were drinking, laughing.

Valerie's own laughter rippled as she spilled brandy onto the white bedclothes. She lifted a glass to Susannah's mouth; and suddenly she was pulling her down beside her, covering her with kisses.

Susannah writhed away. "What—" Why was Valerie here? She remembered running up the stairs with her. They had been with others, but now, all at once, the three of them were alone. Valerie was peeling down the edge of Susannah's gown, while Nicholas pried the slippers from her feet. "Why—" she tried again.

"*Il veut regarder, il s'amuse,*" Valerie said, expertly unlacing the back of Susannah's dress.

"He wants—" Susannah puzzled.

"To watch, *chérie*. To see us." Valerie smiled down at her. Her eyes were like an ancient cat's: tranquil, unblinking. And Nicholas's eyes too now: they saw nothing strange. He leaned on his elbow, and his eyes glinted in the candlelight.

"You promised," he said. "Do you remember?"

"I promised—when?" Susannah sat up on the bed. Valerie was throwing off her shirt and scarlet breeches. Now, bending above Susannah, she brushed a lock of her straight, black hair across the bare tops of the younger woman's breasts. Susannah trembled, and tried not to move—to show that she had felt anything. For it was too strange. Nicholas did not answer her question, but only moved to help Valerie. Together, they pulled the clothes from Susannah: skirt, underskirts, petticoats, shift. When she lay naked, Nicholas held her hands fast in his. Valerie's lips and tongue darted, featherlike, about her neck, her breasts.

"*Chérie*, you are frozen. Do not be afraid."

When Nicholas let go of Susannah's hands, and Valerie coaxed her friend's fingers to her own breasts, which came to tiny, rose-colored points. "But you are lovely," she said, laughing quietly. "Perhaps I have always wanted to."

Does she mean it? thought Susannah. *Or is she acting, to please Nicholas?* Valerie gazed deep into Susannah's eyes with her narrow, inscrutable dark brown ones; and the loving gaze, up close, became as

blank as her face: a mask. Susannah reached up and
touched the fine-grained, powdery skin. What was
beneath it? she wondered. Did Valerie really love her,
or care for Nicholas? Was it possible? Or did she
merely love them all, men and women alike, with this
same, absorbed gaze, meaning nothing?

And as her friend's fingers dove inside her, twisting
and fluttering, now beating a pulse at the very spots
where she was weakest, Susannah struggled, too late,
to twist away. *Not this. Not a woman* . . . But Nicholas pressed down on her shoulders and held her there,
and she could not stop it. She cried out, feeling herself
coming to the height: the longing breaking, descend-
ing in waves. When she opened her eyes, Nicholas was
above her: inside her.

His eyes glinted like dull iron. "Do you see," he
said, "what a trifle pleasure is? Anyone can give it
you. You are a wanton creature, Susan. Wanton."

It was strange how his words made her throb, inside, and want him more. Tears came to her, with the
second wave of pleasure. "Only—because you
wanted," she said. Her voice struggled to escape her.
"I love you, not—"

"You love pleasure, my dear," he said. And what
he said next seemed to make no sense, even when Susannah tried to think about it later. "Now you are my
creature. You have proved me."

The library was warm, its fire too lively for the season. A log tipped over and crackled; on a sofa Nell
Cameron was wetting her finger tracing the actor
Curry's lips in wine. Tom Gant had just won a contest: for the tale of the most arousing coming-to-
manhood. And now, not about to have his place of
honor taken, he cried out, "Who shall test me?"

"Well, you'll not be tested alone!" shouted Carrick.

"Then a contest!" Gant mopped his brow. "All the
gentlemen—"

"Then let the choice be the ladies'," said Nell Cameron coyly, "which gentlemen we are to try." The ac-

tor lying in her lap sat up, startled. "Let the men drop their names in the basket," said Nell. "*We'll* have the pick of 'em."

"Aye!" called Tom Gant hoarsely. "Every man to a new lady—every lady to a new man!" There were groans and calls for drink as the five men found paper and signed. They dropped their slips of paper in the basket of the marble nymph standing by the fireplace. Looking variously reluctant, modest, and flirtatious, the ladies drew: Valerie, Nell, Lydia, Sarah, and at last, Susannah.

She held her breath and opened the slip of paper. Its scratch of the pen read: "Ogilvie." She caught Niccholas's eye but received only one of his antic smiles. *Go ahead*, it seemed to say; and now, along with Tom Gant, Valerie and Nell, he was drawn from the room. Who had chosen whom, Susannah could not tell, but when she saw Nell leaning familiarly on Nicholas's arm, an unreasoning jealousy struck her. *They have done this before.* She was suddenly sure; and her stomach clenched. She could not help it; she could not feel free, not in Valerie's way. Free of jealousy, free to fly from one man to the next, without regret. If only she could be so, it would be simpler. . . . Her eyes darkened to the shade of night as she turned and looked at Ogilvie, who was waiting.

"Don't be afraid," he said. She fumbled for words and could not answer. He gave a narrow smile. "I play this game, you'll find, rather as spectator than— gladiator i' the ring." He moved to lock the door, to draw the curtains. And yet he was right: she was not afraid.

"Why do you talk," she said, "always of *games*?"

Ogilvie poured out a glass of brandy; when he handed it to her, his fingers did not touch hers. He sat on the sofa, some distance from her. "What better word than *game* for the relations between men and women?"

"Why . . . there is love. That is a surer word."

Ogilvie sipped his brandy. But his movements were precise, his words unslurred. "Do you think so?"

"Yes. Of course. It is—" Susannah stopped, looking down. Perhaps she was sounding foolish. "Do you ever even—*think* of love?" she said.

"Oh, yes. I do think of it." Ogilvie frowned, as if with distaste. " 'Tis a fine story."

"I did not believe in it either." Susannah was silent for a moment; but then the urge to talk came over her again. "Once, I thought—it would come when I married." She looked at Ogilvie.

He was shaking his head, smiling. "But no?"

"No. And that was how—when I saw Nicholas again—I knew it must be real. I had met him before, you know. Almost two years ago, at a ball. I don't think he remembers it. But I knew him at once, when I saw him at your party. And I knew—" She paused. Ogilvie's light eyes fixed, still, on her face. "Love might be nought to do with marriage. But I must have it—I must *take* it—all the same." Susannah looked up and saw the amused curl of Ogilvie's lip: heard his chuckle. "Well! How can you laugh if you do not know it? What have you against it then?"

"All of experience."

"Well, then—I don't wish your experience!" Susannah looked up, apologetic, hearing the sharpness of her words.

"If only you had the force to keep it from you! You know—" Ogilvie's face grew serious. "I did not choose it."

"Choose—what?"

"The incapacity—to love."

A silence fell, which seemed to Susannah too awful, too heavy to break. Sarah's words returned to her in a rush. "Perhaps," she said slowly, at last, "it will return."

"No. I am fairly sure—not." Ogilvie would not look at her now. He stared at the fire.

"Have you seen a physician?" she tried gently. "For some ills, they work wonders. . . . "

Ogilvie drank again: let out a sound, nearly a laugh. "Doctors! For this ill, they've no wonders to dispense. Oil of orrisroot, powdered oyster shells, hot baths, cold baths . . . I've tried 'em all. Only one of the doctors had a reason—and he'd no cure. He said . . . 'twas a disorder of the spirit, manifesting itself in the animal—faculties."

Susannah did not know what to answer. "Perhaps you should go live in the country," she tried. "Make a change of life . . ."

"A change of life!" Ogilvie shook his head. He pulled himself up now and drew her hand into his; and so, for a time, they sat together, silent, watching the logs in the fire crack and tumble. Ogilvie smiled. "What, pray tell, should I do in the country? To be sure, my family—the worthy rustics—try to fetch me back to it. Stoneborough Abbey has great need of me, they say! So I should take up the honest, toilsome life of a country farmer. No London, no drink—a sweet country wife, who would not mind that I was incapable of—" He winced and turned his head away.

"Come, Anthony!" she tried, squeezing his hand. " 'Tis not so bad. For near seventeen years *I* lived only in the country. . . . "

"Aye, and would you leave Nicholas to return there?" Ogilvie turned back to her; through a fringe of hair he watched her, as she shook her head.

"No! Why should I?"

"Before . . . you grow unhappy?"

"I shall not grow unhappy," she said with certainty: and wondered. *What can he mean?* This weakness she felt, these doubts—about that time with Valerie, about Nell—they were but small matters, and would pass. Holding Ogilvie's hand—glad of his concern, all the same—she watched the fire.

There was a knocking at the door: a steady thump that made them look behind, then at each other, wondering. It turned to a loud pounding; and outside, the voice of Nicholas shouted, "Leave off! Ogilvie! I know what you're at—"

Susannah jumped up and ran toward the door. Behind, Ogilvie was balancing himself against the sofa, trying to stand. "Come, old Nichol." His voice rasped. "Keep your patience—"

Ogilvie searched for the key and turned it, and the
door slammed back against him. Pushing past him,
Nicholas stood at the threshold, looking: staring.

"What have you done?" he shouted: and, in a lower
voice, "I shall be destroyed."

His eyes were wild. Susannah had not seen him so
before. When she came up, took his hand, it did not
calm him.

"Well? What have you done?" He stared at her:
again at Ogilvie. He did not seem, even, to notice that
they were both dressed, standing, composed.

Susannah looked over at Ogilvie, bewildered. For
she had never seen Nicholas so.

"What is this?" Nicholas snarled, raising her hand
suddenly, fiercely in his. He squeezed so hard she
thought her wrist would snap. "What is this? These
looks of—complicity. This plotting."

"Please," said Susannah, straining. "We were talking. We are but friends."

"Friends!" Nicholas let out a curse. "Nay. I misdoubt it. You can be nought but lovers of long standing. None but lovers can be calm and familiar, so."

Ogilvie started forward, raising a calming hand.
"Nicholas. You surpass yourself this time. Truly you
do—" But at the edge of the carpet he stumbled, and
crumpled dizzily onto the sofa. Nicholas pulled Susannah closer, still holding her arm, and brushed one
hand roughly against the curls at her forehead. For a
moment, Susannah thought, there was affection in his
dark, glaring eyes: and bewilderment.

"She'll not be your friend!" he shouted at Ogilvie.
"She is not yours!"

He pulled Susannah away then, out of the room,
his hair tousled and his shirt unfastened. "I was
wrong," he mumbled into her hair, as they moved
upstairs; and then, in their room, tearing at the hooks
and laces of her dress. "I was wrong. I had thought—
I would not mind it."

"But it was a game," said Susannah softly, evenly.

"Nay. It is no game. If you left me for another, my
own little one—I'd wish him dead."

* * *

No explanation ever came for the change in Nicholas Carrick, although all at the house on The Circus could see it. The playwright scarcely flirted with Nell Cameron or the damsels walking in the Orange Grove; he threw himself, with a fury, into his work. Every afternoon, heroic couplets resounded against the walls of his bedroom.

" 'Death, thou vainglorious!' " he would proclaim. " 'We shall not bow to thee!' Nay . . ."

> *"Death, be thou vainglorious—*
> *Sing not thy siren's song,*
> *For man shall march victorious*
> *Past thee his whole life long!"*

He would pace, and declaim again; at last pen would scrabble against paper. He concluded the fifth canto of *Cyberion*, and still he worked: for the news of the rebellion in France had fired him with the notion of a vast comic-heroic stage piece. He would call it *Palais-Royal* and collaborate with his fellow author Wray in setting it to music.

His mistress, for her own part, came into a restless glow, a beauty; so that those other women who, before, had barely rated her pretty, now took reluctant notice of her. Susannah's eagerness to please her lover alternated with a fear of losing him, which, more and more, drove her to chatter: to laugh and move without ceasing. She danced for whole evenings at the Assembly Rooms with Nicholas and whatever swains he would permit her. She learned piquet and played with a frenetic devotion: Ogilvie, as a token of their friendship, had agreed to back her. She was learning, in this company, to talk without thinking: for merriment counted for more than knowledge. She talked to the men in the house at tea, at supper, her face growing pink when she thought she had answered brightly: in the way that would please Nicholas. For, as ever, he

disapproved of bluestockings, and looked angry when
she turned dull or serious.

"Hee!" the lawyer Beaton giggled. " 'Pears she's
quite sick with love." And his friends nodded, secure
in their immunity from that particular affliction.

Toward the end of his stay in Bath, Anthony Ogilvie proposed to hold an assembly. It would be nothing
like the usual town assemblies: at his house he vowed
to banish stately minuets and dowagers. There would
be drink aplenty and country dancing; whoever arrived at his door would be admitted, until the house
could take no more. Upon all this he gave quite clear
instructions. As for the rest—he had a distaste for
practicalities, and left them all to his servants.

So that on the appointed night at August's end the
people of Bath found Ogilvie's doors thrown open.
There were barrels of ale and wine waiting, and tables of viands: oysters and capons, pigeons stuffed and
pigeons spit-roast; mutton pies and apple pies, trifles
and fools. Enough, in fact, to plenish the servants'
hall even after some two hundred guests ate their fill.
One Madame Carini of Italy was to open the ball with
a song; then, by special favor, the poet Nicholas Carrick would declaim lines of his verse.

"Hmph. Conceited puppy," snorted Jonas Hench.
His companion, an apprentice milliner of seventeen,
was still gaping at the handsome orator, whose name
Hench could not bother to remember.

He glanced around, his face furrowing and reddening as he saw more familiar faces in the room than he
liked. Respectable society had not shunned this event,
as he had hoped; his loud-voiced young friend was
sure to attract some curious stares.

"Lud, but he *is* handsome!" she shouted at the close
of the rousing last lines of *Cyberion*. Nicholas Carrick
bowed away through the double doors of the ballroom as the crowd's applause grew ever louder.

When the guests had eaten and drunk, the orchestra took up a jig to begin the dancing. Madame Carini led the party's host out onto the floor, followed quickly by other couples: hedgehog-coiffed gallants and tousled dandies whose short-cropped hair fell fashionably in their eyes; older ladies in stiff silk faille and so many younger ones in white muslin that Jonas could not venture to tell them apart but by the colors of their sashes. Nor could he find any means to distinguish country wenches from fashionably countrified ladies.

Hopeful of his anonymity in the tussle of hair and feet, Hench let himself be led out into the dance, nodding uneasily at Horace Beaton, a London lawyer of his acquaintance. As his milliner dragged him among the galloping feet, he chanced, for a second, to look straight through the crowd.

"Good God. It isn't—"

"*Who?* Jonas, love. Who is it?" The girl giggled and shook her curls.

"Nothing, pet." They danced on. "In this, of all places," murmured Hench.

When midnight tolled on the hallway clock, echoing on smaller timepieces throughout the house, shining faces turned up toward Nicholas Carrick, who had climbed atop the piano and now announced a "Scottish reel." Few of the company knew the steps; but they formed a line which wound its way around the room, as the fiddles and Madame Carini warbled:

In Dun-Edin, there lived a lass,
As fine as Highland lady . . .

Carrick's wavy-haired partner threw her whole heart into the dance. As she skipped and spun the onlookers at the walls got a glimpse of white-stockinged leg, which caused them to applaud.

"Good God," said Jonas Hench, again. "It *is*." He watched, aghast, as two gentlemen lifted Susannah up onto their shoulders: the Scotch poet-orator and a sandy-haired man he could just manage to identify as the host. Susannah rode around the room now, singing, with glee in her eyes: faster and faster, clinging onto the men's hands as if to the reins of a willful steed.

> *And how the Lowlands, they were blest—*
> *Come kiss me, Highland Ka-tie!*

The two men winked up at Susannah and, taking hold of her ankles, charged out of the double doors of the ballroom.

"G'd Jesus!" murmured Hench. "What'll I tell Maria now?"

"What, love?" said the milliner.

"Well, I must!" said Hench, distraught, paying no heed to his listener. "Aye, I must. She *ought* to know. Such goings-on . . . how can I put it?"

"Here?" whispered Susannah. In the darkness of the dusty cupboard her pupils widened until her eyes were nearly black.

"Yes. Here, now." Nicholas breathed heavily, and took hold of her.

"Someone might come—"

"So much the better." He closed the door, and all light vanished. A group of revelers passed outside, their laughter so near it almost seemed that they must hear and see them. Susannah brushed up against a cobweb, and gave a yelp. But Nicholas held her waist in his hands and pressed her to the wall. "Yes," he said again, the word a slow hiss. "Do you refuse?"

She gave no answer. He pulled her skirts high and lifted her above him, her toes barely touching the ground. The talk outside, the quarter-hour chimes, and the distant strains of a new dance came through the walls.

"Yes," Nicholas said. "Do you hear? Do you hear the music?"

Chapter 17

———— ✻ ————

"Good Lord! The booby." Maria spoke aloud to the empty library of Cheveril Wye. Outside the day was bleak, and the room's windows—designed, at great cost, to lean out over a sea-thunderous coast—cast a gray and shadowy light on Jonas Hench's letter from Bath.

"What in God's name—" Maria began to pace, cane in hand, around the edges of the circular carpet. It, too, was designed by Mr. Adam, and as yet no one in the house—not even Maria—dared to tread on it.

"What," she said, "in God's name, am I to make of such an idiot letter?"

James Cheveril was wandering, bored, down the hallway outside. He had little in Devon to occupy him; weeks ago he had dispatched gifts of game to the thirty or so constituents who controlled his votes. He tried, in a melodic voice, "Are you busy in there, my Maria?"

"One tiny note more, dear. Then I shall be free." Maria strained her voice to the limits of sweetness; to her relief, her husband moved away again down the

corridor. "Booby," she hissed again, at Hench's
schoolboy handwriting.

> *I warrant you, dear Maria—Lud I dont know*
> *what to make of it but there were sartinly, most*
> *sartinly two gentlemen making familiar with*
> *her Corps, prancing about the Chamber with her*
> *atop their shoulders, like as if they shared her*
> *betwixt 'em. The One foppish Authour working*
> *his hand right up her Leg, whilst the Other (our*
> *Host, a Gentleman about 30 most dissipated), He*
> *talked in her Ear and carressed her Hand, in the*
> *same quality of affection as the Other—*

The letter went on for three such heated pages; but
nothing that followed made it any clearer which man
Hench identified as his sister-in-law's lover. Maria
hurled the letter into the fire and took up pen and
paper. For twenty minutes she scribbled furiously,
oblivious of her husband's calls.

His letter dispatched, Jonas Hench continued at
Bath for another week, soaking in the waters and buying trinkets for his milliner mistress. He considered his
compact with Maria sufficiently kept: he had reported
what he had seen of Susannah's activities. The American girl's rejection, some years ago now, in an upstairs corridor of Hench House, was but one of many
personal slights he preferred to put from his mind;
and he harbored nothing worse now toward Susannah, than the vaguest of resentments. To his relief, a
few days after Ogilvie's ball, the gossips of the Pump
Room accounted "that house of license" at The Circus
disbanded, its occupants having returned to London;
so he regarded himself as quit of his duties of observation. Only once he was back in the country at Henshawe did the matter of his sister-in-law return to
trouble him.

Now as he sat in bed next to his wife, three trenches
dug themselves into his normally smooth, shiny forehead.

Augusta looked up, misty-eyed, from *Ferdinand, Count Fathom*, balancing the book against her belly, which was round with the beginnings of a second child. "Pray, what is it, Jonas? Is the black bile in your stomach again?"

"Nay, I merely fret. 'Tis nothing." As if to prove it so, Hench cast his robe off and planted himself, flat, between mattress and feather bed. He stared up at the gathers of the canopy. Augusta peered at her husband through her spectacles.

"There *is* a trouble," she said. "Now, do tell me."

Jonas shook his head. "You won't want to hear it, Gussy. 'T's to do—with your brother and that harlot of a wife he—"

"Jonas! Please—such words. 'Twill mark the baby."

"Hah! An' I thought you'd given up your superstition for that Mr. Rousseau. . . . "

Augusta, however, was not to be distracted. "I will hear what you have to say, Jonas, but only if you will forbear to use such language." She folded her arms tightly over her stomach, quelling—she hoped—the baby's kicking and the anxious beating of her heart. She had not seen Susannah in months. Perhaps, it was true, their paths had diverged. Motherhood and Greek had occupied Augusta; what occupied her cousin, she did not know. Yet they were friends. . . .

"Hem! You know, Gussy . . . p'raps 'tis better not . . . "

"Tell me."

When Augusta shot a glance at her husband that mixed stoicism with suppressed curiosity, Hench harrumphed and gave her an abridged tale of the party at Bath.

When he was done, Augusta said only, "Oh, dear."

"Y'see, m'dear, how the woman's not fit for your society!" Hench coughed and nestled deeper under the covers.

Augusta stayed silent for a moment: searching for the words, the appropriate philosophy, for such a solemn occasion. "Friendship," she pronounced at last, "cannot be, I am aware, anything other than a bond of permanence."

Jonas Hench snored gently.

"And yet—does it not seem so to you, Jonas?—at times, it imposes a duty of conscience. . . . "

Augusta frowned. Without looking again at her husband, she rose quietly from bed. It was clear to her now what conscience obliged. To friendship—more than that, to *family*. However hurtful it might seem . . .

She searched for a candle and her spectacles, and proceeded into the next room, where she began to write.

"Dearest Harry . . ."

For a long time she could get no further. Her husband's account had been annoyingly imprecise. *If only I had been there myself!* she thought. *She* might have spotted the false intrigue to which Susannah—poor cousin!—had surely fallen victim. *Poor Harry!* If only he had taken her north, she should never have been exposed to such rumors: such situations. She did not even know which of the two men she should report to Harry as being his wife's supposed lover. She decided at last on neither. She might describe Carrick in veiled terms, as an "Epick Poet."

At the third try, she achieved a letter which she thought both compassionate and restrained. Susannah, she was sure, had committed no real fault. The Susannah *she* knew had believed in romantic love. She had known nothing of arranged matches—let alone liaisons! Yet if rumors circulated, Harry must know. Then he might come south and bear his wife away from them.

Harry stared at the two frantic missives, both dated a week ago: the fifteenth of September.

I have it now, Henry, from the <u>Most Reliable Sources</u> *that your wife has taken a lover, a rich indolent young Rake who lives the merry life in London in expectance of his father's estates. . . .*

He turned from his mother's letter to Augusta's.

I tremble lest the Rumour be false and cause you upset—nonetheless I fear for Susan's happiness and yours, lest she fall to the advances of that impov'rished Epick Poet!

"Good Lord, Fermanagh," said Harry at last, although, in fact, his serving man had quit the room some time ago. "What am I to make of this?"

"Rich indolent young Rake" . . . *"impov'rished Epick Poet"* . . . Harry felt an unexpected *thump* in his chest. The image of Susannah's face rose in his mind's eye, astonishingly clear. And then, with a sharper pain, he saw that face turning, full of joy, toward a stranger. . . .

"Harry?" called a soft voice behind him.

He turned, smiling as a real face—kind eyes, graying chestnut hair—forced the imagined one from his thoughts.

"You have had news?" said his visitor.

"Word of my wife's—doings," Harry said, with a bitter twist to his mouth.

Margaret Hallward moved across and took his hand, looking up at him.

"I have come to see it now," he said. "After this, and—her last two letters, which were quite heartless . . . It was a mistake, to marry her. She was young—I hoped too much of her."

"Do not talk of mistakes," said Margaret evenly, "especially ancient ones, which can only hurt in the remembering. Come by me."

After some turning and pacing, Harry knelt beside her and laid his head in her lap. "It was"—he spoke suddenly—"a childish passion. Foolish. Nothing like what I know with you—which is true friendship."

She stroked his hair. "I shall be so sorry," she said deliberately, "when I must leave."

"That is not for some time yet—surely? Your husband is—well enough without you. And does your sister not need you here?" Harry looked up, anxious, but her eyes searched the walls. They roved and wandered and would not meet his.

An icy autumn wind whistled through the streets at nine in the morning as Nicholas Carrick made his way home from The Three Georges. He squinted into the gray, dim light of day, and lunged out into the road after three hackney coaches, only to see quicker customers jump aboard ahead of him. He plodded under Temple Bar, up Drury Lane, without even a glance at the girls beginning to ply the streets. His feet moved mechanically under him, all the way across the wide, empty thoroughfare of High Holborn; all the way to Great Russell Street and his grandfather.

A little light filtered into the Baron Blackcroft's room, revealing the dust on his orrery and scientific volumes. Nicholas bellowed in the doorway, "Grandfather? *Grand*father!"

The Baron was awake, as ever. "Son? Is that you?"

"Damn me, Grandfather. Of course it's me. Rather—to be correct, *it is I.* . . . " Nicholas swept up his coattails in an exaggerated bow, lurching into the post of the staircase.

"There is a young lady here to see you." The skin around the Baron's blank eyes wrinkled, with his cryptic smile.

Nicholas squinted and leaned into the room. "Who? Susan? *Where*, Grandfather?"

"I am here," a lilting voice answered. White teeth and a pair of bright eyes flickered at Nicholas in the darkness.

"Excuse me?" He shielded his eyes—or rubbed his head. "What, may I ask, gives me the pleasure of . . ."

Claudine moved into the light of the hallway. She wore a dress of dark-red silk faille and a white linen cap with red ribbons. "I have come to return your money." She smiled.

"My money?" Nicholas stared. "Oh, aye! Now I remember." A smiled tugged at the corner of his mouth.

He ran a hand through his wind-tousled hair. "*That* money! I vow, madam—there's no need of it."

"Oh, yes, there is, sir." Claudine smiled, once again showing white teeth. She reached down for a cord buried in the ruffles of her bodice; she tugged, and a leather sack of coins popped out from between her breasts.

"No—no, my dear. I insist—"

She took Nicholas's hand and pulled it toward her, placing the sack onto his palm. It was still warm.

"Very well. If you wish—"

Claudine backed away, turning, laying a hand on the post of the stair. She took a step down.

"Where is it you work, Mr. Carrick?" she said suddenly.

"Work?" Nicholas gave a covering laugh. "I don't work, Miss—"

"Claudine."

"Miss Claudine—" Nicholas paused and smiled. "I don't work so much as put on plays."

Claudine looked straight up into his eyes, her own, the green-brown of a cat's, unblinking. "I know. I should like to be in them."

"Well!" Nicholas gave a cough. "The present one, you see, is cast. I'truth—there's scant parts for women in a play about the French Rebellion—"

"I should play a man, then! Or a boy. Oh, please. Please, Mr. Carrick—Nicholas. Let me try?" Claudine looked up, beseeching. She saw Carrick's eyes, then his feet, shift.

"Ach, well. This afternoon then. Two o'clock. Come to the pit, by the Drury Lane door. . . . "

She scurried down the stairs, not waiting for the last of the instructions, twice calling out her thanks along the way. Outside, she let out a *"Whoop!"* for all the street to hear.

I'm going to Drury Lane! Nicholas Carrick fancies me, and I am going to be an actress! She ran down the road as far as Plumtree Street, then wove southward through the lanes and alleys that led past Covent Garden to the Strand. She pulled a face at Bow Street Magistrate's Court, where poor hapless girls got sent to

Bridewell, and paused to admire her reflection in a draper's window. Her silk dress, petticoats, and red-leather shoes, bought secondhand from a shop by the Temple, had taken up six months' savings at Mrs. Inverness's. She angled her face up at one of the square panes. "Oh, please, *please*, Mr. Carrick. Would you let me try?"

She whispered the words, but inside her head she heard the wheedling voice, sweet as honey. The shopgirl was watching her suspiciously from inside, so she moved on.

"Oh, please, *please* . . ." she cooed to herself. "God's blood! Make way, boy! Can't ye tell when a lady's afore ye?" She kicked aside the urchin who stood, bewildered, in her path. "I'm an actress an' he knew it. Carrick knew it! *Hold* yer bleeding hand!" She scowled up at the greasy-haired maid who was about to tip a chamber pot over the ledge above her. Feeling like a queen in her red-leather slippers, she pranced right beneath the threat and out onto the Strand. She would not go back to Mrs. Inverness's house until tonight: she knew she'd have the devil's time getting out again. So she whiled away the morning peering into the shop windows of the Strand and Fleet Street. From the street vendors she bought an apple tart, and red silk roses for her cap. She bought a pamphlet, too, called _The Lady's Way: Or, the Path to a Virtuous Womanly Life._ For halfway down from Great Russell Street it had struck her: what if, at the theater, they expected her to read? She had only recently seen the use in it, and tried to call back the few lessons the sailor Farquhar had given her. Mrs. Inverness's son had helped, too, when he wasn't playing the Turk.

" 'The lot of Woman is Obedience,' " she read aloud, planting herself on the steps of St. Clement's Church. " 'Obedience and chastity'—ha!—'and withal, submission to her Fathers and her Brothers. The every wish of her Husband rules her.' . . . Faugh! Let 'em tell you half what they're wishin' for."

Her reading had attracted a small audience of sweeps and pickpockets. "Go on!" she snarled at them. "Get off, or I'll call the watch on you. Git!"

Why, that's half the fun of having an audience, she thought—*getting rid of 'em.* Happily, she clicked her red-leather heels as she saw off her second lot of urchins. She had gotten so busy filling time that when two o'clock rang in the belfry overhead, she barely paid it any notice. At the end of a passage in her book, she looked up and saw the bells still swinging. "Lud o' Hosts! It's two." With a stream of curses she quit the steps and ran headlong up Drury Lane.

She stopped under the arched doorway of the theater just long enough to straighten the roses in her cap. Tossing her pamphlet on woman's lot onto the floor, she charged through a pair of curtains into the darkness of the pit.

There was a creaking and bumping onstage as hands shifted tall, painted scene flats into place. Two actresses, wrinkled and pale without their stage makeup, idled at the side of the stage, parrying insults with the actors, who stamped and swaggered before them. As more stagehands tinkered with oil lamps and colored paper, the light in the chamber shifted from yellow to a dark pink, and the faces in the light took on a feverish cast. Claudine spotted a dark head below the stage front: Nicholas. Beside him, a man with spiky hair that appeared bright orange was jumping and waving his arms at the actors. "Where're the others?" he shouted. "We need enough for a *rabble.* . . ." His eyes lit on Claudine. "Nichol! Is that your friend? . . . Act One, Scene One, ye lugabouts! A small farm in Normandy!"

Nicholas caught Claudine's eye and jumped forward to restrain his collaborator, Wray. "Hold on, man! Here's another one for your rabble."

"Rabble!" Claudine pouted.

Wray turned away from the stage, running his hand from sweaty forehead to damp orange-pink hair. "Well, what more would you be?" he said. "A mulatto wench—'tis hard to place. Though I grant you, there's novelty in it. Can you sing?"

"Like a very Italian!" Claudine clasped her hands in front of her and filled her lungs with air.

Wray leaned back, hands on his haunches, appraising.

"Favor us with a song, Claudine," said Nicholas.

Claudine's lungs froze. She could not think of a song, for all her life. The only tune that ran, absurdly, through her head was one the men on the *Rosaline* used to sing.

"Rule, Britannia!" she belted out at last.

Britannia rules the waves!
Britons never, never, ne-ver shall be slaves.

And true it is, too, she thought, smiling to herself.

"That old saw!" chuckled Nicholas. "Well! And why not?"

Claudine's tight smile eased into a broad one, and as Nicholas laughed, so did she: doubling over, offering up an eyeful of bare skin.

"She's loud, at any rate," said Wray affably, waving an arm to summon one of the ladies from the stage.

"Do I have a part?" Claudine hopped up and down on her red heels. "Do I, Nicholas? A singing part?"

"Every part's a singing part," said Nicholas lazily, his gaze lingering on her. He took no notice of the pasty-skinned actress who had come down from the stage.

"Ah, Belinda," said Wray. "Show this lady to the tiring rooms. Er . . ." He waved a hand at Claudine and Nicholas, who were still staring, glassy-eyed, at each other. "What is your name, miss? . . ."

"Mrs. . . . Mrs. . . . " Claudine looked wildly around her. *I am to go onstage! And soon I'll have a rich keeper and gowns and . . .* "Mrs. *Bryce*," she said at last. In fact, she had had her stage name planned for a long time. *Bry's . . . Bryce.* Why shouldn't she claim the name that was rightfully hers?

She did not quit Mrs. Inverness's right away; for as long as she could juggle her two professions, she did. The theater would not pay her until a week's rehearsals had passed, and then (she discovered, to her dis-

may) only fifteen shillings a week. Why, she spent
fifteen shillings a week on food at Mrs. Inverness's!
She nearly went to Nicholas Carrick to ask for more.
How did they fancy an actress was supposed to live?
Oh, she knew well enough they all had their protectors
. . . but until those came along, what did they do?

"Why don't ye come an' live with me?" the pasty-
skinned Belinda asked her one day. They were waiting by the stage door in boys' clothing: in the second
scene of the play they acted as revolutionary messen-
gers. Claudine regarded the other actress suspiciously;
she had never been so friendly before.

"It's me . . . brother, you see," said Belinda uneasily, rubbing the pouch under one of her eyes. "He
lived with me, but now he's up and left fer the wool
mills, i' Leicester."

Her keeper's gone and left her, thought Claudine.
Aloud, she said, "Oh, I have a place already. At Red
Lion Square."

"You mean Mrs. Inverness's?" Belinda's eyes widened. "What? Be you one of Mrs. Inverness's whores?
Well, well!" She gave a spiteful cackle. " 'Tisn't many
of *your* like we get in here. . . . Nay, your whores are
too grand for us—"

Claudine grabbed Belinda's neckcloth and yanked
her toward her. "I warrant you wish *you* was good
enough to work there!" She shoved her away.

"Mercy me!" Belinda fanned her face. "We're all of
a kind, you know."

Claudine gave her a sidelong glance. "What manner of place is it you have?"

Diffidently, the other girl described her room, as if
she were not at all certain she wanted Claudine there.
Claudine, equally disinterested, asked the price. Eight
shillings a week.

Eight shillings! Claudine was aghast. That would
be half her money, even before she bought her dinners
at the cookshop. But soon, when evening performances began, she knew she would have to leave Mrs.
Inverness's. "How do you come at eight shillings, pray,
on *our* little wages?" she said ingenuously: just ingen-

uously enough to hint that of course she knew how the other girl managed—she whored, of course.

"I pawn." Belinda opened the stage door a crack to look. The first scene of Act One was still dragging on. "You pawn?"

Belinda shrugged. "I buy a shawl at Mrs. Gonegal's—credit, see—an' pawn it at Mr. Jenkin's fer ten shillings. There's shops in Distaff Lane, still thinks I'll pay—I get caps and shoes there, then I pawn 'em. When I gets paid, I pays a few off, an' if they start to come for me, I can always move house. What—have ye not got credit, Claudine, what fer to pay the rent?"

"Have ye no man to pay it for ye?" Claudine countered.

"Ha! 'Tis a rare man what pays to keep full-time what he only wants twice a week."

"You watch! I'll have a man to myself, 'fore the end of this play. I'll be through with bit parts like this one, too."

"A half-color wench like you!" Belinda snorted.

Claudine stood tall and shook her head proudly, ready to strut onstage. "I'll look a damn sight better in the lights," she hissed, "than a flour-paste strumpet like you!"

A week later, she moved into Belinda Harrison's room on Great Queen Street. By the end of rehearsals for *Palais-Royal*, her wages had moved, unaccountably, from fifteen shillings a week to one pound five, though she had never spoken to Nicholas Carrick about it. Indeed, she hardly spoke to him at all, except in passing. For she was beginning to learn principles: some, just now, from Belinda and some she had known all along. Like, *Never let a man have cheap, what he might in a few months' time have dear.*

Chapter 18

Susannah pulled the bedclothes up below her chin as she lay beside Nicholas at Southampton Street. The room was chillier than usual, for Mrs. Hall had forgotten to bring in more firewood, and London was unusually cold this year, for the end of October. Winter had come early: soon there might be snow and another frost fair on the Thames. *How long ago the last one seems.* She remembered the outings, the trinkets, the tavern feasts with a pang, for now she and Nicholas did nothing like that. They met in these rooms and took their supper—perhaps it was twice a week. Sometimes they still spent the night here, but more and more often Nicholas rose and dressed, after an hour or two, pleading some engagement at the theater. And though the games he wished Susannah to play grew ever more varied—once they had both walked, masked, through Covent Garden market and pretended to come together as strangers—he seemed less willing than once he had been to surrender himself to passion. To let go—to come inside her, as he had, sometimes, at Bath—or to risk being seen with her, anywhere in the world outside.

"Why—" she said aloud, and stopped. She did not know why the word had escaped her.

"Eh?" Nicholas sat up under the covers.

"Why do you—never . . ." Susannah began slowly. She *would* ask it, she thought. Even now, his seed lay in a sticky pool on her stomach. And there was something, in that, always unsatisfying and unsatisfied. . . . "Why do you never 'die' inside me, as you used to?"

"Because," Nicholas said, with a sigh and a slanting smile, "if I die inside you, my dear, I should mostlike plant new life there. Where it should be most inconvenient."

"I know!" Sometimes Nicholas's fatherly airs exasperated Susannah. She did not know quite when they had begun to. "I know I might get with child. But what would it matter?" She sat up, letting the blankets fall, and took hold of his arm. "It shouldn't matter to *me*, you know. What if I did have a child? What if . . . we were to go away together, like Lady Framer and Lord Asprey?"

She was referring to the autumn's great scandal. Fashionable Lady Caroline Framer, she of the arrow-straight brows and jet hair, had left her husband, sailing for France with the bankrupt Lord Asprey. Mortified, Lord Silvius Framer clung to the remnants of her jewels and her dowry. Rumor had it he would disinherit their son, for fear he might be some other man's work.

Nicholas smiled but looked absent; he swung his legs over the bed and detached Susannah's hand from his arm. "I've to dress," was all he said. "We've a repetition in an hour."

"Why don't you answer me?" Susannah felt deflated.

Nicholas pulled on his breeches and sighed. "All right! I'll answer. I can't run away to Italy with you, Susan, because—thanks to my grandfather's everlasting belief in the virtue of labor—I've a living to make, here. Now, I cannot think of anywhere *else* I might earn a living as I do. Can you?" He searched around the room for a comb, brushing dust off the tabletops as he went. "Hang that Mrs. Hall," he muttered.

Susannah stayed silent, for she had no reply at hand. It was true: Nicholas couldn't write for the French stage, or the Italian; he was at a loss with all languages but English. Like most gentlemen, he had a little Latin, but that would scarcely be of use. . . .

"Nicholas!" Beaming suddenly, she jumped from the bed. "Of course there's another place you might work. America! Why, by now theaters must be abuilding there—and they'll need authors. Why, in the city, in New York, there is my house. You might come to New York with me, and—"

"No, Susannah. *No.*" Nicholas's voice was loud: surprisingly angry. He glared at her as she pulled a shift over her nakedness. Her eyes, which had searched his, lowered, and she did not press him further. Silently, she dressed again. She pulled her long hair up out of the way while Nicholas pulled the back laces of her bodice closed, as usual. She walked down the stairs ahead of him, her fur-lined cloak wrapped round her. Outside on the pavement, he took her arm: and her resolve not to speak again broke.

"Why will you not think of it?" Her face, in the light of the oil lamps, looked thinner and paler than it had in summer.

"Because—" Nicholas led her gently down the street, around the broken paving stones and puddles. "Because I am an old man, Susan. Too old to begin life again in a foreign land."

"Once," Susannah said, "you ventured to all sorts of foreign places." She paused and, as Nicholas did not answer, went on, "At New York no one knows me. We might live as man and wife, and no one should know different. I could—I could keep a farm. I could raise animals—horses!—I've always wanted to. And you could write. You should write for the theaters—I am sure they have no one so good as you in New York! And I should help you. I should stay by you and help you write."

The thin rain quickened as they crossed Covent Garden, scattering the buyers and fruit sellers beneath the brick arcades of the houses.

"Help me write!" Nicholas chuckled. "Nay, Susan—I think not. Womenfolk are better not to meddle in such things. You might tend your sheep. . . . "

"Horses."

He laughed again and walked faster down Russell Street so that Susannah had to run to keep beside him. "Like Mr. Voltaire, you imagine us happiest in pastoral tranquillity! But, in earnest, Susan—" He took hold of her shoulders and looked gravely down on her. "It shouldn't be so. I should grow old on your farm, and you should grow bored. You forget the dullness of the provinces, after life in the world's great city."

"I shouldn't mind, if you were with me."

"Ah! You say so now." Nicholas smiled, and again grew strangely lighthearted; and Susannah despaired at this more than she had despaired at his seriousness. He had dismissed her idea after all.

Nicholas said evenly, "In a few years' time a girl like you might so easily have a change of heart. She'd no longer want a decrepit old crow like me."

They had reached the side door of the theater. At other times, arriving here, Susannah had asked to come backstage; Nicholas always put her off, saying what great gossips players were.

"I'll not come in," she said, to forestall another speech of caution—which she thought she could not bear just now. "Why," she said suddenly, "do you talk of changes of heart? Have *you* had one?"

"No, pet. Dearest." Nicholas touched her cheek, beneath her cloak. "You mustn't think that, if I talk of what can and cannot be. Why, we shall continue as we are."

His voice was low and persuasive, as ever. He bent down quickly, searching for her mouth, and she yielded it, her hood and loose hair falling back from her head. She didn't care if they were seen. *He* was the only one to mind: she knew it now.

"Besides," said Nicholas, standing back again, "some might say I haven't the heart to change."

But he smiled, and Susannah knew he was jesting. She walked away toward a row of hackney coaches, and Nicholas plunged into the dark pit of the theater.

"Hail, bonny gentlemen! All hail!" he cried, waving at the scene movers onstage. "Have you got the tower painted?"

"No, sir. Not yet—" began a stumpy man, hammer in hand.

"Well, be quick, eh? We're playing in a week." Nicholas spun on his heel, surveying the pit, where Wray and Kemble, the theater manager, sat conferring over papers spread out on the floor. He brushed the ash and orange peel off a bench, so as to join them, but then changed his mind and headed for the stage. He grabbed a spike and found foothold on a stair, and leapt up.

"Nichol! Old Nichol. A word with you—" Wray trotted up to the stage, his anxious, beaverish face glowing pink. "There's trouble."

"Trouble? Can't be any greater than we're in already! Three girls who can't sing, an orchestra with no horns, the Tower of the Bastille unpainted . . . I'm off to counsel the ladies on their melody."

As Wray waved his arms about and sputtered, Nicholas worked his way toward the tiring rooms. Humming "Rule, Britannia" to himself, he moved through a maze of torn backdrops, trunks, and chandeliers, emerging, at last, in the space where the ladies were dressing.

"*If* you please—" protested Belinda at the intrusion, and glared. But the other two girls smiled their welcome. Claudine Bryce looked down bashfully at her bare legs and scurried behind the nearest screen to put on shoes and stockings. Joan Catchingham, the third actress in the play, beamed up at Carrick with round brown eyes and fluffed her henna-red hair out over her shoulders.

"Methinks you're late, sir. We near began without you."

"Aye. But your caterwauling, sweet, I'll forbear to miss."

"Caterwauling!" The actress drew up, affronted. "I'll have you know! In my girlhood I was *noted*, sir, for the best singing voice in all St. Albans."

"My girl, I jest." Carrick kissed her appeasingly on the nape of the neck.

"Caterwauling it is, too," muttered Belinda to Claudine, around the screen, and Claudine emerged, still in her petticoats, to watch. The two had found a way of getting along, in the two weeks they had lived together: instead of railing at each other, they turned, like mated lions, with bared claws on the rest of the world.

"Look at her!" Claudine laughed carelessly, as if she did not *mind* Nicholas's taking up with Joan Catchingham. Though, of course she did—if only because it complicated her own plans.

"The silly sot!" chimed in Belinda.

"The clap-hunting tart!" Claudine used the word freely, now that she had come out of the trade.

Carrick was still fondling an aggrieved-looking Mrs. Catchingham. He reached for the breasts that humped above her tight bodice.

"Hold yer hand!" said Mrs. Catchingham shrilly. "And where were you two nights past, when ye promised me—"

"Betimes my memory fails me, Joany. . . . " Nicholas's hand persisted, but the redhead batted it away.

"With yer fancy lady-mistress, were ye? I bet she'd like to know of yer goings-on. Yer memory fails ye, does it? Who'll ye fergit next time, me or her?"

"Trollop! For God's sake, close your mouth." Nicholas grabbed Mrs. Catchingham's painted chin and pulled it toward him. She eyed him warily.

"Joany," he said more gently. "There's no truth in what you say, you know it well. . . . "

"There is," said Mrs. Catchingham through clenched teeth. "Lady Warrington's 'er name. I've seen her i' the boxes." She shook her head, freeing herself from Carrick's grasp; now she smiled, and patted her red curls. "You think a blue-blooded tart's *different*, don't you? Ha! Men are fools. We're all the same down *there*."

For a moment Nicholas looked as if he would lunge at her again. But instead, folding his arms tight, he backed away. As he caught Claudine's and Belinda's eyes, he wished them politely, "Good day." Mrs. Catchingham smiled, and seemed to regard this as her victory.

Belinda could not resist a hiss at her roommate. "Now d'ye believe me? He still keeps that rich lady—or she keeps 'im. Has done for a year, almost. I told you!"

Claudine glowered. Swinging her hips and skirts, she made her way to the painting table. Staring into the small square of mirror, she powdered her face until it was milk-colored, with only the slightest hint of tea.

She *would* have Carrick. Oh, she'd not do it foolishly, like Joan Catchingham, and share him. No—she would take him all to herself, once he got rid of Susannah for good.

She daubed her lips with red rouge, practicing a triumphant smile.

Nicholas sauntered out toward the stage spikes, yawning.

"Finished with the ladies' singing lessons, have you?" Wray looked annoyed. His yellow brows merged into a line across his forehead.

"Aye, they'll be much improved, I warrant. . . . You said there was some trouble?"

"The Lord Chamberlain wants us closed." Wray's voice was loud and clear; some of the players on stage turned to hear it as he spoke again. "Aye—as I said, man! Closed! That's why I begged a word before."

Nicholas stared at Wray in disbelief. "He cannot."

"Oh, he cannot, can't he? What, pray tell me, can't the king's men do when they've a mind? As our play's about the French, and as things there grow worse for the monarch every day . . ."

"But—can he not see?" Nicholas spluttered. " 'Tis but a mock—a farce! There's nothing in it to displease him."

"Our George," Wray sighed, "grows moonstruck, and stubborn with it. He fears for his life—perhaps he's right to. Who knows, in these times? . . . We're calling it off, old Nichol. We have to."

Wray barked a summons to the players, clapping his hands. When he told them the news, they hissed and booed: two angry men at the back brandished their swords. " 'Twill be our turn next!" one of them called. "We'll have their heads, we will—nor only i' France!"

"But—" Wray called. "But! Listen to me, gentlemen. I'll have you in another play, within the week. The gentleman here"—he nodded at the manager behind him—"has offered for us to perform *Othello*."

The crowd of actors booed again: for they liked Carrick and Wray and their songs and their battle scenes. *That* old, made-over tragedy could never take the place of *Palais-Royal*.

Chapter 19

❧

December came, and each night snow dusted the rooftops; it gleamed, brittle and white, at sunrise, turning translucent and vanishing by midday. The vendors at Covent Garden sold only the limpest of hothouse roses, and root vegetables so covered in mud that they looked like piles of stones on their carts. Susannah knew the turnings of the seasons in London well now: the bright, deceptive winter sun and the fast-closing days. They should pass quickly, and the nights in a long, dull sleep: and yet they did not. She did not know why.

In the last months she had seen less and less of Nicholas. Since the king had censored his play, he had been busier than ever. While the makeshift *Othello* played at Drury Lane, Nicholas huddled with Wray at Great Russell Street, rewriting: changing the setting of their revolutionary stage piece to a mythical "Livonia," making the objectionable king a mogul emperor, and—in a bold stroke—penning a long epistle dedicatory to King George. "He'll not refuse us now,"

Nicholas had crowed, "when the play is writ to his own glory!"

And he was right: at last the Lord Chamberlain had rescinded his objections. Today's rehearsal was the last before *Treason in a Foreign Land* was to begin its run.

Where is he, then? The rehearsal had begun this morning. Then, Nicholas had promised: without fail, this time, he would come here to Southampton Street. . . .

Susannah felt the anxiety growing, a hard, familiar knot in her stomach. At times, lately, it grew so painful that she had gone to the doctor to ask for a remedy. But he had found nothing wrong and gave her his usual counsel for what he called "cases of nerves." *Herb teas, bland diet, restful sleep* . . . Susannah gave a little laugh as she paced the cold bedchamber. For when did she come at any of those? To take her mind from Nicholas, she had tried, these weeks, to be ceaselessly busy. There were parties with Valerie and long evenings at the theater; games of piquet, glasses of wine, an appetite grown suddenly voracious, then absent. And sleep . . . When she tried to sleep, her fatigue left her. She was alone, the hours stretching empty before her, the cords of her nerves tightening in the hollow of her body. . . .

Outside, the candles in the windows on the street outshone the purple-gray of the sky: nearly night. Nicholas might be outside, hurrying to her: perhaps with a bottle of wine or a bunch of dried flowers. Susannah pushed up the casement and leaned out the window, looking. Two streetwalkers in masks and patched cloaks wandered aimlessly down the pavement. A couple of towheaded apprentices capered round them, crying out taunts, making one of them snap her fan. A slow cart horse, stopped in his paces behind them, whinnied.

Susannah counted seconds, to make the time pass. And she watched. She began to hope that some men would come, for those women. They waited, she waited: perhaps it was an omen.

One of the women at last disappeared with a fat, cloaked figure into one of the doorways. The other one looked lonelier now, as she kept on walking. Still Nicholas did not come. Susannah's arms had stuck to the ice on the window ledge, and her skin stung as she pulled them away.

She closed the window and sat on the bed. A fleeting hunger came and passed: for there was no food here, nor anything she could think of that she wanted to eat. *I will give up, I will go home,* she thought: but then, she would be alone in her house, unbearably. Knole would be out, visiting his lady friend in Lambeth; the servants would be supping noisily below. The hall clock would tick and chime, and the silence, as she tried to read, would grow ever more oppressive.

She walked to the window again, but by now it was black night, and she could see no one in the street: still no Nicholas. Her candle picked out a haggard, strange reflection in the glass; and staring at it, suddenly, frightened, she ran with her flame to the mirror.

I am old, she thought: but of course she was not. It had only looked so, for the glass was warped and rippled. The face in the mirror had reddened eyes, hollow cheeks: but when she leaned in closer, it became her own again. *It is the light of one candle,* she thought, turning her head: a single light would always make shadows—strange hollows. But her skin, with its paint and powder, still looked yellow; and there were wrinkles around her near-black eyes. With a faint smile, she wondered, *Can the doctor restore my looks with his herb teas and rest? After all, I am not yet twenty. . . .*

She heard a key at the door and turned, her heart beating in a rush, with relief. But when she stepped toward it, she saw that it was not Nicholas at all.

It was Mrs. Hall, the landlady; and she looked as startled as Susannah felt. " 'Scuse me, Mrs. Temple!" she said. "See, I was afeared you'd removed."

"Removed?"

"Well, I hadn't seen you in nine days entire, an' you know, the rent's six weeks past due."

"Past due," Susannah repeated. She could not seem to make her tongue work. She had been so certain that the sound at the door was Nicholas.

"Aye." The landlady folded her arms. "These six weeks."

Susannah stared and then, to hide her discomfiture, walked toward the window. She had heard no mention of the rent—but then, she never had, since they came here. Nicholas had arranged for the rooms: it was a gentleman's business, he said. She would gladly enough have paid, if she had thought it a difficulty. . . .

"I am sorry," she said, retrieving her poise. "If only you had spoken of it sooner. . . . " She searched in all the room's drawers and in the pockets of her cloak, at last finding half the seven pounds Mrs. Hall said she was owed. She apologized profusely, and some of the suspicion disappeared from the landlady's face.

"Yes, yes, misunderstanding, Mrs. Temple," Mrs. Hall echoed her words. She smiled, looking Susannah over. "An' was that you I saw at Drury Lane last week? Acting the play—'twas a mighty good one. *Othello*."

Susannah shook her head, mystified.

" 'Twasn't you? Well, perhaps I misremember. An' with those perukes and the way they paint themselves . . ." Shaking her head, the landlady retreated. "Hm! I'd been quite sure of it. Oh, well, then . . . Good evening."

Disconcerted by the scene with Mrs. Hall, Susannah could not stay in the room longer. She threw a pitcher of water on the low embers of the fire, pulled on her cloak, and ran downstairs.

This was worse, far worse, she thought, than Nicholas's usual forgetfulness. For six weeks he had forgotten their rooms, their place. Did he care so little?

She tripped on one of the cobblestones, and let out a cry. Shaking her hurt foot in the air, she bit her lip to keep from swearing. It did not matter anymore, she knew. She had done things no "lady" ever would, and yet . . . The habit was too fixed in her now. No curse would come. She walked quickly, limping a little, across Covent Garden. Her cloak was growing damp, weighing her down, but she did not think of going home. She turned into Russell Street. Nicholas might still be at the theater. There was a chance. . . .

The guardsman at the Drury Lane entrance looked to be asleep; he did not notice her. She slipped into the front hall and through velvet curtains to the pit. At first she saw nothing in its blackness. She stood, reeling a little—for her stomach was still knotted and empty—and gradually, up on the stage, a few moving figures picked themselves out of the dark. As a yellow-haired man passed in front of her, she called out, "Pardon me, please, sir. Where is Mr. Carrick?"

"You have business with him, madam?" The man spun, beer spilling from the mug in his hand. His yellow brows rose, and he waved up at the stage with a flourish. "There!"

Susannah stared at the platform and saw no way up onto it. "Excuse me, sir, but—"

"By here." The man grinned, and waddled ahead of her, beckoning, and now she saw steep steps dug into the stage's side. He stood beside them, offering her his arm for balance. "Why, *you're* not an actress," he said, almost accusingly.

Susannah's eyes widened. "No." She could feel the man looking up her skirts as she scrambled over the stage spikes; and she hurried on, across the deserted platform, past piles of discarded props and into a dark backstage passage. She heard laughter farther on, and shuffling feet and the clink of cups.

In a vast, windowless room at the rear of the theater she came upon a crowd: forty or so men, in peasant dress and bright soldier's uniforms, others in everyday suits, and a handful of ladies. She could not see yet if Nicholas was here. But the crowd kept moving, pressing her forward. She heard a toast—saw a cluster of masked men raise their glasses—and as she turned, and inched closer to them, saw Nicholas. He was behind them, half hidden by their bodies: raising a tankard of ale to their toast, basking in their congratulations, as the crowd swirled, the scene shifted, the men moved on. Susannah pushed closer, in vain, while he shook the hands of men in frock coats, kissing their ladies on the cheek. *Why, there is Claudine.* She was certain it was Claudine: a dark figure, in a peasant's laced bodice, jumping up playfully behind Nicholas's shoulder. It was *she* Mrs. Hall had meant, then: acting at Drury Lane. Susannah's heart thumped, and a strange apprehension seized her.

A red-haired woman, also in peasant garb, beamed up at Nicholas.

"Well!" she said, wrapping her arms around his neck. "Come, then. Gi' me a kiss."

At once Susannah forgot Claudine. She stared at the red-haired woman and at Nicholas's familiar smile, familiar look, back at her. For a moment he edged away from her embrace. Then with a whoop, he tossed the contents of his tankard into the air and repaid the redhead with a long, vigorous kiss.

Susannah let out a cry, but it was lost in the din of the chamber. And once the shock of the moment had passed, she knew that she must be foolish, wrong. She had no reason to be jealous of the girl. Nicholas would only think it prudish. So once he was free, and conversing with the masked gentlemen again, she stepped forward, like the other ladies, to congratulate him. She threw back her hood and smiled.

"Lady Susan." Nicholas took her hand, and gave her a peck on the cheek. He smiled blithely at her, as he had smiled at all the other ladies who came before him.

"I was waiting," she began, in a low voice: but decided, hearing herself, to seem more carefree. "Well! I thought, if there were celebrations, why should I not join them?" She felt Nicholas's hand working loose from hers.

"Indeed? Lady Warrington," he said. Another actress was tugging at his shoulder, and a boy had brought him a fresh tankard, which he took. "I am glad you could come," he said. He bowed to Susannah, turning now to an actress behind him.

Stunned, Susannah backed away. The tears welled in her eyes. She did not know what she had expected: a familiar word, a whispered promise—not this coldness, beyond all need for caution. She stumbled backward.

"Susan." A firm tenor voice addressed her. An arm in black velvet took hold of hers, and Anthony Ogilvie's face, masked and mischievous, appeared beside her. "Come away, let me give you supper," he said. "You look as though you need it."

"Oh, Anthony, I—"

"I know. Dear Susan. Don't cry."

Somehow they crossed the stage and the darkened pit and came to Ogilvie's coach outside the theater.

"What of—your friends?" Susannah said unsteadily, as she climbed in: for, thinking back, she realized that the other masked gentlemen talking to Nicholas must have been Gant or Beaton or others of Anthony Ogilvie's wide acquaintance.

"No matter," said Ogilvie. "They're minded to stay." The coach thundered out into the road, and in a few minutes they pulled up at an inn, in a lane off the Strand.

Inside, a serving man took their cloaks and led them upstairs to a private dining chamber, where two dark oaken armchairs waited before the open fire. Ogilvie hung his hat and mask by the door.

"Anthony!" Susannah cried, seeing him properly for the first time. "Oh—you look dreadful."

"My compliments to you too, m'lady." Ogilvie gave a wry smile, which did little to efface the impression of ailing given by his reddened eyes and hollow cheeks. "I've suffered toothache," he said. "Nothing more serious! Lately it has abated—I think I'll not need to have it out." He gave her a piercing glance and looked

about to speak further; but just then the waiting man
came in to take his orders.

In the meantime Susannah wiped her eyes and
smoothed her hair and struggled for composure. She
was ashamed of her tears at the theater. Perhaps
Nicholas had only been showing caution; no dissem-
bling was too great, he sometimes said, when one was
abroad, in public view.

She tasted her glass of wine and felt queasy.

"What, can you not drink, to ease your troubles?"
Ogilvie gave her another twisted smile.

"It—it gives me pain," said Susannah. But she found
the second mouthful of wine went down more easily.

"Then you are in a sorry state, my pet."

"But—"

"But no protests! I declare you should go to that
country house of yours and have a rest. From all of
us here in London, and especially—from Nicholas
Carrick." Ogilvie looked hard at her through his fringe
of hair, and refilled his cup.

"I couldn't," said Susannah dully. "And besides—
how can *you* advise me so, when you'd never leave
here either?" She remembered the talk they had had
at Bath and, looking down at her cup, went silent.
But her companion seemed not to notice. He set to
arguing with her, good-naturedly, on the merits of
the country versus the city for health, and recovery of
the spirits. In the middle of it all, their supper came.

Susannah ate at first cautiously, then hungrily, the
roast beef and wine wearing away at her queasiness.
She wished that Ogilvie would eat, too, but he only
twirled a fork disinterestedly above his plate.

"You should leave him, Susan," he said suddenly.

She swallowed. He had not mentioned Nicholas's
name, but she knew at once whom he meant. "Leave
him? No. I couldn't."

"But he gives you nothing, he does not know your
worth. Other men would—"

"I couldn't love another man so easily as you say!"
Susannah's voice rose in protest: but she knew there

was no hope of making Ogilvie understand. For hadn't he once admitted to . . . no feeling at all?

"I know," he said, relenting. "It is hard. I am only saying—to give it thought. For I know Nicholas, and all his faults. His passion for what eludes him . . . I have loved him longer than you, Susan."

"Loved him?" The words struck her as strange.

"Aye. As a man can." Ogilvie paused. "It is a far more enduring thing than—" But there he broke off, and sat in silence. The boisterous shouts of drinkers and gamblers rang in the tavern below, and the clink of silver and laughter from the men and women in the room beside them.

Susannah finished her meal and stretched before the fire. The ache in her stomach had passed; she might almost be content, but for the memory of that red-haired actress, with Nicholas. *It signifies nothing,* she tried to think: the actress had thrown herself at him. *Nothing more.* Yet, the scene replayed itself in her mind. She looked down sadly at Ogilvie, who was drinking, staring into the fire. He had ordered a third bottle of wine, which they were near finishing. Misery loved company, so they said. . . .

"I am not so miserable," she said suddenly. Defiant, she gulped down the last of her glass and poured more.

"What of your husband?" said Ogilvie, looking up.

Susannah wondered how this connected with what had gone before. "My husband? He is not miserable—he has his work."

"Do you never think of going back to him?"

Susannah shook her head and stared at her glass. She tilted the wine in it to and fro. "I don't think he should want me. Why, he scarce even writes me anymore."

"What is he like?"

"Oh, he's rather—like you, in a way. He was my friend, once. But then he was different, too—he's vastly learned."

Ogilvie looked affronted.

"Oh! I didn't mean . . . I've been a fool, again. What I intended . . ." Hastening to apologize, she lost the words she sought. "Harry is," she said at last, "peculiarly clever. He is a sort of prodigy, for remembering. So that, I think—people can't help but disappoint him. He ends by being fonder of his books."

Ogilvie drained his glass. "Then he was not old, or hideous?"

She shook her head.

"Why did you seek elsewhere?"

"We . . . parted." The memory of it grew hazy, nearly painless, beneath the night's deep tiredness and the wine. "Do you know," she said, wondering, "I can scarce call back why. I think it must have been—only pride."

Ogilvie asked her no more about Harry. Instead, they talked of Sarah, of Valerie: of the other people they knew. It was odd, Susannah thought, how poorly Ogilvie rated them all.

"Of course Sarah's a poor, lost sheep," he said, "who but waits to be converted to a faith. And Valerie—and Nichol, too—they are the priests and the players. Devotion is no more than a toy to them. A means of entrancing the rest of us."

"Not Nicholas," Susannah protested. "He is different. He has more—feeling."

Ogilvie turned to her, looking earnestly at her through the fringe of his light hair. He reached for her hand. "Upon our friendship, Susannah—I would ask a promise. Though I scarcely expect you will grant it."

"What?"

"Leave Nicholas be, for a time."

"I don't know. I couldn't—"

"The closer you follow him, the further he escapes you. I see it, Susan, and I am—most sorry." Ogilvie's gaze flickered away from her for a moment, but returned. "Do without him—pretend you've no need of him! He may yet seek you. Go to the country or stay here, no matter—but care for *yourself* for a time, dear Susan."

Susannah looked up at her friend: trusting, doubtful. "Seek him no more? Do you think it will—come right?"

"Yes."

At last she answered. "Then I will do so. There. You have my word."

The inn grew quieter. She did not know the hour, and no watch cries or clock chimes penetrated the walls. Ogilvie dozed in the chair beside her. Though the promise she had given still made her anxious, for she did not know how she could possibly keep it, in time she stretched out in her own chair, too, and fell asleep. In the middle of the night, she thought, or dreamed, that Ogilvie was kneeling, scrabbling on the floor, searching for something. She saw him lift up a bottle, take a draught; he subsided back into his chair. But by morning she had forgotten it. They rose, sleepy-eyed, at dawn, and made their way out into the courtyard, where Ogilvie's driver dozed inside the coach. During the ride home, Ogilvie fell back into a deep sleep, against the seat. In the light of day, his face looked ashen. He could not be so well as he said, thought Susannah. After all, toothache could be a great affliction. She promised herself to call on him soon, to make sure that he was recovering.

Chapter 20

———— ❧ ————

The time passed slowly; and the promise grew no easier to keep. Every day for a week, Susannah nearly broke it and wrote to Nicholas. She told herself he would not understand the meaning of this sudden silence: and yet, on the point of writing, she always stopped. For perhaps there was wisdom in Anthony's words. Perhaps one man could know another, in friendship, in ways a woman, in love, could not. And Nicholas would be drawn to her, by her remove. He would miss her.

A second week wore on, and Nicholas did not write or come to the house to seek her. An aching fear gnawed at her belly: that perhaps he had not even noticed her distance. She wanted to cry out, to howl. *When will he come?*

Housework, the doctor's bland diet—this steady sobriety—seemed almost as painful a punishment as Nicholas's silence. Sometimes she felt limp, lethargic, so that nothing could rouse her: not Knole's humble jests, not even the suspicion that Ernestine had pilfered money from the cashboxes. She thought of taking the housekeeper to task: but, as she was about to, the strength left her. *What does it matter?*

Yet at other times she was seized with a restless energy. She would crave company: Valerie's, Anthony's, Sarah's. At home, she took furiously to listings and rearrangements. She wrote out tiny labels for the drawers of her tea chest: *Assam, China Black, Pekoe, Darjeeling.* . . . She washed her hair two or three times a week, even though Peg clucked that it was unhealthy. For her hair could take up a great deal of time. She would lather it twice, and scent it with lavender, and pick out every tiny knot with her comb as she dried it by the fire.

When Christmas Eve came, she tried to fill her house with friends. She played piquet with Valerie and her latest swain, a colonel, and accepted the toasts of bald Horace Beaton. Sarah came, but Ogilvie did not; and in the end, somehow, the evening felt hollow. She felt a sharp pang of regret for home: for Adela, and, as in a long time she had not felt it, for her father. A melancholy came over her, which she tried to assuage the next day by attending St. George's Church. She mouthed the prayers but did not really hear them; and the longing for family—even some of her English family—would not leave her. She missed them: Augusta, her little son Jonas. *And Harry.*

On New Year's Eve, still in low spirits, she sat down to write him a letter. She wished she could tell him how she felt, as once she might have. Instead, she wrote of the weather and the changes she had made about the house; of Knole's plans, yet distant, to marry. "I am glad to think of him with a home of his own, and family," she wrote. It was then that the tears began to trickle from her eyes: persistent, inexplicable.

The year turned, and still she had no word from Nicholas. She knew that his play had just ended its run: eighteen days, a long one for Drury Lane, where the plays could change weekly. Determined to keep her promise to Ogilvie, she had kept away from *Treason in a Foreign Land*—though she could not close her ears to the town gossip, which declared it another of Carrick's successes. Soon, she supposed, Nicholas would have scant need to write for a living: his plays and continuous reprintings of *Cyberion* would bring him the fortune to live at leisure. Eventually, too, he would become the Baron Blackcroft. His fears for public opinion would be at an end. If he would not go to America, might he not live openly with her here—at least then? But even as she thought of this, and began to hope, Susannah shook her head. She looked up from the books she was arranging at her pale reflection in the glass. *It will never be; Nicholas has said so. And I will not ask again.*

"Well?" Claudine tossed her curled hair back, catching her own eye, then Nicholas Carrick's, in the tiring-room mirror.

"You acquitted yourself well tonight." Nicholas stepped back, with a look that traced the outlines of her body, in detail and shamelessly. "Even if," he added, "yours was not the song we'd written."

"No." Claudine dabbed more rouge onto her lips. "Better." She looked back at Carrick. "You think so, too." *If he doesn't, the more fool him!* The French maids' tune was a dull thing, and none of the actresses singing it had an ear for tune to start with. The only way to save it was to spice it up: to pepper it with innuendo, with frogs and French letters. So tonight, at *Treason*'s third showing, she had done so, adding, in a loud stage whisper, to the song's written lyrics. She had heard the chuckles, then the laughs in the pit. And she had known, then, that *this* was the way to win a following. Everyone who saw her would remember her now. "So what's to be our next piece, here?" she said.

Nicholas gaped: but she knew he was teasing. "*Our* next piece?" he said. "Do you suppose there has naturally to be a part for you in it?"

"And why not?" Claudine turned. "I've played *Othello* now, and *Treason*—"

Reaching swiftly for her hands, grinning, Nicholas said, "Come out with me, tonight."

"Is that a bargain?" Claudine said tartly. "I make no bargains! I've reformed meself, you know. . . ."

But her look was provocative, only dissolving, after a few minutes, into one of trembling hesitation. Her lashes fluttered against her cheeks. " 'Tis not that it isn't *hard*," she whispered. "Refusing you . . ."

"So it should be!" Nicholas laughed and tried to steal a kiss near her mouth. But she twisted away.

"What's to be my next part?" She smiled calmly.

Later Claudine was glad that she had not surrendered too quickly. Carrick was surely handsome, but he was not her only admirer. When she returned home that night, she found three notes from different men and a bouquet of silk flowers.

"Are ye going to meet 'em?" said Belinda, eyeing the notes hungrily. "Some of 'em sounds rich."

"No." Claudine nibbled the end of her fan. "I'll bide." For after all, she had business to do. Business with the theater, with Nicholas—with Susannah. And all of it too complicated for the likes of Belinda to understand.

She found out the next day that she was to play the country girl, Rose, in *The Recruiting Officer*. Carrick himself ran up to her to present her with the script. With a quailing look, she flipped through its pages: she had not done so much reading since she started acting, four months ago.

"What?" Carrick looked concerned. "Do you not wish it?"

Claudine smiled and cocked her head. "I'd *rather* the lady Melinda—but the maid'll do."

"May I accompany you home?"

"Why, Nicholas. Have you naught else to do? What of your lady-mistress?"

"My—" Nicholas's face went dark. "Who taught you that? 'Tis folly!"

"Come, come. We all know of 'er, much as you try to hide 'er. What, has she up an' left you?" Claudine studied her nails, unconcerned. "Well, we all know their ways! These fine ladies . . . They'll e'er go back whimpering to their husbands, as it's them what has the money."

"You've a fantastical imagination, Claudine," said Nicholas tersely. And then, as she looked up, the strain in him seemed to break. He smiled and took her arm. "Come, miss! Shall we to an inn? Where shall I take you?"

"I didn't say as I'd permit you," Claudine answered, with propriety. "But I'll admit I've a fearsome thirst."

At The Three Georges, once Nicholas had drunk a good deal and was beginning to stare at her, she asked, "Do I 'mind you of someone?"

"No! And yes, and . . . no, not in truth. Why should you?"

"Your lady-mistress?" she teased.

"There is none," said Nicholas unsteadily.

"Aye, there is. Tell me truly."

"Aye, well—"

The answer decided her: *not yet.* She had vowed she wouldn't have him until he got rid of Susannah. So she climbed out of the hackney coach, leaving him on the pavement by her lodgings. And though she knew she had been right to stick by her intentions, she did feel a pang of regret when, that night, he did not come to the theater—nor did he appear again for almost a week, after. His disappearance, after only one evening in Claudine's company, caused the other actresses no end of merriment at her expense.

One evening in the middle of January, Susannah sat sewing in the downstairs parlor. There was that win-

try stillness to the room, and the street outside, that
always unnerved her: a silence so complete that she
thought she heard her own heart beating. Her ears
were so alert to every sound that when she heard
hoofbeats, still distant, across the square, she drew
her breath to listen where they tended. They drew
closer now until, outside, she heard the thump of feet
on the pavement. She stopped her work and waited,
still, listening to Peg's voice, and another, in the hallway.

The door fell open. Nicholas stood in the dark of
the hall, his face flushed and haggard.

"Susan."

He said no more. And when Susannah opened her
mouth, she found only silence. "I—I'd—" she
achieved at last and stabbed the cloth and her finger
with her needle.

"It's Anthony," said Nicholas. "Anthony is dead."

For a few moments Susannah felt nothing but a chill
disbelief. "Dead?" she managed to repeat. She heard
her cloth drop to the floor. "He cannot—"

"By his own hand." Nicholas's voice was rough.
"There was—laudanum at his bed. The priests—" He
gave an eerie smile and staggered forward. "*They* will
not know of it—Gant and I took care of it—long gone!
Before they got there—" Nicholas fell into a chair and
buried his head in his hands.

Susannah heard the words, but they meant nothing
yet; and she moved forward, with a numb, deceiving
calm, and stood over Nicholas. " 'Twill be all
right. . . . " she whispered, stroking his back.

He looked up with haunted eyes. "But—don't you
see? It can never be all right! He was my best friend!"

Susannah recoiled at the anger in his voice. And now,
as Nicholas spoke on, the truth reached her.

The night Anthony died, they had gone to an inn—
he and Nicholas, Tom Gant, and the playwright Wray.
They had drunk; they had stayed late. "And there were
girls," said Nicholas. "Anthony—took one in his lap. He
took her home. And we were all so merry. . . ."

A new chill came over Susannah then, but she did

not speak of it. "What—will we do?" she said. "Without him—"

Nicholas raised his head, and opened his arms to
her. For a long time she leaned there, beside him, on
the arm of the chair, stroking his hair while he buried
his head in her lap.

"Why did he—drink it?" Susannah choked on the
words. "That—medicine . . . It was poison!" She remembered Valerie's words. *Opium, laudanum. To stir
the imagination.* Men took it also for pain: but was
Anthony's pain, in his teeth, so bad as that? He had
said not. . . .

"We saw him—take it, before," she said slowly.
"We might have known. We might have—stopped
him."

But Nicholas did not seem to hear her. He stroked
the folds of her skirt. "Come out!" he said suddenly.
"Come out with me now."

"We can't." Susannah shook her head.

"Yes!" Nicholas raised himself up, fixing his eyes,
narrow and reddened, on hers. "You *must* come out
with me, Susan. Don't you see? I cannot bear to be
indoors. The specter—it is too horrible, Susan. I think
of him. In that room, on his bed . . . Please! You must
come with me. You are my only friend."

"Where?" said Susannah, trembling, standing as
Nicholas rose beneath her. He pulled her with both
hands toward the door.

For a second she stopped. "You know," she said quietly, "before now, I had formed a resolve—to see you
no more."

"What?" Nicholas started. "Why? You never said."

"It was—" Susannah began. *It was because of Anthony,* she nearly said. But she stopped herself.

"Come then," said Nicholas, turning forward, with
his arm around her shoulders. "Fetch your cloak, Susan. Aye—your mask! Your fanciest dress! We shall
go to the Clarion, to Vauxhall. . . . Well, are you
ready, then? Come!"

He held her round the waist as she rode in front of
him, out into the cold rain and the darkness. The horse

twisted and railed against the carriages coming at them. "Please, Nicholas—slower," she cried. "Where are we going?"

"To life!" he breathed. His body was warm, almost feverish, against hers. "We must seize it in our hands—"

"But it doesn't matter, we might go in," Susannah tried. "We are safe. . . . "

But they rode on, until they were far east, near the Thames, and there, at last, Nicholas pulled up at a tavern.

They went into one inn, and another, and yet another, each darker and more fetid with the smells of the river. Nicholas slaked the enormous thirst that had come upon him, talking always of life, of death—"Do you see?" he would cry, and he clung to Susannah's hand as if she were about to vanish. She drank too, and felt the words blur on her tongue, wishing she could bring him back to her house, or to Southampton Street: to calm. "We might—stay in one place. It would not matter," she said at last, in the din of the third tavern.

"No! I'll not let us die yet. When we grow still— we grow old and die." Nicholas's eyes were wild, and fearful. "Nay, I'll not go indoors. Not yet." His hand roved under the table, her skirts, until he touched her bare thigh. "We'll fight it. . . . "

"I—I don't know." Susannah felt what little resistance she had ebbing. For after all, she had kept her promise, until the cruelty of chance brought Nicholas back. He needed her as much now as she needed him.

The weather was too wintry for the pleasure gardens Nicholas talked of; but still he refused to retire indoors. At the third inn he left his horse and hired a coach, which he called out to the driver to take where he liked. From its dark interior they could see little of the streets outside. As other carriages clipped past, the eyes of their horses would shine briefly in the light of a torch. The beat of their hooves receded; the oil streetlamps floated past like hazy moons. At last there were no more lights, and it was quiet.

"Where are we?" said Susannah.

"I don't know, pet. I told him—away." Nicholas sighed; he seemed almost calm, and leaned his head on her shoulder.

"Are we in the country?"

"Aye. Perhaps we are." Nicholas turned suddenly, and knelt on the floor of the coach before her. He pressed his hands to her hips and drew her closer. "As before?"

He threw her skirts up and out of the way. Susannah looked around, at the enclosed darkness and the night sky. They seemed a dream: the dark shadow of Nicholas a dream, too, his touch but a trace, a sketch, a shadow. He unfastened her cloak and worked her gown loose from her breasts. He twirled his fingertips round them. She felt her nipples hardening, her flesh swelling, desiring, below. It was real: this was not the numbness of a dream. When she said *no*, she knew the refusal came too weakly and too late. And Nicholas did not withdraw, did not stop, gave her no respite until the very end.

"So you are still mine," he said. She thought he smiled, with something of the old, antic look in his eyes. The carriage had gathered speed and bounced more violently beneath them.

"No," Susannah said. "Not—" *Not as before.* But Nicholas kissed her and stopped her from saying it.

They drew into the center of the city again, and at Southampton Street at last he consented to go inside. They spent the night in the attic rooms, the fire roaring; and as if by some unspoken pact, they talked no more of Anthony, or of death.

The heir to Stoneborough Abbey was to be buried in Nottinghamshire, as was fitting, but in London his family held a memorial service for his friends. Mourning rings, mourning gloves were given out; and at about the same time new talk started up in the town: not of overdose, nor suicide, but of the terrible, sudden "flux" that had killed Anthony Ogilvie.

"For by such accident," intoned the priest, "might
we all be taken, at God's mercy . . ."

The pews of St. George's, Hanover Square, were
crowded and still, the occupants subduing their rustling
and coughs: their apprehension at the sound of those
words. *By such accident*, Susannah's mind echoed them.
She sat alone, at the Warrington family pew. *Was it
accident?* It might have been. From pain only, Anthony
might have taken the laudanum that night. And, from
the wish to kill pain, attempted too much . . .

Susannah stared down at her hands: gray gloves,
embroidered with the Ogilvie crest. *No one knows*.
No one here knew what could cause a man so young—
not thirty—to despair. Perhaps she was the only one
here who guessed it. The girl from the tavern, the
failing that haunted him . . .

She saw his face, gaunt and sad, as it had been the
night they supped together. And it seemed to her now
that it was the face of a man trapped. Trapped by a
circle of friends, a way of living. By appearances he
could not live up to and did not know how to forsake.
Anthony! she wanted to tell him: to make him believe, as she never could before. *You can change. You
can leave here. . . .*

The priest bowed his head and gave benediction. At
the back of the church she shook hands with Anthony's
parents. They were white-haired, rosy-cheeked, courteous: and she wondered now that Anthony had grumbled at them and called them "worthy rustics." She could
imagine them, cheerful and prosperous, drinking ale
with their tenants, riding out to the hunt. *Why, it is a
good life*, she thought suddenly. *What had he to fear
from joining them?*

She saw Tom Gant, Horace Beaton, and Nicholas, in
their wide-brimmed black hats, among the mourners.
But Ogilvie's other friends—Valerie, Sarah, Lydia
Cram—had not appeared. The men shifted on their feet
and looked uneasy; and once they had spoken to Anthony's family, they hurried from the church. Susannah's gaze followed them as they dashed off down the
street.

Nicholas, catching his coattails up in one hand, waved to beckon her. "We're off to drink to Ogilvie!" he called. "To see him off in less gloomy manner—"

But she shook her head. The service had left her a weary peace, which she did not want to disturb. In these last weeks Nicholas had been all she could ask: passionate, constant. Anthony Ogilvie had been right: she had no need to run after him. He would always return. By herself she turned the corner into Hanover Square.

Nicholas Carrick twisted his hand free of Claudine's as they scurried around the corner of Southampton Street.

"What you 'fraid of?" said Claudine, grabbing it back. "Come on!" Ignoring his unease, his shifting eyes, she led him up the stairs, skirts flying. "Here?" she said, stopping at the first floor, the second, the third. "Ooh!" she breathed, when they finally arrived, and she bent in the doorway to look at the garret rooms. She spun, as if they were a stage set, and took their measure. Then she looked at Nicholas. " 'Tis but a reading," she said, in a teasing voice.

Nicholas smiled back. The worried lines in his face seemed to vanish. "Aye," he said, and his eyes dwelt on her. "A reading." If something—the furnishings, the scent in the air—reminded him of Susannah, he did not show it. *The noble lady?* he had answered Claudine, some twenty minutes ago. *Nay, she's gone from me.* Claudine had clung to him so, then, and begged him to help her learn her part. . . . Southampton Street was but a step from Drury Lane; and Susannah was not due to meet him here till tomorrow.

Still, the dark girl's swelling bosom as she caught her breath—her wild, corkscrewing hair and downward gaze as she walked closer—cast a strange shadow across his face, and he stumbled back against the hearth. The script of *The Recruiting Officer* slipped from Claudine's hand. "I can guess why you recruited *me*," she said, laying one smooth hand on the mantel behind him. Her body nudged his, and she giggled. "Why, your breeches'll catch fire, Nichol!"

Nicholas's eyes flickered sideways, avoiding her, but returned. They rested on the still brown-green of hers. "Why, I wouldn't have thought you so cold," she said. She stepped backward, unbuttoning her bodice.

Her gown dropped onto the carpet. "Well?" she said. "Is that all you're going to do? Stand there, like some limp-pricked son of a—"

With a rush of strength that surprised her, he charged forward and pushed her down to the floor.

She tossed under him, biting and wrangling, until, in the end, she had her own way. She lit on top of him, teasing his body with her lean, brown one: riding him, twitching, swaying, until her strength was exhausted. She clutched at him with every muscle in her body, and was repaid in kind. For he was a lusty lover—*no limp-pricked son of anything, to be sure*, she thought. When it was over, she untwined her legs from his and stood. For a minute she stalked, deerlike, triumphant, around the room; then she shot back into the crimson-covered bed.

"What are you at?" said Nicholas. His eyes flickered with amusement.

She did not answer but grinned and writhed under the bedclothes: leaving her mark. Soaking the sheets in her own, and Nicholas's, wetness. For a moment he looked annoyed, but now he stretched out again and pulled her close. He was on the verge of beginning again, when steps sounded outside the door. With a groan, he rose and reached for his shirt. But the door opened, before he could, and there, red-cheeked and breathless, stood Susannah.

She stared at him, puzzled at first, and a smile rose to her lips, and vanished. She stared harder: now at his nakedness, now at the bed, where a shock of mahogany hair spilled out above the covers. Her eyes were wet, but she did not speak. Gathering her pink skirts, she turned and fled.

Nicholas did not move, nor did Claudine, but beneath the bedclothes her body shook with laughter.

Susannah's new silk dress trailed in the mud, and she hobbled to the end of the street, gasping for breath.

No coach was there. The driver had taken it back to the square, as she told him. And now, but for the chinks of light from shuttered windows, dark engulfed her. She slumped against a wall and felt rain from a gutter spout drip down on her head. Her stomach ached, and she knew now that this was agony. If she had felt it before, that had been nothing. . . .

She had thought he was hers again: how wrong. How often, she wondered, had he done this before? Told her that those rooms were their sacred place. And then . . .

The dark hair, the huddled shape in the bed: they were Claudine's. Now she knew she could believe nothing he had ever told her. For, into her sacred place, he had taken her half-sister, who hated her. She knew now that she could not tell him her fear, which had seemed, until a moment ago, the fulfillment of a long, secret wish. She could not tell him of the joy to which she had woken, that morning, her mind resolved after a week of anxiety: of the glad restlessness that seemed to pull her out of the house, into the teeming streets, past maids, merchants, peddlers, children. . . .

She had wandered past Drury Lane, asked after Nicholas. Not really minding that he was not there, she had crossed Covent Garden toward Southampton Street, thinking to stop there, to tidy the rooms, as she did on occasion. To lay a welcoming fire, for next time . . .

She knew he might not be glad of it: might take no interest. Yet, *mine, to raise, to love as my own*, she had thought, her face warming, her eyes shining with an irrepressible joy. At Covent Garden, with a sudden superstition, she had closed her eyes before picking a silk nosegay out of the flower seller's basket. *Pink*, she had seen: pink primroses. *The babe will be a girl.*

Chapter 21

───────── ❧ ─────────

Susannah stared into the pitch-blackness of her bed
and felt her heart drumming against the shell of her
body. Her hair was damp, but she had nearly forgotten why: the long walk home in the rain was a dim
memory. But she remembered the garret rooms as if
she still stood before them: the harsh reds of the carpets and walls, the woman in bed, Nicholas gaping.
For once, he had had no words. She shivered. Her
body would not stop shaking, even though Peg had
toweled her dry and wrapped her in blankets. At the
first sight of her, Peg had clucked and fretted; the
cook sent up three potions against the chill. *It is not
a chill*, Susannah had insisted, but her body still shook,
as if with sobs that made no sound; with pent-up frustration. With anger.

The house grew quiet, and midnight struck beyond
the square. Her limbs still shaking, but less and less
now, she climbed from bed. She pulled back the curtains and sat still on a chair by the window, staring
out at the black sky, and thinking.

* * *

"M'lady?" Peg called softly. It was morning. The
bedroom door inched open. "M'lady? There's someone below as asks for you—"

"Tell him"—Susannah's voice was hoarse; only in
the dark early morning had she found sleep—"I will
not see him."

"But—" the maid began to protest.

Susannah pulled herself up in bed, awake, puffy-
eyed. "I *do not want* to see him," she insisted. "Don't
let him in."

With a worried look, Peg curtsied. Once she had
sent away the caller—who was but a messenger boy—
she ran up to the bedroom, to rub Susannah's chest
with soothing spirits.

Another caller came that day, too, but with a curt
answer Peg shut the door in his face.

The next morning Susannah was dressing: pulling
on a chemise, a petticoat, combing her hair. She
moved slowly, mechanically. Still, the scene of Southampton Street replayed itself in her head. And another knowledge drummed, insistent, in her ears. For
if it was true, it would not go away: not be forgotten.

Yet it might not be. Her monthly flows, usually regular, were still only a week late. She felt no queasiness
but that of her grief; no swelling, no stirring of life,
such as she had expected a mother must feel from the
beginning. She would go, today, to find out. *Perhaps
it will not be.*

There was a clatter out in the hall, but she ignored
it. The maids were always making such sounds.

Then she heard rapid steps on the stairs, and the
crash of a spindly table. The door of the parlor beyond her bedroom flew open.

It banged hard against the painted wall; and Nicholas Carrick stood in the doorway, breathing hard,
watching her.

He looked bigger, in this small-proportioned room,

than was natural. "Susan." He gave a twisted smile. "What fools your servants are. They'd not admit me."

She turned her head away from him. Her hair, falling loose around her shoulders, hid him from view. She would keep it so, she thought. Not look at him. His breath, his strange smile, the lights in his eyes, made her wary. "I told them—to send you away," she said. "I do not want to see you."

"Ah, but they do not understand." Nicholas gave a sharp laugh and moved forward. "Think they to keep me back from what is mine? They have no right."

Susannah stepped back. She knew how vulnerable she looked, in her thin underclothes, her only weapon the silver brush in her hand. But she held it firm, her arms folded across her chest, guarding herself. As Nicholas Carrick moved toward her again, she edged back and quickly around him, toward the door. "If you do not go," she said now, from her distance, "I shall have to summon them. The servants."

"Do you think they can protect you from me?" Nicholas gave another smile: more crooked and sinister than the last. In the doorway, Susannah reached behind her, for the servants' bell; but the table that held it had tumbled down. Nicholas, in his rush, must have knocked it.

"You owe me a duty," said Nicholas, in a low voice, "at least to explain—"

"You are not my husband. I owe you no duty." Her blue gaze on his angered face fearful but level, Susannah edged farther back, toward the stair post. Nicholas stepped close to her, and she felt his warm breath, smelling of whiskey.

"You cannot understand—how your holding so small a thing against me wounds me." His eyes lowered. "I vow it was nothing. A trifle. It is man's weakness."

She looked at him, almost with pity. For—whatever he said—how slight a claim a lover truly had upon his mistress. Such "weakness," in a husband, might have to be forgiven. But in a man to whom she was bound by no tie but that of passion . . .

"You must go," she said, and her voice sounded cooler than she had expected. And as Nicholas began to speak again—to beg, then to demand—she ducked down quickly and reached on the floor for the servants' bell. "Ernestine! Warwick! Peg!" she shouted.

His words stopped suddenly as he saw the two elder servants coming up the stairs.

"Show him out now, please," she said. She looked— *for the last time,* she thought—at his two-sided face, once dazzling, now simply familiar. She knew that, shamed thus, he would not come back. Yet she felt little sorrow. She would feel his absence, she knew. Time might weigh on her; she might long, sometimes, for his kindling gaze, his touch. But perhaps, in that month she had spent without him, she had already begun to bear it.

The streets in Cow Cross grew so narrow that the driver was reluctant to attempt them.

" 'Twill be on my conscience, miss, leavin' ye here," he said, and his spotty boy's face quivered with concern.

Susannah counted coins into his hand, avoiding his gaze. "If you can wait," she said, "I'll be back in a shake." She tried to smile.

" 'Scuse me, miss, but—'struth, you don't know—"

It was true, thought Susannah. *I do not know.* But she had to go on. She did not know the district, this northeast fringe of the city. Its alleys were treeless, nearly windowless, lined with tenements. A gang of children ran, barefoot, past her, a scrawny dog barking at their heels; and she walked on quickly, lifting her skirts above the dung on the paving. She knew only one name and address here. She had to come.

The women in Valerie's circle dropped the name amongst themselves, like a talisman. *Aye, Mrs. Rattle,* some of the older ones would say. *Bless her, three times she's rid me of my misery.* Susannah had never liked to hear these things. She knew that sometimes these women bore children; that midwives, like this Mrs. Rattle, saw them delivered and given away.

She knew that she could never have such a thing done; in many ways she did not think like Valerie's friends. But she was growing certain now that she faced what they called their "trouble": woman's fate. She had waited two days longer than she had intended to make this visit, to give the monthly curse its chance to come. Still, there was no sign of it. *Either way, I must know.* Now she stood at the corner of Field Lane and Cross Street, begging instructions of a ragged woman heavy with child. The woman curled her lip and stared at her: at last, pointed down a street, to a narrow passage. She followed it, walking on a path of dry straw through the mud. Looking up, she saw chimneys, a blank sky, and the leaning gables of attics. For a second she saw different gables, another place: outlined against a blue sky, near the frozen Thames. She remembered Nicholas teasing her: arguing, pulling at her arm. . . .

That is past, she thought: and yet it seemed more real than this white winter day. She saw the far house across the courtyard, where the woman had pointed. Holding her breath, she ran up four flights of its steps and tried the door, which sat ajar. A voice shrieked, "Don't come in!"

She stepped back, frightened.

A moment later the voice called, "Now, ye can come in."

When she entered, though from the alarm of the cry, she expected to find some visitor, she found no one in the bare room but the midwife, Mrs. Rattle. She was tiny and pink-skinned, with eyes set wide, like a frog's. She wore a limp woollen gown and a mobcap, beneath which her head was completely bald. Susannah stared.

"I han't seen you before," said the old woman warily. "D'ye know ye're disturbing a delivery?"

Susannah looked around the room and saw nothing: a plank bed, dusty floorboards, a mantel covered with bottles and jars. A row of odd-shaped metal instruments hung behind Mrs. Rattle on the wall. *What delivery?*

Mrs. Rattle waved her hand toward a corner, where a heap of black fur lay in a puddle, heaving and writhing. It was a cat, Susannah saw now: a cat, delivering kittens. She might have laughed with relief; but she could not. "I think—" she said, and her throat grew dry. "I think I am with child."

Mrs. Rattle's frog eyes flitted over her. "How many weeks?"

Susannah shook her head helplessly. "I don't know. Perhaps—two weeks? Or three?"

"Have you used any preventives? Savin, lavender, camphor . . ."

"No, nothing," said Susannah. She had not heard of such things. "Except—" And she thought of the interruptions, in bed: the precautions. Which Nicholas had abandoned, since he had returned to her . . . "No," she said at last. "I haven't."

The woman gave a little, exasperated sigh. Then she motioned Susannah to lie down on the bed and with an assortment of noises—*hmms* and *ahs* and clucks—groped inside her. Susannah squeezed her eyes shut. For a moment, before they entered her, she had glimpsed Mrs. Rattle's hands. They were large, the fingers stained red and twisted, as if from the efforts of many deliveries.

"Is it?" she said, her body shaking. "Am I with child?"

"Could be." Mrs. Rattle wiped her hands on her apron. "Most likely, if you missed your flow. 'Tis rare it's another reason!" She let out a sound, which might be a laugh, or a gasp of air. Then she studied Susannah, her frog eyes unblinking. "Course, it maught go away, yet. Maughtn't it."

"Go away?" said Susannah, sitting up. Beads of anxious sweat trickled down her forehead. "How do you mean?" She heard the black cat yowl, as something pink and impossibly large began to issue from her.

Mrs. Rattle bent down to stroke the cat's fur. "All

God's creatures, aren't we, Puss. Born to pine, and suffer . . ."

Susannah had never thought so, but she held her tongue as the midwife reached, now, up above the fireplace. "Don't fret," she said. " 'Twill be over quicker than you think." Susannah decided that she must be addressing Puss, not her.

"Here," said the old woman, turning, with a bottle in her hand. "Castor oil. A spoonful a day. And—" She knelt and unlocked a chest, from which she drew different dried leaves, and wrapped them in paper. "Rue also, and savin. Boil them up, a spoonful to a cup, and drink it, midday and midnight. Also, my dear, a hot bath, every day. To stir the blood . . ."

"Why?" said Susannah. "Does that help it grow?"

Mrs. Rattle stared.

"I mean—the babe."

The old lady seemed to stare even harder. " 'Tis a medicine to be well *rid* of it, my dear."

"Be—rid of it?"

The midwife blinked, and nodded slowly. "Mind you, it doesn't always work . . . If the thing's quite firmly taken hold—there are other measures." She gave a fleeting glance at the instruments on the wall.

Susannah felt the sweat turn icy on her forehead, then felt hot again. Puss mewled and clawed at the floor. "You don't understand," she said. "That's not what I want."

"A great many girls think so," said Mrs. Rattle calmly, "at first." She laid down the bottle and the packet of herbs she had made. "But, in truth, dear, if you don't have a husband . . ."

"I do." Susannah did not know why she had come out with the words. She did not want to tell Mrs. Rattle anything more, now that she knew what the midwife was about. How she solved so many "miseries" . . . What she did might well be needed, by some. *But I won't need it. I shall manage.*

Perhaps the woman meant well, after all. Her face now was kind. "Well, if you have a husband," Mrs. Rattle was saying, "behoves you find him. After all—

there's many a seven months' babe born in the
land. . . . "

But Susannah scarcely nodded. She knew only the
hurry, now, to flee from here. And gathering her
cloak, handing the old woman a guinea, she fled. She
hurried down the sunken stairs, across the court, along
the straw path of the alley.

She did not like to acknowledge the midwife's sugges-
tion. *Many a seven months' babe born in the land* . . .
The notion had come to her, before, in her worry;
and she had rejected it, not liking such deception. And
yet there was truth in what the old woman said. To
raise a child alone—without money, without a husband, without even the halfhearted assistance of
Nicholas—would be no brave act of love. It was next
to impossible.

She ran through the court, down the lane, to the
waiting coach. "Hanover Square," she told the driver,
breathless. As the horses were starting off, she leaned
out the window. "No! Not Hanover Square. To Earl
Street. Please—I must go first to Earl Street."

Valerie had lived in Earl Street since she broke with
the brewer Fellsacre the last summer. There, she
shared rooms with another lady, mostly absent, and
admitted one or another of her succession of lovers:
an elderly country knight, a sergeant, a young musi-
cian who had lived with her till his company, like the
poet Brown's, had palled. Despite her revolving for-
tunes, Valerie remained confident: some man would
always be there to support her.

Through the walls along the stairway Susannah
could hear the clatter of crockery, and babies' cries.
Some of the rooms here housed whole families; and
Valerie's, though less crowded with people, were
cramped and scattered with belongings. But today, as
Susannah opened their door, she found them empty.

"Valerie? Are you here?" she cried.

"Yes, *chérie*. This way."

Valerie stood by the bed in the next chamber, car-

pets, china, silverware, and clothing heaped before
her. A trunk lay open on the floor. She moved around
the bed and Susannah kissed her, distracted. "What
are you doing?"

"Why, I am leaving. *Évidemment!* I return to
France." Valerie beamed, and her powdery face broke
into a nest of fine lines.

"To France?" Shaken, Susannah could only repeat
the words. It was impossible. Valerie had always
talked as if she despised her own country so. . . . "You
never told me."

"Of *course* I would have tell you, my dear." Valerie
squeezed her hand. "I sent a boy, to find out when I
could come see you. But *someone* sent him back, with
the message you are ill! I am glad 'tis not so, *chérie*."

"You could have written," said Susannah, looking
down as Valerie returned to her packing. She felt
childish, sulking at her friend so. But she was sad to
lose her.

"Ah, *chérie!* You know how I hate to write." Valerie shook out a petticoat. "You know, you look ill,
Suzanne. Your hair is very dull." For a moment, she
studied Susannah again. "Perhaps, *chérie*, if you wash
it in chamomile . . ."

Susannah stared. "My hair? But . . . Valerie. I have
no time to think of that! I am with child."

"What? No, it is not true." The words came rapidly.

Susannah wondered for a moment if her friend had
understood: for she was still folding underclothes and
stacking them in her trunk mechanically. Yet she
wanted to confide; and Valerie, she thought, might
reassure her. The only other friend she had left was
Sarah. And Sarah was not a woman of solutions.

She took a breath, and the story rushed from her:
of Nicholas, of her visit to Mrs. Rattle. And then, to
her surprise, Valerie did not pity her. Her face was a
blank. "But you are fortunate," she said.

"Fortunate?" repeated Susannah.

"Yes." Valerie's lips pinched together. "*I* cannot
have a child."

"I didn't know."

Valerie shrugged. "For a long time, it did not trouble me. Then one doctor looked inside me—I do not know how he knew, but he said I was not builded to have one. And you see, it has never happen since." She gave Susannah a crooked smile. "So! I shall have no one to comfort me in my old age."

Susannah did not answer: did not speak her first thought, which was that Valerie had always seemed the most unlikely of mothers. "I did not know you wanted any child."

"Oh!" Valerie shrugged again, and her eyes shifted away. "I do not say I want. But I cannot have. You see—it is as well you shall have family."

Susannah found it was not so easy as she had thought, to tell Valerie of the rest of her plan. Valerie, who had always followed her affections; who declared, at least, that she would not bed a man unless there was love, or desire. Susannah looked at the room around her, rapidly growing bare. Everything Valerie had been given by men, or had purloined from her various lodgings, she was taking. Prints, mirrors, inkstands, candlesticks. Susannah recognized the Grecian vases from the apartment furnished by Fellsacre, and the tortoiseshell combs Valerie had once displayed to her as the gift of a man fifth in line to the British throne. "What will you do in France?" she asked at last.

"Silly question! I return home. For soon in France there will be a new—*philosophy*. Bread for all—egality! Vast changes." Valerie dropped a sack of coins into the bottom of her trunk.

"Changes! But everything there is chaos. And the mob . . ."

"There is no mob," said Valerie, lifting her chin, "but the free French people!"

"I think—it is folly," said Susannah, slowly. Too preoccupied with her own worries, she could not think clearly on Valerie's words: and she knew little enough about France. "What of—all the things you used to

care for here? English clothes and English food and—
marrying a duke?"

"An English duke!" Valerie laughed. "But, you see,
I never will. Oh—I have thought so, once. I thought,
in England, your world is not so—elaborate. So that
I may find my way in it, and—" She shook her head.
"You all have your place here—as in France. Your order—princes, bishops, fools! And you know, I think
it will not change, here, in a hundred years." She
breathed on a silver candlestick and polished it with
the corner of a sheet. "I think I have got myself a deal
of lovely things, here in England! But for France . . .
I am sure the blood is over. My friends in the Assembly, they write me so. They will keep the king in the
Tuileries, where he cannot do harm."

Susannah nodded; but something in Valerie's talk,
she knew, did not make sense. "And your father?" she
said. "The count d'Aubusson? Do you not fear for him
at all?"

Valerie laughed—her own particularly merry, de-
scending ripple. "Oh, Susan. *Quelle histoire*. When I
think how all you English believed it!"

"Well?" said Susannah, indignant. She leaned
against Valerie's windowsill, watching her friend's
face shift expression. "Isn't it true?"

Valerie giggled. "Well! Perhaps if you imagine very
much. . . . When I was five, a maid is come to my
mother's shop, from the Comte d'Aubusson. 'What a
pretty name!' I think. But that is all I know of him."

"And your father . . ."

"He was a sailor. Richard Crow."

"Then he was English?"

Valerie breathed on a mirror and polished furiously. "Yes," she said. "If you wish."

Susannah mouthed the name to herself: "Valerie
Crow." No, it certainly did not make the impression
"Valerie d'Aubusson" did. "That means—" she said,
puzzling, "you are nearly English."

"No, *chérie*! Not I. I should never choose that.
Oh! There are good things to this country—the theaters, Vauxhall. . . . the cream, the English riding

clothes. . ." Valerie went on polishing objects, admiring them and stowing them away.

"But I thought you cared for . . . people here."

"People? Ah, well." Valerie smiled brightly. "There are people everywhere, and they are much the same."

She doesn't care, Susannah thought. Her own problems, she knew now, were as remote from Valerie as the painted scenes in the grottoes at Vauxhall. Susannah crossed the room and settled on the edge of an empty bed. "I shall be going north soon. To Harry," she said. She did not expect much now by way of encouragement.

"To Henry?" said Valerie blankly, still polishing.

"I must! Because—if there is a child—"

"I see," said Valerie with a nod, and smiled.

"Though I am not sure. Sometimes—I can scarce remember his face. And I wonder, if that is so—how can I possibly think of . . ." She looked up, pleading that her friend would understand. Valerie met her eyes at last. "I don't know, Valerie, how I will manage to—"

"Of course you will," Valerie said crisply.

Susannah could only stare. Had her friend abandoned all her precepts at once? "But—" she said. "If there is no love?"

"It is not a matter of love!" Valerie laughed. "It is simpler than that. It is marriage." Susannah started to protest, but Valerie's words broke through hers. "*Henri* will do as duty bids him, I am sure! Then for nine month—per'aps less—you must tole-rate each other. . . ."

"We could not tolerate each other so long, before," said Susannah.

But she might as well have spoken to herself. Valerie talked on. "Nicholas—of course he was a fancy. *Un amour* . . . You will have others. . . ."

Susannah did not hear any more. She stood, gathering her cloak, to leave. For it was clear Valerie belonged to another world than hers, with its own solutions, which were not hers. Valerie always had.

"My dear." Her friend followed her to the door.

"You had best wear some rouge when you go to see *Henri*. You are pale. And try the chamomile. . . . Oh, my dear. I shall miss you."

At the door they embraced for a last time; then Valerie dashed back into her rooms to scribble something on a piece of paper. Susannah glanced at it. "Mme Brunel," it said, "*Mercière. 38, rue du Temple.*" *Mercière*—the word was like English: 'mercer,' ribbon merchant.

"That is my mother," said Valerie solemnly, with the air of bestowing a great confidence. "You know, I am not much for writing! But—will you write me there, of the baby?"

Susannah nodded, and could not quite speak.

"When she is come, maybe you will name her after me!"

The words coaxed a smile from Susannah. For scarcely anyone granted, when talking of an unborn babe, that it might turn out to be a girl. Yet Valerie seemed sure of it. The flowers at Covent Garden had said so, too.

They set out three days later: Susannah and Peg, in a rickety yellow-and-black post-chaise. Warwick had hired it, for the berlin was under repair; and had looked at her queerly, nostrils quivering, when she asked him to do so. As if to say, "Your *haste*, my lady . . ." But, of course, being Warwick, he said nothing.

The driver, Barrow, looked as hard-used as the vehicle. He doubted, he said, that they would make it to Exon in four days, even changing horses. "That's i' summer, m'lady—" he said, with a dubious look at the coach, and shook his head. He spoke little, after that, except to say that inns and hostler fees and turnpike fees were all "the ladies'" to cover.

"And the highwaymen, m'lady?" said Peg, her eyes wide, as they set off. "He didn't say it, but I know well enough they're out there."

"How do you know?" Susannah wondered whether to believe her.

"My gran's uncle, _he_ was one. On his account she ne'er left London in her life. And so she told me. _I've_ not left London these eighteen years—till now." Peg pressed her lips together, resigned. Susannah, looking uneasily over, from time to time, at her quaking companion, wondered if she should have chosen Sally or Ernestine to come instead. But she knew and liked Peg best; and in truth she had not had time to test the maid's opinion. She had been in such a hurry, in the last few days, to pack her trunks and bid her few friends in the city farewell.

She had found Tom Gant, pink-faced and nearly as jolly as of old, in his lodgings. He wrapped one arm around her waist and the other about his mistress Lydia's, and announced, "I'm for the church! To Oxford. My father'll stand for my debts no more." But Lydia did not look too distressed at this; he had promised to visit her on his jaunts to London.

Sarah Hutchings was making a change, too. Susannah found her unpainted, doleful-eyed, wearing black.

"Your are in mourning?" she had asked, surprised.

"Yeth. For Anthony, God bleth him."

"But—you did not go to his service."

Sarah shook her head violently. "No, my dear. I knew mythelf unworthy." She told Susannah that she was leaving the next week, to take a post as an old lady's companion, in Bristol.

"No one shall be left!" Susannah had exclaimed.

"No. Perhapth not." Sarah's eyes had rolled heavenward. "As it ith writ. We have all been—rent, and torn athunder."

Susannah conferred for a last time with Knole, with whom she was leaving all her business while she was gone.

"And of New York—" she began.

"I know, m'lady." There was—almost—a twinkle in Knole's eye. "Don't sell, whate'er the price!"

"You understand me, then." She smiled.

"Yes, my lady. Your piece of the earth. And for those . . . larger rents, of which we shall be in receipt?"

"Put them directly in the bank," said Susannah. "I will write Mr. Chilliam for what I need." *Or*, she wondered, *should I say*—"*we*"? But the notion of living with Harry again—of sharing his house and table—seemed far too strange.

Knole, ever smooth and professional, did not ask into the purpose of her journey. "May I wish you good speed?" he said. He was there, as she and Peg departed, seeing their pouches of traveling money safely hidden inside the carriage. And there, with Warwick and Ernestine and the others, at the corner of the square, waving farewell . . .

They were not far past the London turnpike gate when the chaise lost its first wheel. It tumbled on its side, throwing Peg on top of Susannah.

"If this is travel afield I don't see the use 'n it," Peg muttered. For nearly an hour while Barrow mended the wheel, Susannah tried to soothe her, talking of the great castle where they were going to stay.

"I don't see the use 'n old castles," Peg said. "Dreadful cold—an' the wind moanin' in the cracks, like ghosts."

The February damp had turned all the roads to mud, and by nightfall they had only reached Huntingdon. They put up in the leaking attic of an inn, and all the next day drove, in a steady rain, past dun-colored fields and low clusters of cottages. Only the crowds they met in the inns, at noon and night, livened the tedium of the ride. There were rich farmers who courted with Peg, evangelists, governesses and gentleman-amateurs heading for Scotland. For a time their talk would distract Susannah; then thoughts of what she had left, or what awaited her, invaded her mind. Peg would see her eyes grow glassy, distant, and hurry her away, explaining, "M'lady ails."

But by the third and fourth days, Susannah did so

less and less. She began to see something exciting, unfamiliar, even in the cloud-dark sky and the earth of
the winter fields. They were moving north, she
thought: to lands she had not known before, bare
lands, and far away from Nicholas. When she thought
of him now, the wrenching feeling beginning, again,
in her heart and stomach, she would lean her head
outside and breathe the smoky air, and it relieved her.
She ate well at the inns, and the wind stung red into
her cheeks.

"You're looking *better*, m'lady," ventured Peg,
tucking Susannah into the alcove bed at their third
inn, at Darlington.

"It must be the air," Susannah said, her voice muffled by the blankets. "Peg—do you still mind coming
north?"

" 'Twasn't that I had the choice, m'lady," said Peg,
reluctant. "But maybe my gran *was* too feared of
highwaymen. We han't seen any these three days."

"No." Susannah was silent, thinking of other things.
"Peg?" she called in the darkness.

"Yes'm?"

"Will you sleep by me? I grow—afraid."

"Afraid of what, m,'lady? Ghosts?" said Peg eagerly.

"Yes," said Susannah, for lack of a better answer.
We are almost there. The journey's unexpected relief
was giving way to an uneasiness. She had written to
Harry to say she was coming: still, he might not have
received it. He might not want her. "Yes," she said at
last again. "I grow afraid of ghosts."

The horses picked their way through the stone bed
of the road, which, this last day, had climbed up to
high, bleak hills. The ground was dark with gorse and
heather, the land empty but for a few windswept cottages. Only luck held the wheels fast to the carriage
in the rocky roadbeds; and twice they sank in mud
and were stuck. Barrow cursed as the tired horses
strained to pull them free.

The second time Susannah climbed out. They were in Northumberland now. High above, the stars twinkled, and all around them was silence and velvety dark. No scent tainted the cold night air: no whiff of animal or human, oil- or wood- or coal smoke. They were almost there: she could feel it.

"Come," she said to Barrow. "There must be something you can do. Anything! So we get to the castle tonight. . . ."

"Tonight!" The man shook his head. "Not tonight, Lady Warrington. I can't see to mend—nor'd we find it."

Susannah let out a cry of frustration. She stamped her foot, and it stuck in the mud. Suddenly she wanted badly to be at Exon: to see Harry, smiling or angry, however he might be. To know if he might receive her—forgive her—and what would be her fate . . .

After a night's fitful sleep in the carriage, Barrow repaired the wheel and they drove again. They found an inn, changed horses, and went on, at what seemed a snail's pace against the vast backdrop of hills. Susannah drifted to sleep on Peg's shoulder, but was shaken awake as the coach halted.

The coachman opened the door and pointed out. "There, Lady Warrington. I can see it, but I dunna how to get t' it."

"But it's beautiful."

The coach driver stared at her as if she were fit for Bedlam. In the distance, square and dark against the sunset, stood a tower keep. The last of the day's bright light shot off its parapets, while beyond, over the empty land, blazed a rose and lavender sky.

"Dunna how to get t' it," repeated Barrow. "No road."

Peg also looked unmoved by the castle's beauty; and when Barrow refused to take the chaise down into the pathless vale ahead, she climbed up, ruffled and disgruntled, onto the back of one of the cart horses, behind Susannah. And so the two women rode up to the castle door: the maid straddling the horse, clutching onto her mistress, whose long hair flew loose and whose blue cape was encrusted with mud. Susannah kicked the horse on harder, for now she saw a figure in the distance.

Harry stood at the door, looking startled, then astonished. He had not changed greatly. Rather, he had weathered: grown to suit the angles of his face and body. He looked almost—*handsome*, thought Susannah: though strangely aloof as he extended his arms to her with formal poise. Peg was watching; behind Harry, a manservant with the black shadow of a beard was watching, too. Susannah jumped down and walked quickly into Harry's embrace. For a brief moment his arms wrapped loosely about her; she leaned her cheek against his chest, and the warmth of him surprised her.

Chapter 22

---- ❧ ----

Footsteps echoed against the castle walls as the man-servant, Fermanagh, led the guests to their chamber. Susannah's candle cast light no farther than her knees, and her feet caught in hollows between the stones of the floor. Already she missed the light and warmth of the Great Hall, where they had eaten supper.

"It is . . . a very vast place," she said in a tremulous voice, turning to look at Harry behind her.

He only made a low sound in his throat and gave a nod. A gust of wind whistled through one of the slits in the outer wall, catching Susannah's cheek, cold as a handful of snow. She cried out in surprise, and Peg, treading quickly behind Harry, murmured, "I told you, m'lady. *Spirits.*"

Fermanagh stopped before a tall door of wood and iron. He pulled at its handle, and it opened with a creak.

"This is our room?" said Susannah. Fermanagh's lantern picked out the white shape of a bed. "Where is yours?" she asked Harry.

"Down the stairs, across the hall—and up again."
He smiled obliquely.

"And—" A smile quivered, too, on Susannah's lips,
though this place still frightened her a little. "Are you
sure there are no ghosts here?"

"None of—the kind you might fear," said Harry
mysteriously, and stood back to let the women into
the room.

Susannah and Peg exchanged glances; then Peg tried
a timid smile on square-jawed, dark haired Fermanagh. Harry looked unafraid, himself, of spirits as his
long legs swung off down the hallway.

He didn't even bid me good night, thought Susannah, looking around at the small room, with its single
bed and threadbare carpet. *Perhaps it was a mistake,
to come.* "Will you stay with me, Peg?" she said.

But even once Peg warmed the bed beside her, she
trembled. *With cold?* she wondered. Or with the
strangeness of it all? The confident strangeness, especially, of her own husband . . .

Harry had taken Susannah and Peg on a tour of the
castle just after they arrived; and Susannah could tell
at once that he commanded it in a way he never had
his old home, in the south. He revered this place, in
all its antiquity; he knew its every secret passage and
moss-encrusted carving. With the castle's only servant, Fermanagh, he had an instinctive understanding, so that a nod or a sign brought them food and
drink. When he spoke now, the words came without
a stammer, and with only a shadow of his old hesitation. But he spoke to her only, it seemed, unwill-
ingly. His words were few, and his eyes steadily
avoided hers. When she had asked him, "However
have you spent these two years?" her own strained,
lighthearted tone was answered only by silence.

When the sunlight rippled through the windows of
her tower room the next morning, all was silent. There
were none of the sounds, the rattle of wheels and the
vendors' cries, that, in the city, started up at day-
break. Fermanagh brought the women breakfast, his
eyes twinkling as he watched Peg moving drowsily

about the room, laying out her mistress's clothes and shoveling coals into the hearth. He said in a low growl: "You'll take dinner at three, in the Hall with Lord Harry."

Susannah suppressed a fashionable-Londonish gasp, at such an early hour, and saw Peg's eyes widen, too. Soon, when Fermanagh had taken Peg away to the kitchens, she was alone, with the whole empty day stretched out before her. She dressed slowly; she drank more tea; she tried the various cupboards and doors of her room and the hall outside. Still, Harry did not come to speak to her, to entertain her. It was rude, she thought, but there was no remedy, and she decided at last to explore further in the castle. She crossed the long, empty chamber above the Great Hall, adorned only by a dusty coat of armor, and, trying several passages, came to a spiral stair that led her up to the roof.

She poked her head out, clutching at the stair's column, for the wind outside was fierce. Beyond the uneven stones of the rooftop lay a gray and boundless land. She jumped up and made her way to the parapet.

And for a moment, as if by a miracle, the wind died; there was a damp warmth to the air. The sun broke through clouds, turning the bare country of Exon golden brown. To one side of the castle she saw the steep valley, beyond which the road took up its tenuous path, and to the other side, a low, gray habitation that must, she thought, be Lord Exon's house. The fields beyond it were dotted with stocky Cheviot sheep.

If Valerie could but see this—or Sarah, Susannah thought and laughed to herself. She was thinking on them, and London, still, when Harry's voice rose behind her.

"Here you are."

She turned and saw him looking grimly up from the stairs, as if she should not have come. He took a deep breath and leapt up to join her.

"I . . . did not know where to find you." Susannah

smiled, uneasy. "It is—" she said. And, "I—" Harry started. Both of them fell silent. A cloud covered the sun, and they watched all the scene around them drain of color.

"Why are you here?" said Harry at last, leaning on white knuckles against the parapet.

"I—" Susannah half turned, and could not answer. Harry ignored her gaze on him and looked steadily out at the hills. At last he turned, with a thin smile. "It grows cold. Will you come into my study, and—and see the ghosts?"

He extended a hand to her as they crossed the stone roof, to the stairs. Heartened by his invitation, she reached to take it. His skin was warm, lively—and suddenly he drew away. She did not know why, but tried to ignore it. "Tell me, Harry," she said, in a high, distant voice. "How *do* you survive the winter in such a desolate place?"

At first he did not answer her question. "Your voice, Susannah, has taken on an unfortunate London . . . callousness."

"I don't know what you mean. I cannot hear it."

Harry changed subject. " 'Desolate'? It is only desolate here if one is determined to see it so."

He looked straight at her, as if in challenge; but then, before she could answer, motioned her to descend. They followed the bends of a corridor and came at last to a long, bright chamber: his study. Like Susannah's room, it faced out of the one wall of the keep whose slit windows had been replaced with wider, paned ones. Like all the castle's chambers, it was scantily furnished, the gray-and-green tapestries on its inner walls reflecting the colors of the land outside its windows. There were a chair, a writing desk, and on the floor a walnut chest. Harry knelt and turned the key in its lock, revealing leaves of parchment, golden and rippled with age.

"Oh," said Susannah, disappointed. Was this all he had to show her?

Harry beckoned, and she knelt beside him. "The Exon manuscripts," he said. "They come to us from some eight centuries ago." He smiled hesitantly and held a page out to her. She touched it; it was velvety and soft.

"Mm," she said, trying to sound appreciative, shifting her knees on the cold stone floor.

Harry settled beside her, curling his arms around one knee. He wore boots and a plain, brown broadcloth suit—and yet, thought Susannah, this country style of dress suited him. He wore his hair clipped short now—though surely not to follow the fashions of distant London. His blue eyes shone against golden curls and wind-tanned skin; he looked older than Susannah remembered, and less frail. *He looks well,* she thought; and feeling her face flush strangely, she bent her head down toward the parchment's crabbed black writing. "What language is it?" she said.

"Latin, and Norman French. Do you see—" Harry leaned forward, with all his old eagerness at instructing. "Here its a word—*vivthe*, like *vie*, for life. . . . " Susannah prepared herself to be left behind. And yet the even tenor tones of his voice held her. She followed the words on the page as he explained. And she understood. He talked of William de Warenne, who wrote these pages; of his loyalty to William the Conqueror and his fears of renewed war.

Yet William de Warenne sounded a live, hearty man: no ghost. "Is he—the spirit you talk of?" Susannah said.

For a moment Harry seemed to forget why he had brought her here. "Oh—yes," he said at last. "The only spirit."

She studied his face: staring past her, pensive. And she thought she began to understand him now: more than she ever had, watching him pore over dusty books. "Why—you belong here," she said, with a start. "You have come to think—as if you lived in William's time. Are you—sorry you live now, and not then?"

Harry smiled suddenly. His tanned face glowed. "No. For, to do as I do now—I should have had to enter a monastery."

"A monastery?" Susannah repeated.

"And I think I should have made a most discontented monk . . . . At least," he added evenly, "I have so far."

Susannah turned her head away as she crept back along the floor; but if he noticed her embarrassment, Harry did not show it. "Shall we go to dinner?" he said.

They ate in the Great Hall, whose high walls were hung with shields and faded tapestries.

"Then, you never feel lonely here?" Susannah called: for the whole length of the table stood between them. Fermanagh was lighting the candles.

"Come, sit closer," said Harry, with a shadowy smile; and she could not tell if he was laughing, secretly, at the distance between them: the vast Gothic pomp of what should be an intimate dinner. With Fermanagh, he moved her heavy chair to the side of the table, near his. He poured red wine for them both, out of a silver tankard. It was strong, still cold from the cellar, tasting of metal.

"You asked me if I felt the solitude," said Harry. "In fact—I feel less solitary here than I did at The Marches, or in London."

Susannah looked down, discomfited, and saw her fingers writhing in her lap.

"Of course you have not met the neighbors." Harry's blue eyes twinkled. "Humphrey Smalt—that is Lord Exon—will surely like you, as you share my name. . . . It was my name, you see, that decided him on showing me the Warenne papers." Catching Susannah's glance, Harry broke suddenly into a gruff, wavering voice. " 'War-enne. Warenne-ton . . . Why, God's blood as he must be your ten-times great-grandfather! Welcome to the family, boy!' "

Susannah laughed. She had never seen Harry mimic anyone so before. "Is it true about the names?"

"No. At any rate, my *mother* holds to the belief that we were in England well before the Conquest. For otherwise we should be French! And she can't—can't abide that tongue, for she's never been able to speak it."

Sussannah was torn between laughter and incredulity. Was Maria just as miserable at French, then, as she?

Fermanagh brought in a roast duck, with onions and wild mushrooms and cherry conserves. Susannah wondered fleetingly how he procured such game from what looked a bare land: for last night's meal, of venison, had been even more splendid.

Harry talked of Fermanagh, when he had gone: of how the Exons, glad to see the old castle inhabited, had lent him their servant, who had grown up in it from a boy. "I don't know that either of us shall change from here," Harry said. "It suits his liking for tranquillity—and mine."

"You mean—you would stay for good?"

"Yes." Harry seemed to flush, from the wine, but he held Susannah's gaze. "How long do you mean to stay?"

"How long? Well, I . . ." Susannah shrank back in her chair, startled by the question. *Does he wish me to leave, then?* "I don't know," she said at last. "A few weeks, perhaps . . . Are you never to come back to London?"

Harry refilled her glass, with a thin smile. "You've become quite a partisan of that city, for a planter's daughter."

Choosing not to show she felt any insult, Susannah searched for a change of subject. It was safer, perhaps, if they did not talk of themselves. She searched, and conversation seemed to evade her, and she did not know how her companion liked her silence: how the candlelight made her face glow and turned her eyes to inky pools; how, to Harry, now, she seemed scarcely changed from the blushing, awkwardly outspoken girl he had met on the fields of The Marches. But as she spoke he heard the arch, knowing tones of London punctuate her speech; and he wondered how much, in his mother's and Augusta's letters, had been true.

"Tell me more of your book," Susannah said quietly.

Carefully, he answered that he was corresponding with a London publisher; also he wrote regularly to Gibbon, at Lausanne. He was planning a second volume now, and a third on medieval England.

But disconcerted, perhaps, by his earlier question—*How long do you mean to stay?*—Susannah could not listen well. She grew anxious, preoccupied; her stomach was suddenly surfeited.

"—do you think?" said Harry, finished speaking.

"I am sorry," she said. "I can—scarce understand such things." She gave, unconsciously, the downward-looking smile that Nicholas had found so appealing and the disclaimer, "Forgive me. Think me a dullard, if you like. . . . "

"Of course—of course I do not!" said Harry quickly. Then his voice changed. "Or is slow-wittedness . . . the fashion for ladies, in London?"

Susannah looked up now, hurt. "Why must you task me with everything you—disapprove of in that city?"

"It pains me," said Harry curtly, "to hear you speak of stupidity—as if it were a trait to be desired. I know—you *could* learn anything you set your mind to."

I should hope so, she thought, angrily; but Harry gave her no time to speak the words.

"Good night," he said abruptly. He helped her from her chair and walked away down his corridor. Fermanagh came in to put out the lights.

She spent that night alone, and the next, with Peg on the truckle bed beside her. She despaired of enticing her husband to bed with her; nor could she imagine confiding in him, so harsh and cold he had grown to her. *I am with child. . . . * She tested the words and knew she could not speak them. She saw no sign, now, in Harry of the old, appeasing love for her that had forgiven so many small slights. And, more than she expected, she feared the final rejection that must come when she told him.

Sometimes, when he was not regarding her, she studied him. She watched as his long, blue-veined fingers fastened round a goblet; as his brown-clad legs took the corridors in long strides. She saw his mouth quiver, when he knew she was watching. Whenever, by chance, their hands or arms brushed together, he would draw away. And she decided that he must not wonder, as she did, if the warm current that passed between them was not an ill thing but a sign. . . .

She did not dare to ask him that. She asked him other things, of no consequence. She asked him for books to read, and he gave her two: one, surprisingly, a *Dissertation on Horses*, and the other, a Mr. Blake's *Songs of Innocence*. These Songs were simple; they had nothing of the epic or the mythical voices Nicholas Carrick had liked to talk of. This Blake was an unknown, a London engraver; yet Harry said he himself would not write poems again, unless he could attain the simplicity of these.

Susannah read the words aloud, sometimes, walking by day in the stone corridors of the castle. Sometimes, a shaft of light from the slit windows would fall onto the colored pages. And she was called back to a good, easy world that she thought she could never live in again.

> *When the voices of children are heard on the green*
> *And laughing is heard on the hill,*
> *My heart is at rest within my breast*
> *And everything else is still . . .*

But her heart was not at rest. First she had passed three days at Exon; four went by, and now five. Time was escaping her, and she knew she must act. But she did not know how.

*   *   *

It was late, past midnight. Susannah sat in the wooden bathtub in her chamber, shivering. She had long ago made herself clean, for Harry. When she climbed out, Peg would scent her with rose water. And then she would have to dress and make her way down the long corridor. . . .

"Come, m'lady," Peg said gently, and as she climbed to the floor, rubbed her dry with warm towels. Susannah thought she felt a tenderness when they brushed against her breasts; and perhaps she had grown slightly plumper. But the first, she knew, came and went unpredictably; and the second could be due merely to Fermanagh's food. If she was a month with child, there was nothing to prove, yet, for certain, yes or no. . . .

Can he truly have changed? she thought. For once, when they were first married, Harry had wanted her without cease. So now she knew what she must do. She would go his room—after all, he had not forbidden her—and slip, naked, in the dark, into his bed. She feared that her plan might be too direct, but she had no other.

She took the candle in its dish from Peg, and slid her feet into their square-heeled slippers. And pulling her thin robe closer around her, she ventured out into the pitch-black of the hall. All was silent. Feeling for the walls, she made her way downstairs. Gusts of wind shot in at her through the lookout holes, making her candle flicker. In the Great Hall, she heard a scrabbling of claws, but when she bent low with her candle, saw nothing. *There are no creatures*, she told herself. *No ghosts.*

Upstairs again, behind Harry's door, she heard a whistling, deep breathing. He slept. She lifted the bolt and slid through the doorway. Far away, by the window, Harry lay curled up in the bed, like a child. The night sky cast a bluish light across his face. She would come to him. . . .

She laid the candle to rest on the hearth and slipped

out of her gown. The thin cotton tumbled to the floor without a sound. She shook her hair loose over her shoulders; she could hear Harry's steady, rasping breaths. She stepped closer, and saw that a smile filled the blue-tinted hollow of his cheek. He slept like a little boy, peaceful and trusting.

Once, she knew, he had trusted her, he had married her; and she had given him no love in return, and little patience. Could it ever be different now? For again, she had come to him selfishly, keeping her own secrets. . . .

Go! For your own sake, she willed herself. But she could not move anywhere but backward. Tears stung her eyes as she picked up her robe and candle and retreated.

She watched his face, the next morning, for some sign of recognition. But none appeared. Harry's skin was ruddy from a walk out in the cold. Since it was a sunny day, he suggested they ride out to visit Lord and Lady Exon.

Fermanagh fetched the two horses, Scamp and Elixir, from the stables. They were brothers, equally restive, and galloped off at a far faster pace than Susannah expected. *Wait*, she had to cry out, twice, and Harry seemed, perturbingly, not to hear her. He galloped ahead, through sheep fields and mud, all the way to Lord Exon's low gabled house; and when he lent her his hand to dismount and she breathed, "What were you trying—" he did not answer. He turned to their host, who had issued from the doorway with dogs yapping at his heels, and she realized, then, the meaning of that *Dissertation on Horses*. Harry had taken an interest in them—and he had learned to ride.

Lord Exon was a round, jovial man: an agricultural experimenter. He rotated crops and bred farm animals, ever carefully making notes; in twenty years at Exon, he had improved his land beyond measure. The men now hacking swedes out of the frozen ground had year-round work here, though it was hard. Lord Exon had improved their cottages and done far less— it seemed—for his own comfort, and that of his wife, Mary Anne.

She was perhaps forty, and small and brown as a sparrow. She fussed and cooed over Susannah, exclaiming, "London!" as she ran back and forth from the feeble fire to the wooden settle where they sat. "Well! I've only been once there. My sister, Margaret, bless her soul, was there thrice. . . . "

Harry, who had been taken to a far corner to see Lord Exon's seedlings, heard the last words, the name mentioned, and gave a start. He examined Susannah's face as she answered something mild and polite about the city; and noted, relieved, that she suspected nothing. How blue her eyes were, he thought, in this light; and how gentle her voice. It had almost lost London.

"Say! How's yer 'History'?" Exon nudged him out of his reverie.

Mary Anne turned, waving dismissively at her husband. "Always he asks! And ne'er he'll remember."

"I will too," retorted the lord. But the argument, Susannah guessed, was carried out merely for form. As Lady Exon murmured back sweetly, "You've no more history, m'dear, than the last almanac," Harry searched for Susannah's face: her smile, her glance at him, half-hidden behind the wing of the settle. Now she was asking Lady Exon what animals they kept.

Perhaps I did misjudge her, he thought. For if she had become a Londoner, truly, she would have no patience for the country: no use for northern people. She would be wrapped up in that city world, just as his own mother was. . . .

"I say! You're i' the clouds," said Exon, stuffing his pipe with leaves. "Are ye staying for dinner?" He did not wait for an answer. "Mary Anne! 'Tis a poor welcome we give our guests. They'll be parched and hungered."

Mary Anne nodded patiently, as if all had been attended to before. As she stepped lightly toward the door, Susannah followed, but the round-bellied Lord

Exon pounced on her before she could leave. "Virginia tobacco!" he announced, waving his pipe before her nose. "So, d'ye know it? Do the ladies o' Virginny smoke it?"

"*Some*, maybe—" she started back, jesting; but Exon did not require an answer. He seized her by the hand, and Harry round the shoulders. "Aye, ye're well matched!" he pronounced, pushing them together. "Hold hands, why don't ye? Ye've been gone from him long enough, Lady Susan—"

And Harry did not know if he flushed redder, even, than his wife, as he felt the charge of her skin, again, touch his.

They ate and drank ale in the parlor, and their boisterous host would not let them leave till three. Several times during the meal, Harry thought, Susannah sent him glances: searching looks, laughing looks. And sometimes, as in the old days at The Marches, they seemed to be laughing together, silently: and he did not like to think on it. Nothing now was the same.

He remembered how once she had ridden so well that she put him to shame. And now, as they mounted to ride home, a demon took him, and he let Elixir's reins looser and rode harder than ever before. The hills slid away beneath him with a reckless, impossible speed. There was no path; he charted it through the bends of hills and valleys. The cold water of a brook splashed his thighs as he crossed it. And—though he still disliked water—he charged on, gritting his teeth. The hooves of Susannah's horse drummed on the hard ground behind him.

"Your Elixir!" he heard her call out, aggrieved. "I vow it, Harry—you've put him under a spell!"

He turned but for a moment: long enough to see the sharp blue of her eyes and the fire of her hair in the afternoon light. And he knew if spells were woven, they were not his: perhaps not hers either, but cast by some force beyond them. So that he could not hate her—could not believe any wrong of her. So that they were drawn together, and it took all his will to keep apart.

As they neared the last valley, and the way to their castle, he turned abruptly to the left, into unknown ground.

"Wait!" she called again, and he did not know if there were tears in her voice, or laughter.

"I warrant—you'll not take me," he called out, loudly and slowly. He rode on, and with a drumming of hooves, she caught up: drew even by his side.

"There!" she cried out, breathless, but he did not dare turn now to see her.

They rode as far as Kielder Castle, the Duke of Northumberland's hunting lodge. It was empty now; its new, gray-green stones took on a sterile sheen in the twilight.

Susannah looked up at it without reverence. "I like ours better. It's real," she said, and as Harry lifted one eyebrow, quizzical, at her words, she said suddenly, "What did you mean to do? Have me thrown?"

His look grew apprehensive, and a little guilty.

"Don't worry! I *shan't* be thrown," she said, with more bravado than she felt.

"I feared you'd lost the habit of riding in London," he answered. Now, as they returned in the gathering dusk, he led the way at a gentle trot. Susannah stared at his straight back, the hard muscles of his legs pressing on Elixir's flanks as he rose and fell to the horse's pace.

It cannot be that I desire him, she thought. And at once she knew it was true. She trembled as he kicked his horse on now: she feared somehow that he would escape her. Freeing Scamp's reins, she bent close to his ear. "Go, go on," she breathed. She sucked in cold air as he gathered speed, feeling her skirts and hair flying. But as she began to gallop, so did Harry. he looked back, smiling; now the last hill rose beneath them. Harry was still ahead, dismounting at the castle gate. Scamp slowed, and when he had arrived home, Susannah slumped across his back, breathless.

"You may descend, my lady."

A hand lifted her left foot from its stirrup, and Susannah, climbing down, tumbled into Harry's arms. She felt his face, warm against hers, and his arms, which seemed to want to pull free. But she clung on.

When she opened her eyes, she saw his face: dark, retreating against the sky. Then she saw him approaching, pressing her closer, kissing her.

His lips were warm and soft. When he pulled away, she said, "What will we do?"

Harry did not answer. Smiling, with one arm still around her waist, he pulled her in through the high doorway, toward the shadows of the stairs.

Chapter 23

❀

Long into the morning, they lay naked in Harry's bed, the sun streaming on them through windows glistening with frost.

"Look!" said Susannah, pointing out. "It is like . . . a blessing."

"Superstition," mumbled Harry into her shoulder.

"What? 'Tis religion I talk of. Don't you believe in it?"

"Scarcely, with you here. You make such things pale—arid questions of the mind." Smiling, he laid his head on Susannah's chest. His short hair tickled her. "I think I am happy at last," he said.

"I, too." She stroked the side of his cheek. *Can it really be this simple, after all?*

Harry had been bolder, more skillful last night than she had expected. And she, by contrast, had grown strangely shy. She had stood still, as if she knew not what to do, while he placed kisses upon her neck, her ears. His kisses moved downward, and he worked at the buttons of her coat, then the layers of cloth beneath; and she felt what had been like fear begin at last to melt away. *All will be right now. Not as before.* He had laid her down on the bed, peeling the last of her clothes away: the ankle-high boots, still muddy from their ride, the stockings, the last chemise that clung to her skin. "Will you let me?" he said in a low voice, and before she could know what he meant, his mouth was moving down over her breasts, past her waist, below. "What?" she whispered.

He did not answer but buried his lips and tongue in the murky forest there. No man had done this to her before, and she wondered, for a moment, that he wanted to. She wanted to writhe beneath him as his tongue worked and delved, and yet a strange shyness again overtook her. He sucked the tiny head of flesh at her body's opening, and the pleasure was so intense that she wanted only to escape it, fearing what would come next: what she would cry out, or do. She gasped and wriggled to free herself and, reluctantly, he emerged. She smiled up at the shadowy, hollowed face outlined by the moonlight. Now he bent and kissed her breasts, burying his fingers in the furry grotto where he had laid his mouth before. He pressed his face—strange, fishy, smelling of her—against her neck, and his rod pushed at her sex. She had not remembered the size of it. Her fingers stretched around it, pulling it toward her. He rocked slowly against her, as if afraid to hurt her with too much force, so that finally it was she who thrust herself toward him, reaching up to his smooth buttocks, and pulling him into her. He wrapped his arms round her, and, like a single creature, they writhed and rose and fell. And she thought there could never be enough of it, even if he ran up against the wall inside her: no matter if he forced and broke through it. A slow pulse began below, and she cried out, wishing it did not have to end.

All through the night they had talked and dozed, and twice again taken their pleasure. Though she lay in the sun, Susannah gave a shiver, remembering.

"Poor little one!" said Harry. "You are cold."

She gave another, involuntary, shudder at the endearment, and as Harry pulled the bedclothes over her, he looked down at her with concern. "What—what troubles you?"

"There is much you do not know about me—" she began.

"Shh." He kissed her cheek. "You needn't talk of it now." But Susannah saw the cloud pass over his face as he spoke. "We both," he said slowly, "have had our faults. Does it do any good to speak of them—"

"Oh, yes." Susannah turned toward him, her eyes darkening. "I am sure it does. . . . What, do you mean that while I was gone, you—had a mistress?" Valerie had said it: *All men have mistresses.* By now she was used to the thought; but still, her own words sounded harsh and crude, to her, in the air. Harry did not answer. "I—do not mind, you know," she said. "I cannot. Who is it?"

"The friend—the sister of—of a neighbor." Harry looked down, his brow wrinkling, testing Susannah's reaction. Tentatively he reached and drew her closer, playing with a lock of her long hair as he talked.

"Tell me."

"Are you sure?"

"Yes, tell me."

" 'Twasn't love, to be exact," he said, "but a sort of . . . kind friendship. She was older than we—twoscore, perhaps. I knew her six months, before she had to return—back to Manchester, to tend to her husband. You see—" Harry's eyes narrowed, and he stared past Susannah. "He had a fever, and she had to go home to nurse him. And—though he recovered, she—when she caught it after him—she did not."

Susannah did not know how to answer. She felt Harry's sorrow intruding, invading their very marriage bed, but she knew she could not begrudge it her: whoever she was, this stranger. *The sister of a friend* . . . For a moment Lady Exon's sparrow face, her talk of a sister and "bless her soul" crossed her mind. "I am sorry," she said in a small voice. "I know she deserved you more than I do. And yet—"

"No," said Harry abruptly.

Susannah searched his face, but found no sign of why he had stopped her. And wanting, now, to bear the hurt of it, to hear the worst, she said, "Do you miss her still?"

"No. For—for you are here. Let us talk no more of it."

"All right," said Susannah quietly. "But you must know, in my turn I—"

"No. Don't," said Harry sharply.

"I thought myself in love," Susannah murmured. "I know that is no great reason to forgive me it, but . . ."

"Then there was—but one?"

"Yes," said Susannah, mystified at the question. "He was—"

"No." Harry shook his head, and his fingers dug into her arm. "Do not tell me. I do not need to know."

"Why? It is such a confusion, still. Sometimes I feel I *must* speak of it."

"You might—we might both regret it." Harry's voice grew lower, kinder, and he stroked the soft skin at the base of her throat. "Women, I think—are not prone to that kind of—unreasoning envy, that—"

Susannah turned her head to look in his eyes, puzzling.

"I should wish nothing good to come to him, Susan. Indeed"—Harry's mouth set in a thin line—"I should *like* to think him dead.

In silence, Harry rose and sought out Fermanagh, who brought them breakfast. He ate without speaking, peering out into the sun; and Susannah, drinking her chocolate, grew uneasy, afraid. Perhaps she had been wrong to insist on speaking of the past. They finished eating, and Harry turned toward the wardrobe, as if to dress. But after a few moments there, he spun; he came to the bed and knelt beside her.

"Can we—" he said, "forget—what we said, just now?"

She took his hands in hers and kissed them. She felt a sudden, foolish affection for these hands: for their smooth backs, covered in thin golden fur, and for their

long, tapered fingers. "Yes," she said. "I think so. Let
us be—as husband and wife. As we should have been
long ago."

But Harry's face grew clouded again, his eyes rov-
ing toward the window and the sky. "Perhaps no one
can forget so much."

She felt him beginning to withdraw from her, even
before he had moved. And she knew that she would
not let him leave. Not again. "Oh, yes we can," she
said fervently, sitting up and drawing his mouth toward her, kissing him. "I swear I shall make you forget."

"How—" Harry's lips curled, almost into a smile.

She knelt on the bed, pulling him closer, until the
whole length of his body pressed against hers. "This
way. If there is no other."

For a week they scarcely emerged from the room,
so absorbed were they, suddenly, in the secrets of each
other's bodies and in the half-secret tales of each other's pasts. The late-winter rain drummed, safely distant, on the walls of the castle; and, wrapped up in
bed or curled on the wooden chairs of the hearth, they
paid it no heed. Fermanagh, unsurprised at the
change, brought his master and mistress their meals
in the warm bedroom. Peg was more surprised at this
turn of events than he; but then Peg (thought Fermanagh, paternally) was but a giddy London girl,
whom he had a good deal to teach about the world.

"Tell me, does he approve?" said Susannah, pouring the tea, one morning after Fermanagh had left
them.

"His looks are all dour disapproval, to be sure."

"Well! A lifelong bachelor—perhaps he doesn't understand." Susannah spread a slice of charcoal-tasting
toast with jam.

"Oh, no. I think you have him wrong."

"Why?"

"Clearly enough, he's in love with your Peg."

"No!" The phrase "in love" in her husband's voice gave Susannah a curious tremor.

"Have you not seen it? Then, you only confirm my suspicions."

"What suspicions?"

"That ladies haven't any of that gift of perception with which we credit them. A man may be in love with them—but they act quite blind. Why—do you remember when we first met. I am sure you didn't—" Harry stopped suddenly, and looked away.

Sensing his embarrassment, Susannah broke in with a false cheer. "Never mind! 'Twas long ago." And yet an old guilt pricked her. *Did I know?* When Harry and she had walked about the gardens: he, stammering, eager, talking of politics or slavery . . . She had ignored all but his words: or had she chosen to? For everything in England had been so new. And the hurt of her father's death, though Harry had tried to help it, could only heal with time. . . . Perhaps only in time would she have been able to love anyone. "Well! So much has passed," she said. Searching for a diversion, she seized the last cream cake from Fermanagh's tray. "The last," she cried, "till Fermanagh poaches our dinner! Who's to get it?"

They tussled, tearing the cake from hand to hand, finishing with their mouths covered in cream and jam. Susannah laughed high and nervously, tumbling down on the thin rug while Harry licked the traces of cream from her cheek. Beneath her, she could feel the uneven stones of the floor.

"Ouch!" she yelped. "Stop!"

"What? Do you wish me to?"

"No." She stroked Harry's linen-clothed back, drawing him up to her until his face was near hers. "Never."

The days of the end of February flew. There were but a few, untouched things they could not talk of. But all else was theirs: the realms of their bodies, of religion, and childhood memory. Harry talked of his early amours: the small girlfriends he had had and the

maids he had longed for—though conscience and ti-
midity had kept him from attempting them.

"What?" Susannah answered, surprised. "Not even
one?"

"No," he said. "No one, till you." He pulled her
closer in bed. She listened to the rain tapping the windows and did not know what to make of his answer:
for she had begun to think all men were the same.
Like Nicholas. They had appetites, which they simply
satisfied. Maids, shopgirls—*actresses*, she thought ruefully—all were fair game.

"Mark you, I was miserable!" Harry said now,
cheerfully. "And if any of the ladies of The Marches
had come to me and offered themselves . . ."

"Your mother likely scared them away," Susannah
said, too quickly to remember: Harry had never liked
to hear ill of her.

But now he did not seem to mind. "She tried her
best," he said equably, and chased Susannah under
the covers.

One day in the beginning of March, when the
ground was thawing and the worst of winter was over,
Susannah felt something rush from her. She knew that
feeling; she let out a little cry. She ran to the bare
chamber that used to be her bedroom and there, on
her petticoats, found the brown, scant stain. The curse
had come.

It was no curse, she thought now—far from it.
"Thank you, God! Thank goodness," she murmured,
pressing her cheek against the cool glass of the window. The sky outside, thick with clouds, even seemed
to lighten, sensing her relief. "Thank you," she whispered, and added another prayer, which she did not
dare yet to speak out aloud. *Let me bear a child, now.
And let it be Harry's.*

The blood had come—painless and scant, but
clearly there. And she was glad, for she felt no doubt:
it marked the end of all connection with Nicholas. His
anger, his melancholy, his conceit. She wondered now

how she could have lived for so long in that dream-world: convinced that he would change and begin to love her. First love—so she had heard—could be tenacious beyond reason: remaining, clinging to a hope, when hope and love themselves had dwindled to mere words. Second love, she knew now, must be the one that endured.

She ran through the corridors, suddenly longing to see her husband.

In his study, Harry raised his head from his book, his eyes wearing their old, familiar lost look: as if the world beyond his pages never ceased to surprise him. His blue eyes shone in the gray light from the windows. "Y-es?"

" 'Tis nothing." Susannah skidded to a stop. "Or—'tis foolish. I only wanted to—" *To bear your child*, she thought, but could not speak it. "To see you," she finished. "To know you were here. What is that you're writing?"

"N-nothing—" Harry shook his head, distracted, sliding some sheets of paper under a volume of Johnson. "Nothing of importance. Verses. Nonsense."

"Verses? What sort?"

But he was strangely secretive. Instead of answering, he reached up to her, gathering the folds of her skirts in his arms and pulling her into his lap.

The flow lasted three days then, and did not come again, the next month, when it was due. It seemed—and within another month Susannah was certain—that she was with child, Harry's child. No sooner had she wished it than it was granted: and she did not dare cloud her good fortune with doubt. Had it been granted too quickly? Had what she had been so certain was a child, really been nothing? She had heard of the curse being delayed by eclipses of the moon—or human worries. She had heard, too, of curses coming during pregnancies, though—she reassured herself—they surely could not last as long as hers had. Childbirth was a rocky terrain, poorly understood by doctors, often best traversed with the aid of superstitious midwives. Her maid Peg was superstitious, but no midwife, and could only agree with her own guess as to the babe's time: between All Hallows' Eve and Christmas. Yet that was a long span of time. Babes might come early or agonizingly late. Until hers came, Susannah knew, she could not be rid of a lingering worry. She could only whisper a prayer at her window: "Keep my child safe, and let it be my husband's. Let it be Harry's."

Summer came reluctantly to Northumberland, but at last the ground grew soft and green. Lord Exon's ewes lambed, and his orchards began to flower. Susannah and Harry walked out now, instead of riding. Holding hands, they would climb to the top of the hill nearest the castle. All around, they saw nothing but empty land—no habitations, no other people—and yet they were not lonely.

They walked for miles sometimes, through the tenuously farmed Exon property, or to the banks of the North Tyne, where it curled its rocky path through the Cheviot Hills. There, Susannah would urge Harry into the water and, as it swirled around their knees, attempt a minuet. They tumbled together, laughing, their clothes growing soaked: and Harry seemed to forget, now, that he feared the water. They would charge back up the hill, like soldiers, or cantering on their heels, like horses.

One day in May they walked out later than usual. The sun was setting in a red haze beyond the hills as they climbed up to their watching point.

"The babe," Harry said suddenly. "Can you hear it? Does it—make splashes?"

"Seldom. 'Tis a quiet thing, yet. You think it a very fish!" They reached the summit and stopped.

"Let me hear."

"What?" Susannah laughed, imagining he would hear nothing. The child was still only a small swell in her belly. But Harry dropped to his knees anyway, holding her hands.

"I can hear it! I am sure—" Harry's hands squeezed hers, in pulses. Susannah heard only the wind and smiled, looking down at her husband. "Its heart beats," he murmured. " 'Tis really—truly there."

"Of course," she said, tugging at his hands. "*I* know 'tis there if you don't. Now come up!"

Helena Stillwell, who had come to stay with her sister at Henshawe, gazed with pursed lips at the spread of lawn outside the orangery, as Augusta's footman, Mohammed, served tea. Augusta was reading out a letter, in which Helena herself took little interest.

" ' . . . have been living most harmoniously at Exon . . .' " murmured Augusta. "Then"—her voice rose higher—"it is true. He is with Susannah!" She nibbled agitatedly at a currant bun.

". . . wish *we* had such a fine large garden," mused her sister, her mouth settling between two sullen creases.

"Are you *listening*?" said Augusta.

"I was about to say the same to you." Helena's gaze flitted enviously again around the onion-domed, glassy chamber. Mohammed, in his purple turban, bowed and departed; outside, in the shade, a nursemaid dozed beside the cradles, toys and blankets of the two sisters' four small sons. Augusta had borne a second son, Horatio, in January: right now his ears were being boxed by his eldest cousin, Edmund Stillwell, who was beckoning his brother, John, to join in the fun.

And Augusta, who was normally more attentive, was absorbed in Harry's letter. Some months after she had written him, conveying the news of rumors, and her concern—he and Susannah had reunited. "Susannah is with child," she said. Her voice was unnaturally calm.

"What?" Helena spun. A wave of tea splashed her saucer. "She cannot be." The lines alongside her mouth deepened, and now not only her narrow face, but her voice, were reminiscent of her mother's. "Why, she left London only—"

Augusta did not answer. It was true: in these last months she had lost some of her former faith in Susannah. Her mother, for one, had repeated Jonas's accusations. . . . All the same, she wished Harry happy, however it befell him; and partly for that reason she did not add to her sister's thoughts. For Helena, disappointed in her husband and style of life, grew every year more jealous and carping. The mention of Harry's wife—who came dowerless and now had use of ten thousand a year—always inspired her to new complaints. Augusta fell silent, for she did not particularly wish to hear them.

Susannah's belly grew, as did Harry's "History." Sometimes she poked fun at both. "Let us see which is finished first—and which weighs the greater!" she giggled, while Harry wrote. She twirled on her heels and clutched her stomach—for the baby inside had given a sharp kick at her whirling motion.

"Well, I know which is the greater labor." Harry made a grim face and wet his quill again.

"'Labor,' darling? Please don't 'mind me of that!" And Susannah's worried expression was only half playacting: she really did fear the pangs of birth, with no one near but childless Lady Exon and Peg to reassure her.

Harry looked up, alarmed. "If you think it is near—" he began. He had talked of returning to The Marches for the baby's birth. But Susannah preferred not to think of it.

"Can I help you copy?" she said.

"'Twould be too much trouble," said Harry, looking away. "And it is still in the making as I write."

"You mean you'd be ashamed by my scrawl." Susannah smiled.

"No, I—" Harry flushed. "In truth—I do not want it read, till it is done."

" 'Not yet.' 'Tis very like the babe."

Harry nodded as Susannah left him, continuing with his quill and sheaves of paper. Every day at dinnertime he emerged from his study spattered with ink, but somehow his fair copy was spared the blots. It grew to a pile above a foot high, which, in July, was delivered onto the mail coach for Harry's publisher in London. But that was only the first volume. Harry wrote on.

Summer peaked, the hills around Exon turned green and lush, and they would walk out over the hills at evening now, for the sun lingered in the sky till ten at night.

Susannah spent her days sewing, attending to bills, and helping Fermanagh brush down Elixir and Scamp in the stables. Once he had gotten over his surprise at seeing her dirty her skirts in the muck, Fermanagh began to talk to her. He pointed out the animals' strengths and weaknesses: the massive hindquarters that gave Scamp endurance; the nervous temper that showed in Elixir's eyes.

"At The Marches, there's a great stables," Susannah mused aloud. "Room enough for twenty horses. I wonder that they use so little of it."

Fermanagh shrugged, and left her to her thoughts.

"Why—with those stables, and all the fields about, we might keep twice the horses there are now. Stallions, and foaling mares . . . I wonder what Scamp and Cythera would make, together." Susannah brushed Scamp's black coat harder. "*I* think we could raise the best horses in Surrey. Would you come south with us, Fermanagh—to manage it?"

Fermanagh stared, at this fanciful talk, and shook his head. "I wouldn't like the South, missus. Not my place."

"Peg's from there. From London."

"Aye. Well—" But the waiting-man shook his head again, digging his shovel into the back of Scamp's stall. Susannah could draw no answer from him, yet, even though she and Harry—and Peg, she suspected—all wanted him to come.

She could understand it, though. Many days, looking at the hills and the time-blackened walls of Exon Castle, she would feel reluctance overcome her—whatever fine plans she made for their return south. At The Marches there would be visits from Harry's family, with, she knew, all their questions and judging looks. In London, somewhere, there was Nicholas. In either place, her fragile harmony with Harry could, at one blow, be destroyed.

Sometimes she sat with Harry in his study, sharing his writing desk for her correspondence with Knole and the bank.

Once, while she was in the middle of a letter to Mr. Chilliam, his pen fell strangely silent. She looked up, her eyes an unworried bright blue against the sprigged head scarf that held back her hair. "Darling? What is it?"

Harry looked glum, and shook his head. "I wonder—at the things I cannot account for. Sometimes"—he smiled wryly—"the span of my ignorance seems so great—I wonder if I would do as well to invent."

"Well, invent then!" said Susannah, unconcerned. "Isn't that what most authors do?"

" 'Tis not a deception I—countenance. To invent people's superstitions, habits, ways of thought . . ."

"Why, *those* cannot have changed," said Susannah with certainty. "Surely men have always had the same things moving them: love and jealousy and greed. . . . *Greed* the most, I think," she said, thinking briefly of her aunt.

"Perhaps I shall not understand mankind," said Harry. He gave a slow smile and picked up his pen. "For—I think I am not greedy. All I want in the world is to be here with you."

She thought often on those words as the child grew more cumbrous in her belly. She should not go to bed till November, she knew; and she tried to hide her fear of the approaching birth from Harry. For as yet he did not talk of leaving.

But at last, in late August, he spoke of it. "Shall we go south next month?"

"So soon?" Susannah's stomach knotted. She tried to put him off with reasons. Why, they did not need to leave yet. Lady Exon thought her fit and sound; there was a midwife at Otterburn, only a short ride away. . . .

"Too far," said Harry. "And you should have a doctor."

But it was not only that. Harry himself seemed, more and more, to feel the pull of home. "After all," he said, "The Marches is our land. Where I was born, and my father before me . . ."

"But what does it matter?" Susannah said weakly; she knew it was a losing fight. The history of Harry's family weighed on him in a way that could only be strange to her: a history fixed in that one, green plot of ground, The Marches. They agreed, at last: they would ride south in early October.

"Then I will write to my mother, and Augusta," said Harry. "And they will let Helena and Agnes know—"

"Your mother? Augusta and all of them? Must you?"

Troubled, Harry watched his wife's face grow anxious. "They will want to see us—"

"Oh, no. Not me, Harry. They will not want to see me."

"Of course they will. They don't hate you. What— you can't imagine—"

Susannah shook her head, with a sad laugh, and took his hands. She could not meet his eyes. He was *part* of that family. He was not a woman. He could not know. . . .

He drew her against him, and she laid her head against his chest. She heard the thump of his heart, sure and certain. "It is only"—she shook her head, feeling foolish—"we have been so happy!"

Chapter 24

❧

In London, life was treating Nicholas Carrick well. It was true, he had taken to hard drinking for some months at winter's end, but by May of 1790, when *Treason in a Foreign Land* gave its final performances, he had righted himself again. He had consulted one doctor Theosophilos, healer to fashionable London, whose regime of green fruit and beetroot juice was known to restore lost youth and vigor: both of which he immediately spent upon his new mistress.

He had installed Claudine Bryce in the garret rooms at Southampton Street, which he could well afford now that Drury Lane had advanced him three hundred pounds for his new play. It was to be titled *As Good as His Word*, and it would take on all literary London: for what use restraint, when his other works were selling and playing so well? Its hero, a well-meaning cipher, was to run the gauntlet of patrons and critics in his quest for poetic fame; no nobleman or author of Carrick's acquaintance would be spared. He spoke little of the play, however, to his friends, or even to Claudine. As she hovered over his shoulder, one warm June day in Southampton Street, he crouched even lower over the sheet he was writing.

Annoyed at his secrecy, Claudine stalked to the fireplace, where she threw two empty bottles of beetroot juice down, hard, on the hearthstones. As Nicholas started at the sound of their splintering, she ran over to examine the paper under his hand.

"You're no Romney, to be sure. What're you doing?" She squinted at the awkward pen drawing: a big-bosomed woman with wild, waving hair.

Nicholas snatched it away. "None of your affair."

"Go on! I've a right to know. 'Tis *your* damned pieces that gi' me what to eat and drink. Can ye not finish?" Claudine stared him down with fiery eyes. "What about it? Are you lazy, or just a damn fool?" She paced the little room, her voice, even her body swelling, as if to fill a vast, echoing hall. She ranted on: at Nicholas, for having spent all his advance money; at the Baron Blackcroft, for refusing to give him more; and finally, at Drury Lane, and all its actresses and players.

When she was halfway through, Nicholas said absently, "You still talk like a fishwife." He scribbled in tiny letters:

treachery
gets its
reward.

Then, as if angered at himself, he scratched out the words until they dissolved into a snarl of black lines.

Calmer now, Claudine planted her bare feet on the floor beside him. She looked down: he made a foolish, foppish figure, she thought, in this summer heat—in his starched shirt, green shoes, and green-striped stockings. He hunched lower over his paper, black brows converging. "Will I be the principal woman?" she said.

Nicholas looked up, startled. "What?"

"In your play! Will I have the biggest part?"

"No!" he said quickly. And, again, "No. The irony! It couldn't . . ." He gave a strange chuckle.

"What?"

"Besides, you do not suit it."

Affronted, Claudine tossed her head and stamped her way to the dining chamber. She opened and slammed the doors of the miniature sideboard. "Lud, but I've a thirst! Haven't we ale?"

Nicholas made no answer.

"Lud, Nicholl Ye'll lose me one day with your sulking, unmannerly ways." Claudine looked up to see if she had sparked a reaction. But she had not. "Nought but beetroot juice," she grumbled. "Worse'n piss water. I'm going to the inn." She thrust her feet into shoes and clattered downstairs, enjoying the noise of her heels on the steps.

When she came back an hour later, she was relieved to find Nicholas gone. He had left her a note in his pinched writing, which she stared at for a moment before tossing out the window. She rarely bothered to decipher men's notes. The ones that came to her at the theater rarely offered her more than a drink or dinner. *Funny*, she thought, how men tried to get free from an actress what they were too mean to pay for from a whore. . . .

She riffled through her pin box, looking for the change to buy a seat at the Haymarket. She went to that summer theater every night if she could; she liked to compare herself to the other actresses. She rated only one of them higher than herself—but Mrs. Siddons, of course, was a tragic actress, while Claudine knew herself to be a comic one. Soon, to be sure, the suitors would come; though so far only one caller at the tiring rooms had intrigued her. He was called Captain Travers; he was fortyish, with a rough, handsome face and long whiskers. "Might I call on you?" he had said, and slipped a gold chain bracelet into her hand. Claudine had demurred, then, for Carrick was near. But Carrick, in truth, grew a bore of late. Crazed he was, sometimes, with his cartoons and hidden scribblings. And she had her own way to make. . . .

Until it was time to leave for the Haymarket, Claudine stood leaning out of her window. She liked watching the world go by, here. Sometimes she broke a piece of slate from the roof, and pipped a cart house or an urchin between the eyes. It reminded her of olden days, which did not seem, now she looked back on them, so bad.

At the beginning of October, Harry and Susannah drove from Exon Castle to The Marches. Fermanagh had, at last, been coaxed into driving them; and he took them by a different route, Susannah thought, than the one she had come along before. For now the fields looked greener, the low villages cheerful and thronged with travelers. *Can it all be in my mind?* she thought; and she could not account for the deferential courtesy with which she was received now at the inns, where farmers jostled to help her, with her great belly, into and out of the coach. Fermanagh took the road slowly, for her sake, and on the fifth day of traveling they had still not reached Surrey but pulled up at an inn near Windsor to sleep.

She could not explain why a feeling of foreboding came over her that night. She could not even rid herself of it when Harry held her close in the oaken cupboard bed. He traced his fingers over her swollen breasts.

"You cannot want me—big, and awkward as I am," she said.

"I can," he said, laughing. "You forget, I've not—dallied before with a woman with child."

Susannah laughed a little at that, for that was what it did feel like: dallying, playing, with the babe intruding its presence between them. Soon they would no longer manage it, she supposed: and, despite the awkwardness, she thought she would miss it. The lovemaking soothed her, and in time the baby's kicking ceased inside her. She closed her eyes, drifting,

and came to a room: a long gallery. She walked past
the familiar rows of portraits; the figures in the frames
were strange, aloof, incurious. They wore the costumes of past days: square headdresses, coifs, and lank
curls. And only as she moved closer did she see that
every face was the same. *Maria's.*

From the middle of the long drive she could see
them: one watching figure, then two, then suddenly
a crowd of relations spilling down the white stairs.
Fermanagh sped the horses on, taking the last length
of the drive at a gallop.

"I told you." Harry wrapped his arm around Susannah, with a close-lipped, tense smile. "They—all want
to see us."

They pulled up at the steps, and as he handed Susannah down, the whole group seemed to draw back,
in suspense. A few heads turned toward Maria, who
stood, stock-still, to one side, bright eyes staring. And
then, in a rush, they moved past Susannah. Harry had
descended from the coach, and his sisters, Helena and
Augusta, fluttered around him in their white dresses,
like doves. Susannah and Maria looked at each other;
and now James Cheveril, who had stood, aimless,
among the men, strode over to embrace Susannah.

"My dear! You're as lovely as ever. Now we hear
that you're to be a mother—"

But there he stopped. Maria's very stare, her stillness, accused him of treachery. He swallowed his grin
and dropped Susannah's hands. "Well, man!" He
turned to Harry, with a loud heartiness. " 'Tis almighty good to see you again, I vow. . . . "

Already Susannah wished she had not come.

That afternoon a great dinner was laid for the new
arrivals.

"Do you see?" cried Maria, raising her glass to her
son. "The Marches remembers you—however little
you think of *it*." She grinned at the footman who

poured her more burgundy, and then at Harry, who looked blankly back at her.

" 'Twill be over soon," he whispered in Susannah's ear. But neither of them believed it. The toasts had not even begun. The conversation that whirled around them was upon all the old, once-familiar subjects: James Cheveril's recent Devon election, Mr. Hastings's trial, the prospects for a regency. Susannah looked around silently at the family, most of whom she had not seen in two years. Augusta, who avoided her gaze, had grown plumper with motherhood. Helena, like the limp sash of her dress, had grown more faded. Maria was thinner; she had passed the stage when she could still pretend to youth. Her flesh-tipped, long nose stood out more, now, against her bony face, and her hair, once a graying dark brown, was now uniformly soot-colored. The well-fed husbands—Hench, Stillwell, and Cheveril—murmured together, as they had always done, of stocks and shares and the hunt.

Questions came at Susannah—now from Helena, about that strange, dark Irish coachman, and now from Cheveril about when "the youngest master Harry" was expected. Maria turned to her son.

"When," she said, lifting her eyebrows, "do you go away again? Or have you come to see The Marches as your proper home?"

Susannah felt her heart lurch with all the old dread; and Harry reached for her hand under the table. He spoke in a terse, tight voice. "We regard this as our home. As it always has been."

Maria's mouth curved into a benevolent smile. "How splendid, Harry. We shall have a *long* visit, then. Tell me, Susannah, is there more Burgundy in the cellars?"

Susannah wondered why her aunt asked; for it was she, evidently, who had ordered the meal. "Yes, Aunt Maria," she said. "There must be."

"Then, might you run below, dear, and send for more? That young butler was grudging. Four bottles for the ten of us! And . . ." Maria looked up as Susannah pulled herself to her feet. "Would you take *this* to my closet, dear, while you are out? I would ask one of the maids, only—they all seem so *new* since my days here." She undraped the fox mantle from her shoulders and held it out on one thin hand.

Susannah reeled; her belly felt heavy as she walked, and she clutched the backs of chairs as she made her way around the table. The room grew silent, and she thought that she would never reach her aunt's side. Harry was opening his mouth as if to speak, and James Cheveril stared, perturbed, at his wife. Susannah felt her face grow red, as the anger surged in her and could not escape. "*I would ask one of the maids, only—*"

"Here, Aunt." She took the fur. "I suppose—" *I suppose you are not used to having maids. I suppose you have no servants left at Kensington,* she wanted to say. But her voice balked at the rudeness. She knew everyone was listening. "I will go to bed now," she said in a low voice. "Please excuse me."

She clasped the fur—*those wretched animals*, she thought—and stumbled into the hallway. At the foot of the stairs in the entrance hall she stopped to catch her breath, looking up with loathing at the Roman statues in their niches. Apollo, Venus, the senator . . . *I hate them all.* Even they seemed to look down long noses, despising her. She wanted to throw rocks at them: to break them to bits. She loathed this house— loathed Harry's family, and their scorn. And now that she had come, she did not know if she would ever be free of it.

For an hour or so she hoped that Harry would come to the bedroom. She longed to talk to him: to empty the hate from within her and hear his calm, light voice reassure her. But he did not come. Hearing the faint sounds of dinner continuing downstairs, she did not know whether to blame him for staying away, or the others for keeping him. Feeling heavy and weary, she poked a tong at the fire whose sparse embers were dying in the chill. The marble bedroom was as cold and unwelcoming as it always had been. She and Harry must change rooms, she thought—tomorrow. They could take any other room: Harry's old, book-cluttered chamber; perhaps even the room where they stored superfluous Chinese furniture, and relatives, in the west wing. . . .

Well, it can hardly grow worse, here, she thought, with a shadow of a smile, standing by the fire to un-dress. She could hear the wind whistling between the shutters and the windowpanes. She crept into a bed in her shift, and was silent when Harry slid in beside her.

"Dearest—are you asleep?" he whispered.

She shook her head.

"I am sorry," he said, "about—about my mother. She—"

"Never mind." Susannah's voice was drowsy, dis-tant. "It will pass. . . . "

"But—" said Harry, then thought better of speak-ing. He leaned up on one elbow, stroking Susannah's back and looking, worried, down on her little, bulg-ing form. She had not heard his mother's questioning, once she had gone. *Why, Henry? Did she tell you what she did in London? Why did you give her the use of our money?*

With any luck, he thought, she never would.

In the next few days everyone in the house seemed to grow easier. The conversation at meals turned gen-eral and political; Harry was even given the chance to talk, now, of his "History." Maria gloried in what she took to be her husband's growing influence in the Commons; Jonas Hench trailed her footsteps like a hungry hound. But Augusta seemed not to mind this; indeed, she seemed oblivious. She kept strangely silent at dinner, excusing herself early to put her sons to bed. At tea she shook her head as trays of seedcakes and macaroons passed by her, so that even her hus-band began to wonder what was wrong.

"Mighty broody, dear," was Hench's comment, as they sat sipping tea one day with Harry and Susannah.

"What?" Augusta sniffed. "Do you expect me always to chatter? Is that what you think me—a chatterer?"

Her voice had such a high, peaked sound that no one took the subject further. An awkward silence took hold.

Susannah said, "When is your next child to come?" She had noticed the beginnings of a bulge at Augusta's middle.

"My next?" Augusta echoed, her eyes widening. "Oh—not for some time yet. Not till—some time after yours." Her eyes fixed, for a second, on Susannah's larger belly. Then she bowed her head and sipped her tea with concentration. Hench suggested a turn in the gardens.

While the men walked ahead down the gravel path, Susannah searched for a subject she could take up with her cousin: anything that might put her at her ease. For she felt the estrangement between them. "Do you write, still, Augusta?" she said, in a reedy, uncertain voice. "I remember—you used to write great numbers of poems. *Pastoral* poems."

Augusta walked quickly, her hands folded in front of her.

"Do you still?" tried Susannah, again.

"Write? Ah, no." Augusta's eyes darted up at her. "I find I am too occupied. Of course, you would not know the demands of a family, having had no child. . . . "

Susannah wondered at the sharpness of her cousin's words. *After all,* she thought, *if this is but my first child, that is none of my doing.* She smiled—she hoped encouragingly—and said, "Your boys have grown up so. And they are both so handsome! How old is Jonas now? Two? He looks more. . . . " As she talked she thought she could hear her tongue rattling in her head. And yet she feared silence more, and could not stop. "I suppose their education must be a great undertaking. Will you have them taught at home, as Harry was?"

"If Jonas sees fit." Augusta looked at her hurrying feet.

"Do you hope for a girl?" said Susannah. "Now that you have two boys, you must. . . . "

Silence fell, and Augusta answered at last, faintly. "Jonas would be pleased, I think, at another boy. And of course I should hope for—whatever he wishes."

"But that isn't like you!"

Susannah spoke without thinking; and Augusta turned wide eyes on her. "Whatever do you mean?" she said, in the same, faint voice as before.

"Why, once you—had views of your *own* of things. Oh, I don't know." Susannah faltered. "I don't know what I meant. Forgive me."

They continued down the path, side by side, in silence.

One late afternoon, toward the end of October, she was made to think again of the baby's sex. Most of the household was out riding, while Augusta read to her sons in the nursery and Harry, in the library, studied proofs from his publisher.

Susannah walked slowly down the portrait gallery, which was still her favorite room in the house. The waning sun cast bars of light across the parquet floor; there was a golden, dusty haze in the air here, and a seldom-interrupted peace: for the Warringtons paid little tribute to their ancestors, except in their harmonious arrangement along the walls. Susannah passed the tumbling spaniels, and her gentle-eyed aunt, Amelia Blackpole. She stood looking at her mother, whose blue-tinted skin seemed to hint at her fragility. Surely she belonged here, she thought, more than in that wilderness where she died. One day, perhaps, Harry's picture, and Susannah's, would hang here: and those of their sons and daughters and grandchildren. . . .

"What are you doing, my dear? Meditating? Or praying?"

Susannah turned with a start. Her aunt, beside her, smiled faintly, leaning forward on her gold-headed cane.

"Praying, Aunt?" Susannah edged away. She averted her eyes from her mother's portrait: for her peace with it had been disturbed. "I was but thinking. I do not pray so very often."

"You had best pray now, my dear."

"What—" began Susannah.

"You had best pray your creature be a girl. For if—" Maria tapped her stick. "*If* I knew a boy bastard was to inherit The Marches and all that belongs to it— why, I would raise all flood and hellfire before I let him see a penny. You mark me."

Susannah froze in place. She saw her aunt's malevolent smile. It seemed incredible, still, that she had spoken such words. And now she saw her turning away.

"You wait," Susannah said. She felt her face suffuse with blood. "How dare you talk so? In *our* house."

"You still call it *your house* when you deserted it for whoredom?"

Susannah did not know what came over her then. All the rage suppressed, against her aunt, over past weeks—past years—rose up inside her. "Do you think you can insult me so and remain here?" she said. "Do you think you can eat our food and drink our wine— and order me about like a maid, without the least shred of civility?" She stared at her aunt, whose eyes narrowed to black pinpricks and whose mouth was pinched into a quill-thin line. She felt herself grow strangely calm. "You cannot. You shall stay here no longer, Aunt Maria."

And she saw, even as she spoke, that Maria was turning her back on her: walking away.

"Well? Did you hear me?"

Maria moved slowly down the gallery, a lean, beruffled, limping figure. She half turned her head. "Do not be overbold, miss. *Yours* is not the last word."

Susannah heard the tap of her stick, and her footsteps, as she made her way out and through the passage to the wide front stair. She wanted to run behind her aunt, but she knew on the slick floor she might easily fall. She cradled her round belly, listening, waiting; and she knew, even before she heard Maria march upstairs, where her aunt was going. To Harry. Thinking, no doubt, that he would side with her against his little, inconsequential wife . . .

Her heart beating quickly, from fury and fear, she climbed the stairs, as silently as she could. Down the hall, the door of Harry's study was half open.

"Mother—"

She heard the warning tone of Harry's voice, as it rose, clear, then halted itself. And she thought of the sway Maria had once held over her son, and could only pray that it was gone.

"If you do not make yourself clear, I shall suspect the worst." Harry's voice was calm.

"Your wife has presumed to order me from house."

"She . . . has," Harry repeated slowly. "What for?"

Moving near to the doorway, Susannah heard her mother-in-law's feet, and her stick, scrape against the carpet.

"Why," said Maria almost ingenuously, "I do not *know*, Henry! You know how breeding can affect a woman's moods. . . ."

Without thinking, Susannah moved up to the door and into the light. "That is not true!"

Harry looked, startled, at her, then back at his mother. "Then, what is? Someone—one of you. Tell me."

Maria coughed.

"She called me"—Susannah forced out the last word—"a whore."

"My dear son." Maria raised herself up on her stick. "I merely pointed out what you are a fool not to recognize already. Clearly she is great with some other man's child than yours."

Susannah searched for Harry's gaze, across the long distance between them. *It is not true.* She mouthed

the words; and with her eyes she pleaded, and shook
her head.

"Go from this house, Mother." Harry's voice was
low. "If you have so little regard for my wife—you
do not deserve to live here."

"Henry—" Maria's voice rose in reproof. Her eyes
bulged, and she raised her stick in the air.

"No, Mother. You have said enough. Go from this
room. And from this house. Now."

Harry watched as she turned away, defeated, his
face still and hard as stone.

Maria hobbled down to her room, where she started
to throw her clothes into a messy heap on the bed.
James Cheveril entered, pink-faced and tousled-
haired, after an afternoon's ride.

"What on earth are you doing, pet?"

"Packing. We are leaving, James."

"Leaving?" Cheveril echoed and, "But when?" Maria turned dagger eyes on him and marched away into
her fur closet.

"Hee, hee." Cheveril gave a feeble laugh. He
reached for a brush, which he drew through his thinning red hair for solace. *He* did not know where they
might go next. Not to Devon, for his parents had refused to share their house with Maria again. And
surely not to Kensington, for the house there was be-
sieged by creditors. When Maria returned, he urged
an apology—whatever the trouble was. When she refused, he threw up his hands and went searching for
a brandy.

Dinner that evening was attended only by Harry's
sisters and their families. And all night, curious souls
streamed through the corridors. Helena and Augusta
knocked, in turn, at their mother's door; and, in their
nightgowns, visited each other, commiserating.

"If *she* goes," said Helena, her mouth drooping, "we
must go, too. And I had thought the country air would
be so good for the children. . . . "

"Come to Henshawe," said Augusta absently,

frowning through her spectacles. And, to no one, she whispered, "Why?"

Those rumors, she thought. Her mother must have spoken of them. These three weeks, they had troubled her, too; though all seemed well now between Harry and his wife, she had not been able to bring herself to speak to Susannah as before. In time, she had told herself, she would: for forgiveness', or at least appearance's, sake. . . .

"*Harry*," puzzled Helena, "is grown strangely willful."

At ten the next morning a coach and driver pulled up at the front steps. The Stillwells and Henches lingered on one curving slope while Harry and Susannah waited at the bottom of the other. Pale and tired, Susannah leaned against a stair pillar while Maria shouted and waved at the footmen who loaded her trunks.

But at last they were done, and Maria could put off the departure no longer. Cheveril stood behind her, running hands through his hair, looking sheepish. Maria gazed mournfully up at The Marches' pilasters.

"My own house!" she said, with a sniff.

"Mother," said Harry stiffly, extending a hand.

"Henry?" Maria looked up at her son so dolefully that, for a second, he was certain that she would beg reprieve. She clung to his hand; the spectators on the steps shifted forward. The horses shuffled in the drive, their breath clouding the air.

"Where do you go now?" Harry removed his hand from his mother's. And as he studied her face through narrow eyes—watching the mouth twist, the head toss proudly, as she searched for an answer—there came a cry, a sudden shuffle and motion behind him.

Susannah had crumpled to the ground, against the pillar. He turned and ran to her, wrapping his arms round her waist, while she clung to his shoulders. "What is it?"

"I—I don't know. I think I—" Susannah winced as the waters rushed from her, soaking her gown.

Now everyone clamored round her: Helena and Augusta and the servants. And Harry and the footmen lifted her up, carrying her between them, up the stairs and inside, while the butler Warwick barked, "A doctor!" and maids were sent scurrying for blankets and water.

In the commotion, Maria was forgotten. She stood bereft at her coach door. Her husband returned to her from the house, with a smile. There was no concealing his relief.

"Can't go now! You picked a devil of a time to take our leave. I warrant you'll soon be seeing another grandson!"

Chapter 25

———— ❧ ————

The old wives' tale had it that a seven months' babe was safer than one of eight. So this, Susannah knew, must be unlucky: begotten in February, born the end of October. . . .

"No! It can't be time," she cried as Harry and the footmen bore her down the hall.

"We'll put you to bed, m'lady, and see," said Peg, who scurried along beside them.

"But it can't be," said Susannah again, weakly, with a pleading look at her maid. Peg, with all her superstition, must understand. She felt the quick, sharp clutch of pain; but quickly it passed, and she was being laid down in Maria's great, curving tent bed. "Why here?"

But no one answered. Peg and the other maids clucked and clattered about her: taking off her outer clothes, stoking the fire. A second, stronger wave of pain gripped her belly. She winced, clutching the featherbed, and lost count of time. Shadowy figures seemed to move around her. Men—Cheveril, Stillwell, Hench—poked their heads inside the door, and retreated, while women—her two cousins and Maria—flapped around the bed like great light-feathered birds.

She let out a strangled cry. And when she opened her eyes now the only faces she saw were Peg's and Harry's. They held her hands.

"You must keep your strength, m'lady," said Peg. Her round face was full of furrows. "You'd have the babe born *today*, would you not? For tomorrow—'tis All Hallows' Eve."

"Peg!" Harry rebuked her. He leaned closer to Susannah. "Pay no heed. 'Tis but superstition." He wiped her forehead with the cool cloth Peg gave him.

"But what of an eight months' babe?" she whispered.

But Harry knew nothing of the old wives' wisdom. By the time Dr. Wallace arrived, the pains had come and passed twice again. The doctor reached beneath the sheets to grope inside her, squinting and tilting his face up at the ceiling. Peg, who waited by the fire, eyed him suspiciously. She mistrusted man midwives and had often told Susannah so.

Dr. Wallace withdrew his arm at last. His bald head shone with perspiration. "Very well—" he puffed. "Very well, Lady Warrington. To be sure—you'll have the babe in no time." He extended his arms for Peg to wipe clean, and withdrew from the room for a drink.

There were more pains, which he attended—they grew stronger and closer-spaced—yet the delivery seemed to make little progress. The day was waning. "Can you make it—come no more quickly?" Susannah whispered. She was damp with sweat now beneath the heavy bedclothes.

"God's will, you know! First deliveries are ever slow," said Dr. Wallace, beaming and swallowing a glass of port. Belatedly he motioned for a dose of the same for her.

The clenching and cramping again mounted and peaked and, in a rush, subsided. Susannah breathed out, holding Harry's hand, for he had come in again, and waited for the few minutes' respite she was due.

"Don't clench your teeth, Lady Warrington," called Dr. Wallace jovially. "Such pretty teeth! 'Twould be a pity to wear them down."

There was scarcely any rest this time. She was being stabbed, pierced, attacked from inside. No one had told her it would be like this.

"Harry, don't—don't leave me yet," she cried, clawing at his hand. She dreaded the moment when the doctor would banish him: when she would be left to his hands, and mysterious instruments. . . . "Darling," she whispered. "I am so scared. What if I die? . . . No!" She cried out again, for the pain grew sharper. "No—I know I won't. I mustn't. Oh! I—love you so much."

"And I—" Harry shook his head, and his eyes welled with tears. "Trust to God you will come through it—" Squeezing her hand, he went quickly from the room.

The pain rolled over her in waves. And soon she no longer knew that Harry was gone; for the pain mounted, pressed upon her, obliterated all else. For a second she saw Dr. Wallace grinning at her, red-faced: swallowing more port and rolling back his sleeves. *Why does it take so long?* she thought, before all the words and fear subsided into exhaustion.

" 'Tis midnight!" she heard someone call. *Now it is All Hallows' Eve.* Dr. Wallace checked the lay of the child again, and clucked. He gave Susannah a brandy and, when time passed, another. She was vaguely aware of clutching the bedposts against the pain, of something pulling at her hair, and of screaming. . . .

The child was a girl, a tiny girl, and sucked in her first breath as Dr. Wallace slapped her, just before three on the morning of October 31. Susannah opened her eyes and saw a red, slimy small creature beside her, with a surprisingly black shock of hair, before she slid away into sleep.

"Where is my hair?" Susannah lifted her head and did not feel the familiar tug, the weight of it. Its thick, waving locks ran nearly to her waist. . . .

"Where is it?" she cried, for it was not there. Her head was light. She tugged at the short ends that hung above her shoulders and started to breathe quickly, in a panic, feeling lost.

Peg answered her call at last. "Shh, m'lady." She stroked her forehead. "They'd to cut it. It'd got so tangled to the bed and in your fingers. . . . We'll fix it, when you're up again. Shh."

And so Susannah seemed to wake repeatedly to a world where things had mysteriously changed. The pink creature, with its black hair, her baby, had lain briefly by her side and gone away. Harry would appear by her bedside, then vanish, and she would wake again, to discover that half her hair had gone: or that her breasts were sore and bound up in cloth.

"It aches," she whispered to Peg, touching them. "Why?"

"Dr. Wallace said the babe'd be put out to nurse, m'lady."

"Why?" Susannah shook her head, still drowsy, and rubbed her eyes. "Why . . . did he say she should be put out to nurse?"

" 'Tis what most ladies do," said Peg, with a shrug. "P'raps he thought you too weakly or—"

"But—" Susannah raised herself in the bed. "I'm not too weak. Why—I can take her. Augusta did. A long time ago, she said something about"—she searched for the words—"a state of nature! Why not?" For the first time in she knew not how many days, she felt awake, and defiant.

Peg shook her head and clucked. " 'Tisn't oft done—"

But Susannah insisted. She saw no sense in lying here aching when she might feed her daughter. She had barely seen her yet. So the baby was brought to her, and Peg did what she could to help. Harry came in shortly after, and stared at them in surprise.

"The state of nature," Susannah said, with a little laugh.

The baby was thin, with a wizened face; her eager mouth and tongue sucked greedily. But already, when she had done, she looked fuller and better pleased than before. As the milk leaked from her, and the ache began to subside, Susannah, too, felt better.

"My mother and sisters want to see you," Harry said; and Susannah's heart lurched at the prospect.

"What day is it?" she said.

"Still All Hallows'. Ten o'clock at night."

"I thought it was later."

Harry peered down at the little girl, now lying replete in her lap. "Well? And from which part of the family do you take?" he said to her. "Mine—or your mother's?"

Susannah's heart lurched again; but then—*I am being foolish*, she thought. There was no accusation in Harry's face: only curiosity. He touched the tip of the baby's nose, which was smaller than his finger. Now Susannah saw it too: there was a tiny bulb of flesh, a droplet at the end.

Harry gave a laugh, and tickled it with his finger. "A very Warrington!" he said. "Already. There, Susan—do you see it? The Warrington nose!"

The next morning the family gathered to drink to the health of mother and child. Susannah lay in a fresh dressing gown beneath the counterpane, and had Peg arrange the springy curls of her hair as best she could beneath a lace cap. The maids handed her little girl into her arms, dressed in a long white gown. While the men set into the canary wine and the enormous yellow christening cake, the women leaned over the little girl's narrow, bewildered face, clucking and wiggling their fingers. She stared back with dark blue eyes, unmoved.

"What are you going to *call* the child?" Maria demanded.

Susannah looked at Harry, and he looked back, just as mystified.

"Well!" said Edmund Stillwell. "I suppose you'd expected a boy." He glanced, self-satisfied, over at Helena.

"No—" said Susannah.

"Not all women are so fortunate as we have been, in bearing boys," remarked Helena to her younger sister.

"*Hem!* Well!" Jonas Hench slapped his thigh. "P'raps they'll be in better luck the next time!"

"Do you mean you have not *thought* of a name?" Maria insisted.

"No," Harry said calmly, exchanging glances with his wife. "We hadn't."

"We thought we should see the child first," said Susannah, "and then decide."

"Another of your intellectual views, eh?" said Cheveril. But Harry ignored his, and all his relations', railing. He moved around the room, pouring wine and playing the host. He spilled canary on the carpet and Augusta's dress. When the baby began to howl, her sound was nearly lost in the genial noise of the gathering.

"Virginia." Susannah repeated the name, walking across the frosty lawn. She and the little girl had come out for their first breath of outdoor air, wrapped from head to toe in blankets. Harry carried the baby, to spare Susannah's strength, but gradually, as she moved, steadying herself on his arm, she felt stronger. She walked a few paces on her own. "Virginia?"

"It was only a thought." Harry flushed. "I thought— as it is your place, and you were fond of it . . ."

"Do *you* like it?" Susannah said to the little girl. She talked to her as an adult, for her face looked so aged and wise. When she and Harry had suggested names to her before, she seemed to have decided opinions. "Margaret" made her cry out in protest, and, to Susannah's relief, she drooled sullenly at "Maria." At "Virginia" she widened her eyes, as if inviting a repetition. But, "The

name of my state?" asked Susannah. It was not an often-
used name for girls, even in America.

"Why not?" said Harry. "You felt an attachment to
the place. And—it will offend no one."

They exchanged looks, both thinking of his
mother—who already assumed that this child was a
little Maria. Susannah laughed to herself.

"What is it?" Harry cocked his head at her.

"I was only thinking now—when I was climbing on
the ship, my father called out to me: 'Don't forget
Virginia!' But I misdoubt he expected me to call my
daughter after it."

Harry, looking down at the baby, was suddenly
taken with verse. " 'O my America! my new-found-
land,/ My kingdom, safeliest when with one man
manned . . .' "

It took Susannah a moment to recognize the words:
they came from one of his old verse books: John Donne.
"Heavens!" She tried to nudge her husband out of his rec-
itation. "She is young yet to understand *that*."

" 'My mine of precious stones, my empery . . .' What?"
Harry glanced over shyly, and away. "The words—" he
said slowly, "are not for her. They are for you."

Susannah felt her heart give an unexpected beat.
She squeezed his arm tighter. "I too—"

But he looked away, still. And now they came to
the edge of the woods, and stopped.

"Do you never wish to go back there?" said Harry
suddenly.

"America?" Susannah tried to give a shrug. "I have
stopped hoping it, I suppose. I—"

"But do you not miss it?"

"Yes."

"Then we should go there together."

Susannah stared at her husband: at the baby. But before she could wonder, or make objections, he went on.
"For all these years I have lived out of my own times—
but I know, there is much to learn *in* them, too."

"What do . . . you mean?" Susannah's heart beat
quickly.

Harry lifted their daughter up to face him, looking,

with a mocking smile, into her eyes. "I am not too old to begin my travels—am I, Virginia? To take your mother back across the seas—journey the length of America, and study its democracy . . ."

"But—" Still, Susannah could not believe these words. That Harry would sail away with her: take her to the places he talked of now. New York, Canada, the West Indies . . .

"What? Does she object?" said Harry teasingly, again to the child in his arms. "Then you and *I* shall go together. When you are older—my Virginia."

But for the time being, they were busy enough at The Marches. On the seventh of November, Virginia Anne Harriet Warrington was christened at the Bothwell church. Susannah had not conceived of the need for so many names; but Harry said everyone in his family had at least three. So once they had decided on Anne, after Susannah's mother, she had sought about for a name that was like Harry's.

Virginia lay quietly in the vicar's arms, entranced by the clockwork rhythm of his voice.

"We receive this child into the congregation of Christ's flock, and do sign her with the sign of the cross. . . . "

She let out a sharp wail as the cold water touched her forehead. Susannah bowed her head and heard the shufflings of the crowd behind her. The church was full of all its usual parishioners, including the neighbors, the Chathenhams and Northfords—who, Harry said, would naturally expect to attend a christening feast afterward at The Marches. This they saw as their right; and reluctantly, to spare Susannah too much exertion, he had put his mother and sisters in charge of it. Maria had given him a brittle smile. "I am glad I can be of some use to you, Henry . . . . "

Susannah knew she could not be quite at her ease till her aunt was gone. She gave a secret smile now, at the thought of that inevitable day. The vicar tolled, "So should we who are baptized die from sin, and rise

again unto righteousness, continually mortifying all
our evil and corrupt affections . . ."

Susannah remembered how one morning while she
was nursing Virginia, her mother-in-law had come to
her alone.

" 'Tis a girl," Maria said. She smiled, unblinking.
"I am glad."

"I too," Susannah had answered steadily.

"What very black hair she has." Maria stroked Virginia's head with a knotty hand. "How very odd,
when neither you nor Harry is so dark."

Susannah had met her aunt's gaze as calmly as she
could and held Virginia closer. "The doctor tells me,
when 'tis so, it passes off in a few months and grows
back a different color."

"I see. How very interesting."

Susannah had clenched her teeth and smiled: just
as she did now. *She will go soon. Harry promises it—
she will.*

". . . and daily proceeding in all virtue and godli-
ness of living," finished the vicar.

Virginia was handed back into Susannah's arms, her
forehead still wet and glistening. And Susannah looked
down, and knew how impossible it was to trace, in
those twisted, yelping features—the turquoise eyes,
the bulbed nose, the dark lashes—the provenance of
any. A certain father. Until Virginia was a great deal
older, Susannah could only rely on her own instincts.
She is Harry's.

"A christening's made the very devil of 'er!" remarked old Sir Nestor Northford, passing them. He
squeezed the baby's hand in his thick fingers. Virginia
went on crying.

The feast that afternoon filled the whole of the dining chamber and the card room next door. Old Sir
Nestor, Lady Chathenham, and a great number of
virtual strangers besides, proposed toasts to the happy
mother and father. And though they both crouched
down in their chairs, turning pink with embarrass-

ment, they did seem, to all around, to be truly happy.
Several times during the feasting Susannah dashed out
to attend to her daughter, whose hungry cries she
heard somehow through all the walls and corridors
between dining room and nursery. The toasts went on
until nine o'clock, and before long they were general.

"To the ladies!"

"To Lady Maria!"

"T' the ladies we've yet to know!"

But by noon the next day, all the guests were readying
to leave: most, like the Stillwells, for London, while the
Henches and Cheverils departed together for Henshawe.

"Time we stopped being a burden on you!" James
Cheveril explained, with a wink at Susannah. She
shook her head and started to demur politely; for she
had always liked Maria's husband. But she was relieved when Jonas Hench came up to hurry the Cheverils into his coach.

Augusta kissed little Virginia, and gave Susannah a
constrained good-bye. Her eyes looked teary. "Perhaps you will—sometime—come to see us?"

"Yes!" cried Susannah gladly; and she and Harry
stood on a bend of the steps, holding hands and waving as the last coach rolled away.

"We are—alone," she said, in a bewildered voice.
"After all this time."

"Yes," said Harry, bending down to kiss her. "And
whatever shall we make of it?"

Maria watched them out of the side window of the
Henches' coach as it rounded the bend in the drive.
Her eyes narrowed, and her face contracted beneath
the garnet ruffles of her hat.

"Pet? Are you well?" said Cheveril.

She answered in a terse, thin voice. "Yes. Perfectly."

Chapter 26

———— ❧ ————

In January of the new year, Harry's *History* came out. It had notices in the *Times*, the *London Evening Post* and the *Gentleman's Magazine*. And more to the young viscount's surprise—for he had thought his book a Whiggish, republican one—it extremely pleased the king. A letter came from His Majesty's secretary in praise of *A Full and Impartial History of the Conquest of England by the Normans*; and when Harry began to grin and swell with pride, Susannah had to remind him, "The king is mad, everyone says! So 'tis no wonder. . . . "

But she delighted, too, in the baroque praise of the reviewers. "Hear this one!" she would cry, and pace Harry's study and read: " 'To examine our history in its obscurer parts, must be a more than arduous endeavour, and the author of that task endowed with a rare fortitude. . . . ' " *She* did not doubt Harry's fortitude. Already he had begun on his next volume, even though his friends—the poet Potter and his old tutor, Bayliss—were urging him to London, to partake of the society and acclaim due a successful author.

But Harry still held to his aversion for that city. "No one writes there," he said, "but boasts of writing. Nor discovers aught but claims, at a hundred routs and teas, to have come at the foundation stone of philosophy. . . . " Susannah suspected, also, that London held disagreeable memories fo him, as for her; but she did not try to test him out. For in their last months here, they had been so peacefully happy. With her aunt departed, Susannah felt The Marches becoming her own again. She no longer hated it, the way she had on that night of her return, when she had stared with such loathing on the marble statues, and wanted to smash them. That now seemed a distant, lost moment of folly. For every day, with the changes she made in it, she saw the house becoming lighter, more comfortable and beautiful. She banished the supernumerary furniture of the downstairs rooms to the attics and decorated the halls and tables with greenery.

On Christmas Eve she had held the traditional feast for the estate's tenants—a feast that had not taken place since Harry's father's time. There had been wine and food for two hundred; dancing on the lawn, and a pageant in which Virginia, wearing a cherub's wings, was borne aloft down the gallery by the lord of Misrule. Virginia—or Ginia, as they had started to call her—had grown, in the last months, as solid and healthy as she had been wizened at birth. Her black hair fell away and was replaced by a brown fuzz, but her eyes stayed the same, bold dark blue as her mother's. She suckled greedily, and perhaps in those moments with her—of undisturbed quiet and half-adult, half-whimsical talk—Susannah found her greatest happiness. A happiness shared with Harry in becoming a family, which all the Christmas festivities had seemed to celebrate. . . .

But now it was February, and in this chill season the demands of London came, ever more insistent. Maria, who was staying at Hench House, wrote that Harry ought to take some part in the social Season: Harry could ignore *that* demand, but not so easily the fawning letter that came from the Royal Society of Antiquaries.

Even Susannah was intrigued. " 'If you should grant the favour of an Address to our humble Assembly. . . . ' " she read aloud, by the library fire.

" 'Humble'?" Harry raised an eyebrow. "They are no humble gathering, as far as I know!"

Susannah looked up. "Who are—" In the distance she heard Ginia's cries.

"Oh—Walpole, and Carmatheron, and Ford . . ."

Susannah did a little dance in the cold; the milk, she could feel, trickling from her. "P'raps you should go then!" she cried, as she ran toward the great staircase and the nursery. "I'd come, too, to hear your great address, darling. Let me bring Ginia—you might practice it on her now!"

She spoke playfully, carelessly; and she was surprised, a few days later, when Harry asked her if she had started the servants packing for their trip to London.

"London?" she echoed.

"Y-es," he said slowly. " 'Tis good a time—as any— to make a visit." He smiled. "And, as the Royal Society waits . . ."

Chill winds sliced through the pit and galleries of the Drury Lane Theatre as box doors opened and slammed, causing a hundred candle flames to flicker against sooty walls.

In a high box of the second tier, a scrawny mouse-blond matron hissed, "*What* is it we are meant to see, Mother? I know I shall catch a chill. I really cannot avow to any approval of the theater. . . . "

Her younger sister Augusta, whose plump face looked more anxious than aggrieved, kept silent.

"We shall see," said Maria calmly, opening her tortoise fan and moving closer to the box's rim. "We shall see."

Her husband, who dozed, behind, against a wall, his cushioned stomach regularly rising and falling, she ignored—as was her policy, of late. Of course Cheveril was useful; he escorted her, and never bothered to question her projects and plans. That afternoon, he had taken her to Darly's print shop in the Strand: and there she found her suspicions richly rewarded. There _was_ some matter in Carrick's play, then. For there, among all the politicians and their mistresses, was a fresh cartoon from the presses. In it, on a stage much like that of the Drury Lane, a blowsy, curly-haired actress was orating, while a noble lady, nearly her mirror image, watched from a box, much distressed. "O, she is much like me!" the lady cried, her words neatly scripted and circled in white. . . .

The orchestra plunged into the first sinfonia; Augusta leaned forward, a diamond pendant dangling above the neckline of her blue dress, fashioned, in the newest mode, out of a sari from India. She played nervously with a length of fringe, her eyes darting about the great hall: for though on another occasion she might have reveled in the vaguely illicit entertainment of the theater, now she could not put from her mind the suspicion that her mother had some sinister reason to lead this expedition. The bows of the violinists leapt and dove; her heart sank and fluttered with them. For the play was by Nicholas Carrick, whose reputation as rake nearly exceeded his renown as a writer. If he was the one Jonas had meant, with Susannah . . .

Helena Stillwell did not think on such things. She had distilled, from her mother's grumblings about Susannah, only a dismissive dislike of the girl; Helena's coolness toward her at The Marches was merely that of disinterest. The little American's fate—indeed Harry's—were but peripheral matters to Helena. She looked down at her garnet necklace and cheap fichu, wondering if they drew sufficient attention from her gown, some years out of fashion. She wondered if her son Edmund's genius was sufficiently appreciated at the Merchants' School; and why her husband Everett refused to order a portrait of her. When the play sheet passed into her hands, she glanced at it only briefly.

As Good As His Word,

or

The Tale of a Young Author's Quest for
Preferment,
Perform'd, by permission of His Gracious Majesty
KING GEORGE,
at his own THEATRE ROYAL, Drury Lane.

The Author, N. CARRICK, *Esq.*

The Players,

MEANING, *a poet* .... Mr. DRAYTON
MELISSA, *a country girl* .... Mrs. CATCHINGHAM
The Lady CITTADAGUERRA, *a Contessa* ....
.... Mrs. DARTWOOD
COCOTTE, *her Maid* .... Mrs. BRYCE

The list went on, but Helena did not bother to read
it. Augusta, however, did.

"Citta-da-guerra," she murmured, holding her
spectacles close to the page. It seemed a strange
name. "City . . ." she translated slowly, "or—town
of war." She stared at the play sheet, appalled.
"Warrington."

As the Third Music pounded to a close, Maria
shifted her bench to the front of the box, favoring her
daughters with a tight, expectant smile.

"Mother," said Augusta, *"why* are we here?"

Maria did not answer.

"No! I'm not coming back. Are you addled? D' you
take me for a fool?" Claudine's voice rang out across
the dressing room, for the time being empty of players. A lone tiring woman, picking her way through
the petticoats on the floor, had seen the scene fo-
menting there and fled.

"Aye," Carrick answered slowly, approaching.

"P'raps I'm addled. I must have been, to take up with a whore like you."

Claudine sidled along the wall, jostling the dressing tables with their wigs and paint. "Leave off, Nichol," she hissed. "You do look an arse." As she reached to draw the hood of her cloak up over her ringleted hair, two ruby rings flashed on her fingers.

Nicholas seized her wrist. "Where'd you get those? Whoring?"

"No." Claudine's gaze softened. She seemed now to weaken, to melt: so genuinely that even at a foot's distance, no one might detect the skills of the stage. "Come, Nichol. Don't be cruel. Don't think that."

His grip on her loosened. Laughing, she wrenched her arm free and ran.

Nicholas followed, but his pointed kid shoes were not made for running. "This'll be the end of you—slut!" he shouted. "I swear to you now you'll ne'er work again!"

Claudine tossed back a contemptuous look. "I earn my keep, Carrick. They like me here. And *you* can't do a pissing thing about it."

Before he could call out again, she was at the door and up the two steps out into the street. Carrick heard her voice, changed now, warbling a greeting to someone whose voice and face were obscured by the night. He glimpsed the red of a soldier's coat and the flash of medals; and now he sank down, stunned and breathless, against the wall. He stared ahead, unblinking, his dark eyes sparkling like a madman's.

"Well, Mother?" said Augusta, tears rising in her eyes. The coachman slammed the door beside her. " 'Tis our name, and . . . well, what is it? That—*woman* in the play, Mother . . . What does it all mean?"

The coach lurched and began to move through the clustered carriages and shouting crowds outside Drury Lane. As it pushed forward, bystanders too close to its wheels—a play crier, two orange-girls—yelped and stumbled away. *The play is like that. Causing havoc,* thought Augusta. And now her mother was saying— holding her hand—"It is no matter to *us,* my dear, if that girl's follies come back at her, at last."

Maria thought further as they drove, though naturally she did not speak all her reflections. Carrick's play had been all she had hoped. She had heard he would slander everyone he knew. Indeed he had. Susannah's name, her flagrant misconduct, would become common street gossip: so that even Henry, buried in his country library, could not ignore it. She knew her son, after all. He was proud. Surely he would divorce, at last, rather than tolerate the ignominy. . . .

She drew in a quick, excited breath, for an idea had come to her.

The golden coils of the mirror frame surrounded the face, which was blurred, in the smoky glass, like a portrait: the hair, grown out now to a froth of red-gold and brown; the round nose; the mouth a smudge of pink against pale cheeks.

Susannah shook her head. For the eyes were not right: they were frightened. For all that her face had thinned and showed, pleasingly, the shape of its bones—its twenty years—the eyes were round as a child's, and would not change. *We are going to Carrick's play.*

Only this afternoon, a messenger boy had come, from her aunt. He bore a note, which she had read with a growing trembling: *Henry, do see this play. My footman will keep you seats on the third tier tonight.* Toying, first, with the idea of destroying the note—but knowing, in the end, that it would be found out—she had taken it to Harry. "*Good as His Word?*" he had murmured. "I don't know it. But we may as well. 'Twould please you, my Susan?"

She had nodded. She didn't know what else to do.

Staring in the mirror again, she wrinkled her eyes and tried a smile.

"The *Belle* in her *Stratagem* said it. 'Vanity, like murder, will out.' "

She spun, startled, and saw Harry. "Vanity!" she protested, in a high, unnatural voice. "Why—I scarcely look in the glass. Scarce ever . . ." Her voice wavered.

Harry, smiling—*he notices nothing strange in me*, she thought—was searching in the pockets of his coat. "I know. Women care but for the glass's regard—and other woman's."

"It isn't true!" cried Susannah: playfully, to cover her fear. *You will not even see Nicholas*, she told herself. *It is only his play—not him.* Then what could explain this tightness in her throat, or this strange sense of foreboding?

"There." Harry drew a satin case from his pocket. He held it out to Susannah, who looked up, with eyes almost as wide and blue as they had been in the mirror's reflection.

She gasped as she unfolded the cloth. Never before had she been given anything so lovely. Three sapphires hung in round pendants from a chain scattered with diamonds. The blue stones matched her eyes. Harry drew them up around her neck and felt for the catch to close them. "But what did I do?" she said. "What is the day, that—"

"None. No special day. Jewels are no use to me, you know." He gave a quick, self-deprecating smile. "But they may serve to make the *ladies* of the theater jealous."

"To be sure, they will be! But I care not for that either—" Susannah stood, her eyes glowing, and, seeing that her husband still looked uncertain of his success, turned and hugged him.

She hurried to finish dressing, and when she had powdered her face and perfumed her hair, stood back before the mirror, beside Harry, to inspect. He wore a suit of black velvet, with silver buttons and tails cut away at the front. She wore a new costume, devised with Peg: a gown of iridescent blue silk that shone lavender, with lavender ruffles at her neck, and a turban of the same shade on her head. Her dress was the color of her jewels, of her eyes.

"Then let us go." She made her husband a mock curtsy. *Of course it will be all right*, she thought. She touched the stones at her neck as if they were charms, to bring good fortune.

The coach could not leave them off within even fifty yards of the theater, for the six o'clock crowd had begun to mob the doors. Bodies hurtled and shoved and seethed around Susannah as the coachman handed her down into the street. There were eager playgoers and orange-girls, pamphlet hawkers and play criers. The criers clanged their bells, shouting out,

> *As Good as* an'thing on the stage!
> The quality's up in fits of rage!
> But if ye know t' laugh, be not deterr'd—
> Come see Mr. Carrick's *As Good as His Word*!

"Darling? Harry?" Susannah reached into the air behind her, for his hand. She had forgotten how loud, how hurried, this place was: how the cries and people would carry her back. *Valerie, Tom Gant, Anthony, Nicholas. No . . .*

Harry put his arm around her and drew her through the crowd. "What is it, Susan? Is something amiss?"

"No . . ." said Susannah, longing more and more for home. "I miss Ginia," she said at last, sheepishly. Just then, "Is that 'er?" she heard a voice behind her cry.

"That 'er?" another echoed.

She wondered who they shouted for: a stage actress? She turned to look.

"That'll be her! She looks like 'er!" One of the criers dropped his bell to the ground, pointing; and now others, vendors and apprentices, rounded to join him, arguing, pointing and staring at her.

She did not know why they stared so. She forced a

way in through the theater door and hurried up the
stairs ahead of Harry, shaken.

"What was it?" he said.

"I don't know!" She touched the sapphires at her
neck for comfort, and fell silent. As they moved down
the first-tier corridor, blank faces passed her: groups
of people, familiar once to her, from earlier, theater-
going days. Lydia Cram, Tom Gant's friend, rushed
past her and down the stairs without seeing her. And
she thought now that she must be in a dream: first
she had become a spectacle, then invisible.

"Don't you wish to look out?" said Harry when they
took their box.

"Not—not now," she said. She had grown fearful.

A half hour later the curtain lifted on a painted
grove of orange and lime trees. The principal actor
walked onstage, explaining how his hopes for poetical
preferment depended on a lady famous for her lech-
ery. . . .

Susannah smiled, with the beginnings of relief. This
play was as silly as every other piece Carrick had had
his hand in. A dark, lithe figure in maid's dress jumped
out now from behind a bush.

"Claudine," she whispered.

"What, darling?" Harry leaned closer.

Susannah shook her head. She knew she should have
expected it. Claudine had become an actress long ago.
Nicholas had helped her. But, what matter, now . . .

As the stage panels parted, revealing a sumptuous
bedroom, a woman—the actress Mrs. Dartwood—ran
onstage, padded bosom flopping, red curls flying.
"Cocotte!" she shrieked. "Where is my poet for the
morning?"

Susannah smiled a little as the audience all laughed.

"I am *yores*!" she watched the Contessa declare, in
a strange, flat country accent, to the poet Meaning.
"I avow you, Art, sir, is my Passion. And though I
may have been quite bereft of it, in my youth—in my
peaceful and ordered land, America—"

There was a chuckle in the pit.

"And in my native state of—Virginity—"

The chuckles turned into guffaws.

Susannah drew back, with a horrible thought.

"Susan? Are you well?" said Harry.

But she only shook her head. He had not guessed. She sat frozen in her seat, watching as the Contessa stumbled and pranced. Riding onstage, in a man's breeches, astride a horse, she demanded an ode from Meaning to the animal. Soon Meaning was wooing her, embracing her, while her scholarly, cuckolded count toiled at his desk, oblivious. . . .

"I cannot watch anymore," she said, in a low voice when the interval came. She would pretend to be ill, perhaps. *Anything!* They must go. . . .

Harry looked at her closely. "There is something . . . in the play," he said slowly. "What is it?"

Susannah twisted her head away from his gaze, her eyes filling. "Don't you *see*? That woman—that hideous—contessa . . . She is meant to be me!" Without looking, she could sense Harry stiffen.

"But—she is nothing like you."

"Yes." Susannah stared ahead and mumbled, "She is a fool . . . like me."

"I'll not have you say that." Harry spoke coldly, shortly. "If—this is slander we must stay and hear it out. And then I shall find this Carrick. And take it up with him."

Susannah sat numbly through the second act and the third, knowing it was too late now to make excuses and escape unharmed. She watched the Parade of Critics—all of Carrick's enemies caricatured. She heard the footmen, above, and the men in the pit, below, guffawing as the Contessa, three poets and the Count tumbled so violently in the great bed that it fell to pieces. Numbly she looked on as, again, the hero slavered over the Contessa's hand.

"I swear, my dear," he pronounced, "thou art a rose without thorn! For—see? I pluck it from thee!" As he tugged at the rose in the Contessa's bodice, it sprang open, revealing a profusion of petticoats and stuffing. The footmen in the gallery howled. . . .

Susannah shrank back in her seat. "I must breathe,"

she stammered to Harry, and rose and moved out into
the corridor.

The door of the box clapped shut behind her, and
she leaned against it, her heart pounding. The play's
muffled words continued, on the other side. *Nicholas's
words. His very words, when he met me.* She remembered how he had pronounced them, in his grandiose
way, and torn the rose loose from her dress. *A happy
marriage must be perfection, a rose without thorns.
And you're just as likely of finding it.* Her skin turned
cold. She thought, *He will destroy us.*

She waited, but Harry did not come outside to find
her. She went back into the box at last, in time to see
the Contessa, on her horse, join the Parade of Critics
at the play's end. *A rose without thorns* . . . Despite
Nicholas, those words had been true. She had found
a happy marriage, even if it rested on the enormity of
a secret. . . .

"Harry. Let us go," she whispered.

Onstage the players were taking their bows: Meaning, his sweetheart, Claudine, the Contessa. Mrs.
Dartwood tossed her false bosoms into the pit, to loud
cheers.

Susannah looked down at her jewels, her dress, her
smooth hands, and they did not comfort her. She was
no more than the Contessa: fat and simple. . . .

On the stage Claudine was still curtsying and catching flowers. Harry stood, without a word, and led
Susannah out.

Onstage now, taking his applause in a scarlet coat,
was a figure they did not see. But he had seen them
leaving: from behind the curtains he had watched
them all through the play.

Nicholas Carrick bowed; with a look of disdain, he
beckoned Mrs. Bryce forward. He bowed again and
then—to the astonishment, then the loud cheers of all
the house—he jumped across the spikes and off the
stage. He ran, and fought, and grinned and pum-
meled his way through the audience until, gasping for
breath, he plunged out into the narrow lobby of the
theater.

Chapter 27

———— ❧ ————

Nicholas stopped below the stairs, and looked up with shining eyes. "Lady Susan."

She did not answer but stood quite still. He watched her, and the short curls around her face seemed to change to a fiery halo; her eyes, on him, to radiate a blue and incandescent anger.

"Susan," he said, in a smaller, pleading voice. "Do not go. Do not berate me."

She drew in breath, and her husband spoke.

"You. You are Carrick then. Your play is vicious slander." After the steel-dull sound of his voice, a silence fell.

"Well!" Carrick's gaze swept the lobby. "Slander, is it?" An audience was gathering: trickling, curious, through the pit doors and down the far stair. Striding forward, he cried, "Then let your wife be the judge! She who takes love, and its abandonment, so lightly—"

Susannah let out a strangled sound. She nearly backed away, but as soon she wanted to strike Carrick with all her strength: to silence him. She ran down the next steps until Harry took hold of her arm and stopped her, saying, in a low voice, "He is—vile. Ignore him."

"Play not the fool, Lord Warrington," hissed Nicholas. "You were scarce married before you were made cuckold—before your wife was trying such acts as would befit the most accomplished whore—"

Harry took the last step, and his hand slashed across Nicholas's face. "Never say such things." Harry's voice scarcely rose. "Never again. I swear I will have you—"

Nicholas staggered back. Tears were in his eyes, and he looked only at Susannah. "Forgive me—"

She did not trust her voice to answer him. She stood alone now, her back to the paneled wall by the stair. He rushed toward her.

"Susan." He seized at her hands. "It is you I wanted. I don't know why I—"

"Don't." She spoke as if from a distance. And now, as he tried to pull her closer, she cried, "No!"

She tugged her hands free and hit him: and again, she did not know how hard, her fists colliding with his head, his cheeks, the hard bone beneath his eyes. She saw him reel back; felt the crowd pressing behind her, calling and shouting. And then Harry's arms closed around her, bearing her away.

They were outside now, in the quiet. She clung to Harry's neck and hid her face against his shoulder, smelling only his scent, trying to hear only his breathing and his steps as the tumult of the crowd died behind them.

"You do not—"she sobbed, now. "You must not believe him."

Harry did not answer. They fell into their coach, where it waited at Covent Garden. She wiped her eyes, and was stunned at the darkness of the square: the peaceful silence. Nicholas was far away now. "Did you believe him?" she said.

Harry looked away. "I do not know."

*   *   *

In her dressing room Susannah slowly peeled away the pieces of her gown. She had let Peg go to bed, so alone she unfastened the turban, the bodice and skirt and let the damp silk fall from her to the floor. She knew she would not wear it again.

Harry was still below, speaking to the coachman. She did not know what he was saying. He had not told her. During all the long ride from Drury Lane, they had not spoken. She had wanted to: but the words always came to a strangled stop in her throat.

The sapphires around her neck were cold and seemed to press against her heart. *Only today*, she thought, *he gave me these. As a sign of his love. And how I have repaid him. . . .*

More minutes passed, and still she was alone. He did not come to her. It was never hard, in this house, to recall the chill, the ominous silence, which, years ago, had preceded their separation. Yet she tried to fight off that foreboding, that fear. *Harry will come*, she told herself. *He will come up to me.* She heard Ginia's wails, above in the nursery, and climbed the stairs, heavy-hearted, to feed her.

By the door the nursemaid dozed in her pallet bed. Clucking, trying to calm her daughter, Susannah bent to the cradle. Ginia's gaze lit, entranced, on the sapphires about her mother's neck; her eyes danced up toward them even as she nursed at Susannah's breast.

But Susannah could not laugh now at her daughter's glee; and though Ginia sucked for minutes on end, the ache in Susannah's chest seemed not to ease. She had thought never to hurt Harry again. Yet this night had hurt him, perhaps, more than anything she had done. For her desertion he was made—like the count in the play—a laughingstock. . . .

He would be happier, she thought, with a sharp pain, *had he never known me.* Had he never taken her back: never married her at all . . .

"Darling Ginia," she whispered. "How can I make it better?"

Ginia only smiled at the baubles on her mother's neck and yawned. Susannah covered her up in her

cradle, and crept downstairs. Looking down, from the
hall by the bedchamber, she saw a single, dim light,
below. She moved down the carpeted steps to the chill
first floor, to the parlor.

"Harry?"

No answer came. She moved into the doorway,
where she saw the flickering light. A single candle
stood on a table, shining light on Harry's back. For
he sat turned away from the light, in a stiff chair,
facing darkness.

"Harry—" she said, and all words of sense flew from
her. She could explain nothing, nor excuse it. And she
ran across the room and dropped to her knees beside
him. "I am sorry!"

She stretched out a hand and laid it on his leg,
where the black smooth wool of his breeches was
stretched taut. He did not move. She laid her other
hand there, and crept closer. She could not see his
eyes.

"I—know," she said quietly, "you may not be able
to forgive me—"

She saw his head move. His hair gleamed golden in
the light. And now he shook his head again. His hands
moved to cover hers. They clasped them, held them
in place.

"You wanted me to tell you—nothing," she said,
"of Nicholas. Yet perhaps I must." She waited, and
Harry did not stop her. She took a breath, to steel
herself. "I once—was his lover. As—tonight has made
you know. It was not so short, and unimportant a
thing, as perhaps you thought." She paused. "For near
a year, I believed I loved him."

Harry turned now, suddenly, stiffly, until the right
side of his face shone in the light. His eyes were narrow, and he opened his mouth before the words came.
"Do you—still? Is it that you are come to tell me?"

"No!" Susannah shook her head. She threw herself
against his knees, wrapping her arms about his body,
clinging to him. "No! He is nothing to me now. You
must believe me. You are all I care for in the world.
All I can ask is—your forgiveness."

For a moment Harry did not answer. His hand reached to stroke her hair, trembling. "I do forgive you."

Susannah looked up. Her eyes were bright. "Then it is all—past us. Truly."

He nodded. Then he drew her up to her feet, and they moved, their hands and bodies fastened close, toward the door. At the foot of the stairs, then the first landing, then the second, they kissed, his hands running over the curves of her body. His lips tugged at hers, and his tongue searched her mouth, her own tongue colliding, curling against it, sliding past.

In their room, they drew the green bed-curtains closed until all they could see was a thin strip of firelight, and each other. Peeling away his own clothes and her thin gown, he kissed a trail down through the valley between her breasts, his member hard and high as a young man's, pressing against her. She stroked its smoothness, and held it in her two hands, and in her mouth and between her breasts. She wrapped her legs around him and he curled beneath her on the smooth, dusty-smelling brocade, tracing his fingers very gently round her sex. Sometimes, since she had borne a child, this had hurt her, but it did not now. She felt the wetness as his fingers slid and fluttered inside her. She buried her nose in the golden fur on his chest; she licked his tiny, flat man's nipples with the tip of her tongue, and he cried out: and again, when, lying half above her, he entered her. At the sound of his cry, the echo of their daughter's, the milk began to leak from her swollen breasts. She started to cry and did not know why. She was too happy. "Take—take it from me," she whispered, kissing his damp hair, and he bent his head, while still he rolled inside her, sucking and licking the milk away.

The next day dawned in a gray mist over London. At Hanover Square, Susannah and Harry still slept. Under the onion domes of Hench House servants were waking, splashing water on their cold bodies, while

their masters dozed; running in and out of chambers on their private errands.

A sleepy and ill-shaven footman knocked on Maria Cheveril's door.

Maria stepped out into the hallway. "Well?"

"We saw her. Like you said—lady with red 'air—"

"You did pick the right one—" Maria frowned.

"T'be sure! *I* remembered 'er. From the 'ouse—"

"And you drew some attention—"

"We shouted, like you said. 'That's 'er!' We got some notice by it. Only . . ."

"Very good," said Maria impatiently, reaching in her purse. "There. For your friends," she said, dealing out six shillings. She held up one more shiny sovereign. "And—did you ask, at Hanover Square?"

"Yes, m'lady. They're leaving. Today. For the country."

Maria smiled and sent the man away with his coin. *Leaving for the country.* It said unfortunately little. She had hoped for news of a quarrel, anger: of Henry leaving the house. But, no . . .

She feigned an appetite for breakfast; feigned interest in a novel; and was relieved to send her husband away to Parliament in the afternoon. Augusta, heavy with her third child, stayed reading in bed. And Jonas—*Jonas, damn him!*—still had not come to her with news.

For she had taken the opportunity of sending him, too, to *As Good as His Word.*

The Buddha clock in the parlor struck two. Maria squinted out the window. *Where is he?* The door closed behind her with a heavy thump.

"Jonas!" She fixed her face into a smile.

The nabob looked pink and grim. In encouraging tones, Maria asked, "Did you find the play amusing?"

"Amusing?" Hench's eyes widened, then flopped closed, much like the Buddha's. "I—*Hem!* Maria. You know, I—I'd taken you for a woman of some—per*spic*uousness. Did you not notice—"

Maria let out an annoyed sigh. "Come straight, Jonas. Did I not notice *what*?"

Hench coughed and grumbled, and shifted in the sunlight. "I say—let's draw the curtains, Maria," he said. And then, his eyes shifting, he proceeded to tell his mother-in-law what he had seen.

"I see," she said some time later. "And then—"

"Then, sudden like, he jumped the spikes, and—" Hench mopped his brow, which was beaded with sweat. " 'Twas a right bagatelle, Maria. Everyone saw it. The playman—y'know, now *he's* the one I must've saw, at Bath—"

Hench described screams, fits, blows; caught up in his story, he drew out the fight; he embellished. Maria did not stop him. "She *is* a filthy slut," she murmured.

"Wh—?" Hench was startled. "I—"

"Do not mind me." Maria smiled. "I talk to myself, like a foolish old woman. Go on."

Hench did. When he had come near to the end, Maria said, unexpectedly, "What was he like—this Carrick?"

"Hm . . . dark, well-looking enough. I s'pose he—"

"No." Maria's dark eyes were searching, insistent. "I mean—how did he seem? Is he merely angry? Or is the man still—besotted. In love."

Hench nodded at the last. "Oh, I would say so. He grabbed her, an'—"

Maria's gaze dimmed. Her curiosity was satisfied. She knew three certainties: that Henry had been made aware of the truth, that he and Susannah were going to The Marches, and that the playwright, in a confused state, might yet be used. As for Henry—pace and think as she might, she could make no guess at *his* state now. He was going home with Susannah. *Why?* If he was forgiving . . . Maria's knuckles grew white on her cordial glass. *It will not do.*

When she was alone in her bedroom, she picked up a quill and ink and began furiously to scribble. Circles, squares, designs. *He must divorce. He must not forgive. We cannot let him put Carrick from his mind. . . .*

A dim notion struck her: then stronger, more certainly. It was midnight; Cheveril was still at the Commons. Maria took off her shoes and tiptoed into Augusta's room, which lately her daughter kept separate from her husband's. Behind the bed curtains, Augusta wheezed steadily; Maria set down her candle and began to search through the papers in her desk.

Here was a bill for wine—the desk creaked. Here were two letters from Jonas and an inept love poem in Augusta's hand. And here, at last—dated "10th January, 1789," pushed into the back of a cubbyhole—was a letter from Susannah Warrington.

Maria knew that ungainly, looping hand from long-ago lessons: from notes accompanying bills, returned. Refusals . . .

She smiled, and her long teeth glittered in the dark. Clutching the prize, she retreated: limping with energy toward her own room, where ink and a long night's work awaited.

In the morning she handed a sealed note to her bought kitchen maid. "Take this to Mr. Carrick, Drury Lane Theatre." She pinched the maid's chin. "Mind you, miss. Not a word—"

"No, m'm!" said the maid in a quavering voice. "Not to no one."

She ran toward Drury Lane without looking at the paper or stopping. For the note was well-sealed; even had she tried to read it, she would have extracted little sense from it. It said (in a large, looping hand, very like Susannah's):

Dearest N.,
I am in a Misery. He is taking me away, there is nothing for it, & now, with the knowlege in my Heart of your Betreyal—
O I cannot live, my deare one! I cannot give you up, no matter how you use me—I would beg

you come to me in the Countrey, only I dare not
hope it. But if you can—<u>between 3 and 4 Fri. the</u>
<u>25th</u> I know we'll be safe <u>& alone.</u>

But, perhaps, better forget! I am a fool & gave
you up, & there is no going back. You slighted
me such as I aught not forgive—but remember
me stille, sometime, as your

SUSANNAH.

"Jonas?"

Maria's voice that night was weary as her son-in-
law opened the door of her darkened bedroom. The
broth she ordered for her dinner sat untouched.

"Maria?" said Jonas Hench, wondering. "What ails
you? This morning, you were quite—"

Maria sighed. "Somehow it has—come over me.
This sad business with Henry—and—perhaps 'tis the
city air. I seem to be coughing a quantity"—she
wheezed—"of black bile."

"But—m'dear! I'm terrible sorry. Y'must take care!
I'll send Gussy. *Hem!* A doctor, p'raps. A—"

"I think," Maria said softly, suppressing a cough,
"that the air of the country might cure me. Would it
be a terrible burden—if I were to go for a few days
to Henshawe?"

"What shall you do, once we're back?" said Susannah. She jogged Ginia in her arms as the coach pulled
steadily through the Surrey country.

Harry gave a weary smile, and shrugged. "Continue with my second book. Or . . ." His eyes dimmed,
and his voice trailed away.

Susannah watched him. "Do you still . . . think on
it?" she said.

Bare trees flew past their windows, and a field. In
the silence, Harry took her hand. "In a year," he said,
at last, with certainty, "that play will be forgotten.
Completely."

"Yes." Susannah squeezed his hand. "Quite forgotten." And from that moment on, for her, Carrick and his play no longer mattered.

And if a question still troubled Harry's mind, he did not ask it. He could see no reason for his mother to send them to that play. No reason, at least, but an inexplicable malice. And this, he did not want to raise with Susannah. She played so peacefully with Ginia now. It seemed best to forget it.

The second coach, carrying Peg, the cook, the nursery maid, and Warwick, had gone ahead; and when the Warringtons arrived home, late in the afternoon, the dutiful butler came to them at once with a tray of letters. Harry waved him away. "Not now, not now!" he said, smiling, with an uncharacteristically feckless look in his eye. "I may safely say, Warwick—that we have had enough of society."

"But, m'lord—"

"Pray, Warrick—do us one service? Should anyone call, today or tomorrow—say we are away. Unless it is family—and most urgent." He returned the butler's nod and raced up the front stairs behind his wife.

"Strange behaving, it is," said Warwick, passing Peg and Fermanagh in the hallway.

"And well so!" she retorted. "What should they want wi' that society. Rude as it's been. I could tell you tales of London. . . . "

"No. Pray do not, Peg," said Warwick, and moved stiffly toward his habitual hall chair.

That day and the next were sunny and undisturbed. Harry and Susannah spent a long first afternoon and evening in their bed; and when the next day dawned bright and warm for February, Susannah took Ginia out for a walk in the garden. Harry turned to his letters: mostly from readers of his *History*, asking for introductions or help in their researches.

"I never guessed," he said wryly to Susannah, "that I would acquire such a number of friends. . . . "

So Thursday was short and quiet, and so Friday promised to be: except that in the middle of the afternoon Maria came unexpectedly to the house.

"Mother?" Harry kissed her coolly, in the front hall. "What brings you here?"

"Oh—I can scarce tell you!" Maria was heated, flustered from her ride. "I warrant you shall not believe me! . . . You know I came quite alone to Henshawe. I was unwell. And now . . ." She glanced furtively around the entrance hall. " 'Tis our curate at Bothwell! He's taken leave of his senses. He's determined to resign—and over some trivial matter of Latin!"

Harry stared. He had awaited some reference to the play of Tuesday night—perhaps an apology. But his mother's talk wandered on, and despite himself he grew intrigued.

"The poor man," she said, "has *sat* at Henshawe, crying heresy for over an hour—and will not leave! I told him it was no matter for *my* comprehension. I should scarce think it grounds for our poor curate's resignation. . . . what *if* the archbishop has misconstrued St. Augustine?"

"Which work of St. Augustine?" said Harry. But his mother did not seem to know. She gazed at her son with lost eyes and hung onto his arm; and after a minute's more wheedling, she had succeeded. Harry went ahead of her through the house and out to the flower beds, where his wife was talking to the gardener.

"What a curious story!" she said, when he had explained. "Shall I come, too?"

"No!" said Maria quickly. "That shan't be necessary."

"Well, I wish you luck then. . . . Will I see you back soon?" Susannah's eyes avoided her mother-in-law and rested on Harry.

He assured her so, and the two drove off. Susannah stood on the front steps, frowning up at the mottled sky. She did not know what she mistrusted about her aunt: about this silly-sounding errand. Anyway, Harry had looked intrigued at the task; and he would be back soon enough. Marble-shaded clouds passed over-head, at times letting the sun through, at times prom-ising rain. She went indoors, talked to Peg for a time, washed, and changed into her riding coat.

As she was walking out along the gravel path to-ward the stables, humming a tune and planning the course of her ride with Cythera, she heard wheels clattering in the drive. She spun round to listen. *How strange.* Could Harry be back already?

Chapter 28

———— ❧ ————

Susannah gathered her skirts and ran to the front drive. The gray clouds clapped overhead. Soon the rain would come. Thinking, annoyed, of her promised ride, she stood at the edge of the drive and watched, curious, as the unfamiliar, shabby black coach drew to a halt. It was not the Henches' coach, returning, after all—nor was it that of any neighbors she knew. A small figure in a black cape descended from it and looked, wondering, up at the house.

Nicholas. She could not understand—she could not believe his audacity. Dropping her skirts to the ground, she moved forward. In a cold voice she called, "What are you doing here?"

He stared back.

"Well?" Her voice shook, though she tried hard to control it. "You can have no—business with us."

Carrick gave her a puzzled look. "Why—I come at your command."

"My command?"

Again, overhead, thunder broke, and a slow rain began. Susannah pulled her cloak up to cover her head, but Nicholas, who stood, hands folded, before her, did not move. Drops of water trickled in gray rivulets from his shiny and jet-black hair.

"Might we go inside?" he said.

"No. I—I think not. You cannot stay." She studied his face; it seemed almost a strange object, of no meaning. Brown eyes, lightly outlined in black, hunting her own. Lips parting, saying, "Is it not as you—expected?"

"What?"

The coach driver glanced back, saw the interview continuing, and drove away, stopping his vehicle farther down the drive. And Susannah, catching sight of it, cried, "What is he doing? You're not to stay here. I don't know what you want with me—with us. Have you not done enough already?" She could not blink, for fear of crying, and she backed away, not knowing where she was going, under the dripping trees.

She turned and ran along the side of the house. *He will not know the way*, she thought. But she did not know where she meant to go herself. Her footsteps threw up the wet pebbles of the path, and now the rain poured through the bare branches above her.

"Wait—"

She heard Nicholas call, but did not stop. Now his footsteps sounded on the path behind her. But she would soon be around the wing: by the terrace doors. . . .

"Wait!" he cried again. Breathless, he came up beside her and caught her arm. "I understand," he said. "You have turned against me. Changed your mind." He looked at her, beseeching, through damp black curls.

Staring, she pulled free and started to walk again. She would not have him in her house: that she knew. If he must talk—he would do it here. And before Harry returned. That was certain. Calmly she repeated his words. "Changed—my mind? I changed against you long ago." Her feet moved, almost of themselves, relentlessly along the path toward the lakes.

"I would take back every word of that play. I swear it! It was—a great mistake." Nicholas spoke quickly, panting, searching in vain for her glance as she walked on. "I wrote so, only because you—deserted me. How did I deserve it? I still loved you—"

"Loved me?" Susannah stopped in place, incredulous. She tried to give a hard, cold laugh but couldn't For now she saw Nicholas's eyes, deep and dark as wells. "You loved me?" she said in a small voice. "Then—why did you mock me so?"

They stood apart beneath the open sky, the rain still falling. Susannah's cloak hung wet and heavy on her head. She drew it down, watching Nicholas. "I doubt I could forgive you now. But—why?"

He moved toward her, but she backed away, her eyes wide and mistrusting. "It wasn't you," he said at last, "but an illusion, which I had created—from pride." He stopped, and then went on, looking past her, growing more certain. "A man's mind works in such a way. I knew, to rid myself of love—I must despise it. I must be utterly cruel."

Susannah wondered at the logic in his words; her brow furrowed, but he did not seem to see her puzzlement. His voice grew deeper, angrier.

"You had no faith. You knew I was no pretty-voiced gallant, and yet . . . To scorn a lover for a husband! What worse infidelity can there be?" He gave a bitter laugh, and moved closer. "Come, Susannah. You wrote to me—you know you are still mine."

"No." She tried not to hear the words: tried to tell herself, *He is acting only*. She wondered what he meant, saying she "wrote" to him, but she did not understand it, and now his words flowed over her, like the cascading rain, unstoppable.

"Come. You don't love him." His dark eyes glinted, and swiftly he moved forward, seizing her arms.

She twisted but could not get free. He had the strength, and the advantage now, as he had not that night in the theater. "I love my husband," she said in a low voice, "in such a way as you could never understand—"

He caught her wrists behind her back and pulled her closer. Their chins nearly touched, and her eyes shied from his. "No," he said slowly. "You'll never be his." He began to smile, his eyes sparkling and intent. He kissed Susannah's neck and the soft point of her chin. She struggled to bend back, away. "You were mine first," he said. "And that is all that matters."

"No." But for a moment the old Nicholas, the voice and warm scent of him, seemed to return, and when he pressed his mouth against hers she did not fight free. Then she stiffened. She twisted in his arms, thinking, *This is impossible, it cannot be.* And then a great weight hurled itself upon her, and knocked her and Nicholas both to the ground.

She rolled away, and did not know where she was. Her head pounded, and there was a shouting. She looked up, and it seemed, a great distance away—

"Harry." Her voice was weak; and his figure seemed only to grow taller against the sky. She tried to stand, but was struck down again by dizziness. And as the sky spun round her, she saw Nicholas rising, charging at her husband. "No!" she cried. But they were scuffling, kicking, struggling. Suddenly Carrick gave a thrust of his arms. He broke free and ran for the lakes. Harry followed.

Susannah struggled to her feet: fought the dizziness to find their path. Through tangled branches, to the bridge of land between the two waters.

They veered from one side of the bridge of land to the other. Nicholas grabbed at Harry's clothing, his hair. Harry kicked and broke free, but now the other came at him again, his head lowered, toward the lake, not stopping. Susannah called out, but she went unheard. Harry spun on one foot, and fell backward.

The waters below cast spray up into the air.

"What have you done?" Susannah screamed. "You coward! What have you done?"

Carrick moved toward her, staring, as if he didn't know. That Harry had weak lungs, could not swim, feared drowning. . . .

He reached for her arm, but she struck him away. "Go! Leave me!" she cried out. "Do you understand?"

But still he lingered, while she knelt, her heart pounding, at the edge of the lake. Harry lay face down on the glassy surface of the water. And yet he was not beneath it, not sinking. "The Fool's Lake," she murmured. God have mercy, Harry would not drown. She scrambled down the bank and knelt beside him in the water. He was heavy, but she pulled at his shoulders with all her force, lifting his face from the water so he could breathe. His eyes were closed, his skin deathly pale. But his chest shuddered, as she pulled him up and turned him over. He gave a heaving cough, and water poured from his mouth. Susannah knelt on the stone floor of the lake, holding him, wondering how she would move him from here. And as she looked up at the lake wall, she saw Carrick.

"Go! Go away," she shouted.

He did not answer. He spread his hands, and knelt as if to follow her down the steep bank.

"No!" Susannah's voice rose, high and anguished, above the waters. "Go away, and leave us alone!"

Nicholas Carrick stood stiffly, and slowly his small figure disappeared, beyond the bank. Susannah did not see where he went. She stroked Harry's face, and now his lips moved.

"All—all right," he said, and tried to smile.

"Yes." She pulled him closer and kissed him. His cheeks were icy, like the waters.

"You . . . sent him away," he whispered.

"Yes. He'll not come again." Holding Harry's head and shoulders in her lap, she asked him if he could move.

He nodded. Coughing up more water, he bent his legs and rose, leaning on her shoulder. They walked along the stone bed of the lake to the far bank, where the slope was flatter. "Will you rest here?" she said. But he shook his head.

"I am . . . better," he said in a thick voice. "It all— spins. If I can hold you—"

"Of course." She squeezed his waist and looked up

with hope, and they made their way home, in the closing dark.

That night he ate well, almost as if no harm had come to him. His skin had lost the ghastly pallor of the lake, and though he kept quiet, and went early to bed, he seemed to have gotten no worse than a bump on the forehead from his fall. All the same, Susannah fed more wood into their fire before she went to bed, to ward off chills; and she covered Harry with an extra blanket, kissing his forehead. As she put out her light, she said a thankful prayer.

Sometime in the night, she woke. She did not know why. She felt a strange warmth in the bed, and reached for Harry. His sheets were damp—and he was not there.

She sat up, frightened. "Harry?"

She opened the curtains. He stood, a dark, still figure before the fire. Calling his name again, because he did not seem to see her, she shoved off the bedclothes and ran to him. She laid a hand to his face: it was cold with sweat. "You've a fever," she said. "Come back to bed, darling! Shall I fetch new covers? Shall I—"

He shook his head. " 'Twill—be better. An awful dream—"

His voice was hoarser than before. "Come back!" she said. She pulled him into her own, dry side of the bed and covered him.

He shivered and shook now, beneath the bedclothes, and she covered him with her own body, trying in vain to warm him. Gradually his breathing eased, and his body uncurled. Susannah went to stoke the fire and check the windows, and by the time she returned, he was asleep.

For a while she lay on top of the bedclothes beside him, wondering. Should she have called servants, a doctor? She watched him, and still he breathed regularly, peacefully. She laid her head on his shoulder and drifted from watchfulness into a shallow sleep.

* * *

Early in the morning, Harry woke. He was covered in cold sweat again, and coughs and shivers racked his body. When Susannah saw him, she knew she had been wrong: the fever had grown worse. She must send for Dr. Wallace at once. She ran through the empty halls, ringing bells, but no one heard her; the sky outside was still dark, the house slept. In desperation, she thought of riding to town herself. She was half dressed for it when Peg came to the bedroom.

"M'lady? I heard—"

Susannah's words came in a flurry. "Someone must ride to town. 'Tis a fever. Peg? Will you watch with him? Promise—"

"M'lady." Peg held her twitching hands. "Y'must be quiet. No talk of your going. 'Tis Lord Harry? You stay with him. . . ."

Calmer now, Susannah settled on the edge of the bed, where Harry coughed and stirred. " 'Twill be all right," she tried to soothe him. But as much, she soothed herself. Peg would help—the other servants. The doctor would come. . . .

"There," she said, and touched his forehead. It was wet. Hot skin, cold water. Like the lake's . . .

It will be all right, she told herself again. *It must be.*

Dr. Wallace came, with his assistant, Wadrowe, and wanted Harry moved to a fresh bed, downstairs. Harry jumped and started when they tried to lift him. Susannah reached for his hand, to steady him, but he stared at her with terrified eyes.

"You—" His pupils were wide. He blinked rapidly. "No! The dream—"

But then he spoke no more. His eyes grew glassy, and his teeth chattered with cold. Susannah wiped his forehead. "What is wrong?" she said, in a trembling voice, to Dr. Wallace. But she thought she knew the answer already. *The ravings of fever.*

Dr. Wallace said only, "Let us see him safe downstairs."

In the pink downstairs bedchamber—Maria's old room, the birthing room, the sickroom—Harry tossed and slept. Sometimes, staring at Susannah, he would open his mouth, as if to talk. But his throat was so dry no words would come. She gave him water and brandy to drink, but they made the coughing, the fever, no better.

"It is the rheum—aye, the rheum," Dr. Wallace told her, outside in the hall.

"No," said Susannah. Her body seemed to shake. "I have not seen him so bad before."

"Aye, well—" Dr. Wallace shook his head and shifted. "He had such troubles in childhood, i' the lungs. I sense a dampness, a congestion . . . Pray fortune, it will pass."

Turning in desperation from the usually jovial Dr. Wallace to his young assistant, Susannah cried, "There must be something we can do! Tell me. . . ."

"Mercury?" suggested the younger doctor, weakly. "A blooding?"

Dr. Wallace nodded. So they moved into the room with their tools and ministrations: lances and silver bleeding bowls, mercury pills and poultices. The older doctor took hold of Susannah's arm before they began. "I would bid you—leave us, now. 'Tis no sight for a lady."

"I will stay—" she began.

"And—Lady Warrington—I must tell you. These ills—at their worst, they are like a drowning. Sometimes God sends rescue, but—"

"No!" Susannah flinched and turned away.

Dr. Wallace was silent for a time. Then he said, "You had best, my lady—send for the family. And pray."

She stayed, though they conjured her not to, holding Harry's hand as the blade sliced his white skin; she let out a cry, though he made no sound. His arm jerked against her grasp, and the doctors pressed the skin, till the slow blood came.

"Torpid," muttered Dr. Wallace; and she clutched Harry's hand tighter, praying. *Let him not drown. . . .*

When they had done, he looked up at her, wondering. He let out a low cry. "Where is—Susan . . ."

"Here," she said. The tears rose in her eyes. He stared at her still and did not see her. His head tossed from side to side, and his limbs labored to throw off the covers. "Darling, be still," she whispered, lifting the blankets, pressing him down. "Please, Harry. Please—know me. Forgive me."

She knew, in the end, that Dr. Wallace was right. She would be failing Harry if she did not write to his family: for they must hope and pray for him, too. She wrote to Maria at Henshawe; to Agnes, in Somerset; and to the Henches and Stillwells, in London. *With fortune, it will quickly pass,* she tried to write. Her hand shook. She destroyed two letters, and started again. Across the room, in the tent bed, Harry slept. The drawn curtains cast a night pall across the room. Maria's bright decorations, her putti and nymphs, were lost in shadow, and the fire blazed, illuminating the thin, still figure in the bed.

"Dear Augusta," she wrote this time, simply. "Harry is ill. Please, come quickly."

They came—over the next few days, they all came—and spared Susannah the reproaches she dreaded. Of course, they did not know how the accident came about. And only Maria ventured to ask.

"A fall?" she questioned Susannah, in a thin voice.

"Yes," said Susannah nervously. "Into the lake. He lost footing and fell—"

"*Fell?*" Maria's look was steady, penetrating. "I do not believe you. You lie. Do you know, Susannah, that God punishes liars? Do you—"

Susannah spun away, her face burning. "Stop, Aunt Maria! Harry is drowning! I—" Through the door, in the sickroom, she heard a moan. She turned to face her aunt. "He is woken. We have woken him. I must go—"

"It was Nicholas Carrick."

She stared at her aunt but could not find words. *How does she know?* But she had no time to retort: to think of it. She heard Harry coughing next door. He needed her. She turned, leaving her aunt behind, and ran into the bedroom.

In two days Harry grew no better, but no worse. His fever—said Dr. Wallace—had risen no further than on that first morning. The bedroom was kept hot and closed; twice a day Harry was given mercury and bled. His ravings were less frequent; he had moments of wakefulness, even recognition. He knew Augusta, when she came to kiss him, and, another time, his daughter.

He lifted a hand toward her, as Susannah held her out to him. "Ginia—"

There was something liquid, and thick, in his throat. Susannah stroked his forehead. "Don't trouble talking. . . ."

He gave her a vague smile. *Does he know me now?* she wondered: though she knew the thought was selfish. It did not matter. These last three nights she had sat by his bed, willing him better. Though the doctors said it was not needed: though Maria, more sharply, said it could do no good. But she had not been able to leave him. She needed to stir the fire that warmed him, to hear him breathe. To see him wake, to give him drink, and know he was safe.

The third day passed, and the doctors allowed visitors in the room more constantly. Maria, Augusta, Helena—who had seemed no more than shadows to Susannah in these days of fear—came to sit at Harry's bedside, and chatter together on the sofa. Agnes and John Burleigh arrived at last from Somerset, and the others, rushing to them, in greeting, were able to tell them now that the worst was past. Agnes shed the black dress she had arrived in and hurried in brown wool to the sickroom. She gave Susannah a brisk kiss—she was plump and sturdy, as Susannah remembered her—and pushed back the bed-curtains, the better to study her brother. She clucked. "I don't know . . . ." She cast a grave look toward her husband: at the other men, behind him, dealing cards in the corner.

"He's much better," Augusta assured her.

"Indeed, for such a grave accident—" chimed in Maria.

Helena, who was aggrieved that her two very adult and responsible sons were not allowed in the sickroom, merely pouted and kept silent.

Susannah was relieved, in truth, to watch them, and to see that their petty worries had overtaken their fear for Harry. In their days here they had largely ignored her. And she, sharing Harry's twilight world, had not cared. Now she smiled and sought Augusta's eyes; her cousin saw her and looked away.

But this did not sadden her: nothing could. Friendship would come again, with them, in time. She felt a hope, like none she had known before: a warmth toward all the world, an endless patience. She slept soundly that night, on the sofa in Harry's chamber, and woke only at the sounds of dawn: the twittering of birds, servants' footsteps in the hall. Since Harry still slept, she took breakfast alone; but now he rose up on his elbows to look at her.

"You're awake!" she said. "And you are better."

He smiled and nodded. "Susan—" he said. "You must not—shut yourself in here so."

The words came slowly, but they came: her name, too. And, suppressing the joy that made her want to shout, she smiled back. "I do not *feel* shut in here. I want to be with you."

She had buried her hands and one knee under the covers, sitting beside him. A steady heat seemed to radiate from him, but she could not tell if this was fever or merely the normal warmth of recovery. "You are still hot," she said uncertainly.

" 'Tis nothing. Susan. My—black-eyed Susan. Will you do a thing—for me?"

She nodded.

"Leave me a while." Harry stopped for breath. "Go out and ride. 'Twill do you—good. Then, come to me. . . . "

He was so insistent that she agreed at last. She would go for a ride—a short one. When she was dressed in her riding habit, she reappeared at Harry's door. He smiled silently and waved her off.

It was a fine day. Cythera was feisty and capricious after so many days without a run. Susannah took her out on the road to Bothwell, passing some tenants she knew on the way.

"Wishes for the Lord's recovery—" one of the three called to her, while the others nodded. She drew up.

"Thank you!" she said. "I shall tell him. He's grown much better." Searching for a moment, she called up their names. "Good day, Mr. Carty, Mr. Jones, Mr. Jaffet. . . . " She waved as she rode off, her hair flying in the wind.

She galloped through Bothwell and out toward the downs, her happiness lifting her, letting her fly with the mare. A dull wintry sun was warming the earth, bringing spring. Spring already: a year since she had driven north, in confusion—come to know her husband, at last, and borne a daughter. She had been but a girl then: time seemed long, and she chased a shadow. And the only truth the shadow held out to her, she did not see. *A rose without thorns . . .*

But now she knew how fleetly time could pass: a year had passed already, in love. And it was but a beginning. . . . She rode faster, gulping air to the rhythm of Cythera's hoofbeats, eager to be back at The Marches. Her home. To run the length of the gravel path, the gallery, to Harry . . .

Breathless, she descended at the stables, and shedding her hat, her crop, her cloak, she hurried through the house to her husband.

"—sleeping, Lady Warrington," warned Wadrowe from the parlor. She paid him no attention: she knew to be quiet. In the bedroom the air was stifling. She threw a glance at the bed—Harry was indeed sleeping—and opened the windows farthest from it, for air. The outdoor cold began to penetrate the smoky miasma of the sickroom. Soon, she thought, Harry would be free from here: breathing the fresh air of outdoors. . . .

She crept closer to the bed. Harry's face was turned toward her. The covers were strangely still. *He does not move*, she thought; but the thought made no sense. Where was the rising and falling, the—

"Wadrowe!" she called out, in sudden fear. For there should be motion. He should hear her shout. He should move and wake. . . . "Dr. Wallace!"

She knelt down beside Harry. Still, he did not move. She reached for his hand, and it was limp. He did not breathe. "Harry," she said softly, the fear growing, rising. *"Harry!"* The fear clutched her heart, and she threw herself upon him. "I love you!" she cried, kissing his still face. "I love you. . . . " And even when the tears came, and the wrenching terror, she did not let go. Life could come back to him. It was not long gone. It must.

And so she did not let him go peacefully, properly. Hers was not the dignified comportment of a wife but that of a deranged lover, who clings to human life and will not let go, will not be still.

It was not a pleasant sight for the doctors, or for Lord Warrington's family, who, coming into the room, knew at once what fate had decided. Such clinging to the life of an earthly thing—it was not proper. Even the least religious of them sensed it. But by now a duller grief had fallen upon them all.

It was night. Maria Cheveril doubled over in a chair in the empty gallery. She gulped down her sobs and turned away from the clumsy comforts of Jonas Hench.

"It was not my fault!" she cried. "Not my fault . . ."

"Nay, Maria." Hench patted her hand, looking

helpless. He had little notion of how to comfort women; and he knew only that this death had caused three of them—Susannah, his wife, now Maria—extremes of torment. In truth, what he had seen of Susannah in these last days had given him a new respect for her. "Susannah," he tried awkwardly, "maught—be glad, were you to go to her. . . . "

Maria raised wild eyes. "To *her*?" She lowered her head again. "Nay—Jonas. Not to her. Someday the world will know the fault. . . . " Her last words were muffled in her hands. Her shoulders heaved. "Go, Jonas," she said. "You do not know. . . . "

Confused, Hench left her. In truth, he did not feel very sorry to.

"Not my fault," murmured Maria. Quivering still, she remained alone in the gallery of her ancestors: some of whom in their time had done kinder deeds, and a few, perhaps, worse.

Chapter 29

The others left Susannah to herself, for they did not know what to do.

And if they wondered, sometimes, what she did, behind the closed door of the bedroom, they might guess, but they could not know all. For she still believed Harry was with her.

She had locked herself away, for that was the only way to keep him. *He is not gone.* She whispered the words, fervent, fevered. For here were his books, lying open, his ink-clogged quill: waiting as if, any moment, he would come back to them. Outside the windows was the same sky he had looked upon as he wrote: and, in the air, it seemed sometimes, the echoes of his words. As if she might still turn now and come upon him. She buried her face in his pillow and smelled his hair, his skin again. *Do not go.* And the more the scent seemed to die, to fade, the harder she prayed, till the tears would not stop. *Do not go.*

Two days passed. The Reverend Bayliss, Harry's friend, came knocking at her door. "Lady Susan—" he called. "I would not trouble you—"

She did not answer. For what he came to tell her, to convince her, she would not hear. *He is not dead. . . .*

A time came when her tears dried, and there were no more; and she opened the curtains on the gray sky, and it was only that, a gray sky: and Harry would not see it. She stared at the books still open on his desk and began slowly to close them, to stack them. She came upon pages of his notes, and the spiked letters pierced her heart.

For they were poems: she could see, from their short lines, the labored writing, the blackened words. *But he does not write verse anymore. . . .* And yet there were pages of them, twenty or more. And she knew, as she began to read, that she had seen none of these words before. They could only be his. As she stared at the first sheet, a dull ache grew in her chest.

> *I want nothing of thee,*
> *Save conscience claim thee—*
> *My being shall crumble to bones*
> *Ere I'll love thee. . . .*

Me, he writes of me, she thought. And a terror seized her so that she nearly did not go on. *He never loved me.* She wanted to thrust the pages into the fire, or out of the window, into the rain. *"I want nothing of thee . . ."* But something held her back, and she read on.

She moved closer to the window; she tried to harden herself against the words. But the next, and the third verse were no longer so cruel. They wrote of empty hills and gray rock, and the harsh seasons: of friendship. And still she feared what she saw. *They are not for me.* For she knew—she had put it from her mind—that there had been another woman, once. *A kind of friendship . . .* For many months— many times, she remembered it now—he had hidden the verses he wrote from her. And this was why.

She could make no sense of the words anymore. She read through the stinging of tears: she made herself.

I deserve this. And though the words were now of love, she did not understand them. Her body was a crying, aching hollow. She came to the last page and, in small letters, saw her name: *"Susannah."*

But she did not know why, or how it could be. The page shook in her hands.

Ever I'll love thee
Though all else leave me—
Nothing can grieve me long,
Long as I love thee.

I'll live in & of thee,
Where thou goest, pursue thee,
And, as thou lov'st me more,
Love thee more truly—

I pray thee, stay with me,
Delight me, delight in me,
Console me, rejoice with me—
Ever I'll love thee.

It was her poem. The others were, too. The plain, true words he had tried for so long to write.

He does, he does love me—she knew it now. And it was too late.

The Warringtons moved up the hill in slow procession, their black cloaks and overcoats flapping in the wind.

Below, unheeded, a few villagers watched. For they had all heard the news. The viscount, still a young man, but twenty-eight, was dead. And as the line of stumbling, triangular figures halted above, and as the Reverend Bayliss began to speak, some of them climbed the slope, behind, to hear.

This was the only service Harry would have: though Maria had spoken, before, of a great memorial service in London. For she had broken down, inexplicably, in the midst of all her plans. And she had not been the same since then, but only silent and sad.

And when Susannah had spoken to Bayliss yesterday, he had said something strange about Maria: "Let her suffer."

"What do you mean?" Susannah had asked him. She blinked, behind her veil, at the unaccustomed daylight of the garden where they walked.

"I meant," said Bayliss slowly, strangely, "that—" He stopped. "No—I do not know what I say, Lady Susan. You speak of your—faults, yet you must know . . . 'Let he who is *without* sin cast the first stone.' "

But such words made no sense to her. *Harry might still live, but for me.* Sometimes the thought became too much to bear, and—

"God will yet console you, Lady Susan," Bayliss had said.

I do not believe in him anymore, she wanted to answer.

"For when Thou art angry," read Bayliss now, "all our days are gone: as it were a tale that is told. . . . Turn thee again, O Lord, at the last: and be gracious unto thy servants. . . . "

"Turn thee again," thought Susannah. But the Lord would not. She had prayed so long for Harry: and He did not hear her.

She stood on the damp ground and stroked her daughter's forehead. Ginia tossed her head but slept on peacefully. *When she is older,* thought Susannah with wonder, *she will not remember.*

She would not remember how her mother had forgotten her: how Susannah had run, one night, in a sudden fright, through the hallways, to find her daughter in the arms of a fat, strange wet nurse. How Susannah had tried, again, to nurse her; and how the milk, when it came at last, was but a thin trickle, from which Ginia had turned away. Now, the wet nurse fed her. Susannah scarcely felt the ache in her chest anymore. Since that day she had kept Ginia almost always by her. For Ginia was the only person she had left in the world to love.

Yet Ginia was so little, she knew none of this. She let out a sudden cry, above the reverend's words; and her cousin Edmund, on the other side of the dark grave, looked up at her. His round, five-year-old face formed an uncomprehending pout.

To Edmund, as Harry's nearest male relation, all the Warrington estate would likely pass. Already, he was being prepared for that dignity. He came to the funeral, though his smaller cousins stayed at home. Now, as the coffin was lowered into the ground before him, his legs shook, and he let out a whimper. His mother, Helena, and his aunt Agnes, on either side of him, twitched at his hands.

"Thou knowest, Lord, the secrets of our hearts," read Bayliss. "Shut not thy merciful ears to our prayer: but spare us, Lord most holy, O God most mighty, O holy and merciful savior, thou most worthy judge eternal, suffer us not at our last hour, for any pains of death to fall from thee."

Yet they did, thought Susannah. She thought of the dark line of blood on Harry's arm: the racking fever. *Will I teach Ginia such believing?* she wondered. Bayliss's prayer book thumped shut: pages against pages. They had no answer.

The other women lifted their veils and dabbed their eyes. Tears began to trickle down Susannah's cheeks and, her arms taken up with Ginia, she could not wipe them away. She did not believe in this burial: this death. That was why she cried. *Harry is there.* They could not take him away: for she knew he heard her. She still talked to him: in her mind only, silently. She would never be without him. He was there.

She looked again at the little circle around the open grave. At the Burleighs, the Cheverils, the Stillwells. They did not see her. She knew they did not want to. Maria let out a low cry, and her husband seized her hand.

For a second, across the grave, little Edmund Stillwell looked up with hardened eyes at Ginia. *You caused this*, he seemed to say to her: to her mother. And Ginia stared back. For an instant Susannah thought she saw strange things in her daughter's face: a blank, willful stare from her blue eyes, and, in her twisting mouth, a queer determination. As if she coveted Edmund's place and all that went with it—all that, had she been a boy, would have been her own.

But the moment passed, and it was time: to turn, to kneel, to cast dirt into the grave. It was not real. She took up the handful of dirt but could not think, *I am burying Harry.*

Stay with me, she thought. The dirt fell, and slid down the sides of the coffin.

She moved away, out of sight of the others as they followed: Maria and Cheveril, Helena, Stillwell. She turned toward the dark clouds and did not look back at them. Agnes knelt and cast her dirt in the grave; and Augusta. Then little Edmund led the way back to the church, suspended in the hands of his mother and aunt. His light hair gleamed against their black robes, in the thunderous sunlight that comes before rain.

Susannah walked downhill from the grave. The men were mounting the side of the hill now with their shovels. The rain began, dampening the mound of dark earth, but still she did not want to leave. *He is here.* She could feel his presence; she closed her eyes, and for a second he was beside her. The men's shovels flew, casting dirt up into the sky. *He is here.* There was a clap of thunder, and the rain quickened, sticking Susannah's veil to her face, mingling with her tears. Unseeing, she moved on further, toward the rough grass at the edge of the cemetery.

Ginia howled, and Susannah tried to soothe her. "It will be all right." Her voice caught. "It—will—"

Augusta Hench stopped, halfway to the church, and turned back.

"Wh—" began her husband.

"Go on, Jonas." She motioned him to continue ahead. "I—have something to see to."

She hurried up the slope and stopped at the grave;

and in the distance, lost in the rain, she saw Susannah. She stumbled down the wet hillside, on the rough grass. Susannah turned and stared through her veil, and did not speak.

Augusta came closer. She reached forward and drew back her cousin's veil, and kissed her cheek. "Your—poor babe," she said, in a quavering voice. "She will be soaked."

Susannah did not answer.

Augusta held out her arms. "Let me take her."

"No—" Susannah began. "But you—" For her cousin was big with child herself.

With a faint, teary smile, Augusta waited. "I am—all right," she said. "Come back to the house. I will stay by you—dear Susan. If you wish it."

Augusta came to Susannah's room that night and saw Harry's verses.

"Oh, Susan," she said. "Someday—the world will read these! I know it. And they will see—in Harry's short life, he—progressed so greatly and—accomplished such learning!" She laid the sheets far away, to protect them from her tears, and stroked them with a kind of reverence.

The next day they walked together in the gardens, talking of Ginia and of Augusta's babe to come. The old, carefree chatter of earlier times had gone; but in its place had come a quiet understanding. Augusta alone did not seem to resent Susannah's presence here; Augusta alone sat by her, holding her hand as the lawyers read the will.

They had found it at last, among the account books and records of the estate, in Maria's study. It was, it seemed, the only will: though dated some five years past.

The breathing of the group in the parlor stilled to silence. The lawyer they had brought in from London bowed his head, his back to the green walls, with their happy scenes of hunts and horses. His voice rose and fell. "To my many faithful servants . . ."

An audible shuffling and shifting accompanied these routine bequests, some to persons long gone from The Marches. The last such was to William Bayliss: all Harry's library.

"And," read the lawyer, "one hundred pounds per annum."

Susannah heard a gasp run through the parlor, at this unexpected generosity. Bayliss was not here to hear it, having returned to his London parish. Susannah clung to her cousin's hand, for it was harder than she had expected, hearing these words. Even beneath their cold legal terms, she heard Harry. . . .

"To my mother, I desire all due jointure bequeathed of my father, Edmund Warrington, be continued: in addition three hundred pounds per annum."

There was silence at this. Augusta darted a glance back at her mother, whose sagging face, she saw, was unmoved.

"To each of my sisters, Helena, Agnes, and Augusta, two hundred pounds per annum; and all other estates, funds, and receipts to devolve upon Edmund Everett Skowland . . ." The lawyer paused. ". . . Stillwell. And perpetually unto his heirs male. . . ."

The air in the room moved with whispers: perhaps with relieved sighs. The bequest demanded by ancestral precedent had been made. The house, the lands— the income, but for a few annuities—were Edmund Stillwell's, to be managed by his parents until he was twenty-one.

"And being without wife or heir presently," the lawyer read on, "I desire that, in exigency, provision be made by the principal heritor herein named, in due proportion of goods brought to marriage, to such legal Wife as I may take. . . ."

Susannah felt the blood rise to her face, and she heard no more of the words that followed. She knew only a strange sensation of invisibility. She had been unknown to the young Harry who wrote this will. Then, he had been untroubled, and free. . . .

Augusta glanced over at her, worried, but Susannah did not notice. The lawyer concluded his reading and sat down.

"My dear Susan!" she heard Augusta's voice at her side, high and fretful. "Oh! It is a terrible confusion." Behind them, chairs creaked, and the rest of the group began to stand, to move from the room.

Susannah looked up. "Why? What is the matter?"

"But, my dear!" Augusta reached for Susannah's black-clothed arm. "I do not myself understand it," she murmured. "That Harry made no other will. No later . . ."

Susannah gave a shaky smile. "He was ever—careless of such things."

Augusta stared at her with concern. They emerged beneath the stairs into the gallery, bright with sunlight. "My dear," said Augusta, squinting, as they moved to a seat by the windows. "Do you quite . . . understand?"

"Yes." Susannah's voice was calm. "I heard that much. I shall keep—some part of what I brought with me to marriage—"

'But *that* was but a tiny piece of land in America!" Augusta's voice rose, high and anxious. "Oh, Susan! 'Tis most iniquitous. We must see that—in all fairness . . ."

"But perhaps it *is* fair," said Susannah in a hazy voice. None of this talk of estates and affairs seemed real to her. She sat in the dimness of death, of guilt. And Augusta still talked on.

"You mustn't give up hope! There may another will. . . ."

"If there is, I shan't look for it. I don't care! I don't deserve it." Susannah leapt up with a sudden sob, and ran from the room.

And yet, when her tears had dried, she knew she must think of it. *What will I do?* She mouthed the words into the air. To Harry. But no answer came back.

She heard a tapping at her door. "Susannah?" came a sharp voice: her cousin Helena's.

She righted herself on the bed and stood. "Come— come in." Helena entered; so did Maria, leaning on her cane. And Susannah watched, taken aback, as more and more of them followed: the three sisters, standing with bright eyes, and hands folded, in their black dresses; and the four husbands, and little Edmund, clutching his father's hand. They formed a circle round her.

Helena and Maria both started to speak at once. But Helena, with an obedient nod, gave way.

"We have come," said Maria, in a loud and shaking voice, "to discuss what provision shall be made for your future." Her lips quivered, her hand shook on her cane, and her voice was but a shade of its former, strident self.

Helena, with a pitying look at her mother, took over. "We know," she said briskly, "that you must be uneasy, until these matters are decided. You have lands—do you not?—in New York, of which we would not deprive you—but which, as we understand it, you are unlike to wish to occupy."

Susannah's heart thumped. She thought she could not form an answer. None of this mattered to her yet. *There is no future.* She watched, mute, as the scene shifted before her: as some players became spectators, backing away, leaving only Helena and her husband at the fore.

Everett Stillwell pursed his thin lips. "As trustees of this estate, we feel in duty to make clear—that you may continue to live here. Of course, under conditions—"

"In the garden house," said Helena quickly. "Or the west wing."

"Supposing," Stillwell began to drone, "that the needs of a widow are modest . . ." He talked of Susannah's "small income" from rents; of eventual provision for her daughter—a dowry. "In the nature of—three hundred pounds."

Behind him, Maria let out a strangled sound.

"That," said Stillwell smoothly, "is what we discussed. Of course it should be decided more exactly when the time came."

There was a silence, during which Susannah felt she was meant to speak. But she couldn't. Nine pairs of eyes rested on her.

Maria pulled herself up on her cane. "I hope," she said, in a frail voice, "that what we describe will *satisfy* you, Susannah."

In the glint in her aunt's eye, Susannah read some of the old, familiar menace. But it had faded: just as her hair had, in these weeks, to a dull metal-gray. *What will she do?* Susannah wondered, watching her, and, for a second, felt something like pity. Perhaps without Harry, she, too, was truly lost.

She struggled to find the words for an answer. For she knew well enough what was meant by her cousins' proposal. She might lodge in a disused wing here and eat gratefully at their table, providing for her own and Ginia's wants out of a rent of sixty pounds a year. Her heart rebelled at it—but she did not know how to answer. "Thank you," she said. "May I think on it longer?"

Some of her visitors looked affronted at this. She heard their murmurs as they moved together down the hall. Augusta stayed behind, apologetic. "I am sure," she said, "in time, they will be more generous. At least you will stay with us. . . ."

"I don't know." Susannah turned away.

Augusta stared at her. "But what else could you wish to do?"

Susannah ate dinner with the others but excused herself early. Helena Stillwell's beady eyes followed her.

"She might be more grateful," Helena pronounced, sweeping the table with a magisterial gaze. While with one hand she motioned to a footman for water, with the other she seized her son Edmund's round paw, which was fastened round a carving knife, slashing lines through the tablecloth. "*Now*, Edmund," she said, in mild reproof. "Mother. Are you well?"

For Maria's face was trembling: another of her strange fits of grief seemed to have taken her. She clung white-knuckled to her fourth glass of port. "Not *our* fault," she said loudly, incoherently. "Not our fault . . ."

The footmen, at Helena's signal, moved in quickly, and dinner was adjourned.

Susannah closed the bedroom door behind her as the clock in the hall struck eight. Breathing quickly, almost afraid, she bent to light a candle at the fire, which she carried through to the dressing room cupboard. She turned the key in the mahogany door and raised her light to look.

She did not see what she wanted at once. She drew out folded clothes, shoes, old books. She reached behind, in the dark. *Is it not here?* And on the very floor of the cupboard, she saw its silver shining. She laid it in her lap; its raised picture of the Sermon on the Mount was tarnished. She did not remember the last time she had looked in it: for she had so many trinkets and belongings now. But, with a swift wave of longing, she opened it and traced her finger over the rose pin, the silver spoon, her mother's picture. Below them all lay a stiff, folded sheet, inscribed in a childish hand: "LISPENARD'S MEADOWS."

Here were the borders, as she had remembered them: Ten acres, north of Collect Pond and west of Broad Way.

Ten acres. It was not so very small. Ten acres at the heart of a city could be a great deal indeed.

She knew she possessed more letters, more records: that despite her late neglect of this land, Mr. Brown in New York still attended to it for her. She spent the night searching cupboards, drawers, desks, for papers. Her eyes ached with reading in the near dark by the time she opened a drawer in the desk of the up-

stairs study and found it. The first letter. With a rush
of joy, she read:

> . . . *It is pleasingly situated at the edge of the*
> *City and with plenty open Country to the North.*
> *It is possess'd of a House most comfitable of White*
> *Board, in three Storeys, & of extensive Sta-*
> *bling.* . . .

At last, with the picture of that white house in her
eyes, she fell asleep.

The next day, before anyone woke, she walked with
Ginia to the gazebo. All night she had thought of that
place, Lispenard's Meadows, and of a new world:
white, alluring, and clear. But she did not know. She
moved silently, with Ginia heavy in her arms, and her
heels sank into the soft mud.

Don't be a fool, an imaginary voice admonished her:
a voice such as her aunt Maria's once had been. *We*
have offered you all you will need. It is a failing—a
sin!—to want more.

But as she climbed the hill, another voice came to
her. *Don't let them make ye English, do ye under-*
stand? Ye're a Virginian bred, Susanny. An Ameri-
can. . . .

The gazebo's door shuddered in its frame and fell
open. "What do you think?" she said to Ginia, breathing in the musty air. The panes of the windows were
dusty, cracked, and the sunlight within had a strange,
hazy brightness. Ginia's mouth opened wide, as if to
wail, but no sound came, and for a moment Susannah
felt herself suspended. As if, again, it was a spring day
and she was sixteen. For a moment, time waited.
Harry waited for the answer to some question. . . .

Then the clouds came and covered the light. And
she knew that there would be no reprieve. He would
not speak to her. The floor creaked, and in the gray-
ness she saw only the dust on his table and chair, the
leaning wooden walls, the peeling paint. She thought,

with sudden alarm, *They will pull this place down*.
As if she could see into the future: as if she knew. Soon
Maria would be old; her grandchildren grown,
wealthy, lazy, and careless. The viscount Edmund
would be a grown man. And they would have no time
for the past: for Harry or for her. Here in this place,
the years would fly away from her: and life itself,
with all its pains. Its joys . . .

Are there joys? she thought. For their memory was
dim. She thought of hearing music at Gallini's rooms
with Augusta. She thought of Ginia's dark head on
the pillow beside hers. *Ever I'll love thee. . . .*

"I pray thee," she whispered, to Ginia, "stay with
me. Delight me, delight in me . . ."

And Susannah knew that, from now on, for Ginia—to give her all that was good in life—she would
do everything.

She moved down the steps, and pulled the rusting
door shut; and if Harry had spoken to her, in silence,
in verse, she did not know it. She looked down into
her daughter's deep blue eyes. "There is a place," she
said, "that is ours. Shall we go to find it?"

"Lispen—Lispenard's. . . . " Augusta stared at the
papers in Susannah's hands, mystified.

"Lispenard's Meadows," said Susannah.

"But . . . Lispenard's . . . You wouldn't go and live
there!" Augusta scurried across the carpet. Her spectacles flopped down from her nose and bounced on
their cord against her bosom. Her bedroom, with its
carpets and broad view of the grounds, was the same
as it had been long ago: when they had talked, sitting
by the fire, of marriage.

"What can I do, in faith," said Augusta dully, "but
urge you against it?"

"But tell me what you truly think."

"What I truly think?" Augusta looked up, surprised.

"You spoke words. But do you mean them?" Susannah's gaze was intent. "You must know—for all the

risk of it—why I would go. You know the Stillwells
do not wish me here, upon their charity."

"No! Of course they shall be glad . . ." said Augusta
weakly.

"No." Susannah looked, clear-eyed, at her cousin.
"They shall feel obliged." And the two, alike in their
black gowns, with only a white ruffle at their necks,
and their own blue eyes, for coloring, moved close
together. Susannah touched Augusta's arm. "Please.
Be with me in this."

"But—what will you do there?"

Susannah explained, as much as she knew: that Mr.
Brown had written that the land was well-watered for
farming; that there was stabling, where she might
raise horses. . . .

"Raise horses?" said Augusta, still distraught. "You
would work on the land—in the mud?"

"I have before. I do not mind it." Susannah smiled.
"In any case, is it not better than to be idle and de-
pendent here?" She paused, for Augusta still looked
unconvinced. "And also—it is my own country, Augusta. Sometimes I greatly miss it."

"But—" said Augusta, looking up, her objections
failing her. "You shall—go from here forever!"

"Come visit me, then!" said Susannah playfully,
embracing her. Both cousins remained, their arms
around each other's waists. Susannah knew it was
true: she would not see her cousin again. If anyone
accompanied her, it would be servants—Peg and Fermanagh, perhaps, if she could persuade them. "The
Stillwells—your mother and the family—must be
willing for it," she said now. "I will need my passage,
and money to start. It needn't be much. . . ."

"But of course—you will go in fitting fashion!" exclaimed Augusta. Still holding Susannah round the
waist, she pulled back, looking her solemnly in the
face. "We . . . I . . . that is, my dear . . . If you are
so determined, you shall have what you need to live
properly. I shall see to it."

But how? Susannah wondered. She had held back
from raising her plans with her other cousins. For she

doubted that they would like any notion of her future different from their own.

The next morning they met: the Stillwells, Maria, Augusta, and Hench. The Burleighs had left the day before for Somerset. Susannah hovered on the stairs above and saw her relations file into the parlor. The door clicked shut behind them. Coming downstairs, she heard their voices rise and fall, and she knew what they were discussing, though she could pick out no words. She made herself leave off trying to hear, and walked outside. When, her stomach hollow with nerves, she was returning toward the house, she saw Augusta running across the terrace to meet her. Maria and Helena stood at the gallery windows, their faces as still as the portraits within.

"They agreed," said Augusta, seizing Susannah's hands. "They wondered at it, but then I told them . . . how much you wished it." She smiled bravely, but her eyes watered, and her lips began to tremble. "Yes, my dear. You shall go! You shall have your way. How I—how I nearly envy you!"

Epilogue

———— ❧ ————

The Marches, Surrey—1791

It was a clear, hot July day, and a swift breeze blew. A fine wind for sailing. Susannah ran down the drive to the coach, which creaked and swayed under its load of boxes.

"Stop!" she called out to the two men who were trying to lift a commode up onto its laden roof. "There's far too much already. They'll never allow me all that on board as it is!" She smiled and watched anxiously as the men lowered the heavy piece of furniture to the ground.

"But," panted one of them, "the lady Helena said . . ."

"She is too kind already. Please, leave off. I'll go and speak to her." Clutching her black straw hat to her head, Susannah ran up the steps and into the house.

It was true: Helena had been kinder than Susannah had ever expected. She did not know what had prompted this warming in the last few months. But she suspected that it was nothing in herself: it was Maria. For now that Helena so indisputably ruled The

Marches, she would brook no interference from her
mother. Many of Maria's old favorites had become her
scapegoats: and the reverse. The Cheverils had stayed
on at The Marches because their Kensington house
was let, to pay their debts. But Helena made their
position as guests quite clear, and often the dining
room walls rang with her exasperated, "*Mo*-ther . . ."

Maria's mourning sadness was wearing away; but
still she lacked her old conviction. "So, you are going," she had said to Susannah some months ago. Her
voice was hazy, and she stared into Susannah's face
without feeling. "So . . ."

She had moved past Susannah, leaning on her cane.
Susannah could not remember being spoken to by her
aunt since.

Augusta and Jonas Hench had tried to please her by
christening their daughter, born in April, Anna Maria. But even this had aroused in Maria only a fleeting
interest in the girl, and in the thousands Jonas Hench
proposed for her dowry.

Her husband, whispered Augusta, was even prouder
of Anna Maria than he had been of his two sons. "Our
two daughters will be perfect playfellows!" she had
declared to Susannah, just after Anna Maria was born.
And then, with a crestfallen look, she had remembered. "Oh, *why* must you go?"

But both she and Susannah knew the answer. For
the last two weeks Helena had searched the house,
with her sister, for linens, china, and furniture to send
away with Susannah. *Yes, they have been kind*,
thought Susannah. And she knew that it must be, in
part, because she was going.

She ran across the entrance hall, glancing anxiously
at the clock overhead. It was already past noon; they
must leave soon to be in London by tonight. They had
learned from last week's papers that the fleetest of the
boats to New York, the packet boat, would sail tomorrow. *We must be off.* Susannah's heart beat at a
rattle pace. "Helena! Augusta! Aunt Maria!" she

called. She nearly ran headlong into them as they walked toward her together from the gallery.

"Well!" Helena heaved an exasperated sigh. "*There* you are. Where are those two boys? Have they done loading the coach? I gave them *hours*." She charged through the entrance hall, ahead of her mother and sister. Susannah ran after her.

"Yes! The coach . . . That was why I came to look for you," she said. James Cheveril and Jonas Hench wandered into the hallway from the card room.

"What?" said Cheveril, with a friendly toss of his red mane. "Is the ship to wait for you, Susan?"

Hench chuckled. "P'raps with that load out there they'll have to hire a barge to New York. *Hem!*"

The ladies paid their husbands' raillery scant attention. They gathered at the top of the stairs, outside, where some of the servants were already awaiting the departure. Helena grumbled, to see so much idleness. Peg was running, with Ginia in her arms, up the stairs.

"There's no room for us, m'lady!" she said to Susannah. "I know it, sure as doomsday we'll o'erturn!"

Fermanagh, since a month ago her lawful husband, came up behind her. His admonishments to Peg joined Cheveril's pleasantries, Hench's throat clearings, and Augusta's fretful murmurings until Susannah could hear nothing in the hubbub.

"Enough!" cried Maria suddenly, tottering down the stairs on her cane. She waved it at the men loading the coach.

"Heavens," said Helena. "What's Mother at—"

Augusta's eyes widened, too; but they let Maria rail at the footmen, until she grew tired.

Maria hobbled back to the steps, smiling. There was a glint in her eye. "*I* told 'em. Varlets—"

"Aye, you did." Her husband hopped down the steps to help her. "I've always said, dear, you treat them too hard. . . . " They walked up the stairs toward Susannah, an odder couple than ever: Maria, an old, lean woman, beady-eyed, and James Cheveril, fox-haired and growing plump but with a young man's spring still in his step. As they passed, Cheveril smiled at Susannah; but, as usual, Maria did not seem to see her.

Susannah moved to the foot of the stairs, by the Fermanaghs. They would be all her family in America: a strange family, perhaps, but the one she had chosen. She had known the two servants to be attached, in some fashion, since that time at Exon Castle. So it seemed to make sense to ask them both to come away with her. Still, it had been a surprise when Fermanagh had answered her with, "Then, by your leave, m'lady, myself an' Peg'll marry." She had said, "Of course!" and tried to smile her happiness. But the news had pained her. They would have each other, and she was alone.

Alone! she scolded herself now. *You are not alone. You have Ginia.* And yet she knew she would feel alone: perhaps for the rest of her life. Harry was gone, and inside her there would always be this loneliness: even though she tried not to speak of it or show it.

She took Ginia from Peg, into her arms. The child's eyes darted about the curious scene: the servants, more and more of them, pouring out through the downstairs doors; her aunts, in their black gowns, scurrying on the stairs; and her uncles, in their shirt-sleeves, shuffling and smoking.

The driver flapped his reins, and the coach heaved under the weight of its roof, creaking up the drive and toward the steps. It was time to leave: nearly time. And Susannah had not guessed how, in these last moments, the love of this place, even these people, would surge up in her, so that she nearly wanted to call the coach off: to stay. Now the whole staff of the house stood in ranks down the left branch of the stair. Peg nudged Susannah, whispering, " 'Tis—time to take leave, m'lady."

Slowly Susannah moved across the landing. Knole, with his black, shiny hair and dark suit, was the first to leap up toward her. Now he worked for Helena; but he would not be staying much longer. He had plans to marry and to set up an accounting office in the City.

"Godspeed, my lady," he murmured, and clasped her hand. And she reached forward, on impulse, and kissed him on the cheek.

She walked slowly down the rest of the stairs, nodding and smiling and murmuring thanks as the various servants curtsied and bowed. She shook Warwick's hands, and kissed Em, the cook: for she had known them the longest.

She came to the bottom of the stairs: to the door of her coach. And now the Warringtons streamed down after her: her cousins and their husbands and children, one by one, all bidding her good-bye. Jonas Hench came to her, with his two sons; and Everett Stillwell, with Lord Edmund and his brother, John. James Cheveril murmured a gallantry she half heard, about "the wilds of America."

Maria took hold of her elbows and planted a dry kiss on her cheek. "Good-bye," she said clearly, "Miss Susannah. You will soon enough forget us."

Miss Susannah. For a moment she was too stunned to speak. Her aunt spoke as if she were still Miss Bry, the unfortunate cousin. As if the last four years had never passed. . . .

"No," she answered at last, in a low voice. "I shall not forget, Aunt. I shall not forget—anything."

"You shall have all you require, I hope," said Helena. Her voice was cool and imperious.

Susannah nodded, and raised her cheek to her cousin's. They both knew what Helena meant, and did not mention. Sewn into the deep pocket of Susannah's dress were a hundred pounds in coin and a letter of credit from Edmund Stillwell for a further four hundred. Susannah hoped she would never need to cash that letter; still, it weighed in her eldest cousin's speech and her own. *They have been kind.* . . .

Helena backed away, and there was a second's pause. The horses shuffled restlessly in the drive. Augusta came forward, her cheeks already wet with tears.

"I cannot—" She tried to smile, while Susannah, feeling her own tears come, despite herself, bent down, with Ginia in her arms, so Augusta could hug her. Their two broad hats clashed in the air, and Augusta's tumbled back, leading all the men to scramble for it. Freed of its weight, she leaned forward and sobbed wholeheartedly on Susannah's shoulder.

"You know," said Susannah, "you may come and visit me! Ships grow fleeter—safer every year!" But her voice was choked; she knew it was not really true. She would probably never see Augusta again.

Finally they pulled apart, and Susannah bent to kiss Anna Maria in her nurse's arms. In her own arms Ginia was howling at the tears and commotion all around her.

At last Susannah knew she must let go. Leaning on Cheveril's arm, she climbed up into the dark hollow of the coach. It was stuffy and hot and, as Peg had warned, so full of trunks that there was barely room to sit. The coach heaved as Peg and Fermanagh leapt up onto the seat beside the driver, and started, ever so slowly, on its way. Susannah looked out of the window; framed in its glass, the Warringtons waved and smiled. Or, like Augusta, they mouthed words she could not hear; or, like Edmund Stillwell and Maria, stared, pugnaciously or blankly, into the distance. This was their portrait: the way she would remember them. And it stayed in place for only a moment. Already they were breaking ranks, turning, talking; though a few, like Augusta, still waited and waved. They had laden her with gifts: carpets, a gilt mirror, a mahogany writing desk. She wondered how such luxuries would appear in her new house. *A House most comfitable of white Board* . . .

She still knew so little about the place; about what that damp soil Mr. Brown wrote of would yield. "It is a land," he had written her, a month ago, "which might prove rich, but which remains, thus far, unproven. . . ."

I am the same: unproven. The thought made her

smile. "Ginia," she said now, in a shaking voice. "Tell me. Are we great fools?"

Ginia only cooed and batted at a ribbon dangling from the brim of her mother's hat. The coach had turned so that the family on the steps vanished from the side window. They were replaced by roadside, trees, and moving fields. *English fields*, thought Susannah. She knew she would find nothing like them in New York. Perhaps, looking again on America's wild emptiness, she would long for them.

The horses reached the straight stretch of the drive and gathered speed. In four hours' time they would be in London; a month later, at New York. And Ginia, most likely, would know only that new home. Of The Marches, of England, she would have not even the haziest of memories.

But suddenly it seemed to Susannah that she *must* remember. She lifted Ginia onto her shoulder and turned to face the coach's small back window. She felt her heart lurch and her throat go dry. "Do you see?" she said. "The place where you were born. Do you see? . . ."

Ginia made no sound as she bumped, with the motion of the wheels, against her mother's shoulder. But as the house grew smaller, now a white speck, now invisible in the distance, her eyes flickered across the scene, darkening to indigo.

About the Author

LUCY KIDD was born in New York City and was graduated from Harvard in 1987. She was a National Merit Scholar and won the *Seventeen* prize for fiction when she was sixteen. She is married to a Scotsman, Colin Kidd, and lives in Oxford, England. *A Rose Without Thorns* is her first novel.

FANFARE

Now On Sale

CARNAL INNOCENCE

(29597-7) $5.50/6.50 in Canada
by Nora Roberts
New York Times bestselling author

*A seductive new novel from the master of romantic suspense.
Strangers don't stay strangers for long in Innocence, Mississippi, and
secrets have no place to hide in the heat of a steamy summer night.*

A ROSE WITHOUT THORNS

(28917-9) $4.99/5.99 in Canada
by Lucy Kidd

*Sent from the security of her Virginia home by her bankrupt father, young
Susannah Bry bemoans her life with relatives in 18th century England until
she falls in love with the dashing actor Nicholas Carrick.*

DESERT HEAT

(28930-6) $4.99/5.99 in Canada
by Alexandra Thorne

*Under an endless midnight sky, lit by radiant stars, three women ripe with
yearning dared to seize their dreams -- but will they be strong enough to
keep from getting burned by . . . Desert Heat?*

LADY GALLANT

(29430-X) $4.50/5.50 in Canada
by Suzanne Robinson

*A daring spy in Queen Mary's court, Eleanora Becket was williing to risk all
to rescue the innocent from evil, until she herself was swept out of harm's
way by Christian de Rivers, the glorious rogue who ruled her heart.*

☐ Please send me the books I have checked above. I am enclosing $ _____ (please add $2.50 to cover
postage and handling). Send check or money order, no cash or C. O. D.'s please.

Mr./ Ms. _____

Address _____

City/ State/ Zip _____

Send order to: Bantam Books, Dept. FN, 414 East Golf Road, Des Plaines, IL 60016

Please allow four to six weeks for delivery.

Prices and availablity subject to change without notice.

 ## THE SYMBOL OF GREAT WOMEN'S
FICTION FROM BANTAM
Ask for these books at your local bookstore or use this page to order.

FN 19 - 1/92

FANFARE

On Sale in January

LIGHTS ALONG THE SHORE

☐ (29331-1) $5.99/6.99 in Canada
by Diane Austell

*Marin Gentry would become a woman to be reckoned with -- but a
woman who must finally admit how she longs to be loved.
A completely involving and satisfying novel, and the
debut of a major storyteller.*

LAWLESS

☐ (29071-1) $4.99/5.99 in Canada
by Patricia Potter
author of RAINBOW

*Willow Taylor held within her heart a love of the open frontier -- and a
passion for a renegade gunman they called Lobo -- the lone wolf.
Their hearts ran free in a land that was LAWLESS . . .*

HIGHLAND REBEL

☐ (29836-5) $4.99/5.99 in Canada
by Stephanie Bartlett
author of HIGHLAND JADE

*Catriona Galbraith was a proud Highland beauty consumed with the
fight to save the lush rolling hills of her beloved home, the Isle of
Skye. Ian MacLeod was the bold American sworn to win her love.*

☐ Please send me the books I have checked above. I am enclosing $ _____ (please add $2.50
to cover postage and handling). Send check or money order, no cash or
C. O. D.'s please.

Mr./ Ms. _____

Address _____

City/ State/ Zip _____

Send order to: Bantam Books, Dept. FN, 414 East Golf Road, Des Plaines, IL 60016

Please allow four to six weeks for delivery.

Prices and availablity subject to change without notice.

 ## THE SYMBOL OF GREAT WOMEN'S
FICTION FROM BANTAM

Ask for these books at your local bookstore or use this page to order.

FN 20 - 1/92

FANFARE

Rosanne Bittner

_____28599-8 EMBERS OF THE HEART . $4.50/5.50 in Canada
_____29033-9 IN THE SHADOW OF THE MOUNTAINS
$5.50/6.99 in Canada
_____28319-7 MONTANA WOMAN .... $4.50/5.50 in Canada

Dianne Edouard and Sandra Ware

_____28929-2 MORTAL SINS .... $4.99/5.99 in Canada

Tami Hoag

_____29053-3 MAGIC .... $3.99/4.99 in Canada

Kay Hooper

_____29256-0 THE MATCHMAKER, ... $4.50/5.50 in Canada
_____28953-5 STAR-CROSSED LOVERS .. $4.50/5.50 in Canada

Virginia Lynn

_____29257-9 CUTTER'S WOMAN, ... $4.50/4.50 in Canada
_____28622-6 RIVER'S DREAM, ... $3.95/4.95 in Canada

Beverly Byrne

_____28815-6 A LASTING FIRE .... $4.99/ 5.99 in Canada
_____28468-1 THE MORGAN WOMEN .. $4.95/ 5.95 in Canada

Patricia Potter

_____29069-X RAINBOW .... $4.99/ 5.99 in Canada

Deborah Smith

_____28759-1 THE BELOVED WOMAN ..$4.50/ 5.50 in Canada
_____29092-4 FOLLOW THE SUN .... $4.99/ 5.99 in Canada
_____29107-6 MIRACLE .... $4.50/ 5.50 in Canada

Ask for these titles at your bookstore or use this page to order.

Please send me the books I have checked above. I am enclosing $ _____ (please add
$2.50 to cover postage and handling). Send check or money order, no cash or C. O. D.'s
please.

Mr./ Ms. _____

Address _____

City/ State/ Zip _____

Send order to: Bantam Books, Dept. FN, 414 East Golf Road, Des Plaines, IL 60016
Please allow four to six weeks for delivery.
Prices and availablity subject to change without notice.   FN 17 - 12/91

FREE MYSTERY GIFT • FREE BOOK • RISK FREE PREVIEW

Open your heart to soul-stirring tales of love by best-selling romance authors through our Loveswept at-home reader service.

- Each month we'll send you 6 new Loveswept novels before they appear in the bookstores.

- Enjoy a savings of over 18% off the cover price of each book. That's 6 books for less than the price of 5—only $13.50 (plus S&H and sales tax in N.Y.).

- Each monthly shipment of 6 books is yours to examine for a 15-day risk-free home trial. If you're not satisfied, simply return the books...we'll even pay the postage. You may cancel at any time.

- The exclusive Loveswept title LARGER THAN LIFE by Kay Hooper is yours absolutely FREE. The book cannot be found in any bookstore because we have published it exclusively for you.

- THERE'S MORE...You will also receive a mystery gift. This beautiful and decorative gift will be yours absolutely FREE simply for previewing Loveswept.

YES! Please send my 6 Loveswept novels to examine for 15 days RISK FREE along with my FREE exclusive novel and mystery gift. I agree to the terms above.   41236

Name _____

Address _____ Apt. No _____

City _____ State _____ Zip _____

Please send your order to: **Loveswept,**
                                Bantam Doubleday Dell Direct, Inc.,
                                P.O. Box 985, Hicksville, N.Y. 11802-0985

Orders subject to approval. Prices subject to change.   RBBA1